Sykosa.

Sykosa

Copyright © 2012 by Justin Ordonez

All rights reserved.

Published in the United States by TDS Publishing.
PO Box 30032
Seattle, WA 98113

www.sykosa.com
www.tdspublishing.com

First printing, 2012.

Table of Contents.

Prologue: Swim Tryouts. ... 1

Part I: Junior Year. ... 3
    I. ... 5
    II. ... 16
    III. ... 27
    IV. ... 39
    V. ... 48
    VI. ... 60
    VII. ... 73
    VIII. ... 85

Interlude I: Sophomore Year. ... 101
    1. ... 103
    2. ... 112
        Detour One: The Past. ... 121
    3. ... 131
    4. ... 140
        Detour Two: Mother Superior. ... 149
    5. ... 161
    6. ... 170
        Detour Three: The Future. ... 179
    7. ... 188
    8. ... 197

Part I (Cont.): Junior Year. ... 209
    IX. ... 211
    X. ... 221
    XI. ... 232
    XII. ... 257
    XIII. ... 275
    XIV. ... 291

An Open Letter From Niko: ... 307

An Excerpt from Part II. ... 309

Prologue: Swim Tryouts.

A soggy, diluted filmstrip, full of scratches that come and go, rolls 4...3...2... WHITE. Fade in on the locker room. To the left are the showers, and from them comes the sound of fifteen showerheads, a slow cloud of steam and herself, still in her Academy issued one-piece. It's blue and it's covered by the white towel she takes from the rack. She prefers to dry at her locker, where she has the most privacy one can get in a place like this. It's several rows away, yet she doesn't notice how each row she passes is silent, and that the girls in them dress quicker than they usually do, and that they are avoiding eye contact with her or anyone else. It's like how one would behave if they just witnessed an execution and felt guilty about how much they enjoyed it. That's not how these girls behave, but she's too preoccupied to notice.

Did Mackenzie tell me what I think she did?
It makes no sense for Niko to do what Mackenzie says.
No one does anything like that to Donna Harly.
No one.

It's at her locker where she finally notices that something's out of place. On the floor is a bucket and presumably all the water around it is from it. There's also water on the lockers themselves. They're the mini-kind that're stacked two tall and everything beneath the floor of her second story is wet. She just noticed the girls are silent and that none of them are looking her in the eye. She gets it and prepares herself—turning the lock right, left, and right and opens the door.

Wonderful.

Part I: Junior Year.

I.

First period. American history.

Who knows which is worse. At this hour, it's too early to care. Luckily, it's never too early to bitch and moan. And she would do so, save her teacher is already on it. He's up at the board—in shock that not a pupil noticed how his cuff smudged all his bullet points. Like wrist trajectory were her problem. That's a math problem. And math problems aren't her problem for another two hours. Yawn. He's still going on—something about full attention being on…

Her fingernails.

Fingernails, you see, are better than lectures. Particularly these lectures. Particularly this class.

She wishes nail polish didn't break the Academy's Personal Code, then her fingernails could be pretty colors, and she'd feel like a pretty girl. They should let her do her nails in class. It's no different from doodling. It also increases hygiene, and in high school, that's nothing to scoff at. She may paint her fingernails this afternoon, just for fun, then remove it and—

Hang on. Her teacher said something will be on a test.

Never mind, she already knows it.

Anyhow, if she does do her nails, she has a problem. She doesn't know what to do. However, she does know she doesn't want to do something she's already done. If she's gonna do her nails for one night, then it'd be nice if it were a departure of some type. Alas, her brain has no ideas. Being pretty is hard! Yet, she likes it so very much. That does it. She needs to talk to Niko. For one, Niko's her best friend. Two, Niko's gifted in the department of being glamorous. And luckily, Niko's her neighbor, so she drafts a note that she passes across the table.

What should I do with my fingernails?

Niko reads the note in delight, then dies of boredom.

I thought you were gonna share good gossip or something.
No, I want to do my fingernails.
Do something slutty. That's always good for a thrill.
That's a good idea.
Niko always has good ideas. Niko's brilliant!
She wishes she were Niko.
And Niko wishes she were Sykosa's breasts. *That's me, Sykosa! Well, technically, it's my breasts.* Breasts are an urgent topic for Niko, seeing as her prime puberty years have passed, and to Niko's horror, she's all As in the bra and all Ds on her report card. That's harder on a girl than people think. And it's why Niko collapses her cheek on her hand, then inconspicuously stares at those far-bigger boobs. Niko thinks she does it for a second or two. In reality, it's seven or eight. Now, before anyone makes any assumptions, Niko's not gay. She's about as boy-crazy as a girl gets. To the point that she collects boyfriends as if they were Girl Scout badges.
And to be fair, this breast-staring is harmless.
Though every girl has her limits.
Hers have been exceeded. Not by Niko, but by Tom. He also has his cheek in hand, his eyes overcome by her chest—for what is maybe ten or eleven seconds.
Unlike Niko, he's thinking of her as if she were some toy.
He may be right.
In the only snowstorm of the year, as the Academy froze under the sickly sweet smell of a dysfunctional oil furnace, she retreated behind the two bell towers of the Academy chapel. And on that very day, this very boy—in his ski jacket laden with those sticky tags they put on bags at airports—stumbled onto her smoking self and put his tongue in her mouth. It was a bold move. And it impressed her. They didn't need to "talk." Besides, it woulda fucked up the moment. *I get shy fast.* Accordingly, she kissed him until her heart beat so hard she became faint. It meant something. This feeling. She caught her breath. They sat beside each other. Seconds later, she wished they hadn't stopped, so they restarted, then kept at it.

This time without the tongue.

Niko steals the note, then writes a new one.

Why is he looking at you like that? Only I'm supposed to look at you like that!

Niko's the type who admits her faults shamelessly. While its slightly backwards, Niko does so not as a deterrent from such behaviors, but to enable them. She rarely complains. Because that's Niko. And somehow that excuses everything Niko does. That said, she supposes she's predisposed to Niko's jealously over her body, perhaps to the point of flattery. You see, this Tom-thing is nothing. Or if it is something, it's certainly not enough of something. Not enough for her to buy a prom dress.

Why do you think he is looking at me like that?

*Because you * him.*

Not to delve too far into the well of note-passing dynamics, but she—and the Queens—use secret codes in case of confiscation. "*" means fuck, in all forms and conjugations. She has not * Tom. She has not * anybody. Her lips quiver at the *. It feels like something she'll put off until she is thirty. Simultaneously, she also feels like it could happen in the immediate future.

Sometimes she just "knows."

Gross.

Afraid?

No!

But, she is afraid. Everything is too complicated. It should not have to be. She goes behind the chapel. He goes behind the chapel. They make out. Simple, right? It's not. Regardless, if even that must be complicated, then certainly the concept that she wants to go to Prom, thus he should ask her to Prom and then they should go to Prom is simple, right? It's not. You see, he has this best friend, this confidante, this main focus, this everything—and her name is not Sykosa, but Mackenzie.

Or as you will soon find out: "M." That's what he calls her.

So, every day, she faces the fact that, outside of the chapel, they are merely acquaintances. Two pigeons in a flock of nine hundred who dress the same, talk the same, and act the same. That's okay. Pigeons are only pigeons because conformity is only conformity. After all, those goth girls who wear heavy eye makeup and piss off Mother Superior, they're conforming. It's okay to be like everyone else so long as she is always herself. And that is the reason, because there is no other reason, why she makes out with this boy. Other than she likes it. Kissing is fun. She's lying. There is another reason. Another trivial teenage doodad—what the priests describe as an "infatuation" or perhaps inappropriately labeled as "puppy love." When she talks to him, lame as it sounds, she feels like she is being herself, just as she is definitely not herself when with Niko, her parents, her teachers, Mike Holler or Lonny or Donna, and most of all Mackenzie.

Tom's never understood this. He sees no issue in how she feels like a phoenix, but is only regarded as a pigeon—and not only a pigeon, but one pigeon in a flock of... Never mind, conformity * sucks! She blames herself. At first, these back chapel indiscretions barely affected her, and it wasn't until the days turned into weeks turned into their kinda-sorta three-month anniversary that her feelings became...a tad poisonous. And he is wonderful. He's a bit of a perv, but he's quick-witted and pretty, and he kisses her and his jokes are funny. Yet, like she said before and she will say again, he never holds her hand in the hallway or runs his finger along her jaw before they separate for class or cups her cheek and whispers those three wonderful words in her ear.

I, love & you.

It reminds her of this morning, really every morning, when she undergoes her final inspection in her bedroom mirror. Her back is always straight and her shoulders are always proper, her knee socks aligned and her skirt taut, the fabric above the last-buttoned button of her blouse separated to show the faintest touch of her neckline. Then she strokes her hair, examines the fluidity of her foundation and scans her forehead for pimples. Once she determines it's safe to be seen in public, she promises to break up with him if he avoids the whole Prom subject.

She always chickens out.

Niko writes back.

He's still looking at you.

He is still looking at her, and she's beginning to understand his subpar grades. All he does is obsess about her. And she finds it charming. However, in these in between days of April, she has found a new dilemma with him has arisen. His penis. And not only his penis, but her manipulations of it.

Well, her one manipulation of it.

She was between his legs and, above her, a stained glass Peter, Paul, and John peeped upon the five fingers of her right hand, which had released his navy pants, then clamped down on his erection. He insisted that she motion up and down. She did and then watched him lean his head about while listening to him moan. It was encouraging that he was so moved by the movements of her wrist, and she squeezed harder, then went faster. She did so consistently until he called her name in urgency. "Sykosa!" To be followed by a gyrated thigh, a locked jaw and his spray like a garden hose from beneath the spout.

She had to clean this unforeseen mess.

No one told her it was so sticky.

Write about something else.

I need to copy your math homework!

Typical! Both her American history teacher and Niko want her for her math skills. *But, I'm not Asian like that.* The math gene skipped her. Either way, she can't pass the homework now, so she tells Niko to wait, then waits out this class and, over the next hours, the duration of her day. She knows it's over when the bell towers ring dismissal. She crumples her papers into her backpack, stops by her locker for her books, then walks a wing of empty classrooms, out the rear of the Academy and across the campus, towards the aforementioned bell towers that reach high into the sky like castle lookouts.

Behind the chapel, a slab of cement is laid by a locked fire exit. She leans against the wall and then sits like the Chinese people sit in China, her skirt tucked between her legs and her sweater vest pulled over her neck. She fishes out a cellophane-wrapped package and thrusts a cigarette between her lips.

Niko rounds the corner, drops her bag, removes her sweater vest and stretches her shoulders to her toes. Then, her arms, which have disappeared inside her blouse, reappear with her white bra. She tucks it inside her bag. "Really, that's such a disgusting habit." That's how Niko asks for a cigarette. Niko gets one, and it blows out of her mouth. "I swear, did you see how short Ass Girl's skirt was today? She musta rolled it like five or six times. She's such a slut. I heard some sophomore say she was all over Hazu this weekend, and she walked around with her hair all JBF."

JBF is another note-passing code word.

It stands for: Just-been-fucked.

"Doesn't surprise me, she acts like an idiot around him."

"I think Hazu's asking her to Prom. Stupid bitch, I thought he might ask me."

"Would Timmy go with you?"

Timmy is Niko's current infatuation. The devotion of all her romantic energies whenever Hazu (shortened from Haruhide), Niko's real love, is indisposed. "I'd take Timmy, but he hasn't asked. Plus, he's a college guy. I'm sure he thinks it's lame."

"Has he mentioned it?"

"Timmy and I don't talk about things like Prom, but I can't believe your knight in shining armor hasn't asked you."

Niko means Tom.

"He'll ask. I know he will."

"If you don't get asked, you can't buy that dress you like."

"I know. Let's talk about something else."

Niko holds out her finger. "You need to be authoritative. You tell him if he wants anymore anything—"

She interrupts. "If he doesn't want to, he doesn't have to."

Niko's tiny Nokia rings a computerized jingle. Niko presses the plastic against her ear and talks in a sexy slang. It worsens with each twirl of hair. Thus, Niko's caller must be Hazu, the leader of the Speed Stars, a local racing team/hoodlum gang who all drive RX7s. After school, the team loiters in the Academy parking lot where they stand over their engines like cavemen over a fire pit and talk about...whatever boys talk about. Niko joins in to learn how to better control her own 7. Also, Niko suffers a weakness for boys who drive too fast. She likes getting drunk with them—see Hazu—and then dancing inappropriately to obscene rap lyrics.

Be that as it may, this is not actually Niko. It's Niko3.0. More on that later.

Niko ashes her smoke and flakes of gray settle by her foot that stomps the dropped cigarette. "I gotta jet. Hazu wants me to listen to his new speakers." She shakes her slightly shorter-than-shoulder-length hair. It's not as punky as usual. The school limits the amount of product girls can use. "And I need your help with our math assignment sometime."

"Why don't you ask me for the answers again tomorrow?"

"Okay!"

"Alright, I'll try to get it done tonight."

Niko points her finger again. Her breasts poke like teeny-tiny mounds. "You'll try? What's going on? You're not doing your homework, you're passing notes for answers on tests—as if I would know any—and you smoke like a chimney!"

"I don't know, it's..." He came behind this chapel and he kissed her, and she thought her long wait was over. She would have him and she'd finally be free. She thinks she knows why she isn't. *Last year.* It's hard to discuss, and like a lot of things that're hard to discuss, it's pretty much the root of every issue in her life. But, also like a lot of things that're hard to discuss, there's tremendous consequence to discussing it, thus there's tremendous incentive to not discuss it. This incentive has a name: blackness. It's something she's all too familiar with. She even feels bits of it now. She ignores it. "I wish he would ask already." The blackness has a way of splicing her from reality, so like the first day Tom came back here, he's snuck up on her, separating two fingers over Niko's head like bunny ears. She smiles the smile that only happens around him, and she calls to him. "Stop it!"

Niko turns to face his untucked Academy shirt and blazer. "Oh, it's you." Niko puts her finger in her mouth and fakes a hurl before jogging off. "You know I hate those cigarettes, Sykosa! I'll be in the parking lot when you're ready to leave!"

"Okay."

Niko drags her feet to a stop. "In case I forget, don't forget to ask your parents about you-know-what."

"I will."

They're alone.

She looks up at him. He looks down at her. He smiles, and she makes her obligatory evaluation of him. He's dressed like usual—below expectations. Even in parochial school, with its Personal Codes, and in the case of the boys, its button-down shirts, burgundy ties and gray blazers, there're those who cannot keep par. It doesn't bother her much. Boys who dress better than girls are weird.

He talks first.

"What's 'you-know-what?'"

"It's nothing-to-know." As in he shouldn't worry, but she will...later. For now, he's hers. "How're you?"

"I'm fine, yourself?"

"Alright."

A second passes where neither does anything beside stare. She is sure. Positive. *He's about to ask.* Instead, he complains about how school was terrible today. "I'm failing American history. I think it's your fault."

This isn't her story. This isn't her life.

He's usually charming.

"Is it really so hard when I'm around?"

He crouches, then softly kisses her lips. "It's impossible."

That was happiness. She was secretly hoping he'd bend over to kiss her. "I thought about you a lot today—"

He interrupts. It's his bad habit. "What exactly?"

Her response is another soft kiss. It's also really nice.

She thinks this chapel is their place and, geographically, it's the worst place to break up.

Yes. It's a geographic thing.

Kiss me again.

He stands up and she stands up. Her cigarette follows the toss of her wrist and her hair follows the roll of her fingers. She waits in anticipation, aware of his intent. Then his tongue parts her lips and her hands lay on his shoulders. She leans to accommodate his circles of saliva and his hands, eager as always, press against her sides. She forgets that these actions are real and his hands... They feel good. Even though all they do is dig out her blouse and yank her undershirt into her armpits. Too distracted to notice his breast petting progressively traveling to her red and gray skirt, playing with the elastic of her panties and grasping her butt, lifting her onto her tiptoes. She moans. Almost gone, almost lost...until his hand passes the valley of her hips and his fingers tickle the first hairs.

"Hey!" She pulls away to fix her blouse. She remembers that comment about JBF and straightens her hair, too. "You aren't allowed to touch that."

"Why not?"

"Because."

"Come on, it's no big deal. I tell you what, let me touch it for five seconds. You can count."

"No!"

"Why not?"

"I'm not counting seconds while you touch my... I'd rather you just touched it."

"Okay, that's what I'll do."

"No!"

His eyes are mournful. It's cute. His penis pulsates against her side. It's less cute. She grins anyway. In some moment she cannot recall, she became such a sucker for this boy. But even now as her grin dissipates, the goodness vanishes. She kicks at the ground, so he knows he's upset her and to fix it.

He notices.
Unlike the last two days.
"Are you feeling alright?"
"All these girls are freaking out over Prom. It's stupid, don't you think? I mean, we're only juniors, right?" He shrugs his shoulders. *He's never gonna ask.* It's particularly hard since she decided, like, a year ago she wanted to go to Prom with him. For now, she puts her finger through his belt loop and leans against him. *Actually, it was almost a year ago—exactly.* The date has significance not only to her, but to the blackness, so she forgets both, and hopes everyone else chooses to do the same. "Say something."
"Are you sure you're feeling alright?"
"I'm feeling weird, that's all."
He kisses her again and she kisses him back.
Then, he leans to her ear. "Hey, I was thinking, remember that time, last week—"
She interrupts. "That's all you think about!" She pulls away and looks into his eyes—to see he was looking into hers first. And his look beautiful and mysterious. She cannot stand not knowing what he is thinking, what he is feeling. Primarily because she knows he's thinking about her, and her heart tells her it's incredible. She knows this because, last year, he did something incredible for her. It was out of this world and, as Niko said, totally knight-in-shining-armor stuff. *So he has incredible things inside of him.* He just never says what they are! "What're you really thinking?"
He looks bad. "I was thinking about that time, last week..."
She puts her other finger in his belt loop. "Is that really all you were thinking about?"
"No."
Why does he make it so hard? "What is it then?"
"Your hair is perfect today."
It has been a terrific hair day. He's not just saying it.
"Alright."
He pulls up his slacks and lowers himself onto the cement

slab. She lowers herself between his legs and tucks her skirt between her ankles and butt. She notices a pack of scars—discolored, even a little deforming—on his right hand. They are her fault. He got them by saving her, which was part of the incredible thing she was thinking about. It provokes the blackness. She still breathes, it feels like she's getting 5% less air. She's adjusted to ignoring it, and does so—motivated by those scars, much the same as they motivated her last time, and this time, she pets him and pulls down his zipper, lets him take it out since she fears hurting it or something, then once it feels like a fine time to start, she—without his instruction—massages.

The experience isn't quite what she anticipated.

The excitement is gone.

His penis is unchanged and the act is repetitive, and it seems ordinary, like a household chore. To jerk him off is to take out the garbage, necessary—yes, annoying—yes, expected —yes, unbalanced—yes. Everyone produces garbage. Only one person takes it to the curb. Two people sit behind this chapel. One person feels. The other works. She thought he would be as concerned for her own pleasure as she is for his. But, no, that's not gonna happen. His eyes are either closed or watching her hand or watching her boobs or... *And here I was supposed to break up with him if he didn't ask me to Prom.* And other thoughts that never find a way to words. Mostly because she's distracted—by his semen. It dribbles off her hand and onto his stomach. This time she brought tissue and she blots at the divots of her knuckles.

How does he get to me like this?

II.

Niko oversteers her 7 as a cautionary sign becomes a shimmer in her rear view mirror. Her determined face scrunches, little breasts that bounce as she pumps the clutch up this twisting hill. Brake. Brake. Shift. Turn. *Gas! Gas! Gas!* Brake. Brake. Shift. Turn. *Gas! Gas! Gas!* Her engine roars like an oversized can opener and her throat hums a hip-hop song that blasts: *All them bitches. All them hoes.* As time slows—Brake! Brake! Brake!—and the road levels. (This is Niko's favorite part). Double clutch, shift, *gas!* until the shock nearly rips the frame in two, slick rubber leaving smoky trails while the tachometer hits the limiter and... The transmission releases, the needle falls, and the suspension transfers weight, like a swift cheetah, teeth deep into the driveway.

Bending over from the outside, she wishes Niko well, and once in her matted kitchen causeway, she drops her fifty-pound book bag and gives a silent prayer for the noise of Niko racing away. *If you think she's dangerous driving up the hill, you should see her on the way down.* Cut short by her short mother, short like Niko short, who hurries in to say hello. Her mother is very thin and dressed as if today were of some importance, which it's not. Also, her pronunciation is... Her mother was raised in Japan. She confuses articles, sentences with multiple verbs, and misuses "no, not, and neither."

That said, the disparity in her mom's English—as with lots of Asian mommies—is overstated, especially by white people.

"What took you so long to get home?"

"We stopped at Starbucks."

"You should've called and told me."

"I know, I'm sorry."

Her mom isn't the type to let that go so easily, but she does for some reason. "How was your day?"

"Alright, I suppose."
"You want something to eat?"
"No, I'm fine."
"Are you sure? It's no trouble."
She carefully sidesteps into the kitchen. If her mother were to sniff a cigarette, she'd die a most dramatic death, but not before lecturing, "I can't believe you smoke! Are you stupid? You see the commercials on TV, don't you? That stuff will kill you." It probably sounds cynical to describe her mother in such a way, but trust her, the woman is too gifted at theatrics. Her mom won't raise a stink about anything for a year, but then blows up over the smallest thing and will be angry at it for the year that follows. *An unfortunate habit I've picked up.* Especially since last year, when Tom became her hero and her entire life changed in one instant. *Whatever.* Back to her mother, who shouldn't be thought of for her bad behavior, but for her need to over-nourish. It is no accident her mother greeted her from the kitchen, it's where her mother always greets her, as it's where her mother spends her time, beside the stove, constantly complaining, "You never eat enough. Tell me what you want. I cook it for you." That carries hidden dangers since her mother is as relentless about feeding others as she is about depriving herself.

Besides, I might need to fit into a prom dress.
She nabs some crackers.
"Mom, I'm borrowing some of your nail polish."
Her mother follows her to the stairwell.
"Why? Where're you going tonight?"
"Nowhere, I just want to try something out."
"Okay, then, okay. Put it back when you're done."
"Will do!"
Her mother has turned towards the kitchen, but then turns back towards the stairs. "And hang your uniform up."
She's already up four stairs, shouting so she won't have to turn around. "I know, you remind me every day."
"How about you try remembering it every day?"

"I'll hang it up, Mom."

Hitting up her mother's nail polish for something slutty will be a chore, as it's not her mom's style, and even if a color, in the right context, could be slutty, knowing it's her mom's turns all the reds classic, and all the other colors sophisticated. Plus, her mom is meticulously organized, and the bathroom light almost feels industrial. It's like looking at the nail polishes at a department store and wondering why they all look so bland in real life. Still, all this nail pontification has pointed out to her how several patches of skin on her right hand are "tight" in dried semen she thought she had removed, but she supposes she only distributed thinly. It washes down the drain with soap, and having selected a dark red, she heads to her room with a nail file, cotton balls, and other stuff. Inside, she slams shut the door before she clicks on her old RCA television.

I touch penises now.

Oh my God, that thought makes her smile uncontrollably.

And think more about handjobs.

Maybe I shouldn't do my nails today.

Like most things involving Tom, once she starts thinking, she has a tendency to be unable to stop, even if it's about gross sex stuff. Right now she can't deny a biological imperative to the male orgasm. And she does feel a confidence knowing she has some mastery over it. Then, again: *It's a stick. I rub it. Who cares?* Well, he does, for one. She wishes she understood that. Like, she kinda likes his orgasms. They're fun to watch. And she has sexual desires herself. She wants to [fill in the blank] with Tom, she just doesn't need to do it like he needs to. Yeah. Anyhow, she thinks if she did understand it, if he could provide a plausible reason, then maybe she'd be willing to do it more often, and he'd have to pressure her less...

That's a joke. Like there was ever a reason!

He does not love her. He does not listen to her.

He only wants to get-off.

Dickhead.

In Tom's absence, she scrunches her nose at one of her boy

stuffed animals, a Fievel mouse. He sits atop her made bed, and the shiny black brim of his sailor cap lies deceptively over his left eye. She wonders if little Fievel asks little Cindy, a princess in a pretty pink gown and a limp magic wand, to jerk while he feels up her royal panties. He says he wouldn't, but she knows he's lying—the liar! She punches him and he falls onto her teddy bear, and there he stays, acting all injured and making her feel like more of a jerk.

She caves and fixes him, then makes up with him.

"Poor Fievel, you wouldn't be so disgusting, right?" He says he would not. She hugs him. "What's that? Oh, yes!" She kisses his mouse cheek. "I'd love to go to Prom with you!"

Prom!

A cracker is stuck in her molar and her uniform crumples on her floor. Goose bumps prickle along her skin and a swallowed lump forms in her throat. She clips her skirt to the same hanger supporting her blouse shoulders, and once it's hung, she folds her sweater vest square. Done with that, she slips into a skinny pair of pink pajama pants and a spaghetti string camisole, then catches herself at a good angle in the mirror on her cabinet door. So she attempts many other angles, most involving her breasts. She's quite proud of their sometimes D-cup status. (It depends on the brand of the bra). And she has to be proud. If you recall, not only is Niko crazy about them, but so is Tom.

In fact, it's the first thing he noticed about her.

(Sadly, it might be the only thing).

Such details are insignificant! Yes, they are.

On the TV is a sitcom about stereotypical people who're obsessed with themselves and their infighting, their contrived plots and trivial hang-ups. It's called *Friends* and it's her all-time favoritest show and she'll hear nothing bad about it! When her mind spaces from it, she thinks about herself and her infighting, her contrived plots and trivial hang-ups. Particularly Tom and their relationship, and how much she likes having a boyfriend, and then she thinks evil thoughts about stuff that happened last year. Since her brain is so focused on hands today, she thinks of all the scars on his right hand, and of how, unlike with his semen, they cannot be washed away with soap.

Nothing I will ever do will top him, thus everything I do and think and feel feels insignificant in comparison.

She ignores this thought cause she ignores the blackness.

It's not a great coping mechanism, but it is one.

Her left hand is painted when she decides to smoke.

The best part of her bedroom is her bay window, which she can sit on and watch the neighborhood from—and smoke, of course. Once she's twisted the window open, she breathes the chemicals in deep and notices, across from her and atop her fleece blanket, some of her mother's fashion magazines. It excites her since fashion mags talk about taboo subjects, like sex, menstruation, breast and cervical cancer, homosexuality, QUIZZES!, pregnancy, clothes, intimacy, and—this one you were waiting for, so enjoy yourself—how to "please" Tom spiritually, emotionally, physically and visually.

How does he get to me like this?

And why does she love him so very, very much?

Forget him for a second.

She needs to note that her mother rarely shares this trash because society says it propagates an unrealistic female figure, which's true; however, her mother will occasionally—when she feels the need to make amends for something—leave these behind after she cleans. *What did my mom do? I don't know yet.* (But, it's worth highlighting this tidbit of knowledge). In the mean time, she reads, hoping to find ways to make being a woman feel less dangerous. Instead, she settles for a picture of a pretty white girl with freckles and a sun hat who's leaning over a rock on an exotic beach. Her bathing suit has orange flower prints and the bottoms are the less revealing style, a really short-short pair of shorts, which must mean she has no trouble getting a Prom date...

One-tracked mind strikes again!

Anyhow, she wants this new suit for many reasons.

First, Ass Girl is throwing a big party this Friday. Ass Girl's parents are gone for the weekend and Ass Girl, in all her assy greatness, smutted her slutty Ass Girl ass in her face, insisting they get dressed in their super-slinky bikinis and give the boys something to go gaga over in her father's hot tub. Not that she listens to Ass Girl, but Ass Girl is friends with Mackenzie who's friends with Tom and Tom suggested the two of them, if they're both going, go together.

She wants to go with him, so she said yes.

Second, last year, she overheard a girl named Donna Harly crying about rape. She prefers not to think of it. And she prefers it not happen to her. She thinks this bathing suit can help with that, certainly more than her current bathing suit.

Third, her head's in her panty drawer like an ostrich's in the sand, where she snatches a suit of more string than fabric. By impulse, she disrobes, then scrunches the bottoms between her thighs as she ties a knot over either hip. A minute later, her breasts are covered as well. *Yeah...* Basically, after all the stuff that happened last year, she went through a short-lived phase where she attempted to see if dressing like a prostitute could help her feel better about herself. Spoiler! It didn't and she quit doing it. And she's gonna quit on this bikini, as it's not only too slutty, it's not at all practical. Tuffs of hair stick out the sides, and yes, this type of bikini requires a not-so-typical brand of pubic grooming, which leads to...

Fourth, she won't have to shave her pussy for this new suit. She keeps things "trim" down there, but for the most part, it's old growth and it's everywhere. Though, saying she won't shave her pussy begs the question: when did she shave her pussy? Well, it was last year. (Notice something?) And it was partially so she could wear this bikini to Niko's summer parties. While she was surprised that shaving such a sensitive area was so uneventful, she didn't like it. One, she thinks her pussy is ugly. Two, being bald felt Lolita-ish.

She thinks the hair is like the man on the crosswalk.

Fifth, all these reasons remind her of the you-know-what Niko mentioned behind-the-chapel. Should you-know-what become what-actually-happens, she'll need a new suit.

Her thoughts have been disrupted.

Arnold, her neighbor, mows her yard in diagonal lines. Her father pays him to do this because he dislikes doing it himself. Arnold receives two forms of compensation for his labor. One, twenty bucks every Tuesday. Two, he gets to find "convenient" times to mow when she's "coincidently" by her bathroom or bedroom window. What a total perv, and a macho-less slug with pancakes of sweat under his arms and a toilet bowl ring around his neck.

He has the cutest twin sisters, though. She babysits them twice monthly when their parents go out. He usually stays in his room, probably because conversing would be a non-pervy thing to do. The twins say he's boring. They like Sykosa! Recently, they've been frenzied by the loss of their front baby tooth, both on the right side, and both on the same day.

They approached her as she retrieved the mail and pointed to the holes in their mouths. "Sykosa, look!"

"My Gosh, you two look like hockey players!"

"What?"

"Hockey players, they get lots of teeth knocked out."

"We don't play hockey, Sykosa! We lost a baby tooth! It means we aren't babies any longer." Both girls held out their right palm to show off a shiny fifty-cent piece. "Look what the Tooth Fairy gave us! Do you know the Tooth Fairy, Sykosa?"

"You sillies! She comes at night while we sleep!"

"Did the Tooth Fairy visit you when you were little?"

"Of course!" That was a lie. Such customs are unusual in her family. "I'm so happy for you girls!"

Arnold rotates the lawnmower opposite her and she pulls her drapes shut, to become preoccupied with her full-length cabinet mirror again. She traces the pooch of her butt and the pooch in her tummy and the ski slope drop in her breasts. She wants to go to Prom. Her mother's stir-fry smells warm. Back into her PJs, she slides her socks across the kitchen floor. Her butt is in the chair. Her stomach is empty.

Her mother is annoyed. "Why are you not eating?"

She pouts. "I ate too many crackers."

"No, no! I go up there and I bet the cracker box is full."

This food fight continues and her father stays behind the paper. He pretends to be into the world news, but only reads sports statistics. His shirtsleeves are rolled to the median of his workingman forearms, muscles built atop muscles that collide uncomfortably into small digits. He's also flat, save his stomach—his stomach is large, but he's got a flat forehead, flat haircut, flat chest, flat personality, and eyebrows that, as he gets older, consume more and more of his face.

He tilts the newspaper and stares with disapproval. "Aren't parent-teacher conferences tomorrow?"

Her mother answers. "Yes, tomorrow."

"What do you think your teachers will tell us?"

Traditionally, these school situations are no situation, since she was old enough to tie a ponytail, the expectations have been clear: she is an A student and she is a teacher's pet and she is a terrific test taker. These labors, being forlorn as they are, should lead to prosperous Prom dates, the enrollment in a first class university, and then to the performance of her lifely duties in a position of great wealth and stability, preferably as a doctor or an engineer.

Such foresight is lost on a sixteen-year-old girl.

Also, she is eating and talking with her mouth full.

"I think everything's fine. English, science, and Spanish are in good shape. I'm probably getting an A in all of them." Here comes the difficult sell. "But, I'm having trouble with math and American history. I'm trying, but my grades might be a little low because my teachers keep doubling-up tests on the same day. They don't know it, and when we tell them, each refuses to move the dates."

Her father looks displeased. "How bad?"

"Probably C+, B-."

"Sykosa!"

"I know, but they double up the tests..." Which they don't. "And it's—"

He interrupts. "Finish your dinner and go upstairs. You're to study every night this week. When's your next test in... in..."

"American history?" That's better than math. "It's Friday."

"I want you ready for that test."

Her mother agrees. "Yes, and it counts for this quarter."

She nods like nothing is wrong. "I will do good, I promise." Whew, dodged a bullet there, at least until tomorrow.

Oh, that's right, her mom's talking. "How is Model UN?"

It feels like this question comes nightly. "Mom, things are fine in Model UN."

"I'm not getting a call from Mother Superior like last year?"

She drinks cola, her voice echoing in the glass. "No."

"Because if your grades are lower, then Model UN matters even more for valedictorian."

Valediction! Valedictorian! Valedictorian!

"Mom, can we please not do this every night?"

Things get silent for a bit.

It's ended by her mother, who forces an unnatural cough that sounds almost like a grunt. Or a signal. It works, as her father stares with disapproval again. "Who is Tom?"

Her chopsticks tumble and she grabs the soda again. *Maybe he called to ask me out to Prom!* She feels stupid. "He's a boy I'm doing an English project with. How do you know him?"

"He called before you got home. Your mother told him you would call him back."

She doesn't want this to feel like a big deal. She downplays it. "It's alright. I'll talk to him at school."

Things get silent again, and again it's ended by her mother. "Isn't Tom the boy you went to Sadie Hawkins with?"

She gets what her mother is implying, also why her mother left those magazines up in her bedroom.

She wanted me to talk about him with her.

(See, it's good to remember this stuff.)

"He is."

It seems like an innocent answer to an innocent question.

But, last year happened, so nothing with Tom is innocent.

Her father talks like he doesn't know this stuff. "This Tom, he was the boy in the accident, right?"

What happened to Tom was no accident. It was purposeful, but people—like her dad or herself—need it to be an accident. They need to know it's not their fault. They need to....

Blackness.

"He was."

She knows her parents are debating any number of topics. Maybe they want to talk to her about sex. Or what love is really like. Or, if they feel bold, they want to explain how life, unlike what they've presented thus far, is a cold and lonely place, and they're a tad worried she's learned this too soon. Possibly they want to get really specific. They want to tell her how sometimes bad things happen and, yes, it brings people together, but it can also create attachments that, while not bad, are not by such automatically positive. And they fear this has happened to her, and that this boy, Tom, who seemed like an alright guy when he picked her up, may be inadvertently, and by no fault of his own, prolonging her pain and intensifying her suffering.

None of it gets said.

They think: She's only sixteen. There's no way she feels so bad. Kids don't feel things that serious, and I'm projecting my emotions on her. I shouldn't put these thoughts in her head. Besides, other than the occasional second, she seems happy, and okay with life, so let her be a kid and...

This isn't her story. This isn't her life.

I'm no kid.

Her father starts on a generic rant. "He's not a boyfriend, is he? Because you're too busy and too young for a boyfriend. He isn't the reason that your grades have been slipping, is it?"

She's echoing in her soda glass again, and once she's done and she's released the glass, she wipes her wet fingers on her pants. "Dad, I told you, we're doing a project together. And we went as a big group to Sadie Hawkins—you remember, right? It's not what you think," except that it is, and it puts a drive in her to sell this lie, "and, besides, I...I don't even like boys."

"You don't like boys? What's wrong with boys?"

She throws her hair. *Ugh, give me a break!* "Well, I like boys, just none of the ones at my school."

He bellows before covering his face again. "Well, that'll change someday. Now, hurry up and finish eating so you can..." *Dream about Prom?* "...start studying."

He's no fun, not like he used to be. And his fatherly manner reminds her of the you-know-what and how she promised to ask and how this is not-the-time. Maybe she'll mention it later. *Ugh, Niko'll be so pissed if I forget.* It could be for the best. You-know-what, when it comes to Niko, always ends up as wish-it-wasn't, and this time, especially with Niko being so intent on winning Hazu back, screams of glad-I-didn't.

"Yes, Daddy."

III.

A red dawn distills her dreams to a forsaken reality. Her limbs frozen in their comfortable position, desiring a return to this restful world where homework is nonexistent. If the Academy knew how comfortable she was, they'd call off school. She'll get her mother to write a note. One saying her sheet was stretched over her shoulder like a warm cocoon and her hair was perfectly tucked away while Fievel suffocated in the crease of her breasts. It would also say girls need more time for sleep, more time for dreams...
Make boys do all the work.
Her bladder states otherwise.
Her underwear are at her knees, her elbows are laid about her thighs and the toilet seat is cold. She thinks about Prom while she pees. She forgets Prom while she whiffs at her semi-stinky armpits. No time to shower. She wipes herself, flushes, lifts her panties, and glares between the blinds. She has a feeling Arnold's watching her. Perv. Then, she pops three whiteheads and brushes her bacteria-ridden gums.
She takes a quick shower, anyway.
In her room, she wears a pink bra, then a mint green thong. She rarely wears thongs any longer as he gets to her pussy so fast in one, but he really likes them. *I like them, too.* Moving on, she buttons her blouse over her undershirt, then tucks in the ends before she yanks at her shoulders. A glass bottle, square in dimension, is inverted on her fingertips, #10 foundation spread across her cheeks, nose, chin, and pimple-ridden forehead. It's totally cool. The Academy's Personal Code allows for makeup, and the amount allowed is based on grade level, and being an upperclassman, she gets away with a lot. After, she combs, then snaps some hair clips in place before she performs her final inspection. Once she determines it's safe

to be seen in public, she promises to break up with him if he avoids the Prom subject.

Whatever.

Then, it happens, or starts. She hoped to squeak by without mentioning it, but it's here. This weight on her chest. It's the same as what she experienced behind the chapel, when she was taking in 5% less air. It's a sign the blackness is here. She hates the feeling of it. Both because it sucks, and because it means more is to come. *And it'll get worse.* Still, it's odd. She usually thinks about the weight more than she experiences it, yet this week has been an exception—and for good reason.

Next week is the one-year anniversary of Tom's "accident." This isn't her story. This isn't her life.

It's a big deal, and I don't know how to let him know that.

Niko honks her horn, then leans back against the seat. The car is pumping warm air, people are bitching on the radio, and Niko's hair, still wet from her shower, is shiny in patches. Niko has also covered her face to cover her eyes. They're agitated and red from another sleepless night, possibly from hanging out with Timmy, or Hazu if Niko met up with the Stars to convince him that Ass Girl is lame and going to Prom is lame. You see, by the rules according to Niko, it's better he go to no dance if he cannot take her, but Niko probably hung out with Timmy since—both when she sits in the passenger seat, then waits at the Starbucks drive-through—Niko mentions nothing of him.

At a stoplight near the Academy, two cutie boys, who attend the school and were part of Mike Holler's circle last year, pull up next to them. Niko lowers her window and the boys say, "What's up?" and they chat a bit. It sounds stupid, but she likes that someone went out of their way to say hello to her. In fact, she breathes easier afterward, but at the Academy, specifically at her locker, that's gone. She thinks of all her valedictorian, Model UN, and other crap expectations. *I need to get out of here.* So as the bell towers start her day and her American history teacher starts his class, her feet stick to the mud of the chapel while her nipples become so hard they practically eat through her vest, like temptation eats through her will—foil ripped from a new soft pack and a flame against the gray-silver sky.

She wishes he were here.

If the morning weather is severe, occasionally everyone will decide, via cell phones and pagers and whatnot, to meet up for coffee or something and be twenty minutes late for school. Last month, that happened for a heavy rainstorm, and she arrived at the Starbucks with Niko just as Tom did. Despite the public discretion they show for their relationship, they kissed once and sat together at the center of the big table, holding hands while surrounded by friends. She fantasizes about it, but one can only fantasize for so long, especially at the scene of the crime. She replays jerking him off—drawing his penis in detail and wondering how her red fingernails might've blurred had she jerked him off when she did have, for one short hour, red fingernails. Also how, at the midway, her forearm succumbed to overuse, and she had to substitute her strength for the momentum of her body. It bruised her knee and might've done worse, but nope, what happened was he shot his white stuff all over her hand and himself.

She thinks about that for quite a while.

She had always wondered what boy cum would look like.

And...

How does he get to me like this?

She hits off her smoke, then tries to forget it, but she can't. In truth, when they started getting serious, she thought she'd shyly forego his advances for her penances with God. But, even if she could not, then certainly they could find a place for such indiscretions that was not the chapel, that was not God's home. *Tom's got a solution for that.* Lately, he's mentioning how his mom works late, and his home is empty, including his room—unless, of course, they went there after class.

Thinking about it makes her feel heavy.

Feeling heavy makes it difficult to breathe again. She snubs her cigarette and, in class, explains to her American history teacher that she's having "girl problems." He's skeptical since she smells of tar, but lets it pass. She is, after all, one of the Asian girls—too good and too innocent for something so improper. He gives her a packet titled *Review for Test of Chapter 14* and tells her to find her seat. Once she does, she flips her hair over her shoulders, gets a pen from her bag, and finds the usual group has assembled. Niko, of course. Tom, of course. And this goth boy who can never find a group.

Everyone decided to await her arrival before beginning the review packet. She supposes that's expected, and she talks with conviction, knowing she'll have to convince the two biggest lazy asses that all must work. "I'm in big trouble with my parents, so we can't goof around."

Niko has gum in her mouth. "Where were you?"

"Where do you think I was?"

"Smoking! You should've had me come with you."

She rubs her temple and reminds herself to be patient. No one knows she is feeling the weight. Still, she wonders if the Pep Squad (in her mind) is assembling. No, it's too soon.

Relax. "Seriously, we have to study."

"Why? What's gonna happen with your parents?"

It's hard to pass up an opportunity to whine, so she whines her woes to Niko's shock. Surely not! He would never! My dad would never order me to study! Niko then recounts a story, and there are many, of great adventure and irresponsibility. It involves Timmy and his friend Clyde, someone she's never met but who is supposed to be gorgeous, and how they did this or that and it almost ruined the night...

Blah!

She's not allowed out on school nights.

Tom is busy noticing how her nipples have eaten her vest. She makes her obligatory evaluation of him. His top button is undone and his collar lies like some seventies TV superstar. His blond hair is slicked back in hair gel stuff, and he is still comatose on her tits. She wishes there were boundaries. He is, by his decree and not her own, only a tool for her sexual amuse-

ment and not a menace to her schoolwork.
Wait, nothing's getting done! "Seriously, we have to work!" Niko, who's without makeup today, has sprung up from her book bag, and from it she ties a white headband, with three red Japanese symbols, behind her head. Niko sticks her gum under the table, and holds out her fist. "Alright, Sykosa, for you, I will study." Niko opens her text, then reads not three words before she becomes overwhelmed by jitters. "I hate this! I'm never gonna need this useless shit."
    She frowns. "What did I say about concentrating?"
    "I don't know. I wasn't listening."
    "This isn't a joke."
    Niko's eyes roll, her attention finding its true subjects—Ass Girl and Hazu. They're sitting together, similarly engaged in some sub-intelligent conversation. Niko, too, wonders if she'll ever get asked to Prom. "I... I..." Niko wants to say something, but she's become stuck on that goth boy who's tagged along. He has nice vampire hair, and it's sexy how one of his eyes has a bit of eyeliner. Niko feels something funny when she thinks of it, and she doesn't understand it. She ignores it by talking to Tom. "Tom, are you doing anything interesting tonight?"
    "Nothing really, I mean, what's there to do on a Thursday?"
    Niko holds her answer a half-beat since she knows Sykosa will chime in. It is the most important day of the week! Sykosa smiles, because she cannot control herself sometimes, and lifts her head to say in synch with Niko: "Watch Friends!"
    "I take it you both watch it together?"
    Niko shakes her head. "Never, we watch it at our houses and talk on the phone."
    "Wait, you watch the same show and talk on the phone?"
    They speak in unison again. "Yes!"
    "Whatever."
    She giggles, annoyed that Niko used Friends against her. Though, she does feel better, until she feels worse. She tries to sound tough. "Enough of this. Niko, you take section one; Tom, you take section two..." They look like toddlers in a too

big world. She closes her eyes and feels dizzy. Her eyesight becomes fuzzy. This is the blackness. This is what happens when it gets worse. *And it's only first period.* Should the Pep Squad assemble? No, not yet. It's too early. *Relax.* "Can you guys please do this for me?"

"Absolutely!" Niko forms a fist and goes headfirst into the text before, three words later, her eyes get lost and her fist grows limp. *God, this is boring!* It's so boring that talking to Tom is a for-real alternative. "Tom, if you could do something tonight, what would you do?" Sykosa pounds her fist into the table and looks all frazzled. Niko is perplexed. "What're you worried for?"

"Because we need to work on this—"

Tom interrupts. "Why? You're going to get an A."

He better not say what she thinks he's gonna. "What makes you think that?"

"Because you always get an A, even without studying, right? All of you Asians get good grades. It's genetic or something."

Actually, it's cause our parents are psychopaths.

Still, he's such a jerk!

"I get good grades because I do my review assignments, so do something or go sit with someone else." He looks surprised. Niko looks happy. "And you," she means Niko, "of all people know a C+ is failing where I come from."

Niko handles this like a pro, sounding suave throughout her entire explanation. "Look, you need to calm down. I mean, I hate to agree with..." Niko's head drops in Tom's direction. "...but, you can't get higher than 100%."

Niko's right. She tries to relax.

Relax.

Mostly she succeeds, except for the tiny distractions. Like the noise from other groups—it multiplies, then layers, and at the end, jumbles together. Or the fluorescent lights, which magnify, then intensify and cut at her brain. It's maybe 7.5% of the air that isn't making it to her body. It's complicated by her internal voices warring with each other. Her father says she can't go to Prom since she failed the test, but that's immaterial since Tom hasn't asked, and her Mom is at her about her Model UN project and...

Relax.

The problem is that she has been lying. No one knows about her grades. Well, her parents know, but she let them down softly. That wasn't a lie. It was a fib. Her tough voice is gone and she's begging. "This one is extra important. My dad is mad and this will make it better."

Niko concedes. "Look, I'm only saying you're the smartest chick I know. You're practically valedictorian—valedictorian in this Academy!" Niko holds out her hands in exasperation. "*This* Academy, this place of God that's so clearly controlled by the devil." The table breaks out into laughter. Niko is quite proud of herself. Unfortunately, the laughs get the attention of their teacher, who points to his forehead. He's referencing her headband. Niko pretends she doesn't get it and goes back to work. "Like, you'll do fine even if you only study tonight. You should be happy about that, not stressed. I mean, you're such a liberal."

"What?"

"A liberal, it's what you are."

"Where did you get that from?"

Niko sits up, the headband's tails twirling like propellers. "It's from my father!" She punches her fist in her hand, then interlocks her fingers into a stretch. "He says a liberal is someone who feels guilty for stuff that isn't their fault!"

Her head collapses from her neck. "That makes no sense."

"Sure it does." Niko folds one leg over the other and kicks it up and down with a smug, *I've diagnosed the problem, let's move on!* But Niko can't. This time their teacher has walked up to the table and pointed to his head. Niko reluctantly takes it off, folding it in her lap. "Anyhow, there're important things that need discussing!"

"Like what?"

"Did you ask your parents about you-know-what?"

Shit. "I tried, but—"

Niko interrupts. "You forgot again?"

Tom recalls how yesterday you-know-what was nothing-to-know, but now he-knows-different. "What do you mean?"

Niko looks annoyed. Cat's out of the bag now. "Every year, I go up to my family's cottage in Coeur d'Alene, and every year, I invite Sykosa to come, and every year her parents say no, but I have faith that this year, *this year,* she'll sway her father's opinion about her crossing state lines without his presence."

"Well, based on my ability to convince you two to study, I think I'm definitely not going to your cottage." She stops there since she doesn't want Niko to know that not only did she not ask, but she foolishly committed, after Tom's invitation, to Ass Girl's party. "Now, how about—"

Tom interrupts. "I didn't know you owned a cottage there. My family used to have a place there."

"Oh, yeah. It's awesome and huge, and it has a swimming pool, a spa, tons of bedrooms, and a forest with tons of trails behind it. The fridge is always stocked and tons of college kids are there for spring break." Niko freezes, her mind in thought. *Sykosa likes Tom. Tom likes Sykosa.* That sounded wrong. *Sykosa likes Tom because she's suffering temporary insanity. And Tom likes Sykosa, but he's a moron.* That's better. *So, if I get Tom to... Then, Sykosa will... Yeaaaaah.* "Tom, you're welcome to come this weekend!"

He's a bit shocked. "I am?"

Niko acts like "duh!" "Oh, yes, you should come! I'm going there with a bunch of people! Why? Do you have other plans?"

"Nothing, I was gonna finish a video game and maybe watch a couple of movies."

He didn't mention Ass Girl's party.

Why didn't he mention it? Is he lying for me?

Niko doesn't care. She's being sarcastic. "Now I don't know if you can come."

"Why?"

"Is the movie *Titanic?*"

"Ugh, no."

"Alright, you can go. It's just I'd never separate someone from that movie."

He cackles. "Okay."

Niko smiles, satisfied with leaving him confounded. "Sykosa will tell you, I've seen it way too many times."

True dat, and if she has to see it once more—and she's seen it plenty since Niko's father mailed back the pirated VHS from Japan—then she'll birth an entirely new stress syndrome. The "girls, stop being so predictable and stupid" syndrome. The doctors will call it "Sykosa Syndrome." It's catchier that way. The movie is alright though. The boy is cute. And his sketch of Win-slut is the only "okay" porno she has ever seen. Really, it was lengthy. Granted, if she were ever on a sinking boat, she would want—without question—to stay afloat far longer. That said, as she sat in the movie theater while that giant hull lifted into a teeto-totter upswing—the passengers sliding along the deck like shuffleboard pucks—she felt...nothing.

A boat sank, who cares?

For Niko, it's a filthy and passionate affair. Slumming with the poor boy (who happens to be dreamy) and letting him rip off her brassier and fuck her rich cunt. Then, while love still has bearing, he's swept away, telling her to "never let go" and then himself freezing solid. This way Niko can feel eternally in love without ever earning it. Plus, Niko keeps the awesome necklace! How typical of Niko, as Niko loves no one more than Niko, and Niko hates no one more than Niko. *And I love Niko.* Thus, seeing Titantic as a story about romance disgusts her.

Tom agrees. "Don't worry, I think Titanic sucks."

If Niko's skin had daggers like a porcupine, they'd be half stiff. "Be careful, it's unwise to mindlessly say things like that about my favorite movie."

He laughs. "Why?"

"Because I'll beat your ass."

"Will you?"

The boy with vampire hair speaks up. "She will."

"Look who finally speaks! Tell me, how will she do that?"

"Her headband said Aikido."

Niko gasps! *How did he know?*

Tom is unimpressed. "What's that?"

"It's the art of using an opponent's strength against them."

Niko has found her breath. "It is."

Tom is hesitant. "You can kick ass?"

Vampire Hair answers for her. "She can."

Niko sighs. *Aw, you're so adorable, you undead fiend!* She doesn't understand. He isn't as cute as Hazu, he isn't as smart as Hazu, he isn't Hazu at all, yet her tummy is upside-down. *Weird.* "Well, I don't like to brag or nothing!"

Tom feels intimidated. A girl he would fuck shouldn't be stronger than him, and while Sykosa is Grade A, he thinks about fucking Niko, like he does all girls. Thus, all girls should be weaker than him. No, he didn't mean that. He meant... Never mind. "Look, this weekend sounds awesome, but—"

Niko interrupts. "It is! And we have huge parties! They're so much fun and we get so drunk!"

Tom knows of Niko's reputation, and he remembers all the buzz in the Academy over Niko's Coeur d'Alene party last year, but he thought that stuff was overplayed. "I don't know. It's short notice."

Sykosa's filled with...well, still blackness, but also relief. The thought of him out at Niko's cottage, by himself, with all those slutty college girls who fuck so carelessly you'd think their legs were a set of separating doors at the mall, is too much. *I... I need him and if he does something like that...* Let's put it this way, and she doesn't like sounding old and farty, but she hates girls who use the notion that love should be free as an excuse to be a whoreface. To expand on that, she hates hates hates any girl who would use the notion that love is free to be a whoreface for Tom.

How am I gonna go to Prom otherwise?

Niko ruins this relief. "Well, if your mom calls my mom, it'll work out fine."

"How do you know that?"

"Because I'll pretend to be my mom, and I'll convince your mom it's alright."

"Why would you need to pretend to be your mother?"

Niko smiles so big all her teeth are visible. "Because we're going there by ourselves!"

"................." That's what he says. Try it. It makes noise, specifically the noise of his head making all the connections. *Parts of Niko's reputation are true. If this is true, and I go and Sykosa goes and there are no parents, then we'll be by ourselves and we'll... Yeaaaaah. This is perfect!* He has been trying to get Sykosa to go home with him after school for a little while, so they could be together away from the chapel. Don't get him wrong, action is action, but they long ago pushed the limits of what can be done back there. "I want to go! Do you think you could get Sykosa's parents to let her go?"

"That's not even necessary! Sykosa practically lives at my house—they won't check, but someone..." Niko's head drops in Sykosa's direction. "...won't ever ask!"

"You won't?"

It's not that easy, which Tom knows, but since she guesses he doesn't, or doesn't want to, she explains it. "Well, it's—"

He interrupts. "Come on, all Niko wants is for you to ask."

Of course, he interrupted. He doesn't care.

Relax.

She bargains. "Let's just finish this, you guys..." No one says anything. "I don't think it's a good idea, not this year. Next year I'll make a push, okay?" The wall-mounted clock steals her attention. *Class is almost over, and I've got nothing done!* All the stuff with her lungs and her eyesight are still going on, by the way. A new one lets itself be known. An anxiety that has energy enough to build a city. It comes uncontrollably in and out. *Today is gonna suck so bad!* And she speaks. She curses, afterwards. "Besides, we committed to attending another party this weekend."

Niko's neck jerks. "Don't tell me you're talking about Ass

Girl's party? You can't go to her party and not come to mine! That's the shittiest thing you could do."

"Niko, my parents have never let me go to your cottage, even the years your mother actually took you."

Niko is unappeased. "Like-that-matters."

The franticness plummets to a valley where she only wants to cry. *Relax.* The Pep Squad doesn't need to assemble. They need to charge forth! *Hurry, you fuckers!* It's far too early. It'll get worse before the day is out. "Look, if we start working on this, then I will ask, but think of it this way: if I don't get an A, I'll be attending a super exclusive party this weekend, and it'll be in my bedroom by myself."

IV.

Twenty minutes ago, some teacher in some class laid out some scientific method of learning. His useless information got bigger, longer, more complicated, and well...she took out notebook paper, a pen, and she broke it down into the A) 1) a) b) B) 1) a) 2) a) b) 1b) 3). Kinda useless, as her notes were like her life. It started out thorough, but became sketchy, then jumbled until her attention dissipated into the green ocean of unused chalkboard. Outside, the sun shines. Inside, there's only darkness. The blackness is hard to describe, as it's more than symptoms. It's a nothing that becomes everything there is. And what one sees is only a fraction of the trauma inflicted. It can get so bad she literally goes black, and she wakes up seconds, minutes, hours—who knows—later, to the silence, and the shame, and the...

That's an extreme example.

For now, it's made her debilitatingly claustrophobic.

She tells her teacher she has "girl problems."

She keeps the hall pass visible, should Mother Superior, the vice-principal, or whoever's wandering wonder why she walks the main hallway toward a jackknifing auxiliary hallway ending at the gym and the pool, which smells like crotch and bleach. Like always, the cola machine's compressor covers the snap of the key turning over. Outside, there's only darkness. Inside, the light is a drippy yellow, down a causeway, and upon an open space with three individual sinks below three individual mirrors beside a row of stalls. Above, a smoke detector hangs by one last a uncut wire. Straight ahead are the Queens, whose shoddy voices sound clear since the door has auto locked shut.

First off, a lot of information is about to be dumped on you and, unlike Sykosa, you may want to take good notes.

This bathroom is off limits.

Last year, the Administration discovered it was a hideout for Academy girls and, upon inspection, found the trifecta of evil for female parochial students: drugs, pregnancy tests, and eye makeup. Immediately, the bathroom was locked. No biggie, right? Wrong. What the Administration, particularly Mother Superior, never suspected was that Donna Harly used this bathroom the most. Donna was a lot of things. Primarily, she was a drug addict. Her coke binges were so legendary that she was nicknamed the "Yeti." Also, she was Prom Committee President, which is huge at the Academy, and as PCP, her many responsibilities meant she had a master key, which opened this bathroom, which meant she had it copied for a few friends, one of whom was Niko.

Presently, maybe eight girls are aware of its existence.

Forget it. Thinking about this will wake the Pep Squad.

Back on track. Pay attention, because this gets complicated!

Like America itself, the student body at the Academy is subconsciously split by race, a fact everyone would deny if asked. One of these groups belongs to Niko, and it's named the "Queens" (derogatorily known as the "Bukkake Queens"). Its inner core is Niko, Sykosa, and a gang of girls secondarily known as the "Star Sluts" because their boyfriends are in the Speed Stars. Specifically, the Sluts are like a naval fleet. They look somewhat different, but alike nonetheless.

SS1: A corn-fed Asian, like Sykosa, which is an Asian face with white hips, breasts, and legs.

SS2: A conventional Asian, like Niko, which is short, flat, and narrow.

SS3: A traditional Asian, which, to put it mildly, is reserved. She is also clearly Thai.

The other major group belongs to the white girls who're called the "Bitches" (derogatorily known as the "Cokehead Bitches"). Its inner core—and leadership—is shared between Mackenzie, Jessica, and Ass Girl. That's this year, though. Last year, the unquestioned ruler of the Bitches was Donna Harly. Also, last year, everyone was in the Bitches. *Including me.*

What happened was Donna and Niko had a falling out. Consequently, Niko organized the Asian girls into the Queens. Before that, this bathroom was exclusively Cokehead Bitch territory, and it mostly still is, as crazy white girls who're, by the way, so obsessed with weight that lunch is replaced by cocaine and diet pill "Cocktails" are in no shortage.

Somehow, and this confuses her, the Bitches snort some lines and remain themselves, but if she—being Sykosa—draws a line along her thumb, then she becomes another coked-out rice-vag—Donna's term, not hers—like the ones their white fathers abuse on their business trips to Asia. Lots of white girls think the Queens are whores. There're also rumors that Sykosa and Niko are gay for each other, which is untrue, as is the cocaine use. She would never do cocaine, simply because it scares her. Niko would never do cocaine, simply because Niko promised to stop.

Niko is excited. "Sykosa, help me out. I'm telling the girls they need to come to my cottage this weekend. Let them know it will be totally awesome!"

"It will be totally awesome."

SS1 is up against the mirror. She fluffs her hair right, then left, then right, and finally left. "Are you going?"

SS2 has put herself on her tiptoes, looking in the mirror too. "Yeah, are you going?"

She's freed her pack of smokes. "I'm not sure yet."

Niko is unmoved by this. "Look, we had a killer bash last year. What part of it don't you guys want to do again?"

SS1 giggles. "What I remember is that we had that big bash and then the entire Academy had a meltdown!"

SS2 giggles too. "The entire Academy!"

"Meltdown" refers to the fight, which didn't happen the Monday after Niko's big bash, but the Monday after Prom. It's the kind of detail people often overlook. It's the kind of subject no one brings up. It contributes to the blackness. She knows it will come. She had hoped a cigarette and a shit might help. Upon this failure, that socializing would be a sufficient substitute. Although, not all news is bad.

If the Sluts blow off Niko this weekend, then she can too!

Niko is annoyed. "Please! Like it's my fault Mike Holler went off the deep end!" Then, Niko holds out her hand at Sykosa until she has a cigarette. "Besides, why do you all want to stay here? We should leave the Stars behind!"

Obviously, this is what the argument was about.

Hazu, who dates Ass Girl, is committed to Ass Girl's party, *like I am,* and where Hazu goes, the Stars go, and the Sluts follow. How did this Ass Girl dynamic emerge? In January, she transferred in from Texas and, in a short series of months, has infiltrated Niko's post-Donna social theocracy. As you know, it involved Hazu, whom Niko was dating before Ass Girl arrived, and whom Niko is madly in love with.

It's why Niko wants to have this party so bad.

You see, after the "meltdown," everyone assumed there'd be no Coeur d'Alene party this year. It just caused too many problems—and if word got to Mother Superior, then major hell would unleash itself. But, to combat Ass Girl, Niko knows no bounds and is trying to rapidly organize this thing (Niko only had the idea two days ago) in hopes it will cause problems in the Stars, drive Hazu insane, and if luck holds, destroy Ass Girl's party all together.

One other thing.

Last year, Mike Holler was the Academy quarterback.

He was also Donna Harly's boyfriend.

And a loser.

SS1 tosses her hair again. It's long and luscious, and no matter how many times she messes with it, it falls perfectly in place. "I don't wanna leave the Stars behind! Besides, if only we go without them or the Bitches, it'll be just us and no one else! Plus, everyone is gonna be at this party this weekend!"

SS2 concurs. "Yeah, everyone's gonna be at the party!"

Niko's annoyed. "Oh ye's of little faith—wake up! There'll be tons of college guys there, we don't need our boyfriends!"

SS3 is confused. "Your boyfriend isn't coming, Niko?"

Niko coughs. "Well, he has to drive us out in his van."

SS1 gasps. "See, I knew it. I'm not going if the Stars aren't."

SS2 gasps as well. "Yeah, we aren't coming."

"Fine, you guys. You're so lame sometimes."

SS1 shakes her hair a third time, then reaches into her book bag for her own cigarettes. She dresses like most girls at the Academy, in the sense that her skirt is rolled and her blouse is pulled back. However, during weekends, she transforms into a Niko and wears slinky club clothes when she parties, drinks too much, and eventually starts freak dancing her boyfriend in public. (It's where the girl rubs her butt in the boy's crotch).

"What about you, Sykosa? Who're you gonna bring?"

SS2 lights up. Her skirt is also rolled, her blouse also pulled back and, during weekends, she too wears skimpy club clothes. Her boyfriend dislikes dancing, though. For that matter, so does Niko's. Thus, the two often dance like lovers. They freak, hug, and kiss (no tongue, pervs). They have a bond since both feel physically inadequate. "Yeah, who're you gonna bring?"

It's been noticed how Sykosa and Tom are closer, as some girls have relationship Dopplers. They also, of course, know about Sadie Hawkins, which she took Tom to. Now, before he sounds like a big jerk for not asking her to Prom, Hazu had just broken Niko's heart, so seeing as everyone's lives were in romantic shambles, everyone went as a big group.

I wasn't lying to my parents about that part.

The dance was also awkward, so they don't talk about it.

She plays dumb. "Whom do you mean?"

"Tom! Are you ever gonna hook up with that boy?"

SS2 nods. "Yeah, hook up with that boy! Then, we'd all have boyfriends! That would be so cool!"

Should it need to be said: no one knows she hooks up with Tom behind the chapel. "I don't know what you're talking—"

Niko interrupts. "Relax, girls, I invited Tom. Maybe Sykosa will finally get some action this weekend."

SS1 pouts. "How so unfair! Your first hookup out there all by yourselves? That's so romantic."

SS2 has big, starry eyes. "Yeah, that's so romantic!"

Her attention splits since her butt is tight with poop, which reminds her why she came here. She uses the last stall where the light barely reaches. For one, she likes her privacy because girls are strange. Defecate in a normal bathroom and females hang around doing makeup to find out who pooped and feel gross for them. There're other reasons. Last year, when she first got the key to this bathroom, she came here to poop and...

Well, she can't go there.

(Her eyesight gets fuzzy again).

Niko rolls her eyes again. "Whatever, you guys, go ahead and go to Ass Girl's party and—"

SS2 interrupts. "It's funny how you call her Ass Girl."

Niko pouts. "Come here, whore." SS2 rushes over and she gives Niko a hug while Niko lays her arm over SS2 like she is a boy. "You always know what to say to make me feel better."

SS2 giggles. "Don't worry, you'll get Hazu back. You will."

Niko agrees and decides this situation calls for a little reverse psychology. "You girls go to Ass Girl's party! But, you're going to be disappointed because no one throws a bash like me. So, go hang with the Bitches. I mean, you're only welcome because Ass Girl's such a slut for Hazu; otherwise, you'd never be invited and they'd laugh at you for showing."

The Sluts have worried expressions.

SS1 throws her hair. "Should we do a girls' weekend?"

SS2 agrees. "Yeah, let's do a girls' weekend!"

Niko throws up her arms. "Thank you!"

SS2 wraps her arms around Niko again, but talks to Sykosa. "Well, are you gonna come?"

She spaced out, hoping her disinterest would prompt their exit. Then, in the last stall, she'll sit, staring at the door graffiti. First, *Kana's a coke whore*. Second, *I hate myself*. It will begin again. That time, last year, when she was in that stall trying to shit in peace, the deadbolt snapped back and she stayed silent, hoping she would go unnoticed. That happened, and she got the "pleasure" of hearing a distressed Donna Harly tell a story about a boy feeding her a pill. He put his hands on her. Donna pushed him, to find she was pushed back, pushed open, then pushed into. She was his toy. And more than Donna wanted freedom, she wanted it to end. If she surrendered, then he'd shoot in his condom and leave her, like they all do, to cry alone. She breaks free. "What?"

SS2 giggles. "You gonna come to Niko's party?"

Niko chimes in. "She's talking to her parents, but it's super hard with Sykosa's parents."

SS1 has returned to the mirror. "That sucks."

SS2 returns, too. "Yeah, that sucks!"

It does suck, not this weekend, but these last few minutes.

Periodically, she comes here to remember she's like Donna. That boy would've been atop her, her legs forced open and he'd be inside while she played dead, praying this might be one of those memories so blurred by fear she'd never actually remember it. These thoughts aggravate her core. The weight is upon her lungs and her eyes are fuzzy. It's why... It's why—after Donna left with Mackenzie—she wiped clean her cheeks, then her asshole, had no cigarette to smoke since she did not yet smoke, but instead put her pen on the stall door and, right underneath *Kana is a coke whore*, wrote: *I hate myself.*

This isn't her story. This isn't her life.

I do hate myself, though. And I blame myself.

Niko's perked up. "You're all making the right decision. We will be the hottest party in all of Idaho!" That sounded wrong. "I mean, it'll be cool anyway."

SS1 separates and picks at her bangs. "Let's talk to the boys. Maybe they'll want to come."

SS2 does, too. "Yeah, Niko, let's invite the boys!"

Niko vetoes. Hazu is a 100% no-go and a potential deal breaker. After all, Ass Girl is white, as well is her ass, and he's drowning in it. Niko's smart and patient about these things. She knows if she makes Hazu miserable, he'll come back to her. It has to seem like his decision, though. "Let the boys rot. I bet they're calling you complaining about how bored they are without you."

SS1 likes this notion, especially since she expects her boy will do this. "Okay, girls' weekend!"

SS2 agrees. "Girls' weekend!" Then, she smiles big before she hugs Niko. "Hopefully your parents let you come, Sykosa!"

"Maybe, I'm going to try really hard."

The Pep Squad, who wait in earnest, simmer down.

It's still there, though.

She hates Mike Holler. The raping bastard.

It could've been me.

That's the thing. No one raped her. She feels raped anyway. She feels naked when clothed. She feels alone when with company. She feels used, even when appreciated. It's led her to the conclusion that rape is an assault on all women. And why not? Everyone put up with Donna being raped. Everyone would've put up with her getting raped...or Niko, or the Sluts, or anyone with girl parts. That's why rape isn't a crime, it's a statement. And that's why it's hopeless. Which explains why she latched her skirt, adjusted her sweater vest, then exited the stall, exited the bathroom, and went back to her normal life.

Hours later, post-"meltdown," Tom was bloody on the floor.

Apparently, he didn't approve of the statement.

Niko's proud of herself. "Girls' weekend, it is. Keep in mind, Timmy's coming cause he's over twenty-one and that's vital."

SS1 snubs her smoke. "It's cool that you date an older guy."

SS2 does the same. "Yeah, we wish we dated older guys."

"It has its advantages, like the booze."

Seconds later, the Sluts walk through sprits of perfume and say their ta-tas, leaving Niko and Sykosa alone. Niko's in front of the mirror. Her eyes are glued to the nine imperfections on her face. Niko's documented these areas for the better part of her life, and she's failed in all her attempts to hide them. "Are you more excited about this weekend?"

"I guess."

"I don't understand you. I mean, if Tom goes, don't you—"

She interrupts. "I don't know."

That means no.

"I don't get it. What's the matter?"

What's the matter is she likes her relationship being unlike the Sluts'. She likes how Tom is different. If she brings him to Coeur d'Alene, he might become just another "guy," like all high school boys are "guys." Crazy as it sounds, she saw Ass Girl's party as a testing ground for going public with their relationship, and, if that went well, taking their relationship to his bedroom after school. *I'm tired of the chapel, too.* But it's hard. Lots of stuff has been drilled into her by her parents, by the Academy, by Mother Superior. Like, it's insane, but she justifies her sexuality with Tom by the fact that he never touches her vagina. *That's why the rule exists—if I never feel anything, it's not my fault.* And her sanctity as a woman is untarnished. It's a retard theory, but she's bought into it, and it's not even her first concern. It's Mackenzie. That M. *I'm not certain our relationship can handle this weekend.* She isn't certain he cares.

"Don't get ahead of yourself, my parents will say no."

V.

The long, lonely hallways fill with moving bodies and slamming lockers. Teachers monitor these happenings like night watchmen. Far be it for them to understand, but every so often, girls pull hair and boys break noses. Far be it for her to understand, but every so often, her stomach cramps like someone installed a dome light in her colon. She thinks she'll shit soon. She'll go back to that secret bathroom, which will hopefully be empty, to be in that same stall, stare at those same words, think those same thoughts, and fall in love with him all over again.

Don't give in, Sykosa! The Pep Squad—teenage boys and girls in red-grey cheer uniforms with two-toned pom-poms—assembles in her mind. *Fight, Sykosa, fight!*

However, she can't hear the Pep Squad over Tom.

"Did you hear? I was late for another class." Yes, Tom, I sit around and gossip about how late you were for class. Oh yes, that's what I do! "I guess I got enough tardies that they might suspend me." Poor you, oh poor poor you, I'm only having a breakdown! "I hope my Mom isn't too pissed."

Blackness.

She tells herself not to think about him, not to feel for him.

She fails.

It annoying how his every sentence is like a new paragraph. Once again, he doesn't notice. He only waits by her locker. Like a dog. She performs her obligatory evaluation of him. He sucks. Everything that made him cute this morning sucks too. His shirt isn't firmly tucked, his collar isn't firmly straight, his smile is crooked, and a piece of hair has sprung loose from the collected whole.

Why is he such a slob?

Pep Squad: *Don't give in, Sykosa! Fight, Sykosa, fight!*

"I probably can't come here in between classes." ¶ "I wanted to let you know." ¶ "Anyways, what did you think of what Niko said earlier?" His speech is garbled by chewy candy pieces. Each chewy is wrapped in a wax paper housing, and instead of throwing the wrappers away, he puts them in his front pocket. *Slob!* "Hello, are you in there?" ¶ "Sykosa?" ¶ "Are you mad at me or something?"

Don't think about him. Don't feel about him.
Blackness.

"I'm sorry, I..." *I need a hug and chocolate and a laxative, if you can spare one.* She pauses. They don't hug around other people, only behind the chapel. *I'm a slut.* "I'm stressing out over all this crap. You and Niko have these cool parents, but mine are freaks. They're coming to parent-teacher conferences tonight, and afterwards, I'll be locked in my room until I have all As." Inside her locker, she twists material until a textbook slides out. A note's attached to it. *Do homework.* "And I didn't start my homework for my next class. I forgot it yesterday."

"Is it an important assignment?"

No. "Yes, and I have to get it done as soon as possible. Hold this." Her bag unloads onto his unsuspecting arms and he stumbles like the weight of her bag is the weight of the world. *And you know what? It is the weight of the world. And, mind you, a little wimp like her finds a way to hold it every fucking day and why can't he? She'll tell you why. He stumbles not because he cannot stand steady, but because he is afraid to stand steady—afraid to be a fucking man and hold her fucking bag like a fucking man should!* "I'm sorry. It's heavy, isn't it?"

The anxiety is winning. Her thoughts are running.

She thinks how no one's perfect, except for her. She must be perfect, ever so perfect and everything else, or else everything will go wrong... *Relax.* It'll be worse without him. She wonders what he's feeling. He's smiling. *At what?* It's Mackenzie with her fancy Fendi book bag and her Invisalign braces. *Not only will Mackenzie have better grades, she'll have a better smile. Plus, Mackenzie's a better swimmer! Don't forget that! Fuck you.* She hates feeling inferior to Mackenzie in the boyfriend, or any, department. It relates to valedictorian, which barring a miracle, will be won by Mackenzie. It's all bullshit too. Nobody remembers, the Administration included, how Mackenzie spent last year slutting it up with the Bitches.

She was Donna's #2. And Lonny's #1 dickhole.

I wish.

Truthfully, even dating Lonny, Mackenzie never got the "bad girl" reputation. She also knows, for a fact, all the sex rumors about Mackenzie and Lonny were fake. As does everybody. All anyone knows is Mackenzie's a prude, and not in the "waiting for marriage" way, but in the "I don't understand anything about my body" way. Otherwise known as the girls who over-invest in the sexual purity Catholicism encourages.

Hell, Mackenzie probably doesn't even masturbate.

How weird is that?

Moving on, Tom sets down her worldly bag. "M, in American history, our teacher passed out this review packet. I swear, it was hard. I barely finished one page."

"Didn't Sykosa help you?"

She speaks from inside her locker. "He spent all class joking with Niko. That's why nothing's done."

Mackenzie shrugs. Sykosa behaving like a freak-a-zoid, how unordinary. "Well, Tom, I'll help you finish it tonight."

Her eyebrows climb her forehead.

Not if he knows what's good for him.

"That'd be cool."

She looks inside her locker. It's gray.

Sometimes that is all it will ever be.

"Hey, I have the pictures from the Sonics game." Mackenzie un-tucks the flap of the 24-hour photo package. "And this one! Remember, you spilled your drink all over the Sonic Squash?" M giggles, staring at him with a typhoon of brown irises so innocent even Sykosa has the urge to fuck the little bitch until she cries. Worse, they have that touchy-feely friendship. The one where everyone thinks they're hooking up soon. "Take these, I have my own copy. Why didn't you call last night?"

"I'm sorry, M. Were you lonely without me?"

"A little."

We never go to Sonic games, or take pictures, or talk on the phone. The best they do is the infrequent party together or a mini-date on the weekends if she can separate from her folks. *And I... I...* Her hand shakes, her stomach quivers, and this sweeping weight overwhelms her lungs. It's going to happen. *Relax* won't work and the Pep Squad will fail and she will pass out. Right here. Right now. Upon the floor as if she were dead. *Relax.* She can't pass out in front of him. He thinks he saved her and that she is happy. So she tries to keep straight, but her eyesight has been infected by splotches of replicating green until her head gets dizzy. Her muscles drop a bunch of papers. She bends. He does, too, like a good dog. She smells his hair gel. It calms her. And it lets her heart, no longer burdened by her compact frame, pump blood to her brain.

Both their hands reach for a page, and their fingers touch.

He's warm, but scarred.

It's her fault. He saved her.

He did save you, so get it together.

She complains. "I'm such a klutz."

Mackenzie thinks this is lame. "I have to go. Call me, okay?"

This isn't her story. This isn't her life.

Mackenzie's totally lame. That's what you said, right?

Tom's voice is unsure. "O-okay."

Mackenzie playfully hits his arm. "Say it like you mean it! Call me tonight, you promise?"

He sounds less sure. "I promise."

M has gone. So has the blackness. She stacks her stuff and forgets her homework. If he's on timeshare, then she wants her minutes worth. The Pep Squad's in the background. *Don't give in, Sykosa! Fight, Sykosa, fight!* Not only for her salvation, but for her relationship. This is what loving Tom's like—constant attacks from Mackenzie that're quite immoral; yet, because it's Mackenzie, who's so sweet and innocent and lovable, it seems like M's right or even responsibility to try to steal Tom.

It's for the betterment of the species or something.

It's... There's something about white people. She hates to sound racist, but...

She ignores it. "Mackenzie is pretty insistent, huh?"

He looks like he noticed something he wasn't supposed to notice. "What do you mean?"

"Nothing, I suppose."

He believes her and forgets it, which mildly annoys her, but she ignores that since he is talking. His voice is calm, like he were asking her if it were raining outside. "I really came here cause I wanted to ask you something. Do you remember what Niko was talking about in class?" *Like I could forget!* And like she doesn't know exactly what he implies. She knows it like she knows every American knows two things: OJ Simpson is guilty and Bill Clinton had his dick sucked. Like he wants her to go to his bedroom after school, of course he wants to go to Niko's cottage. *To *.* He continues on as if this isn't a big deal. "Are you really asking your parents if you can go? Because I'll have my mom talk to Niko."

While she needs to address the sex thing, the hallway isn't the ideal place. Also, it'd be nice if they could discuss it on a day not so steeped in blackness. *Like maybe next week, after this one-year anniversary is over!* She wants it to pass as if it never happened. Fortunately, one topic commands that type of attention. She has to be careful how she brings it up—if Niko finds out, she'll be pissed. *She knows I committed to Ass Girl's party without telling her, she probably thinks I'm lying about other stuff.* "What makes you think your mom will say yes?"

He's confused. "What?"

"Your mother is gonna let you go for a weekend by yourself with Niko's mother?"

He gets it.

His body gets tense, and his expression is disappointment, yet he looks off, clearly scheming. "That might be a problem."

"My parents don't trust Kana, specially since the 'incident.'"

"I remember that." His face's still disappointed. And he still

carries the same will to ignore it. It's amassed itself in his shoulders, which seem to be holding back lots of energy. She's seen him like this before. He gets an idea in his head and he can't let it go. "But we could be alone together."
Like she said, this isn't the place. "I know."
"Will you try? Just ask?"
It's a split-second decision she doesn't think about.
My parents are gonna say no. They say no to everything.
"Okay, I'll ask."
At the dinner table, things are right on schedule. Her father is behind the newspaper, and her mother has sat down late, as she's always forgotten something for the meal that draws everyone's attention to how tireless her work is. A bunch of nothing talk about everyone's day leads to nothing talk about the day to come—where she mentions Coeur d'Alene.

Her parents don't know everything about last year. Only a few choice people—Tom, Donna, Mike, herself—know it one hundred percent, but her parents do know it was connected to Niko's Coeur d'Alene party. It's probably why her father finds himself struck with indigestion, reaching into his breast pocket for antacids. "You ask us this question every year, and every year you get the same answer."

Like she said, exactly on schedule.
My daddy's saving me like a daddy should!
"I know, Dad."
"Based on what your teachers say tonight, you may go for the weekend. I won't reward bad grades. You must get an A on this American history test."

She has heard her parents say "no" so many times, she just shuts off while they do it. It hurts less. Besides, her eyes have been distracted all afternoon anyhow. She keeps peeking down to see her boobs in her old summer-camp tee-shirt from fifth grade Girl Scouts. She loves how tee-shirts for little girls are cut with no regard for boobs, so when she wears them now, her breasts look about twice their size and her tummy looks about half and...

Did he say what I think he did?
"What?"

He looks okay with his decision. "You're almost seventeen, and Niko's invited you up there for years. I think now that the situation with her mother has settled, and you're older, you can handle a trip like this."

Okay, that was out of nowhere.

And what is it about my life this last year?

It's almost like her life were a TV show—her own little TV show with her own modest, yet significant TV ratings. Then, she turned fifteen and the "male, 18-49" demographic tuned in, and with them came the big advertisers, focus groups, and execs "retooling" her show, which's become a bunch of sex and tiny outfits and a father who turns her over to a teenage boy. She almost wishes he said, "No" and then said it was, "for her own good." *Actually, that's what I was counting on.* Those days are apparently done. At some point, some public service announcement or random article, who knows, convinced him teenage girls are more mature than teenage boys. They perform better in athletics, possess greater pain thresholds, higher GPAs, and in general, know what they're doing.

The problem was no one called on them in class.

It's been fixed now.

Her mother knows that nothing's fixed. She's not as easily deceived by fancy language, maybe because her own English is as spackled as the walls. "Your teacher grades during fifth-hour free period. You call here with that grade before you leave, understand?" Then, her mother glares at her father. Oh my, the folks are gonna have issues tonight. Her mother leaves it. "Just because Niko's mother is there doesn't mean you can do whatever you want."

She's a tad deer-in-headlights. "Okay."

"You need to make better choices than her."

"Okay."

"And you're to behave as if we were there, no exceptions."

"Okay."

Dinner is awkward thereon. She retreats to her head where she tries to figure out her feelings on this. The blackness has no problem with this weekend. She breathes fine, sees fine, but she doesn't want to think about it. Once the food is finished, she goes to her bedroom, where she doesn't have to think about it. Her TV plays a syndicated episode of Friends. That numbs her. *Ah, it's so good!* Six people who sit around and talk about nothing, deal with nothing, fight about nothing, and have a wedding every season or so. Oh, to have situational problems! Real is overrated. She wants to be fake—fake and transparent and to never worry again.

And there is something wrong.

It involves her underwear, all of them lying in a pile by her cabinet door. This pair is pink. That pair is white. Those pairs are stolen. These pairs are not. She's worn them all, but somethings's still wrong. It's the blackness. She thought it was fine, but no, it wants another go. It wants... Like, when Niko went to Coeur d'Alene last year, Niko left as Niko2.0, when Niko returned, she was Niko3.0, and Niko3.0 led a charge against Donna that... *Relax*. The best way to relax is to think about boys. Mike Holler comes to mind. *Wrong boy to think about.* She changes panties and thinks of anyone but Mike—maybe Tom or Hazu or Lonny—the male, in general. She looks at Fievel, atop her bedspread, with that same deceptive eye under his hat brim, watching her butt like it was bacon.

She calls Niko on the phone.

"He said I could go if my conferences aren't too bad, and I ace my test tomorrow." It never occurs to her that lying would get her out of this. She sounds unenthusiastic. "It shouldn't be any trouble. I'll study after we get off the phone."

Niko chews gum. It sounds like two people sucking face. "None of your teachers are gonna be mean, right?"

"I've been good lately, for the most part."

"This means you get to tell Ass Girl to fuck off about her party! You're going to mine!"

This part over joys Niko.

She just stares at her reflection, currently donning a pair of boy-cut low-risers. She looks at her butt like Fievel did. It looks... She can't think of a word. *Not like my butt, I guess.* She takes care in the panties she buys. She thinks they often speak to her core or they have a greater meaning, so to have so many look so wrong is... *Relax.* She puts her thighs together and her free hand pushes them down past her knees. "I think she'll understand. There's a big difference between partying here and doing it at your cottage."

"No shit, there is. This is exciting! Have you told Tom yet?"

I guess I should. "No, not yet." She wiggles a purple thong up her ass cheeks, then pulls it until it lays symmetrically. *What's wrong?* Not to sound like a vain princess or anything, but usually when she finds something she thinks she looks good in, it improves her mood. She persists. Taking off the purple thong, then feeling at her tar-black pubic hairs. She should shave. Everything he's seen of her has been trim and tidy, and her twat should have a similar effect. *Where did that thought come from?* "We don't talk on the phone together."

"You know Tom is coming, right?"

She puts her hand in her hair, shocked. "How do you know he's coming? I don't even know that! How does everyone know more about my boyfriend than me?"

"Your boyfriend?"

Now, I'm going to get it. "I mean..."

Niko sings. "Sykosa and Tom sittin' in a tree, kay-eye-ess-ess-eye-en-ge! First comes love, then comes marriage—"

"Shut up!"

"Then comes the baby in the baby carriage!"

"Seriously, I don't love him. It's not like that."

"Alright, why you gotta take all the fun outta everything?"

Actually, it's Tom who does it—by being so damn confusing. *Relax.*

Some turquoise string panties are applied to her personals. They swoop low and make her belly look washboard flat. They also show a bit of toe, and since showing toe is slutty, Tom will like it. Tom liking it gives her some relief. She's worried about that. Whenever she feels the need to be attractive for him, it's usually a sign he's about to get his way.

"Do you think I love him?"

The gum pauses. "I was kidding."

"Alright, I was just making sure."

She will believe this lie. In these turquoise panties, she will believe anything. Except she clearly needs to lose five pounds. If he sees her naked like this, she will die of embarrassment. She frowns. *Ugh.* This is bigger than wanting to be attractive for him. Somehow, her underwear have come to symbolize her cherry. *It's hard. Like, I know Tom and I have the chemistry to get me to that place.* She looks at her vagina again. Her chest wants to rip. It took a long time to attain what fragile confidence she has in her looks. Mostly it's due to all his lavish attention, but if she picks the wrong panties and her vagina looks ugly, then she'll...

I'm sensitive about my genitals. Let's leave it at that, okay?

Niko's dismissive. "Chill! I know he's coming because his mom called my mom—or me—and I said that I was coming."

Her massive bottom's in the mirror again. Her lips scrunch. The blackness makes it difficult to think coherently. All these different thoughts are competing for space in her brain, but one eventually wins. *Wait, I don't even want to have sex with Tom!* It's true. She doesn't. If she did, she'd have started going back to his bedroom. This realization only makes things worse. He hasn't mentioned sex; only "time alone," and she assumed sex all by herself. Now, she's trying on panties, every single pair she has, not because he plans on having sex with her, but because she expects to sleep with him. She's not stupid. That means she's going to * him. Her mind has already made the decision and this is the part where she freaks out.

She guesses sex could be nice.

I'll give him my virginity as a gift for his sacrifice.

On the one-year anniversary of it, no less.

[BLACKNESS].

She struggles to see. "He's coming for sure?"

"For sure. I mean, don't get me wrong, it took some time."

"It did?"

"His mom was worried there would be shenanigans."

"Cause of what happened last year with Kana?"

"Yeah." Niko moves on. She dislikes talking about it. "And it's gonna be the best bash I've ever had! I'm going out with Timmy tonight to get alcohol and stuff. He called me and cried about his grandmother dying again."

Timmy crying? I don't believe it. "Who's coming with us?"

Niko sits up in bed! That's the best part! "Tom, Mackenzie, Timmy, Timmy's friend and major hottie, Clyde. He plays in some band. He's the lead guitarist. Oh, and all of us Queens! We're probably all going to drive up in Timmy's van, and when we get up there and word gets out about the party, a bunch of other people will show."

What a crew! Niko's so proud. Hazu'll be so jealous when he hears about it!

While she's happy for Niko, she's concerned for herself.

"Why's Mackenzie coming?"

Niko smacks her gum. "Tom asked if she could go, and she came last year, so it's kinda hard to say no."

"Is she bringing the Bitches with her?"

"No."

Odd. "She's going out there by herself—with us Queens?"

"Yep, it's just her."

Just Mackenzie. Just him. *And me.*

She can't ignore this anymore. He apparently wants to sleep with her, or maybe Mackenzie, and she will apparently sleep with him, assuming Mackenzie doesn't, and, as much as she may want to, it shouldn't be free, for her or Mackenzie. Well, Mackenzie can get JBF'd by whatever guy is not Tom. *I don't give a shit.* However, before she gets JBF'd by Tom, she wants to be sweet-talked, taken to the movies, hold hands, kiss and be his girl without fear of being an insurance policy in case Mackenzie won't put out.

Maybe I can just do BJS.
Maybe. That makes her feel worse. Besides, it's not his fault. There're good reasons why they've kept their relationship on the down-low. *You saw how my parents responded yesterday after he called.* Their love is probably a bad idea, and maybe a disaster in wait, but she can't stop feeling for him, nor can she help her desire for him to feel, so she'd prefer to do it where people who don't understand the situation can't judge it.
I just thought we'd have more figured out by now.
"Do you think he wants to sleep with me?"
"Has he said he wants to?"
"He said he wanted to be alone, but I think he does."
"What do you want to do?"
Sleep with him. "I don't know."
Niko sounds resigned. "He'll beg for it. Guys do that."
He's a guy. He'll beg for it. Maybe he'll make the decision for her. *No, he can't do that for me.* She has to know when she leaves if she will or will not, even though she already knows she will. She lowers the turquoise. She feels fatter, filthier, and her hairy pussy keeps being her hairy pussy. She knows. If she is to do something so bold, then these turquoise panties are her only option. Call it ditzy. She'll call it a rabbit's foot. "Promise me something, okay? If I don't want to, can I stick by you?"
"Isn't that sorta the point? We're gonna hang out together."
Relax. "Okay."
"Hey, I gotta jet. Call me when the new Friends starts."
"Sure, I'll study until then."

VI.

Pencil writes across her American history review assignment, then stops as her fingers rub eraser until the page is rollings of Pepto pink and shots of gray that dust her skin silver. Normal dust agitates her nose. *Achoo!* It's funny. Her nostrils affect her more than most people and people have names, so she should name her nostrils. Name the President. Name the General. Name the date. The place. The reason. The result. Three pages of questions remain, answers laid in fifty-five dog-eared pages of underlined passages. Remember this! Don't forget that!

All this history makes her feel like she is dying.

She needs a break.

On her bay window, she wraps herself in her fleece blanket, and bends to cover her toes. That quasi-panic attack knocked her out. She thinks that's the medical definition of the blackness. She's never consulted anyone about it, but she heard a daytime TV personality talking about it once and all the hairs stood on up on her neck and she thought, *That's me.* The TV personality said trauma plays a significant role. That made her feel broken, so she decided not to listen anymore and to pretend like nothing was wrong. That's why no one knows about the blackness—her pretending won't let them. As she knows if her mother, Mother Superior, or the Administration knew about it, they'd try to fix it and she doesn't think they can, nor does she trust them anymore. Thus, she fights it by her lonesome—and, trust her, it does fight, and fight, and like a wildfire, it exhausts her until even it can no longer self-sustain.

That's where she's at right now.

She cannot be sick any longer. She cannot worry any more.

The same compulsion that drives her to panic is driving her to rest. In fact, it's like the street lamp down the road, a post surrounded by indistinguishable insects. It gets blurry, splitting

into a transparent twin that reforms after every long blink before it splits...again...and...she...
Is asleep. And dreaming.
About sock-hops and ice cream socials. About prom dances and prom dresses. About those cute twins next door and being taken away in the Nautilus to meet a cute French boy who likes to build airplanes. About being a television actress who makes a million dollars an episode, walks red carpets, wears fancy jewelry, looks into the camera, and talks about how fame has not changed her. Bullshit. She sought fame so it could change her.
Change her now.
The phone rings.
She sniffles as she depresses the green button. "Hello?"
"Hey."
"Who's this?"
"It's Tom."
She jars, stuck in sleepiness. She thinks this is when he dumps her. He called the other night, says her father, and it must have been to dump her. The handjob was the last hurrah. But, he needs to understand that her parents are crazy and he shouldn't dump her, not if he is worried about...
This doesn't make any sense. "Uh, hi."
"What's up?"
"Nothing, did you need something?"
"One second." One second. "Sorry, I'm on the freeway now. What did you say?"
He never calls.
"Did you need something?"
"Naw, I don't know, wanna talk?" Her turquoise panties are folded in a square atop a pile of clothes she wants to take this weekend. She thinks she should put them on. They might help her phone technique. "Are your parents gone for conferences?"
"Um, let me check." Her alarm clock is on her nightstand. "Yeah, they probably left twenty minutes ago."
"Great, I got food I didn't finish. I'll come over."

She needs to pack. And she has that test tomorrow. There is no time to be his plaything. Then his words hit her. Sleeping does make her hungry. "You have food?"

"Mackenzie and I went out to eat. She helped me finish my American history packet. Have you finished it?"

"Almost. Are you sure you want to come over?"

Him coming over is one of those risks that ends badly. Her parents will come home early. A neighbor will mention the car in her driveway. He'll fall down the stairs and she'll have to call an ambulance. Plus, there's her house. Three bedrooms. Two.five baths. One kitchen. If he enters her little life, he might suffer his own bout of claustrophobia. Or he'll see her furniture. The scratched up dinner table. The two family room couches that're a sun bleached yellow. The tacky sunflower matting in the drawers and cupboards. No one knows, except Niko, her father's a union leader for the ILWU. He doesn't play stocks, investment bank, or whatever everyone else's fathers do. He spends all his money on her tuition.

She feels guilty for being so ungrateful.

Maybe she is a liberal.

"Yeah, I'm coming over. Where do you live anyway?"

"Oh, you have to go north."

"I can do that."

Oddly, she wants him to ask her to Prom and, you know, love her forever; yet, asking him to turn his car around is a burden she cannot bear on him. "But, you're already going home."

"Not anymore!" His horn blares in the background. "I need to exit here, get out of my way!" More adolescent horn beeps and name calling. She imagines his goofy looks and charming eyes. She wonders what he'd feel if he knew she spent all evening trying on underwear. She wonders what kind of stuff he does when he thinks about her. "Is it Lake City or Bothell?"

"Kinda in between. It's Exit 177, then take Ballinger Way until you see the big bookstore, then turn left at the light, left at the stop sign. I'm at the top of the hill."

"I have great news."

"You're going to Niko's this weekend!"

"Yeah, how'd you know?"

"It's a best friend thing. Niko called and told me—"

He interrupts...you get it. "Did you ask your parents?"

Really, what boggles her is why this interruption was even necessary. *Let me finish my sentence!* "Uh—"

He interrupts again. "Forget it. I'll be there in ten minutes."

He hangs up and she pops a whitehead in the mirror. The fuckers only come around when she sleeps. She thought her reflection would look happier. That attack stole her ability to feel. She wants to feel again. Um, change clothing! She decides on her too-tight jeans. She bought them after Niko told her a girl should always keep a pair of jeans that don't fit, that way she always has an excuse to be on a diet. And she's not been on a diet. So she puts her feet through the ends, then grips either side—ready to prove that, in the manner one runs a potato sack race, two objects can occupy the same space at the same time.

Go!

She jumps across the floor, her hands pulling like hydraulic pistons until it's at her hips and the button's closed. *Let's see him finger me now!* Forget the witty remarks—must complete outfit. She chooses a belt with cowboy tassels that dangle to her mid-thigh while her feet slip into some Earthy sandals. Obviously, she leaves the Girl Scout shirt be because her boobs look good in this shirt, whereas they're hidden at the Academy. He also really likes her boobs, so if he sees them in this shirt, he'll think it's worth seeing them somewhere else besides the chapel.

Like at Prom.

For kicks, she puts on shiny lip gloss and parts her hair down the middle. When she does this, someone's kid always says she looks like Disney's Pocahontas. After that, she sits on her bay window and waits for him. She didn't jerk him off today. Maybe that's why he is coming. He is coming to cum. *That's funny.* They did make out, like they do. He liked her green thong, of course, and he grabbed it and begged to feel her pussy, but rules are rules, and once his fingers dug too deep, she feigned anger while he feigned apologies.

She gets it now. He's desensitizing her.

Day by day he's moving millimeters closer to her vagina in much the same way he got his penis in her hand. So you know, it didn't just "happen." It took months. It started with holding her against his erection, then tucking it underneath his belt, then humping her thigh, then humping between her thighs, then loosening his belt to hump her with only his boxers and, in the process, coming his pants what must've been a hundred times. Then, low and behold, one day he kisses her, and she kisses him, and he humps her, and he says it's uncomfortable, and he asks if she'll take over, and it almost felt like her idea.

You know what happened.

She knows it too.

His SUV, a Lexus RX something, is in her drive. He got it a few weeks ago. It's snazzy. It's also the primary reason why going to his bedroom after school is even an option. That's not on her mind, though. He is. And she runs to meet him at the screen door, then perform her obligatory evaluation of him. He's in his uniform minus the starchiness. And his cotton shirt is scraggly where it was tucked in his pants. His blond hair's fallen forward. He has a sinister feel when its slicked back, like a rich asshole who wants to buy her. Lastly, she sniffs him. He smells like carbohydrates. He has two trapezoid containers with the tops that open four ways.

"It's yakisoba."

The sight of it causes her waist to expand, and she doubts, in these pants, she can swallow without having a hernia. "I'm not hungry. You can finish it, if you want."

"I'm not hungry either. I just ate."

He surfs his way around the kitchen, still in his shoes. Lucky boy. If her mother were home, he would be under her omnipresent condescendence. "For future reference, take off your shoes—"

He interrupts. "I'm sorry. Is it a parent thing?"

"It's a Japanese thing."

He walks to the door where his one foot digs his other foot out of unpolished leather, which then copies the motion for its partner. He has black socks.

"There."

It's nice when he listens. She feels like putting her pointer fingers through his belt loops, then giving him an Eskimo kiss. At times, he knows these things—like what she wants, and what she needs, and he's able to give them to her. He does that now. Hugging her, like seeing her, is really special to him, like getting a hug from her from somewhere other than the chapel or away from school matters to him. At the end, he gives her an openmouth kiss like a husband might give his wife when he gets home from work, and he gives her butt cheek a squeeze.

When they separate, her hands are on his chest.

"You're still in your uniform?"

He ignores her. "Do I get a tour?"

"You can see everything from where you're standing."

"Come now, you can do better than that."

She shrugs. "It isn't like your house."

"How do you know that?"

"Fine, how large is your house?"

"I live in an apartment downtown, by the waterfront."

Is there no end to his subtle insults? "Uh, I know that."

He smirks. "Yeah, you do, don't you?"

"I meant house as in home, and judging by your car, my house isn't like your apartment."

"Who cares?"

She realizes she dodged a landmine. It was an opportunity for him to mention his bedroom. Even so, she doesn't consider herself so lucky as to give a tour. She's about to say such, but then she stops. *This is a trial run.* What happens in her house sets the standard for what happens in his. She makes a mental note of that, then finally says as much. "Exactly. Let's skip it."

"Let's do it and say we didn't."

They go through all the rooms. She folds her hands one

over the other and claps when she feels embarrassed. She also feels it's somewhat necessary to be upfront about her poverty, thus she points out the water stain on the hallway ceiling, the chipped tile in the bathroom, and the parts of the carpet that look clawed. He watches with no regard. He laughs sometimes, too. He thinks her behavior is ridiculous. She feels stupid, but it's the good stupid. This is the kinda stuff she would come out and tell people if she trusted them.

She feels intimate.

The tour ends upstairs.

"And that's my house."

They're in the balcony that runs after the stairs between her bedroom and the bathroom. The track lights are turned down to a sunset orange. He's beautiful in it. "And that door?"

She is coy. "What door?"

"That's your room, isn't it?"

"Yeah, it's my room, but you can't go in it."

"Why not?"

She gives him a spoiled brat attitude. "Because you can't."

He fights a deceitful grin. Troublemaker. They stare at each other and, once the rules are laid, he stands above her, big and bold, from his six-foot-two frame. "I'm gonna see it."

"Uh-uh."

He steps right, and she steps left, then he steps left, and she goes right. Her fingertips touch her door, as do her shoulder blades. He touches the slice of her hip that exposed itself when her shirt bunched; it's like charged wires shocking her skin. She gives him a very female look, so he knows to forget it.

He pretends not to see. "I'm coming in."

Boys are fun. "No, you're not."

"Yes, I am."

This isn't her story. This isn't her life.

No, he'll ask! I know this time he'll ask!

"No, you aren't." He licks his lips, then looks left. The fake out. He skits right and she holds out her arms. She laughs. "Tom, no!" She wraps herself around him, blockading him and pulling on his shirt so she might be like dead weight. He spins her around, so she locks her arms against the doorframe. He tickles her sides and she jumps, laughing hysterically. "Stop, Tom! Stop! That's cheating!"

He does stop, but it starts in his pants. When she held onto the door, her ass rubbed against him. Girls are fun. "Come on, you know I'm gonna win."

"I'll never jerk you off again."

"Oh, that's a lie!" He reaches for her sides and she releases the wall. "Got ya!" He scoops her up and she hangs over his shoulder. He's strong for his age. "Let's see you stop me."

"Stop it. Do not go in there!"

He kicks down her door.

"Let's see here... School books? Homework? What's this?" He stops at her desk. Her white and gold soft pack stares him in the face. "Cigarettes, huh? How cliché. You know, in this age of post-Madonnaism, it'd be more rebellious to quit."

She feels silly, but it's nice he's somewhat like himself again. He felt a bit off in the hallways this morning, then behind the chapel this afternoon. She pretends like she doesn't know what it is, but she does. He's nervous. He really, really wants this weekend. She can see how much he wants to have her to himself for a little while.

She won't lie. She feels it, too.

"So now that you're in my room you have some commentary to offer on my life?"

"Commen-whata?"

"Do you have any idea what you're talking about?"

He puts his foot upon her desk chair, then looks above like many a philosopher before him. "I've no idea, but your smart-ass is right next to me. I must be learning by osmosis."

She hits him. "Let me down, I'm serious."

"Wait a second."

"No, let me down."

"Jackpot!" She's spun, her room blurry and her hair against the wall (almost smacked her head). His hands release her and her feet hit the floor, both her bones and the metal desk handles rattle. She pushes the hair from her eyes and sees that he has fallen to his knees to inspect all the panties she wore.

"Wow, you own lots of sexy underwear. I've never seen these."

"Nope, not all of them."

She supposes she could be embarrassed. Though, his liking her underwear, while immature, is not surprising. And he gets to do stuff other boys don't. It's always been that way, and it's way too late to change that. So she waits until either he grows bored or she gets angry. He doesn't get bored, staring at a black g-string of transparent lace and three strings that're held by a silver ring at the top of her butt. He licks his lips, stretching it out, as if to see how big a girl could fit.

Eventually, his eyes move to her poochy butt.

"Let me see you in them."

Her mouth drops. "You wish."

"Hell yeah, I do." He kneels on both knees like they do in the pews at mass. He interlocks his fingers and thumbs, holding them over his head, making her his false idol. "Oh please, do not make me beg, Sykosa. Put it on and show it to me for five seconds, please!"

Those scars, on his fingers and hand, fill her eyes, and... They might be convincing, but not quite enough. "No."

"Please, I cannot live if I cannot see you in them."

"I'll tell you what, put them on for me, and I will for you."

"You've got to be kidding."

Actually, no, she's not. "No, I'm not."

"I'll look dumb."

Her finger snubs his snout. "I bet you'd look cute." He looks unamused. She interlocks her fingers and wells up her voice, like when she asks her father for money. "Oh, please wear my g-string, Tom. I cannot live if I cannot see you in it."

Her impression is a little too accurate. "Sykosa—"

She interrupts. "For five seconds, I'll count them for you."

"No way, I'll feel retarded."

"How do you think I'll feel?"

"There's a difference."

This oughta be interesting. "What's that?"

"Girls are supposed to wear that kind of stuff. Guys don't."

He's sort of right. It's made for girls. Thus, he's got a point. She has her point, too. And her eyes say how she's conflicted. And his are drunk in possibility. She can't do it. She just can't, for good reason or not. Besides, this is their trial run, and it's actually going well. Apparently, if they visit his bedroom, she'll get a really long hug, a good kiss, he'll still be his playful self, they'll still have their chemistry and, really, trying on panties is gonna mess everything up.

She kicks at the ground, so he knows he has upset her and to fix it. "I don't wanna. I thought you wanted to talk."

He's discarded her underwear and stood up. For once, she's so very happy he's so ADD. "Right then, talking. How often do you wear that thing?"

"Hardly ever, and let's talk about something else."

He slouches in her desk chair like a rebel as he looks over her room. He thinks it's a girly room, so girly with so many girl things, girls, yes girls—all he thinks about are girls. To his point, he wants to ogle her, and... *What's this?* She's sitting on her polished maple bay window, her legs drooped over the side, swinging back and forth while her bunched shoulders hang on, for dear life, to those melon tits with the candy drop nipples and... *I got it!* He has it. *I know!* He knows. *She looks like Pocahontas!* She looks as gorgeous as any girl he's ever seen. And this hot girl and her tight ass rubbed itself against him by her door. *She's such a babe.* "American history sucks, but it's okay. Tomorrow we'll be heading east to Coeur d'Alene."

"Did you say earlier that your family owned a place there?"

"Yes, my grandmother did. We visited during summers."

"But not any longer?" He raises his eyebrows. She feels like she intruded. "It's okay, if it's like family stuff."

"She died a while ago. My mother and her didn't get along."

"Your grandmother must've really driven your mother crazy then. I mean, I can't imagine being without my mom."

"Well, you get along with your mother."

I do? "What makes you think that?"

"You seem like someone who likes her parents."

Her parents, and by that she means her mother, betrayed her once. Had her mother been successful in that betrayal, she wouldn't have gone to the Academy, and never met Tom. "We have problems."

"You do?"

"Yes, but they're not as bad as they used to be."

He moves on. Family stuff and all. "Well, my grandma was my father's mother, so after they split, I didn't see her often."

"How long have your parents been divorced?"

"Long time, it seems."

"Do you see your father a lot?"

"No. Your parents are married, right?"

That's why we all live in the same house! "Yes."

"If you had to choose, who would you live with?"

"What?"

"Who would you live with?"

"I don't know. I've never thought about it." He does not believe her, nor does he stop staring as he waits for the truth. She coughs. Divorced kids are fucked in the brain. "So what's Coeur d'Alene like?"

He likes that question. His answer is swift. "It's right in the middle of nowhere. One second you're on the freeway, driving through the mountains and then pow! You break through the trees on a lake. And people are waterskiing and jet-skiing and having fun." Occasionally, at times like this, he has a unique sense to him and he's very poetic. When he sits back and lets the words come off his tongue, they sound slicked in butter. "You're coming, right? I mean, that's why you got these clothes everywhere, isn't it?"

She gives an uncertain look. "I'll know when my parents get back, but I'll probably be going either way."

"What do you mean?"

"My father's strict, but he's also a yes-or-no person. He said

I could go and that means I can, whether I meet his conditions or not." She says this and notices she no longer feels any turmoil about being alone with him this weekend. She'll forget it five seconds after he's gone. What she won't forget is how, if she goes to his bedroom, they're still gonna talk about stuff. He doesn't see it as a sex dungeon or anything strange. "That's how it is. But, if a teacher," *like our American history teacher who might be upset that you screwed off all morning,* is what she'd like to say, but doesn't, "trashes on me, who knows?"

He does appear relaxed in that chair and happy. She recalls his shoulders at her locker. *This weekend really matters to him.* She wonders why he invited Mackenzie. She doesn't ask, but he validates her impressions. "I can't believe this worked out. Yesterday, I was doing nothing this weekend, and now it's looking like it'll be the best weekend of the year. Good things come like that though."

Aw, that's so cute that he would say that.

Good things do come like that.

Like him, for instance.

Still, Mackenzie's on her mind. It's at times like these, she thinks, there's no way he loves Mackenzie. *He loves me.* It's so obvious she can hardly question it, but she doesn't know how to talk about it. "I agree, good things are like that."

"I spoke with Niko and worked out the details. I never heard it in real life, but on the phone, Niko talks as fast as light."

"Yeah, it can be tough to keep up—"

He interrupts. "I think her boyfriend is driving us up."

"Yeah, his name is Timmy."

"Is he cool?"

No. "I've only hung out with him a few times."

"How long have they dated?"

Since Ass Girl moved to town. "A few months."

It takes him a while to speak. "Niko... She seems a bit crazy sometimes."

You have no idea. "She's better now."

"Better?"

"Yeah, she was really out of control last year."
"When that thing happened with her mom?"
"Yeah."

He's stopped caring, kick-spinning the chair and stretching his arms behind his head. "M and I are driving to Niko's after school tomorrow. She said I can leave my car in her driveway and it shouldn't be a problem."

"It won't. You see, by 'driveway,' Niko meant 'parking lot.' By 'house,' she meant 'hotel.'"

"Niko lives in a hotel?"

"No! Her house...it's so big it's like a hotel, ya know?"

"I've never been. Isn't she like the richest girl in school?"

"Mackenzie may be richer."

"Her father's that guy. He owns all those companies, right?"

"Something about shipping, I'm not sure."

"And Niko's mother...of course."

"Of course."

He will have to leave soon. They know that. And they don't talk about it. Once they're out of things to discuss, they lie on her bed. He stays on his side and she stays on hers. *Does he already have a side?* Her head's propped up by her hand. The reception of her TV is poor. That's alright. His tongue is in her mouth. His feet are at her feet. And his boxers are full of jizz from humping her butt. He really needs to go and Friends will be starting. She thanks him for fixing her. It's hard to describe, but she didn't feel the blackness the whole time he was here. And that's great, as she now knows if she goes to his bedroom after school, he'll be as good as taking care of the blackness there as he is at taking care of it behind the chapel. Of course, he says he doesn't understand. She kisses him, watches his SUV drive off and then, in her bedroom, after a minute or two of doing nothing, humps a pillow much the same as he humped her. She doesn't have to deal with the jizz part. The new Friends is an old Friends so she doesn't call Niko. She studies instead. Then she shaves her pussy. And studies for her test again, right after she smokes a few.

VII.

White shimmers graze a polished cherry oak table, the length lined by a white slip presenting an arrangement of food stuffed fine China. Tomato sauce drowned pasta bowls browned on a stovetop in melted Swiss are built around an open grill where shish kabobs and crab cakes simmer. Wine corks fire like cannons across a sea of battle! Pouring from the thick necks of their clear-green bottles to the bellies of long-stemmed glasses. One of them belongs to Fievel, who balances atop his highchair by the rounded question mark of an umbrella. "I propose a toast! To prosperity! To friendship! To everything that's good in life! I say, here is not a toast for one, but a toast for all!" He stumbles, wine split onto his wrist. Princess Cindy excuses his poor demeanor. Her Fievel's such a show-off when he's drinking. And the guests are overjoyed—already raving this night is the best night that has ever come and not near as best as the nights that will follow.

She sits at the opposite end in a Victorian dress with bunchy shoulders and a taffeta skirt, before a fountain of ice carved into an angel amongst a series of serving cups whose spouts overflow fudge upon ice cream and pickles.

She is lonely.

Her alarm clock is buzzing. Her face is washed. Her books are collected. Her #10 foundation is applied. Her uniform is over her body. Her weekend bag is thrown in Niko's trunk. Niko's driving when it hits her. *That dream wasn't a very good Prom premonition.* The bell towers are seconds from sounding. She stands at her locker. He's by her. "I can't remember anything M taught me! I'm back on academic probation for sure!"

Poor, poor Tom. That's a lie. She's happy. Elated. Ecstatic! She wants to disrobe to reveal some super-villainous costume. Sin-exy Sykosa. *Mwhaha!* She rips off the rooftop like it were only one toothpick in a line of many and then, after some contemplation, squishes a fleeing Mackenzie with the inverted depression of her thumb. *Mwhaha!* That little tramp and her cute promises, her cute mannerisms, her cute promises...yeah, those promises! Nothing—*nothing*—could help him pass his test. Not Mackenzie. Not her American history teacher. Not Mr. Wizard. Nor the Pope. And certainly not Mackenzie.

Useless bitch.

"I'll go over the review packet in class. You can pass it."

"No offense, but it might be too late."

She wants to punch his arm. "Hey, I can do it."

"It's not you. I don't think I can remember it."

"Well, you better. You'll put me in a bad mood if you don't."

And I care about that why? "You're coming this weekend?"

"Was there ever any doubt?" She wants to kiss him on the cheek. Instead, she wiggles her pointer finger through his belt loop and pulls him toward her. She likes his belt loops. Good things to latch onto. "Not to sound like Mackenzie, but can you call me again sometime?"

"What?"

She slips her other finger through. "Call me."

He straightens his posture and salutes her breasts.

"Of course, I will!"

"I had fun yesterday, even though we had little time." She lifts onto her tiptoes—*he's so tall!*—and kisses his aloe shaven cheek. Her heels find the floor as his hair gel lingers by her nose. *It happened.* Some non-shame inducing affection. Who knows, maybe he's ready to go public with their relationship. *Maybe I'm ready, too!* "You're the first boy to see my room."

"Hopefully I'm the first who has seen that g-string."

She laughs. "You were."

At lunch, she visits her American history teacher's office. On the wall are posters of FDR, MLK, Our Lord and Savior, and whom she thinks is Karl Marx. His desk is scattered with mini-relics. A novelty size statue of David. Neil Armstrong in space gear. And a dark creature bathed in a red cape longer than his body, bearing guns of a governmental nature.

His smile is surrounded by a peppered goatee. "Come in, what can I help you with?"

"My mother wants to see my test right away. My parents are upset about my grades and they're keeping an eye on me."

"Yes, your father mention your visit. Hang on, let me find it." He shuffles through a folder in his bag, killing time. He wants to reinforce the grades bit. "I also share your parents' concern about your grades. Is everything alright?"

She nods—reinforce the re-enforcement. "Everything's fine! I'm going through a busy semester of school."

"Keep your focus. A student as bright as you should do well."

She dismisses it with a smile. "My dad's watching my grades closely now."

"Well, it seems to have worked."

He hands her a test with no red marks, save the corner where there's a one, two zeroes, and a percentage symbol. She folds it between her fingertips.

I guess this is it. Tom and I are going to...

It's not something that worries her.

Nothing about this day has really worried her. It's him. His visit really cheered her up. *No one takes care of the blackness like Tom.* After he left last night, to right now, she finds she just "does" things. She packed her bag like it was nothing. Got dressed this morning like it was nothing. And treated her test the same. *Now I'll have sex like it's nothing.* Ugh, that was not a good thought. It's nothing she thinks too long about. She can't. Niko's gone...Niko-like when she hands Niko the test.

Promptly, Niko suggests ditching the rest of the day, then leads the way to her 7, mall-bound after slinging off her bra.

I left my bra on.

In a chilly dressing room, she unlatches her skirt and drops her panties. It agitates her vagina. She's sensitive there today, and cold! She examines the follicle runway, a headstone to her former bush, which now resides somewhere in the city sewer. The process began with scissors, but was ended by a razor swiping between her lips, around her entrance and further back by her asshole. In all, it took forty minutes, but as the hot water tank became empty, so too did her crotch become bare.

In reflection, it felt like déjà vu.

This whole thing with him does. It's like the pull that got her to shave her vagina was the same pull that got her to jerk him off or, predating that, him humping her. Actually, humping's a perfect example. She consented because she worried some slut would blow him or something. It wasn't a very rational fear, as Tom's not a ladies man type, but at the same time, it was. She knows she thinks about sex with Tom, and in some way, deep down where Mackenzie has feelings, Mackenzie thinks about sex with Tom, which means other girls, whom she's not aware of, think about sex with Tom, and the longer they met behind the chapel, the more sure she became some girl would see his value, then act on that impulse.

And I'd have to match her.

Or they could start humping.

Like, she weighed his pluses up against the risks of ignoring the erection problem (and she learned fast, if you're gonna kiss boys, it's a "hard" problem to ignore) with all the stuff Mother Superior's told her about sex and, like, humping may not have been ideal, but as far as sins go, it wasn't so bad. It also kept all her clothes on and it minimized the amount of sexual pressure he asserted on her as yet unwilling self. It was an all around practical solution. *For a long time, it worked.* That's changing for him, and she gets that and always knew it was likely, but what's confusing is how it's changing for her, too. No joke, the humping's for him. She gets nothing from it. Or she didn't. Like, yesterday when he humped her, he also humped certain sensitive body parts into her comforter. It was like a five alarm fire and she ground her teeth to maintain control. Worse, she masturbated after he left! Sure, she does that daily, but not in the "I'm an animal, I must hump" way.

Okay, maybe she read too far into it, but it's like...

I'm gonna have sex this weekend. I'm so crazy.

Niko's a room over, documenting the nine imperfections on her face. "Does it look good?"

"I don't know. I haven't tried it on yet."

"What're you doing in there?"

"Nothing, I'll be ready in a sec."

Niko slips her legs into a jean skirt that caught her fancy since it has leather patches sewn onto the ass. Then, she holds up a shirt and her shoulders collapse. *Why, oh why, am I so flat?* "Like I thought, I look all *Little House on the Prairie*."

"Maybe you'll find a shirt somewhere else."

"I suppose. Are you changed yet?"

"Almost."

The bathing suit—the one from the magazine with the pretty white girl—is on a special hanger with a plastic bust. Her feet thread through the bottoms and she scrunches her kneecaps to lift the short-shorts. Next, she ties the top behind her back before she does around her neck. She jumps on her toes. Her boobs bounce like sexy boobs and stay in her suit, unlike her old bikini, which seemed cut to promote mammary slippage.

Niko's getting impatient. "Do you like it?"

"Yeah, I'm gonna buy it."

She changes back into her uniform, buys it, and then shops some more. At the Secret, she searches through a display of clearance panties, taken by a low riding one with "Dangerous" written on the rear. Forgotten for some solid colored thongs, the kind with a thick rear that lays over the divide of her ass instead of between it.

It makes a difference.

She shoplifts four of them.

Niko holds up a high-cut, cut-up club shirt. The kind that girls are only comfortable wearing when they're on drugs. "Do you think I have the tummy for this?"

"I wouldn't wear that for my life and you shouldn't either."

"Are you kidding?" The shirt falls to a wrinkly mess at her feet. "Midriffs are in! I have to lose ten pounds before the summer or else I can't wear all the shirts I bought."

On a good day, Niko's 5'1", 99lbs, soaking wet.

So Niko's exaggerating, as Niko often does. She decides not to play into it. "You look better when you're dressed sexy."

"If I knew, I'd buy that stuff!" Niko's discarded the shirt to examine—in disgust—those same thongs. "Those things are so uncomfortable." That's a very Niko thing to say. Or it's a very Niko3.0 thing to say, as Niko3.0 dislikes thongs, bras, and will, on occasion, grow out her armpit hair. But, last year, Niko2.0 embraced all this shit, and while those days are gone, Niko3.0 acts like they never existed. "Why do you wear them?"

"Cause I like them, and they're not uncomfortable."

The girls return to the 7 and Niko encroaches on the rear of an elderly driver. "Why can't people follow the speed limit?" The car swerves and her feet stomp around. "Timmy should be at my house already. He has all the alcohol with him. Plus, my parents got stuff out there."

"How much was it? I got ten bucks I could give you."

"Don't worry about it." After Niko cuts across several lanes and clears herself to a space of open road, she spins the dial on the radio to hear the weather report. "Did you hear that? It'll be in the seventies! It's April, but who would have thought we'd have such a perfect weekend! I bet you'll get to wear your new suit and everything."

"To tell you the truth, I'm not thinking about it. I just hope this test gets my father to lay off."

"Well, you shouldn't have flaked so much! And for the sake of our continued existence as friends, your grades need to stay up. If you lose your shot at valedictorian, your mother will never let you see me again!"

The puppet master.

For the record, Model UN is slightly more important.

She forgets it.

"I'll get them up, I will." Glares bounce off the paint of the cars this zooming coupe has caught up to, then left in its trail. Their intensity forces her to squint, which forces her to focus on her thoughts. They're the sexually anxious type. That forces her to focus on Niko—the only non-virgin, besides SS1, she knows. "Niko, when you did it the first time..." The tires squeal and butts slide as the stick is jammed forward. The landscape is like a merry-go-round. The seat belt locks and she curses. "Why do you always do that? You know the gate to your home is closed. You're gonna get in an accident one of these days."

"No, I won't! Hazu says I have excellent control for a girl."

Oh, you have no idea how much that sounded like Hazu.

"For a girl?"

"You know boys. They think they're good at everything cause they have muscles. Fuck that, I can work the clutch better than he can. He doesn't want to admit it."

"The clutch?"

"It's this pedal here on the left."

The grind of machinery pumps as a wrought iron gate—the sole entrance to the property as the perimeter's surrounded by a castle-like wall—rumbles open. The gate is imposing and its once pitch-black bars have been replaced by an almost green rust and large floppy leaves that've nearly swallowed the structure whole. When it's open, Niko drives a winding street to her home and stops, sanely, in the circle drive. She removes her sunglasses and flings her hair to see her poor friend pouting like a lost puppy.

"Okay, what is it?"

Not only are her lips pouting, but so are her shoulders, and her knees are turned inwards. "Well, Tom came over yesterday and I told you how he's been rubbing against me."

"Yeah, he's dry-fucking you."

That's...one way to put it.

Her throat's a bit dry. "Yeah, we did that, but we were on my bed, and we were kissing, too, and I had... I had this feeling like we should start doing things together."

"What does that mean?"

"Like, we need to stop doing things separately."

"You mean sex?"

That's...one way to put it.

"I guess."

Niko squeezes her jaw shut in thought. "It's hard to say."

"Why is that?"

Niko half-shrugs and looks away. "Well, you two've kept this on the down low. Some of guessed, but you guys are always behind that chapel. Is that all you do back there?"

No, but she can see how Niko would think that.

"We talk a lot. I've told you that."

"About?"

"About what he's feeling, about what I'm feeling."

Once again, Niko proceeds with caution. Sykosa doesn't see how sensitive she is to criticism of Tom or the circumstances upon how she came to love him. "Do you talk about last year?"

She looks pained. "He tries, but I change the subject."

"Why is that?"

She closes her eyes and squints her face. "Niko, don't make me change the subject."

Niko chuckles. "Okay, you want my opinion?"

Yeah, she does, but she just remembered Niko didn't lose her virginity in a romantic fashion. *Still, what could it hurt?* "What's your opinion?"

Niko's opinion is things need to stop being about Tom. Shit, Niko just fucked over Ass Girl in the ass worse than Hazu does. Ass Girl's party this weekend is screwed. The Stars will lose it when they learn what they missed out on. And doing this stuff to the Bitches is what Sykosa and Niko did together pre-Tom. They were best friends and they stuck to the group and everything was perfect.

Niko doesn't say any of these things.

"I think you're over stressing. They'll be other weekends at my cottage. Besides, I'm finally taking you—my bestest friend and the one person I've always wanted to take—to my cottage, so we can party and act like tramped up super-bitches!"

"I know. I do want to do that."

"Why can't you?"

"Because I want to go to Prom."

"He said he won't take you? Did you ask him?"

Her elbow collapses on the door panel and her fingers push her hair up. The blackness may not have her today, but she can't deny her Prom dream has affected her. She knows she's gonna sleep with him regardless, but things could get messed up between Tom and her if everything isn't handled well. "I didn't ask him, of course. But, he has to know. I mean, pretty soon they're gonna stop selling tickets. What am I supposed to do then? I got excited over it and pretended not to be, and now—maybe he thinks I don't care about it."

Niko is a syllable into an anti-Tom rampage when her door opens. It's Timmy. He smiles like a jackal and looks like a weasel, his body as thin as a match and, unfortunately, not nearly as tall as one. He wears a mesh of trailer trash and hip-hop, his traditional motif, while keeping his true-to-da-streets attitude by scratching his balls in public and spitting every time he exits a vehicle.

"What's with the coldness, baby? Trying to avoid me?"

"Of course not, now get outta of my way." Niko shoves her way out, and he provides her clearance, only to lay his skinny arm over her shoulders. His elbow swings like a loose hinge over her flat chest. "Where's Clyde?"

"In the van screwing with his damn guitar. Clyde, where the fuck are your fucking manners? Get the fuck out here and fucking greet everybody, you fuck!"

In the past, Niko's said Clyde is a hottie, so she watches the passenger door of the van—an early 90s Chevy Astro rusted at wheels and wells—squeal open. Clyde sets down his acoustic before the sun off of Niko's neighbor, Lake Washington, splashes him visible. She runs out of air while breathing while getting light headed and something else. Wow, he's gorgeous. That's unusual in a man. They're attractive, but not like this.

Her problems sink away, like someone cleared the drain of her better sense, then they return.

He did give her that second.

This Clyde.

He's pushed back his dirty blond hair to open her door with his back bent over like a concierge. She twirls her hair around her ear and holds down her skirt as her leg steps onto the pavement. She tries not to stare at him. He slams the door, and after he does, his fingers run across her back, off her hip and she, *gulp!*, thinks he might grab her butt, but he does not.

"Do you mind if I bum a cigarette from you?"

She holds up her smokes like a losing slot machine. "Here."

Timmy is bored. "Are you girls ready? Let's hit the road."

"Um, can you not see that we're in our uniforms? Besides, everyone won't be here until classes are over. Since we have time to kill, Sykosa and I are going to get ready, that way we can start partying right when we get there. Don't you think that's a good idea?"

Niko's bedroom is, technically, a wing of the mansion. She has her big bathroom that leads into her big actual bedroom, with her big bed and her large posters of Leonardo DiCaprio and Bruce Lee. Beyond that, through French doors, is a lounge with pastel purple walls, comfy sofas, and a big screen. There are bookcases on the walls full of stuffed animals, pictures of Niko's mom, and a bar/mini-kitchen. It is in this room that Sykosa drops her book bag before she tunes the TV to TRL to see the same songs that're there every day. Included is this rap song that's been stuck in her head. *All them bitches. All them hoes.* The rapper has a deep voice, and he's very, very black.

"Niko, Timmy's friend is hot!"

Niko's on the bedroom side of the French doors.

"He's probably gonna play his guitar tonight. You should listen and tell him it's great! He has this fragile ego thing." Niko walks towards her bathroom, but takes a left into her walk-in closet—or as it's nicknamed, "The Hallway"—which is an infinite tunnel of tee-shirts, skirts, dresses, and non-thonged lingerie. Currently, Niko bites on the nail of her third finger, distraught over how little she has to wear. "I should've bought that damn skirt!"

"Hey, don't come in here. I'm gonna change, okay?"

"Don't come in here either."

This dialogue was necessary, and hard to explain.

At one time, Niko and she had, what her mother described as, "boundary issues." They're both only children and they definitely thought—think—of themselves as sisters, so they shared beds, bath tubs, blankets, underwear, and—brace yourselves—practiced her favorite masturbation technique: pillow fucking, which—brace yourselves again—Niko taught her how to perform. That wasn't all. Because of Niko, she knew to sit against jets in hot tubs, straddle speakers, where to place her toothbrush, and the correct way to ride a tire swing. Now before anyone calls DHHS, Niko didn't understand sex, so 80% of Niko's sex ideas were pea-brained, non-sexual, and in retrospect, kinda cute.

The problem?

I was nine years old. And my mom freaked.

Her mother's response, and Mother Superior's, was to help her establish an identity. Many attempts were made over the years, but none worked. What did work was Niko joining the Bitches. This happened during sophomore year or, as she refers to it, "last year." And despite how it seems, joining the Bitches was difficult. For one, Donna Harly was leader, so membership required constant submission to her. In Bitches terms, this was called the "Rules" and the Rules were followed without exception. Thus, to fit this mold, Niko1.0 became 2.0, and for many months, worshiped, mimicked, and followed Donna like she were a Messiah.

Until, of course, Niko didn't want to any longer.

All that's in the far past. Niko3.0 fixed those things. As it so happens, while Niko3.0 was busy doing that, she fixed their friendship, as she learned that privacy and independence are part of growing older.

In the last year, she expected Niko to discover the same.

That hasn't exactly happened.

"Like, I was thinking, it doesn't really matter if I listen to him. Clyde is like Timmy's age. I'm not dating him."

"What's that supposed to mean?"

Shit. "Nothing, it's a personal preference thing."

"Excuse me that I think high school boys are lame."

No, you think nice boys are lame. High school has nothing to do with it. She wishes Niko wouldn't date Timmy. He's kind of a loser. "I didn't mean it as a bad thing. I meant he's hot, but I'm not interested beyond that."

"Yeah, yeah, like Mike Holler, I know."

She becomes silent. That name.

"Yeah."

This isn't her story. This isn't her life.

Niko never mentions Mike Holler. Why would she do that?

No time to find out. SS2 sticks her head in the bedroom door and sees Niko pop out of her closet in some punky jeans of zippers and patches and holes on the knees. SS2 gives Niko a hug. "You look so hot! God, you're so beautiful, Niko!"

Niko spanks SS2 on the butt. "Thanks, butt face."

SS2 laughs. She thinks it's funny when Niko abuses her. "When we didn't see you in school, we knew you ditched, so we did, too!"

SS3 walks in afterwards. No one notices.

SS1 follows. Her corn-fed body is in her Academy uniform, as are the rest of the Sluts. She's on the phone. "It's one weekend. – Don't be like that. – We'll party next weekend." Then, SS1 sets her phone on the dresser. "You were so right, Niko, my boyfriend hates that I'm leaving! He's afraid all the college guys are gonna woo me!"

SS2 smiles too. "Yeah, Niko, our boyfriends are pissed!"

VIII.

The cottage in Coeur d'Alene (as it appears through a forest like a castle in a storybook) almost seems like an optical illusion. The lawn is cut and green—alive!—in April. As are the flowers along the driveway that lead to a beautiful rock landscape. It builds to a ninety-five hundred square foot compound—*aren't cottages small?*—with a second floor of too many rooms to count (one full of pictures of Niko's mother from the swimsuit issue), and whose main floor includes a sauna, weight room, dojo, movie theater, and a four-car garage full of three sport coupes and a truck that looks like it belongs in a war. The real eye catcher is the rear deck. It's multiple levels, sectioned off like the house in *Swiss Family Robinson*. It bottoms out to twin spas on either end of a pool, which has its own secret lagoon where people can screw.

Hm.

That's an interesting thought.

Maybe Tom and her will make love in the lagoon. That way she can listen to the waterfall while he gets off. Or they can pretend! They're Honeymooners who've rented this cottage to, um, that's not right. They're recently engaged lovers who've rented out this cottage... Oh! They're traveling students, both on break from their respective significant others when they meet on a crowded beach in Spain and, later that eve, decide to fuck each other. Then, three weeks later, after telephone correspondences that stretch until dawn, he'll take a train to spend the day with her. He'll be wearing cream pants and one of those guayabera shirts like sexy Cubanos do. She'll be in a sundress and no underwear. After checking into this cottage/hotel, they'll tour the city, eat only appetizers, drink too much, and later in the eve, decide to fuck each other. And it's okay because they're studying for careers and other stuff, so this is an important experience.

I can't wait to go to college!

(She secretly read her mother's romance books at 12).

(Niko underlined the sexy parts).

Then she remembers it takes money to do these things.

Depressed, she sits on a kitchen bar stool where she smokes and watches it curl up her transparent window reflection. She does this because she needs a few minutes where she doesn't have to smile and laugh and be polite and meet the needs of everyone around her. This resignation bothers boys, who then go to great lengths to make her smile and laugh and be polite and meet the needs of everyone around her. Their lavished attention amuses her, and thus she smiles and laughs and becomes polite and meets the needs of everyone around her.

Boys use many tricks to achieve this.

Some tell jokes, some become goofy, some act like your best friend, some refuse to talk to you (yuck), some are mysterious and others are TMI-junkies, some talk about sex stuff (pervs), some behave like gentlemen, some become shy (boring!), and others do what Clyde's doing.

He sweet-talks.

Specifically, he continuously curls his hair around his ear so he seems vulnerable. He talks into her eyes so he seems attentive. He looks at her boobs when he reaches for his beer so she knows he is attracted to her. He listens to her problems and tells her all the stuff she has to endure is bullshit so she will think of him as someone wise.

He could go to jail for it.

For now, he sits with his guitar case at his side. It's easier to talk to girls after they see the guitar. "Music is like an orgasm. It gets, like, better and better, faster and faster, or slower and slower, and sometimes slower is better, ya know? Then it all gets bigger and bigger, and before you know it—pow! Music is all about sex. Everything is, if you think about it."

He'll fight her if she disagrees. If he fights her, he'll move in excitement, and his shoulder will block more of Tom, who shares the family room sofa with Mackenzie. His uniform is crumply and worn—*like last night*. His hair is messy and blond—*like last night*. His posture relaxed and fun loving—*like last night*. She wants him to pick her up—*like last night*. Yet, he stays on that sofa like he doesn't care. It's because Clyde monopolized her for the entire van ride. For some reason, Tom has not butt in to claim her for himself and that's unfortunate; she wants to ask him if he saw that lagoon!

Until he does, she drinks the expensive, dust-covered, cellar wine. It makes her drunk and dissociative. "I've never thought about music that way, but I guess you're right. I believe everything has to do with relationships."

"Yeah, sex, that's what relationships are."

Typical guy crap. He's lucky he's a hunk. "I don't think I'll ever see music as just sex or my relationships as just sexual. I mean, we're more than our bodies, you know?"

"Huh?"

She should have defaulted to *Niko's Big Book on Being Cool* where Niko notes—in great length—never to bring up the subject of spirituality to public school kids.

They get confused.

"How long have you played guitar?"

"Since I was nine."

"Did you take lessons?"

"No, I just started to play."

"Wow." He smiles like he knows he's hot and she's unable to resist him. She's unsure if it offends her. Though his smile reminds her of Tom and the look in his eyes when he's gonna be grabby. Then, she relives kissing Tom on her bed. That was a good time. "I kinda envy you. You know what you want. It's not so simple for me. It's like everything is available, or that's how my parents talk about it, but I don't want that."

"You know what I want?"

"Tell me."

"I want to be the greatest musician ever."

Also depressing!

She isn't interested in a man who chases the impossible, but a man who chases himself. Like a dog. That way they can lie in a rut together. That sounded wrong. She fixes it. She wants a boy who is more of a friend than the boyfriend type. That was wrong, too. Hm, she wants a boy who's... Shit. Brain fart. What she wants is a normal, non-pervy boy or boy-like creature who'll serenade her with good dreams.

She used to have that boy, except for the perv part.

She remembers it's impolite to ignore someone speaking to her. "Wow, that's kind of difficult."

Clyde's over read her words. "You don't think I can do it?"

"You could be the best, and no one might ever notice."

And taken his reaction too far. "What do you mean?"

"I don't mean anything, I'm saying—"

He interrupts. "Are you saying I can't be the best?"

"No, that's not what I'm saying."

In an attempt to sound cool and accepting of her opinion, he ends up sounding like a prick. "You know what? Let's forget about it. It's no big deal."

Okay. Fine with her! She'll forget it, if that's what he wants. She'll never think about it again, nor will she mention it. Hey, it's not a problem!

She's whining. "Clyde, I didn't say anything."

"Alright."

"Did I make you angry?"

"I'm not gonna listen to anyone tell me I can't be the best."

She refills her wine glass and changes the subject because she was right. Clyde's shoulder is blocking Tom and she does not like it. Once he's sure she is no longer questioning his guitar licks, Clyde reverts to his old self. She looks at Tom again. The pull—the one she feels around him—hits her. It wants to make him look at her and pay her some mind, then when she's sure she's got him, have him do her in the lagoon.

Maybe I really do want to have sex.

Clyde continues to talk, but she's not listening. She looks at Mackenzie's thin pink lips and their sort of shiny layer, at her

Mary Tyler Moore haircut and bellbottom jeans, and those hands, folded one over the other, her back straight when she sits. She sees Mackenzie and tries to figure out how to act more like her, so Tom will be less distant. And Mackenzie sees Sykosa and tries to figure out how to act more like her, so Tom will be less distant. She looks at Sykosa's lips and their pout, her fine hair, and those hands that work that cigarette and swirl that wine like some spoiled debutant.

Tom continues to talk, but she's not listening.

He isn't either.

He peeks over his shoulder, obsessed with Sykosa and her come-hither outfits, which... How she is buying this guy's crap, he'll never know, as he knows better than most that, with a girl like Sykosa, it's never the conversation that's interesting. That came out wrong. He doesn't only like her because she's mega-hot. There're other reasons.

They're difficult to explain. Basically, he misses her.

"What're you thinking about?"

"My grandma's upset that I'm missing this Sunday at the country club." Mackenzie feels weird. They both talk to each other when both listen to Sykosa. With Tom, everything has a way of being about Sykosa. She knows something's between them, yet he never mentions it. "I'm debating having another special tryout for swim this year."

He's dead pan. He feels sorry for her.

M has a legacy at the Academy.

Her two older sisters are alumni, were captains of the swim team and won state championships. It's basically unspoken that Mackenzie will do the same. However, she's not as talented as her sisters, nor is the team the same since Donna Harly—swim team captain—disappeared last year. M feels a lot of pressure from these expectations. It's why she slaves at academics and will probably be valedictorian; to compensate and be accepted into Stanford, where her sisters are also alumni.

"That's what you were thinking about?"

She apologizes. "It's lame. What do you want to talk about?"

"I don't know—something interesting."

She counts on her fingertips. "Let's see here, you like beer, pizza, girls, and video games. It's gotta be one of those, right?"

"I also like girls."

"I said girls."

He's perplexed. It's a cute perplexity. Both notice Sykosa noticing. "Let's talk about those things. Or we could combine them. Like, we could talk about video games with girls in them or we could talk about eating pizza with beer."

Mackenzie shines. She hopes Sykosa is watching this part. Yes, Sykosa's watching his part. "Why don't we talk about girls playing video games while eating pizza and drinking beer?"

"Genius!" It is genius! Sykosa's more interested than ever! "You're a genius, M!" He shouldn't have called her a genius while looking at Sykosa. That was mean. Also Sykosa's noticed his noticing and stopped caring. He recounts his day. "You tried to help me with that test and nothing stayed in my head. Then Sykosa tried and nothing stayed in my head. My mom says I'll never get into college. She wants to lock up my N64. She'll let me have it after my homework's done."

"Oh no!" Really, Mackenzie worries about his grades, too. He's always teetering on academic probation, but it's unlikely he'll face any disciplinary action for it. The Administration gives him special treatment because of the scars on his hand. "Well, it might do you some good."

He stops noticing Sykosa long enough to notice Mackenzie pull her jeans forward. He thinks it's Timmy and Clyde. New boys make Mackenzie nervous. Last year when Mike Holler and Lonny... He'll put it this way, he knows Mackenzie's a lot of things, and not all of them are good. He also knows she was never a doormat. And he hates anyone who'd hurt Mackenzie— or Sykosa. He hates it so much sometimes he wants to punch something over it.

He did punch something over it.

It ruins his buzz. "How was your day?"

"Same ol', same ol'. I'm glad to be out here though."

"What would this weekend be without my best bud?"

For a long time, maybe twenty-five or twenty-seven minutes, nothing happens. Except Niko announcing she's heading into town to spread the word about the party tomorrow and the prerequisite bash tonight. She returns with a flock of fancy automobiles at her tail like an army of foot soldiers. They park along the drive, on the grass, and then further down by the street. Like followers on an Abercrombie and Finch pilgrimage, scores of muscle-bound college guys and their pretty college girlfriends herd themselves through the thrown-open front doorway.

On cue, Sykosa feels like being social, and she indulges like Tom indulges her panties, to find she subconsciously allows Polo shirts to chat her up about competitive internships, beach homes, and trust funds. She smiles and she smiles and she smiles and they keep talking! Always eventually telling her she's "gorgeous," "sexy," "beautiful," "perfect," "an angel," and in what she overheard one guy whisper to another, a "cum bucket." These descriptors intensify her emotions, both negative and positive, and she drinks alcohol to compensate. She wonders if one of these handsome jocks, not the cum bucket one, will take her to the lagoon, tell her to "shut up" (but, nicely, like maybe add a "please") when she gets scared and then fucking take care of it and keep taking care of it even though it hurts her. She thinks you have to be a bit mean to take a girl's virginity, like those people who pierce ears and make baby girls cry all day.

For some reason, these guys decide her virginity isn't worth it and abandon her. She matriculates to a circle of girls who all dress like Niko, talk like Niko, listen like Niko, and lazily let drop the shoulder strap of their tiny black tops like Niko. She tells all the girls they are beautiful and asks them for tips about their hair and makeup. They, in turn, tell her she is beautiful, and everyone, in turn, hugs and kisses each other on the cheek. One of the girls, unprovoked, drunkenly says to her, "Do you know what guys like?" She's interested, as this girl is exactly the type she feared cornering Tom. Let us not mince words, a Goddamned whore. "What do they like?" "They like getting their dicks sucked."

Yep, Goddamned whore.

Luckily, not all the girls are.

One is skinny, beautiful, becoming a doctor, and holds out her engagement ring. "He asked when we were vacationing. He got down on one knee in front of my whole family!" "That's amazing." "Yeah, he's definitely 'the one.'" "I hope someone loves me like that one day!" "Oh, it'll happen, it just takes a while." "It does?" The girl laughs. "Yeah, you shoulda seen the guy I dated in high school." Never mind, this girl sucks, too. *What's wrong with high school boys?* Then, by some process, they migrate onto the deck where everyone strips to their skivvies and jumps into the pool.

Being felt up by random guys scares her.

Plus, the lagoon is full of people. That makes her sweaty.

Back in the house, she's alone again.

Those girls never saw her exit and those boys are over there, but they're not coming over here so they're useless. This does not surprise her. She has no money, no power, no connections, and thus they have no interest in her. *Whatever, they're not so great!* She decides to aimlessly walk the chandelier lit hallways, bumping into cute boys and then waiting a second. None of them approach her. *Whatever, they're not so special!* She wanders back to the kitchen stool where her bottle of wine waits. She drinks by herself and lights up smokes. She watches people interact and thinks watching these people is like watching a great TV show, which, for socioeconomic reasons, she cannot join.

Then, she feels lonely.

Whatever, they're not so...blah!

Tom lifts himself onto the neighboring stool. His beer is on the counter, the label bloated from bottle sweat. It sweats on her hand. "Do you mind if I have some?" He says to do so, and she does. "You aren't all freaked out, are you?"

"Why would I be freaked out?"

She points to the bottle. "It's like a second-hand kiss."

"Why would that matter?"

She feels lonely again. *Boys and their inability to love anyone but themselves!* "It's supposed to be a joke."

He's silent. His eyes are stuck on her hand, which runs the rim of the bottle along the wane of her lip. He heard once that when girls do that, they're thinking about giving head, which means she may be thinking about giving head. God, he wants her to give him head. Like girls in porn do. Or what if they have sex? Like girls in porn do. No, any sex is enough. He just needs to not screw up. She has to be thinking about having sex with him. She *has* to be. The only thing that can get in the way of said sex is himself, which he's not gonna do.

Nope, not gonna happen.

The problem is that not screwing up is paralyzing him and...

It's making the pressure big, and she's so hot and he wants her so much and how many weekends does a guy get to have a girl like Sykosa to himself? Not many. This has to go well, it... Jesus Christ, he needs to fuck her already!

Ugh, he didn't mean it like that! It's...

He's disrupted by Clyde who plays his guitar somewhere.

Why does she like him?

"You're sure you're fine?"

"Yeah, why wouldn't I be?"

"I don't know."

She returns to her wine.

Resignation overcomes her; she appears more serious than she actually is. Really, she wants to play like yesterday. *Why won't he do something?* She expected to stave off his advances all weekend. She didn't think he would ignore her.

"What're you talking about?"

"That guy, you've been talking with him for hours."

What? "You've been talking to Mackenzie for hours!"

"That's different."

"How?"

"Mackenzie's my friend. Clyde isn't your friend."

Like that matters. You know, this whole weekend, thus far, has been a total disappointment. "I can't talk to another guy? You're so predictable."

"How can I be? You just met him."

Her next words are slurred. She hates how, when drunk, she has a propensity for telling the truth. "You know she's different when you're not around."

"What?"

"I said, 'You know she's different when you're not around.'"

"What're you talking about?"

"I'm saying Mackenzie's two different people."

He holds up his palms, kinda practiced in his reaction. He's worried for a while this might happen. Of course, it happened tonight. He sounds diplomatic. "Please don't get me involved in this stuff between you and Mackenzie."

"Get you involved? What're you talking about?"

He sounds diplomatic again. "I don't know, but you girls and your groups, and all the pranks and stuff. Mackenzie's my friend, and I don't want those problems to be our problems."

Well, there're about to become it!

She looks hurt. "Gee, thanks for hearing me out there." She finishes her wine in one gulp and snatches her purse. She wants to smoke on the deck by herself. "Don't let me get in the way of your cozy friendship, in fact, maybe you should go, I'm sure 'M' needs you." Her foot attempts to plant on the floor, instead it plants on an ice cube. She has a sick tremor as her knee wobbles and her arms reach out. He kicks back the stool and the rubber shoe sole squeaks. His mitts snatch both her forearms. He is *very* strong for a boy his age. She talks to herself. "What a great exit, Sykosa. I suppose it was possible to be a bigger loser." She tugs on her shirt and flings her hair. His face awaits her gaze and his blue eyes don't end. She's frustrated. "Let's just forget this."

He's confused. "What's going on? What did she do to you?"

"Who?"

"Mackenzie."

What's also lame about drunkenness is losing her off switch. "What didn't she do? You know, just because she's puts on this good girl routine after..." Shit. Now, she's done it. She brought up last year. *Oh, I'm an idiot.* "The point is she's pretending nothing happened." Shit. Now, she's done it. She brought up pretending. *That's all Tom and I do.* "She doesn't care about anything but herself, and she left us hanging, even after her supposed best friend Donna disappeared." Shit. Now, she's done it. No one talks about Donna Harly lightly, not in this circle. *Why can't I shut up?* "I mean she's phony, and people want to forget that, including you."

"It's not forgetting."

"What is it then?"

"I forgave her."

There's something about that word.

Forgive.

She feels like she was supposed to do that.

Fuck it. "How could you do that?"

"How could I do what?"

"If you care about me, how could you forgive her?"

He stumbles, then ruffles his hair. "What do you want me to do? Be pissed forever?" He holds up his scarred hand. By the way, she never mentioned how, should he roll up his sleeve, his entire arm is covered in them, too. "I gotta live with this forever, so I had to let everything else go."

"Next you're gonna tell me you forgave Donna, too."

He pauses. "Well—"

She interrupts. "Are you kidding me?"

"And Mackenzie hasn't forgotten Donna. Not only were they good friends, she's not gonna win State without her."

Donna Harly, before disappearing last year, was the captain of varsity swim and the fastest swimmer in King County, and possibly the State of Washington. She knows these things cause she was on the team with Donna and Mackenzie. She swam for the Academy last year and was recruited to do it again this year. She chose to do Model UN instead. Not that she's any talent in the water, but she's better than whatever Frosh took her spot. Not like any of it matters. Tom's right. One cannot replace a Donna Harly, she's a once-in-a-generation swimmer.

And Mike raped her and she disappeared after.

Or that is what everyone thinks.

Mike did rape Donna, she heard Donna crying about it, but almost no one knows the circumstances of the rape and how it came to pass. *Except Tom, Mackenzie, and me.* The blackness will come if she talks about this more. She chooses not to and gets pouty. "Fine, you're right."

He knows better than that. He tries to fix it. It might be too late. Of course, he fucked up this weekend. It didn't even take him one night. "Relax, what I meant was—I just don't want to take sides, and I don't want to make things worse."

She isn't relaxing. "Don't tell me what to do."

"I'm not doing that."

"Then, what're you...?"

"Just stop, okay? Stop."

He cups her cheek and kisses her lips. It's a strange kiss because it ends the frustration in him. She has the ability to do that sometimes. She reminds him life is about more than getting laid. Strangely, after he remembers, he isn't upset, he's grateful, so he opens his legs and leads her by her forearms between them, where she hugs him for a long time without having to strain her calves since she's on her heels. He holds her close, and when he pulls away, she pulls away, and they are pulled together by their lips again. It reminds him of when they first met. He bumped into her in the main hallway one morning and... What happened last year hadn't happened, so they weren't acquainted, but he remembers even then he'd have killed to have her like he has her now—at a cottage, alone together, herself powerless to his lips and his hand in her back pocket, taking a bite out of her wonderful ass.

When it's all said and done, he'd be an idiot to fuck this up.

Her voice is girly. "Oh, you're so sweet."

"You're drunk."

She giggles. "A bit."

"Hey."

"Yeah?"

"I'll protect you. Don't be afraid of Mackenzie, or anyone."

She nods like a lamb. "Okay."

"And I'll call you again, and I did like being in your room."

She rolls her eyes. "Yeah, okay."

"I really did. I thought you had a nice room."

"You don't remember anything about my room."

"I remember every detail of your room."

Sometimes it's fun to watch him dig these graves.

"Tell me about my room."

"Your curtains and your bedspread are pink. You have a Fievel stuffed animal that sits above the others. You stack your books by your desk based on which class you have first in the morning. Your notebooks are stacked beside them. And your planner is between them. You don't actually close your planner. You roll it over the rings so the current day is always on top. You stack all your other books in your closet, and they're a mess. When you try on clothes, you leave the clean clothes on the bed, change in front of your mirror, then throw the clothes to the left, where I found that pile of underwear. You keep your smokes behind the base of your desk lamp, probably so your parents won't notice. Your laptop is in the center of your desk. It's probably the only computer in your house, and your parents only bought it cause the Academy requires our papers be typed. The wall has stuff on it, but what matters most is the bulletin board above your desk where you've spent hours placing photos of Niko and yourself in a way so it looks like you didn't spend hours doing it."

Did she mention his words can sound slicked in butter?

He just did that.

A timid feeling of special significance weakens her stomach. It means, from this moment on, if he says something mean, she'll automatically cry. "Wow."

"Told you I remembered it."

She looks into his eyes and they look...something they don't usually look. His chest is tense. She wants him to relax. "How can you remember all that, but you can't remember a couple dates for our history test?"

"Don't you understand?"

She becomes tense, too. "Understand what?"

"Isn't it obvious?"

Something's going to happen. She knows it.

It's like a giant hiccup that won't finish.

"Wha—t?"

"I love you."

This isn't her story. This isn't her life.

What. The. Fuck?

"Are you serious?"

"I said I love you. You don't believe me or something?"

"No, it's not that."

"What is it then?"

She's not sure, but now if he says anything mean, she won't only cry, she'll lose all sanity. "I never thought, I mean, I knew you cared, but—"

He interrupts. "Ever since last year..."

She knew it!

She brought up last year, and now like last year, he wants to fix it, but she doesn't want it fixed, nor addressed. It's selfish, and she feels like a bitch. She can't worry about that. The one-year anniversary is next week, the blackness is too strong and it's about survival first, decency second. Also, she's unsure if anything's to be gained from discussing Donna Harly. Like they both said earlier, Donna's gone and so is Mike. They left so this crystal globe of the Academy could continue. And she understands she has to play her part in that—that the students, the parents, the teachers, the Administration, none of them will feel safe without the lie.

I don't feel safe with it.

So she tells it to herself endlessly, hoping to believe it.

Wanting to go back to that place...

Sophomore year.

Last year, before it happened, and the blackness started.

Then, Niko shouts! "Get the fuck out of my house!"

At the cottage's entrance, Niko points at the door. Timmy's holding her back with one arm while the other is held out like he's embarrassed. Like he knows the people Niko's screaming at, or he's trying to impress them or something. The Sluts stand with surprised looks—surprised looks she's seen before. No one quite knows what to do when Niko snaps. She blinks off Niko to see the boys Niko's shouting at.

She recognizes no one until...

Scott.

Tom's beside her now. "Who're they?"

Why would he come to Niko's party? "They're nobody. Hey, I have to go, you know, calm Niko down and everything."

"Alright." She walks away, and his hand, the one with all of those scars, takes hers. "Sykosa?"

So much for the lagoon. "We'll talk, I promise."

Interlude I: Sophomore Year.

1.

Swimming sucks.

It blows hardcore chunks of something. Worse, it's not even worthwhile chunks. She swims to one side, then back, then there, then back—like maybe, you know, one day, she might conquer the ocean wide, but she can't and she never will, and if she could, she'd be a moron because, duh, there're boats! *I'll never forgive my mother for this.* Mother Superior be damned as well. It's not melodramatic. Don't believe her? Consider this, don't be deceived by the pool's bleach-y smell, for she long ago learned, as you're about to, that chlorinated water only stinks when combined with bodily fluids. That's right. She willingly—*willingly*—dove into a million gallons of girl piss, girl spit, and probably period blood.

This is too disgusting.

At least it's over. Wait, it's not over.

With Niko as a best friend, it never is.

Niko, version 2.0, skips full-speed across the auxiliary hallway, her blond-tipped shorter-than-shoulder-length hair awash behind her, then awash before her as she, in one step and on one foot, pirouettes like a ballerina. It's a testament to Niko's athleticism, and it testifies further as Niko performs another turn, then a third and flinches on the fourth. Niko's eyes, which were shut, are open—and despite her naïve expression, Niko is aware an astonished pack of string-bean Bitches, who've studied dance since four, stare in a potentially murderous disbelief.

Lots of people are jealous of Niko, herself included.

"Where'd you learn to do that?"

"I don't know. I got bored waiting for you, so I practiced."

"Like right now, you just learned that?"

Niko smiles. "Well, yeah!"

"It was cool."

Niko smiles bigger. "I know! Hey, is your uniform damp?"

Aside from her socks, her skirt, her blouse, her underwear, her backpack, and all of the skin on her body, she has no idea what Niko refers to. "It's not."

Niko presses on. "Well, did you make it?"

"I don't know."

"You don't know? Tryouts ended like an hour ago!"

"I know, I didn't check."

"Well, I'm sure they've posted the team by now!"

"The team" is ladies swim.

She tried out for many reasons, none of them sound, and as one might expect, being as unconditioned for exercise as she was, her body surpassed its physical limitations ten minutes into the first day, and now on her fourth and final, soreness surrounds her abdomen, locks her thoracic region, and, like, it even hurts behind her boobs. Those parts are fortunate, though. Several areas, like her forearms, ankles, and ears—subjected to Mackenzie's drill sergeant-like orders—have lost functionality.

No, her ears are fine. They're under assault again.

Mackenzie, flanked by that same pack of string-bean Bitches, stands in her uniform, but with some very critical differences. Traditionally, whether girls belong to the Bitches or not, they follow the Rules for Academy wear, which state that Academy girls roll their skirts, pull back their blouses, and, for winter, own tad-too-tight sweater vests. It's a "cool" thing, yet Mackenzie's uniform is, and always was, as the manufacturer specified. For that Mackenzie wears this naïve expression, like Niko, as if she were too pure to even notice these "cool" Rules.

Though, at this moment, nothing about Mackenzie is pure.

"I need to talk with you privately, Niko."

Niko is unimpressed. "You could say 'please.'"

"Donna and Lonny, my boyfriend, are waiting for me. We have some last minute details for Prom Committee."

"And you assume you're busy but I'm not?"

Mackenzie is dismissive. "You're going to the dance?"

"No, but you assumed I don't have anything going on."

"I don't have time for games."

"Neither do I, so stop playing them with yourself." This is the standard Niko-Mackenzie posturing. They're in competition for #2 in the Bitches, a position Mackenzie used to outright own and one Mackenzie never earned. It's why Niko's infiltration has been so effortless. It's also why, to aggravate Mackenzie, Niko stuffs gum in her mouth, then yacks loudly while pulling her blond tips into a super-tight nub like a tiny dog's tail. "On the subject of time, save us some—did she make the team?"

Shit, Niko had to bring me up.

She's not mad, but confused. She was sure the locker room was empty when she left. It's not possible Mackenzie snuck up on her from behind like this. She should've seen her in either the auxiliary or main hallways. She'd dismiss it, but this isn't the first time Mackenzie, or Donna, has done this.

Are they...in that bathroom? The one that's locked?

She cuts off Niko. "We'll check ourselves."

"Or we could ask now."

Mackenzie is blunt. "Assuming you need an answer."

Niko pops a bubblegum bubble. "What does that mean?"

"It means you know she's on the team."

I'm what?

In addition to her reasons for trying-out being poor, so was her effort. She finished dead last...at everything. Last from the locker room, last in the pool, and last to finish laps. The only thing she did first was leave. She never wanted this. "That's a joke. Why do you want me on the team?"

Mackenzie crosses her arms. "Why don't you ask Donna?"

"Donna wants me on the team?"

Niko is ecstatic. "Of course, Donna does! You're awesome!"

"Niko, you don't understand. I shouldn't be on the team."

Mackenzie concurs. "No, you shouldn't."

"Why shouldn't she?"

"For one, her fat ass displaced half of the water in the pool. And two, if you two want your own Pride and Rice Parade in our school, then be my guest, but keep it off my team."

Niko pouts big as a bull dog. "Aw, is poor 'Kenzie upset that she got outranked? Too bad, you can't do shit but cry to the Yeti, and we'll see how much she cares."

Mackenzie looks like Niko said a swear. "I'm telling Donna you said that."

"And I'll tell her you're lying. Who's she gonna believe?"

Donna will believe Mackenzie. The Yeti will believe Niko.

It's telling when Mackenzie backs down. "Like I said, I'm late for a meeting for—"

Niko interrupts. "Prom? I heard you the first twenty times."

All the Bitches behind Mackenzie gasp! Them were fighten' words and Mackenzie must respond. Not that Mackenzie worries. Her conservative exterior is often mistaken for being soft, so few know Mackenzie—and her perfect verbal score on the PSAT—turns a phrase nearly as quick as Niko.

"Niko, you're as fake as your tits."

The Bitches gasp bigger.

No one mentions Niko's bra stuffing. You just don't do it.

It shocks Niko. "Yeah, well..."

"Watch yourself. This weekend was one thing, and your hair, okay, it's against the Rules, so what?, but you're crossing the line."

"I don't know what you mean."

"I'm sure."

It's like a prison yard stare down.

Niko's ready, but Mackenzie, too reformed for such brutishness, steps aside, her Bitches, who're in trail, already lost in chatty whispers. "Pride Parade" referred to rituals in the LGBT community, but Mackenzie hijacked the term to fuel the Academy's juiciest rumor. *That Niko and I are gay.* The latest connotation is several students saw Niko and her sucking face at a Starbucks this last Saturday. (Keep in mind, this rumor is most often told in tandem with the rumors about Niko's Coeur d'Alene weekend party, which was not held at a Starbucks in Seattle). The "rice" part is a unique wrinkle since racist stuff is uncommon at the Academy. It implies sexuality for an Asian girl is, in actuality, nymphomania. Like, Niko and her aren't gay, they've simply run out of white men to steal, which allows white girls to feel better about being asexual robots.

Both aspects of these rumors are beyond ridiculous.

And, somehow, like all rumors, there're grains of truth.

Well, more than grains.

Niko relaxes her stance, then puts her arms out like "what the fuck" before she drops her weight on one hip. "What a blind fool. I don't stuff my bra!"

Yeah, Niko does.

"She was trying to get you back, that's all."

"But, I don't stuff my bra. Why doesn't anyone believe me?" She tries to be cheery. "Hey, she doesn't know about BJS!"

"BJS" is an inside joke. (You don't want to know).

Niko winks. "Oh, she knows about it, just Lonny's version."

She gasps like the Bitches did. "Are you for real? Or are you starting a rumor?"

Of course, it's a rumor.

Sweet, perfect Mackenzie would never...

Whatever.

The real problem is as these rumors escalate, so do the retaliations. By tomorrow, all the Academy will see when they see Mackenzie will be a desperate slut down on her knees, and by the afternoon, all anyone will see of Niko is...a desperate slut down on her knees. *The problem's that people will picture Niko with me.* Hey, get that picture outta your head! Anyway, she shouldn't be such a wuss. It's school. And she accepts that, in one as mouthy as the Academy, rumors come standard, but the onslaught of falsehoods these last weeks is overkill, and it brings back too many of her own repressed memories.

It has to do with those "grains."

It's something Niko and her have never fully discussed.

At their sleepovers, after Nana went to bed, Niko would strip skimpy, then watch, rewind and rewatch, every love scene of every movie in the house. Or squint at the scrambled naked people on the cable TV stations. Some nights, Niko'd sneak her downstairs to skinny dip or help her climb the perimeter wall, then dare her to sprint across lawns naked. (Niko's record was three). Other games happened, too, but the details aren't important. What matters is this felt natural, like the moonlight had let something loose in Niko that Niko couldn't quench... until Niko found out how.

To grownups, it's masturbation. To them, it was, "rubbing."

No one knows about it. *Except for Mother Superior and my mom.* So these rumors and her childhood "activities" are in no way connected, but they bother her because they imply that people "know" Niko and her are gay.

Or white man stealers.

Which, for Niko, has been contemporarily true.

Niko examines her sweater vest. Certain her boobs look real —she puts so much time into them! "What's the difference? Besides, can you believe the way she boasts about how Lonny's a junior and she's going to Prom? Yeah, he's your boyfriend— we all know it! No need to repeat it for the hundredth time! That's so lame."

Not so.

It's quite cool that Lonny's an upperclassman. She wishes her boyfriend was an upperclassman. *I mean, I wish I had a boyfriend.* It's also cool Mackenzie's attending Prom. Recently, she went to Sadie Hawkins, and it was quite fun, but that's peanuts next to Prom, especially if the prom goer is an underclassman, like Mackenzie! *Or me—in my fantasies.* For her, doing such is akin to having a September birthday, then driving to school all year while other kids beg for rides.

Wait, that's Mackenzie too. Soon, it'll also be Niko.

Now everyone will see me getting rides...maybe.

"I don't get it. I shouldn't have made the team."

"What're you talking about?"

"I was purposely the worst swimmer there."

Niko is aghast! "What about our plan? You didn't even try?"

God, she hates valedictorian.

"I did, but I... I can't go back to Model UN, and this is the only way Mother Superior would leave me alone over it."

That explanation really sucked. She doesn't try to better it, but instead trades words for pouts.

Niko falls victim to it. "Well, at least you made it. Now you can stay valedictorian, and you can come to the party tonight."

"I told you, my mom said yes to post-Prom and a sleepover this weekend, she's not saying yes to this, too."

"She will if you make it about school!"

Niko believes if something's about school, her mother is powerless to it. "How am I going to do that?"

Niko squishes her face in thought, then grits up her voice. "What if we say it's about Prom Committee?"

My mom's not that stupid. "I don't think she'll buy that."

"No, she will. Prom Committee has an academic credit."

That means it applies to valedictorian.

"It has a chance of working."

"Please try! Scott's coming tonight! I planned it special."

Scott is Niko's boyfriend. *And someone with whom I'm unacquainted.* Usually, that's no biggie, as Niko's M.O. is to gobble up whatever boy wets her appetite, then spit out his remains like, well, garbage. The best and latest example of such is Hazu. A too-cool-for-school rebel-type who, now that he has a drivers license, likes to race cars. Like most boys, he became obsessed with Niko, then ignored the signs he was just another of Niko's doomed affairs. Like clockwork, he was replaced for Scott. The difference is, so far, Scott's bucked all of Niko's romantic trends, holding her affection for weeks.

So now I have to meet him.

That said, it's Niko's fault they've never met. Since Niko, excuse her, Niko2.0's in the Bitches, Niko goes to Bitches-only parties, and since she isn't, she doesn't.

Or she didn't.

That's the other thing. Swim tryouts are Bitches tryouts.

Guess what that means?

Niko's started for the main entrance. She keeps at Niko's

side. She hates following Niko like the Bitches do Mackenzie. "I thought I was meeting him this weekend at post-Prom."

"Right, but let's just do it tonight."

Her stomach dislikes the idea. "It took forever to get my mom to agree to post-Prom. She still thinks you went to Coeur d'Alene by yourself."

Oh yeah, when the rumors about Niko's Coeur d'Alene party hit the Academy circuit, they found their way to the teachers, then the vice-principal. Lots of schools might've turned a blind eye. The Academy isn't that type of school.

Niko had to see Mother Superior.

And so did I.

Niko struggles. "I mean, tonight's your debut! All the Bitches think you're coming."

"Why would they think that?"

Niko rewinds. "I mean, not that they think that."

She's been on swim team and in the Bitches for less than a hour. Yet, everyone knows about it, and everyone knows she is going to this party. It might seem like Niko had rolled out the red carpet for her, but if you had heard the stuff Niko's been saying these last weeks, you'd know it wasn't true. "Why does Mackenzie think you knew I made the team?"

Niko, who's gotten a step or two ahead, stops, then twirls her top half around. "Well, that's a funny story."

"You're the reason I'm in the Bitches?"

Niko shrugs. Her boobs don't shrug.

It looks weird.

"I told Donna she had to take you."

That explains a lot.

Imagine going to tryouts for the week, dragging ass, only half listening, swimming slower than you know you can and showing how little you care at every opportunity. Then, imagine Mackenzie, also exhausted from tryouts, valedictorian, and the effort it takes to keep Donna happy. Now add on hearing that by Niko's influence, the worst swimmer, who was only the worst because she cared so little, made the team, and is thereby

in the Bitches. *It'd drive me crazy!* It also explains Mackenzie's behavior after tryouts. In the showers, Mackenzie said something weird. Her first instinct was to tell Niko. She meant to, but when she visited her locker, she realized it was a prank, even if it was a dimwitted one.
And it was dimwitted because I was dimwitted.
She sees now it was no prank. It was revenge.
"I don't think Mackenzie liked hearing that."
"How do you know?"
Because I just pressed my uniform between towels for the last thirty minutes! She takes the two steps to Niko then, after she speaks, walks off. "I can't believe you did this. You used me to start your war with Donna!"
Niko gets tense. "No, I didn't."
"Don't lie!"
Niko shouts, then follows, after her. "Look, I can fix this."
"I don't want it fixed. I never wanted it done."
"I swear, I thought you did."
"I told you I didn't want a target put on me."
"I didn't put a target on you."
She turns around. Niko's face looks innocent, but she's seen this face on Niko before. Fortunately, they're right at the main entrance, and it's also fortunate the doors are still out. It'd be hard to make a dramatic exit otherwise. They're large, heavy, and the effort it takes to open them is unreal.
"Yes, you did. They can't touch you, so they came after me."

2.

It's wet in the pool, it's wet in the showers, her clothes are soaked and it's raining from the sky. Oh, how water sucks and Seattle sucks with it. And her splash-tastic shoes, in synch with Niko's, hurry down several plains of steps and across the blacktop to her family sedan whose floor is wet from her dropped book bag. (*Water resistant* book bag, and thank God for that. Her mother woulda freaked had her books wilted). She sits in the seat, which seals her chilly clothes against her backside. It knocks her knees, then jars her elbows. Hypothermia has its benefits, however. She's half sure the downpour has fooled her mother.

Nothing fools her mother.

"Did you swim in your uniform?"

"I don't want to talk about it."

"Did you make the team?"

"Of course, she made it!" Niko catches herself, her big mouth aware this statement wasn't kosher, so she slings into her seatbelt, then fumbles over a retraction. "I mean, I think so."

Her mother is impatient. "Did you make it?"

"Yes, but don't get too happy."

"Why?"

Her hands redirect all the hot air vents her way. "I was really bad, and I don't know if they'll keep me."

That was a lie. They're keeping her.

Her mother doesn't know that. "What do you mean?"

"Niko got me on the team."

Niko chuckles, then bites on her hair. By no surprise, this story is eagerly awaited, and Niko's eager to tell it. As soon as she knows what it is! "Well, um, I knew she was struggling—cause she hasn't practiced! So I reminded Mackenzie of what good swimmers we were as kids."

Her mother is impressed. "That was very clever, Niko."

"Thank you!"

Her mother agreed with Niko.

It's official, everyone's retarded. Or perhaps it's her.

When Niko orchestrated this plan, she assumed Niko could not strong arm Donna like this. (Niko isn't even affiliated with swim!) This is real life, where hard workers get rewarded and non-hard workers don't get on swim. *Which means I'd lose valedictorian...permanently.* That was her orchestrated plan. As Mother Superior has, over the years and in a manner suggesting her dog just died, informed her of her oft second place grades and what should be done to address them. It's been a waste. For as much as it stings to concede, Mackenzie's smarter than her.

And dryer.

She needs to change the topic.

Also, the hot air vents are pumping cold air, so she turns them all away faster than she turned them toward. "I'm sorry we're late. Tryouts went over."

"I was about to come in and find you."

"I've got news about that!" Niko jumps at her bag book, ripping at the Velcro, then yanking back the zippers and reshuffling shit until she produces a thin plastic hanger like the "Do Not Disturb" signs at motels. "It's my parking pass! It's effective next week!"

Let's do this quick.

Last month, Niko turned sixteen.

As Niko was still dating Hazu, she asked for, then received, an RX7 for her birthday. It's a super-sexy, fire engine red sports coupe Niko's already spent a fortune "modding" so it's as fast and fancy as Hazu's own. Sadly, Niko also adopted Hazu's devil-may-care driving style. Even sadder, Niko got a speeding ticket. *And my mom found out about it.* Since then, there's been an unspoken embargo on driving with Niko. Mostly, it's a non-issue. The Academy, being the Academy, took weeks to process Niko's parking forms, and Niko, being Niko2.0, was too busy with the Bitches anyhow.

But, now...

She sits up! No longer caring for the treatment of her frozen body. "Mom, that's fantastic, right? You won't have to make so many long trips out here now!"

Her mother struggles. "I don't mind the trips."

"Really? You complain about them all the time."

Let's do this quicker.

Her mother pulls double-duty on rides. It sounds cool, but it adds an hour in both the morning and afternoon. It's left her mother so rushed that, one day, she drove them in curlers and a bathrobe. *My mom doesn't leave the house unless she looks ready to go to mass.* The time sacrifice has been unavoidable. At the beginning of the school year, Niko's mother, Kana, got in some trouble and had to, for lack of a better term, leave Seattle. No one asked her mom to do this for Niko. No one had to. Cause there was no one. Nana doesn't drive anymore and...

We always get the slack.

Either way, that's over. Tomorrow, Kana returns.

It's the biggest of big news in these parts.

Her mother mentions it. "Niko, are you excited?"

Niko is! "Of course! My mom called last night, and she says she is so much happier, she can't believe it! And she said she wants to stay in Seattle, so she won't work overseas, and, like, I mean, I hear it in her voice! She's better this time!"

Her mother beams. "That's fantastic, Niko."

It is fantastic. If it actually happens.

Here's the thing, this isn't Kana's first attempt to come home. It isn't even the first time Kana's been in trouble, so she puts a lid on the outright joy, and gets back to her efforts to reheat. She turns the dials all the way to red, then the fan to 4. The air stays cold. *I hate technology.* "It'll be great to see her."

Kana's picking them up from school tomorrow.

It reminds Niko of something. "Hey, remember you guys don't have to get me tomorrow morning! I have my appeal!"

While we're doing things quickly.

Last weekend, Niko cut her long hair short, then dyed the tips blond. Niko saw it as a bold statement of individuality. Her mother saw it as a cry for help. The Bitches saw it as a violation of the Rules. The vice-principal also saw it that way, but per the Academy's rules. On first sight, the little baldy ordered the blond severed. In response, Niko invoked, from the student charter, an appeal clause allowing Personal Code infractions to be reviewed by three teachers instead of one. It's a bullshit technicality and it's "known" not to challenge the faculty in such a manner.

Since Niko has anyway, she hopes Niko wins.

"They should let you keep your tips! They're so pretty!"

"I want to keep them, too."

Her mother doesn't. "How about you get your hair cut now? That way, Mother Superior can see how serious you are."

"No, I'm gonna wait. I want my mom to see it."

If her mother were recorded on an audio tape, it'd be playing right now. "Niko, you're in a time of your life where you want to express yourself, and that feels more important than more important things, but you focus on making a good impression."

If she were recorded on an audio tape, she'd be playing right now. "Are you kidding? You're getting Niko a haircut?"

Niko talks over that. Beforehand, she held her gum in her teeth, stretching it with her fingers. "I'm making a fantastic impression, by showing how well I know the Personal Code."

Pop!

(That was Niko's gum, too).

"When you say that you come off as being smart."

"Thank you!"

"That's not what I mean. I mean you come off as being, what it is?" No one knows. And no one answers. Her mother's not aware. When driving, her mom's concentration is absolute, her hands glued to the wheel, and her eyes in a constant squint. "A know-it-all. Mother Superior won't like that, and after what she's done for you this year."

And quickest.

Mother Superior has done a lot for Niko, this year and in years past. Niko's special circumstances require discretion, or "secrets," and Niko, being Niko, requires individual counseling, where things (like how Niko needs to listen to adults) are explained in ways Niko understands. For Mother Superior, it's a delicate balance between educator and pseudo-parent. It requires an effort and a love Niko has never fully appreciated, as it's unlike Niko to ponder a life at the mercy of the vice-principal.

Not that I care, I want a haircut!

Until this weekend, she liked her ass-length hair, but if Niko can get her hair dyed, then she wants her hair dyed, too! Or at least styled. Her mother said no—like her mother always does! To anything and everything! For example, every morning she prepares one way for her mother, then in the school bathroom, she rolls her skirt, pulls her blouse—you know, those "cool" Rules—applies her makeup and ear rings. While that sounds doable—like her mom's double-duty rides—try doing it daily, it's annoying. Plus, it's only the surface of her mother's denial.

My mom is convinced my pillowcases wear themselves out.

Go ahead and laugh. She might, too. It sounds harmless, but masturbation is the reason for these big arguments that go on and on and it's...

Not worth it.

Also not worth it is this stupid heating system. She turns a few more knobs, then gets knocked out of the way by Niko, who forces herself between the chairs to fiddle with the buttons.

The air is hot now.

"Mom, that's unreal! You're taking Niko to get a haircut?"

Niko talks over her, adjusting her chest during it. When she stretched, one of her boobs was knocked out. "Mother Superior knows my hair isn't meant to upset her."

"All the same, Niko. Show some loyalty."

She repeats herself. "Don't ignore me!"

Her mother sounds trapped. "We'll talk about this later."

"But you offered to take Niko!"

"It's different."

"How so?"

"Niko needs it done."

Ugh! She hates how Niko gets special treatment. She throws out, then crosses her arms. "I'll dye my hair too if that what it takes!"

"You will not do that."

She knows she won't. "What's it gonna take, then?"

Her mother blinks like a migraine. "There's not enough time to visit your Aunt."

Auntie lives in Tacoma.

"What if we didn't see Auntie, could we do it sooner?"

"She has cut your hair since you were little."

Tradition, to her mother, is like sentimentality to emo girls. It somehow applies to everything. "Can Niko drive me?"

Niko's stretched between the chairs again. "Yes, I can!"

Her mother stalls. "I'm not saying yes to that."

"Well, when can we go see Auntie then?"

"I said we'll talk about it later."

She backs off.

Things could go postal quick, as it seems to do almost daily. All her mother and her do is fight and... It's worth it now. Her mother and her have had issues for two years. Wait, strike that. Issues ever since she met Niko. *If it's not about Model UN or masturbation, it's Kana asking me to keep "secrets."* All that aside, on Monday, Mother Superior asked her to forgive her mother, for present sins and past. Lord knows she tries, but her mother always shoves it in her face.

She tells herself not to lose it.

She dislikes arguing with her mother around Niko since Niko would love for Kana to be involved in her life. But if it bothers Niko, Niko keeps it hidden, as Niko goes for her own agenda, holding herself against her mother's chair, and pressing her boobs into it, so she can better talk into the front, and feel their weight on her chest. "Tonight I'm having a party for the girls on Prom Committee. Next week, next year's Committee is gonna be selected, and we both want to make an impression, you know, so they know us a bit."

Her mother verifies everything Niko says. "Is that true?"
Here we go.
"Um, yeah."
Niko jumps in. "And you know what?"
Her mother wants to know what. "What?"
"Prom Committee applies to, like, valedictorian and stuff!"
Her mother verifies everything Niko says. "Is that true?"
"Um, yeah."
Niko jumps bigger. "And there's more!"
Her mother wants to know more. "What?"
"Donna Harly, the swim captain, is also Prom Committee President! It gets us in good for both."
Her mother verifies everything Niko says. "Is that true?"
"Um, yeah."

The time is now. The air is ripe. Gonna bring it down and give Donna Harly the long kiss goodnight. Or so Niko thought, and her anticipation has left her seething. *"Um, yeah?"* What betrayal! Of all the things that perplex Niko, shit like this is #1. She falls off the chair, then sulks into the backseat with her arms crossed as well. "I'm trying to participate. I want you to be valedictorian, too!"

She tries to be polite. "Thank you."
Her mother agrees. "Yes, thank you—how thoughtful."
Niko's back on it. She missed feeling boobs against her. "What do you think? Can we go?"
"Is your nana going to be there?"
"Yes! It was a rumor that we were alone this weekend."
Her mother hesitates.
It isn't only due to this Coeur d'Alene party.
(We'll do this one quick, too).

When Kana left, and Niko became Niko2.0, her mom, like the Academy, reassessed Niko in full. Before this, asking to go to Niko's parties or sleepovers was a formality, and at school, teachers overlooked their verbatim answers and note passing.

Now, this stuff requires intense scrutinizing, as if it were part of some grand metaphor. It's also subconscious. Her mother, and the Academy, know to ignore the exaggerated stories about Kana, but said stories are in such prominent repetition that her mother has, with the Academy, applied Kana's sins to Niko.

Crap like that made Niko1.0 feel responsible for Kana.

Crap like that makes Niko2.0 rebel and go crazy.

When Niko2.0 does just that, it verifies, for her mother and the Academy, that Niko requires intense scrutinizing. It's why, be it swim team, Model UN, haircuts, or car rides—all aspects of her life are Niko vs. [enter person or organization here]. Typically, this happens incidentally, save this time. Purposely, Niko used her as a battering ram against Donna Harly's oppressive rule, then, just now, failed to apologize for it.

It makes her irrational, so when her mother asks about her homework tonight, she forgets she finished most of it in study hall and lies to hurt Niko back. "I've got a lot to do."

"You do?"

"Yes."

Niko grumbles. "Are you sure?"

"Yes."

"Because it could get us on Prom Committee."

"I wish I could, but I just can't."

She regrets it seconds later. She stands by it anyway.

Goodbyes are awkward, but extended as Niko says, "I've got some stuff of yours." A minute later, Niko's back, out of breath from running with a duffle bag hung from her shoulder like a guitar. Then the real goodbyes happened. It was less awkward, since they're not things of hers, but things of Niko's, or as Niko refers to it, a "Care Package." As she said, her mother views all womanly indulgences as contraband, so from time to time she borrows Niko's clothes, jewelry, money, and dirty literature. This individual package is clearly an apology, seeing as care packages, like a lot of things, had fallen wayside to Niko2.0.

Hell, Niko fell wayside to Niko2.0.

It happened at dinnertime. Her mother had left the kitchen

TV on by accident. The volume was low. The words were clear. At first, no one responded. Maybe cause no one was surprised. Later, on the telephone, Niko was introspective and sad. She said, "I'm in a weird place," followed by, "I want to change everything." For as Kana spiraled out of control, so did Niko, and when Kana crashed into the ground, Niko dove after her, but when Kana emerged from her madness full of promises to fix it, she discovered a hard truth.

Niko was damaged. And it was in the way that can't be fixed.

Detour One: The Past.

This weekend sucked, and she knew it from the start.

On Friday night, she was moody over that, and spent the time watching TV and staring at the phone. She even tried to pen the great American novel. She failed. On Saturday, she perked up. She took a too-long shower, mixed old outfits into new, then in the mirror, forced her granny panties up her crack with her taut fist. On Sunday, she freaked out. Soon, her mother will find out she quit Model UN. *And that I quit in an awful way.* To distract herself, she flipped through childhood photo albums, then from her closet, gathered various leftover school supplies that, for the chosen pics of Niko and herself, became a corkboard she had her father nail above her desk.

It was meant to be a happy monument to their friendship.

Instead, she cried. It wasn't sad crying. Okay, it was sad crying. Over how Niko used to be a fun, cool person who did fun, cool shit, but when Kana left, Niko was left to discover, before the public en masse, that her life was a lie, and that people thought her spoiled ass deserved it. Tickets to that show sold fast. And the Bitches bought out the house. Evil notes were put in Niko's locker, insults were written in bathroom stalls, the prank calls were constant, and when it seemed like it couldn't get any worse, it stopped. In what amounted to the "if you can't beat 'em, join 'em" mentality, Niko—with zero forewarning—joined the Bitches, becoming Niko2.0, or Donna's sock puppet.

"And she totally lost it all on Saturday! She put huge guys—humongous, I tells ya—to shame. One was one of those tough guys who smashes the empty can on his forehead."

"Really?"

"She not only out drank him, she drank it faster!"

"Really?"

"Then, she went crazy! She was, like, yelling at the walls."

"Really?"

"I'm telling you, Donna Harly is insane."

See! Niko2.0's a way-boring, pro-Donna Harly propaganda machine. *Well, usually.* Either way, she's so disinterested that simple things—like holding the phone—require a balancing act between her shoulder, chin and face. She looks like one of those paralyzed people who breathe through tubes. That's just her. Most people are captivated. You see, Niko2.0's transformation was kinda incredible. It was precise, yet organic, transparent, yet clairvoyant, and Niko executed it with such legitimacy that it obliterated Niko1.0. *As was Niko's intention.* It wasn't as easy as that. Like all assimilations, there were sacrifices, or Rules, which demanded Niko tame her hair, change her wardrobe, alter her manner of speech, and pack her chest with tissue.

The fake tits are the worst. It's Niko's Scarlet Letter.

It tells girls, "I'm worthless."

It tells boys, "I'm desperate."

It tells teachers, "I'm dumb."

It tells Niko1.0's friends, "I'm untrustworthy."

And so no one does, and no one blames them. *I don't.* Even a naïve brat like herself, one who hates Model UN and sucks at political science, recognizes indoctrination. The Rules serve one purpose: to drain each Bitch into a compliant zombie. The issue is Niko can't be a compliant anything. After all, an alpha is an alpha, and while Niko2.0 suppresses that, it's nonetheless confused the biological predispositions of the betas around her.

In layman's terms:

Since joining the Bitches, all of Niko's pursuits have failed, including her attempts to circumvent Rule #1: Bitches only associate with other Bitches.

"I can't believe that. I never thought Donna was like that."

"Seriously, yelling-at-the-walls. It happened. Hazu saw it."

"Hazu? He was there?"

"Yeah, I invited him to come."

First off... "I thought you two weren't dating any longer."

"We're not, but we're still friends."

Second off... "You invited just him?"

"Well, him and his entire gang, and their girlfriends!"

This weekend Niko took the Bitches, the boys, and what she guesses was a bunch of other people, to Coeur d'Alene, where Niko had, what Niko already promises will be, an annual bash. Niko did invite her, and Niko even said, "Please try to come!" and "I want you to be there!" but she assumed it was a ceremonial invitation. No joke: Bitches only associate with other Bitches. Niko insisted the contrary, saying, "Ask your mother, please!" and "It's gonna be awesome!" She asked her mother. Her mother said no.

No way, I don't believe it!

Actually, she was pleased. She had zero desire to get served up and sold out to Donna Harly like a lamb to the slaughter.

Had she known this...

The news jolts her. She's sitting on her bedside, organizing her art supplies before her mother sees the mess. "Donna was okay with that?"

Niko takes a deep breath. "Um, yeah."

"But, that's not how it usually works, is it?"

Niko giggles. "Um, yeah."

"She changed her mind?"

"Um, she didn't get the chance. I sorta didn't tell her."

She's holds the phone with her shoulder again. She needs two hands to place her markers. She's a bit OCD, so the colors need to be in the same order as they're on the box. "You didn't?"

"Nope! *And* I have a confession!"

Niko almost squeals like a pig. A bit giddy for a confession. "What?"

"I cut my hair and I dyed it."

No shit. "What does it look like?"

"It's about at my collar and the tips are blond."

That sounds cool. "But, the Rules! Did you ask Donna?"

"Not exactly. I mean, I may have mentioned it in passing."

Okay, slow down.

Sure, by noise alone, Niko's fallen on her bed, and knowing

Niko, she's in a state of marginal dress, like a thong (*that I so wish was mine!*) and no top *(she doesn't stuff her bra when alone, duh!)*, and while this suggests that Niko's pleased by her badness, rest assured, nothing is further from the truth. Hard as it may be to believe, this is the first Niko1.0 thing Niko's done in months. It's logical, too. Niko had a weekend to rival all weekends, and it fried her brain, so she cut her hair, maybe even bought a new wardrobe since she burnt all her Bitches clothes *(you made that up)*, but that's all it is, and that's all it ever will be. *(Damn straight)*. Tomorrow, at school, Niko will fall back in line.

In the end, Niko2.0 likes being Niko2.0.

And I confused magenta and pink.

She starts over in case it happened somewhere else.

"What's going on?"

"What do you mean?"

"I thought you liked being in the Bitches."

Niko is fast. "I do."

"Then, what's...?"

"Since I've joined, like, everything has changed."

It has.

All the major parties happen at Niko's, including post-Prom, even though Niko's not attending Prom. Niko also provides pot or booze for free, then pimps out the mansion's bedrooms like it was a sleazy motel; or in Donna's case has basically allowed her, and by extension Mike Holler, their own bedroom. As a result, Niko's life has turned into a free-for-all. And Niko's life might've always been, had Nana not been there to set limits.

Lately, there don't seem to be any.

"Just stop for a second, Niko."

Niko stops. "What?"

"I gotta ask, how you are getting away with this?"

"What do you mean?"

The markers are done, but the OCD persists. All the caps aren't the same height. This particular set requires brawn. She pushes on the cap. It doesn't snap in place. Those markers are removed from the sleeve, and they're being stabbed into the nightstand. "Like this weekend, Nana let you do all this stuff?"

Niko giggles again. "Um, she wasn't there."

"What?"

"She didn't go. She was ill." Niko steamrolls forward. While this conversation may feel organic, it's nothing of the sort, and Niko is intent on hitting all her major points. "As I was saying, everything's changed, but the real change is Scott. I'm the one who knew him, not Donna, and this weekend, he realized that."

"What?"

"Scott's my boyfriend now."

And an enigma.

Niko speaks of Scott frequently, but her praise usually lacks any and all specifics, like he is a cult leader. "Scott's the best!" "Scott knows stuff about life." "Scott gets things done!" "Scott speaks to the space aliens from across the Milky Way!" (She made one of those up...maybe). Also, in the fall, he had a fling with Donna that ended badly. According to Niko, both were cool about it, but then Donna got desperate to get Scott back, which means Niko got desperate to make Scott her own. Don't judge, it's not cruelty that fuels Niko, but the spirit that drives any understudy to be an...over study. Yeah, um, point is, Niko sees winning Scott as a tribute to Donna and not a "here I am shitting on your face," fuck you.

Of course, Donna sees it as the latter.

Everyone else sees it as suicide.

"This weekend?"

Niko wears a quite-proud-of-herself smile. "Like I thought and I don't think Donna liked it."

"Why?"

"It was his name she was yelling at the walls."

Forget the markers.

She just got hit with the flu. Or something worse.

It's like her entire body started to work against itself. And it fills her with a warning in her every corner. Individually, all of these occurrences Niko described sound almost innocent, but as a collective, each seems bent on the minimization of Donna, while intentionally jabbing Donna over it. It should be zero surprise then, at least to Niko, when Donna lost it at a wall and probably other things, too, as what Donna was witnessing was a new Niko-centric scene, which means Niko's...

No, that's not possible.

Niko2.0 likes being Niko2.0.

"Um, where's this coming from?"

"Where's what coming from?"

She won't fall for that. Niko's planning something.

That's why I feel sick. "These thoughts about Donna and..."

Niko gets proper. "Well, I got some great news today."

"What?"

"I talked to my mom. She wants to come home."

Well, there you go. She's not sick anymore. Or she is, but it's the queasiness that happens when too much good stuff happens at once. And it's welcome. When Kana left, that was bad stuff—*really*, really bad stuff. Since it was Kana who started Niko2.0, it could be Kana who ends the 2.0. With Kana back, Niko might feel safe being herself.

She's abandoned the markers, her hand against her chest.

"Are you certain?"

"Yes, I'm certain. It's going to happen this time."

"That's fantastic. I could cry."

"I know. I cried for an hour."

"What do you feel? Are you ready for this?"

Niko sound tepid. "I'm happy, but I'm in a weird place."

Hm. Déjà vu.

"What?"

To that, Niko cannot speak, but when Niko feels that place, she breaks into goose bumps. Kinda like she just did, and in her closet, Niko exchanges her thong for an extra-long tee. Before that, Niko fondled her tiny breasts while imagining having big ones. It forces Niko to open one of her many drawers. Inside it lies her bra-stuffing crap. Her techniques have evolved this year, so there's lots of abandoned stuff from earlier generations that's pushed aside until Niko finds some tackle weights. (It's what fishermen use). Niko's current breasts are gel packs that sell well in Japan. They do the job, but they're super light, so while her fake boobs work for the world, they don't for Niko. Niko wants the full experience of breasts.

"Everything needs to change."

"Why?"

"I don't know."

"Could you be more specific?"

"I think we need to send Donna a message."

"What message is that?"

"That things will be different. Certain Rules will...cease."

Impossible. The Rules may be Donna's, but they've long been integral to the Academy's culture. Every girl in school rolls her skirt and pulls her blouse to Rules' requirements. One has to do it and do it without thought or question.

"I don't know if you can do that."

Niko's not listening. She's putting stuff in her drawer, then tossing some dirty clothes from her weekend in the corner. "I found something out."

"What?"

"Donna's the one who gave Jessica the nickname 'Cow.'"

Oh, no... The happy queasiness has turned into the full-on flu again. "But that doesn't mean—"

Niko interrupts. "Donna's behind the rumors about us and that shit against me when my mother left—it's her."

"Why? She asked you to join the Bitches."

Niko pauses, like she debates telling the truth. Then, Niko lies. "Trust me, I'm sure. I have a source, and it's a good one."

"You trust this person?"

The doubt annoys Niko. No one trusts her. "Look, Donna's personality is concocted for the Academy. In truth, she has got issues and they've, like, overtaken her. She can barely swim and she's forgotten major Prom details."

"So?"

"Her friends are turning against her."

"And what does that mean?"
Niko turns off her closet light. "I see an opportunity here."
"And that's what this 'message' is?"
"Yes."
It's also a bad idea. As this is bad intelligence.
Info of this type never leaks on Donna. The Bitches are like a secret society. It's cool to be in, but what's really cool is the inner circle, and whoever spilled the beans either, A) misrepresented the situation, or, B) did so without full disclosure of Niko's intent. Simply, Donna'd never throw Jessica under the bus—only a total nutcase would turn her guns on her own soldiers. So this talk, it better be pontification—cause Niko's popular and has always been, but Niko's never been organized, nor has Niko ever had a mean streak like Donna's.

Niko's a happy-go-lucky person, like in those photos.

Or, that is to say, Niko1.0 was.

And to a lesser extent, so was Niko2.0.

Whatever Niko is now, it isn't defiant. It's vengeful. *And I'm an idiot.* Think about it. Maybe with Kana back, Niko will feel safe being Niko1.0. Or maybe Niko is neither Niko1.0 or 2.0.

Then, the question becomes... *Who is this?*

She's finished with her markers, but started on nothing new.
"Niko, are you doing this on purpose?"
"Yes."
Wow. That was straight-forward.
"Can I ask why?"
"Donna thinks she can do anything to anybody."
She's glad Niko finally sees that. She's less glad about Niko's reaction to it. "That's why we hated Donna before you became, you know, her friend, but you can't do this."
"Why not? Donna would do it to you—to anyone."
"That gives you an excuse to do the same?"
"No, but we have to be as strong as her."
"She's not strong. Can't you see that?"
"I'm not so sure about that."
"Niko, I want you to talk to Mother Superior."

"No."
"Then, at least talk to your mother."
"Why?"
What a stupid question.
"Because do you know who you sound like?"
"Who?"
"You sound like Donna Harly."

In a way, Niko knows that, and in another way, she doesn't care. And she's on her bed again, nursing her achy joints. It was a rough weekend. Her goals were accomplished, but... Like, it required sacrifice. One sacrifice was bigger than the Rules. It was something Niko didn't expect. And it cannot be taken back. So there's no turning back. That makes Niko lonely, and she looks to her nightstand. It's a picture. On a beach, Kana has a fruity drink with an umbrella, and Niko has an umbrella OJ meant to mimic; mimicked no longer.

The booze turns Niko brave. It does that now.
She swallows in gulps. "I can't do it alone. I need allies."
She shakes her head. "No way. It'll put a target on me."
"It won't be a target."
"Yes, it will."
"I'll make sure it isn't."
"Niko, even you can't make that happen."
"But, if I could..."
"You can't."
"But, if I could..."

Above her desk, Niko and her are in Girl Scout outfits. She is bored. Niko looks confused. (They quit a few weeks later). Slightly higher, Niko and her are at a swim meet. Niko has too big goggles hung like a necklace. *I look like I've got a monster wedgie.* Beside that, she sits at Niko's ninth birthday in awe of the presents. In the center, Niko and her are, from a few weeks ago, dressed up for Sadie Hawkins while, sprinkled throughout, she has stenciled words like: "Love," "Friends," and "Joy."

Her urge to create this collage finds its origin.
It's not a monument. It's a tombstone.

I'm gonna regret this.

"You've got to promise you won't put a target on me."

"I won't. I promise."

"Then what do you need?"

"Two things. The first is you absolutely have to be at post-Prom this weekend." Niko hacks to interrupt an interruption. "You're not going to the dance, I know, but it's how I'm getting you into the Bitches."

Her stomach falls to her toes. "Into the Bitches?"

"Yes."

"Um, it takes more than a party to get into the Bitches."

"That's the second part. And you're not gonna like it."

"What is it?"

"Tomorrow, Mackenzie's going to announce a special tryout for Ladies Swim, and you're signing up for it."

3.

Her mother is overjoyed about swim. Or, politically speaking, her mother is overjoyed about valedictorian and its renewed viability. It's uncanny. Only her mother can make, "I knew you would get on the team," sound like, "I know everything!" So she does all she can. Watch traffic, hum radio songs, and stomach it with the silent treatment. *Or else we'll fight again, and I'm supposed to be forgiving her.* Throughout this, her soggy panty elastic impresses her skin. She pulls it and it burns, just as this duffle bag does a hole in her heart. Once in her bedroom, she unzips it to find this month's *Seventeen*, some eye shadow, and be still her heart!, a black thong and bra set, lined in pink lace, alongside matching garter and thigh-highs.

She really likes this lingerie.

And it's finding its way onto her body.

Despite the physical discrepancies, Niko's clothes usually fit her, albeit sometimes with a struggle and never with blue jeans. Bras are also impractical, but practical isn't her mindset. Still, her nipples don't fit, but before she critiques that, she softens the angle of her desk lamp, and at her mirror, she bunches her breasts, bares her breasts, shakes her breasts, and works her ass over, including when she puts her head between her knees. She puts her school uniform back on to see what it'd feel like to wear this to school, then an outfit she might wear to a party, one she might wear on a date, and finally she puts on her Sadie Hawkins gown.

She *really* likes this lingerie.

And she is tired of this game.

The thong is on her right ankle, and her legs are spread so her spit-laced finger can turn her clitoris in spit-laced circles. It's a good pace, and she stays there until she plateaus, then switches to similar circles at her entrance. It contracts her kegel like when the doctor hits her knee with that tiny hammer. Though that hammer never numbed her hips or put pixies in her boobs. Soon her forearm seizes (swim tryouts strike again), so she goes tried and true—what's worked since she was nine, which's to chokehold a pillow between her thighs, then smother the satin trim with her open vagina.

It was a solid orgasm, but not valedictorian level.

Mackenzie woulda come better.

She is bored.

Good thing homework awaits, tests are eminent and various other things require her attention. Instead, her dress is in her closet and Sadie Hawkins is on her mind. No, that's dirty. She thinks about boys, and ponders how lame it is to fuck a pillow like a total loser. *God, I hate masturbation.* Ya know, the safety of her bedroom and this house sorta turns her into a slut. She better get a hold of that. *Especially if I'm easing my boyfriend standards.* Hm, maybe she should wait. If she dates "a guy," she might miss "the guy." And if she misses him, logic would suggest, she'll miss Prom with him, too.

On that note, she needs to compile a Prom checklist for next year and start looking at dresses, shoes, and handbags.

Also, she should buy sexy underwear for Prom.

And say thank you to Niko!

"Wow, it's hot, where did you get it?"

"At the Secret. You tried it on already?"

"Of course, it took my breath away."

Niko laughs. "Are you still wearing it now?"

"Yes!"

On her bed, in fact. The thong's back up her butt, but the bra is still on the ground and her dark nipples are concealed by her black hair. She twists her waist and scissors, then spreads her legs—to pose this way, then that—before she lies on her tummy to practice her over-the-shoulder glance and its various degrees of open mouth. She gets sweaty. It's heat from the flash bulbs she nearly feels—like Kana! *It's hot!* At times like these, she realizes if she invests herself, she has real babe potential.

She should try to remember that. She's too lazy to bother. And too giddy to suspect the obvious.

Niko talks like nothing. "I have a question."

One she assumes. "I don't know why I said I couldn't go to the party, but my mom wouldn't have said yes anyway."

Niko doesn't believe her. She doesn't bring it up. "When did we stop telling each other things?"

When your butt joined the Bitches! "I don't understand."

"I mean the reason you didn't ask to go tonight."

She's confused. "And what's that?"

"Your uniform was—"

She interrupts. "It got damp after my shower. That's all."

An awkward silence persists. Niko almost bites her upper lip off during it. "I know what happened. I got on the phone and I found out."

No way did Niko find out. No way could Niko know.

What it was like to approach her swim locker. The room was silent and she felt lightheaded, like the air had been swallowed in anticipation of some great joke. Once she was the punch line, talk returned, as did the oxygen necessary to fully feel it. A tougher kid could've handled it. Whoop-dee-shit for that kid. She's a sheltered, sensitive baby who should've been destroyed. Instead, the lingerie took her to la-la land, but la-la land it was, as Niko2.0—the occasional dirt bag—assembled this Care Package only to butter her up.

She buries her emotions, then slides onto her feet. Soon, it'll be dinner time, so she ties in place pajama pants, and verifies, in the mirror, that, in this thong, her ass imprint isn't too pronounced. *My Mom notices this stuff.* "If you knew, why ask?"

"Who did it? Was it Mackenzie?"

She recognizes the tone. *That's who Niko wants it to be.*

"I think she knew about it, but she didn't do it."

"How do you know?"

"Mackenzie kept me in the shower."

"How?"

"We were talking about something."

"What?"

"You."

That doesn't surprise Niko. "And when you left?"

This is insensitive.

She gets sarcastic. "Don't want to ask me if I'm alright?"

Niko grinds her teeth, then scrunches her cheeks. She never intended to be rude. It's... In the hallway, she asked Mackenzie about tryouts. Mackenzie had to notice she didn't know about what happened. It worries Niko. Donna can't find out she's losing the trust of her Asian friends, it'll fuck up everything and so, yes, sometimes Niko loses herself in the political crapola.

She has no choice.

It's simple: Niko can't fake it all any longer.

Her room is a fantastic example.

On one side, all about her slept-in bed are her Rule-following outfits—mostly skirts and tops, shorts and tee's that are vanilla in flavor and pastel, Easterly in color. On the other side, upon her desk, dresser, chair, or floor, lie skater pants, racer backs, combat boots, and arm warmers of a predominately black motif. In between it all is Niko. Spread out like a corpse on the carpet, her limbs blown out in all directions like she had just survived an explosion, wearing only black, leather chaps, a dog collar and eye makeup so thick her eyes are ultraviolet. In those same eyes are her fingernails, which Niko's painted green on the left, then black on the right.

Before Niko is a choice.

Donna will be here soon. It's up to Niko who Donna will see, but either way, if Niko is to stay in front of this uniform thing, she needs the details...now. "I'm sorry, are you alright?"

No. "I guess. I mean, like, it was hard. Everyone knew. They tried to get out of there as fast as they could."

"Can you tell me what happened?"

Her neck falls over. "Do you care? Or am I a pawn to you?"

"No, I care. I want to help, but you've got to let me."

"Help? You caused it!"

Niko is offended. "I caused it? How so?"

Repeating herself makes her feel like Niko didn't listen the first time, which is probably true. "You used me for your plans, even though I said, 'Don't put a target on me.'"

"Hello—the plan was always to get you on the Bitches."

"Not like you got me on."

"But, there was no other way!"

"Then, you shouldn't have done it!"

Niko snaps back. "Well, I'm so sorry to have misread you, your majesty! I guess I'm just not as good at that anymore."

It bothers her.

Niko used to "know" stuff about her like those kids who tell rumors "know" she's gay. *Except Niko knew stuff that was true and those kids suck ass.* It brings back her moodiness. She forgets it as she packs up Niko's duffle bag in order to hide it beneath her bed. "Just forget it, Niko."

Niko tries to fix it. "Hear me out, swim may be the best thing that ever happened to you."

Nice try. "How so?"

"It can get you stuff you want, like—"

She interrupts. "Making things about school doesn't work."

Niko is annoyed. "Did I say that?"

"No."

"Let me finish." Niko pauses, then sits up. As Niko does so, she touches her abdomen. While Niko recognizes she has no boobs, she's got a nice stomach. It's one of her few parts she approves of, so she often feels the muscles create subtle definition in her skin. Once Niko's enjoyed it, she talks. "You have a free pass to pimp this shit. I mean, how did we miss it? You *need* a haircut. Swimmers can't have hair that long. Your Mom has no choice."

Holy shit.

How did I miss that? "You're right."

Niko liked that tone. "And Mackenzie still has her slumber parties for swim team where, just like when we were younger, all the girls use the pool and the hot tub."

Oh, baby.

"So I'll need a bikini."

"And you'd have to go shopping with them…"

Let's clarify something.

She hates Mackenzie. She wants to be Mackenzie.

Over the years, Mother Superior, her parents, and what feels like society at large, have conditioned her to view Mackenzie as the gold standard. Thus, it was natural when, given the gross levels of nudity that're allowable when team sports are introduced, she compared herself physically to Mackenzie, who has thin ankles, a staunch butt, zero stomach fat, tart titties, and those damn elf ears, which, despite being a genetic deformity, look cute. By no surprise, she wants thinner ankles, a stauncher ass, a fitter stomach, firmer breasts and…forget the ears part. But, there's more! She needs Mackenzie's *Heather's* hair, her fancy pearl earrings, her doll-like undies, a similarly shaved crotch and—if it's vain, vapid, bad for her psyche, and Mackenzie already has it, then she needs it too.

Don't like it? Take it up with God.

Looks matter, and what hurts her most is how Mackenzie is effortlessly high class, instinctively feminine, and tremendously virginal.

And me, and my mutual masturbating childhood, are not.

"Okay, I get what you're saying."

Niko again sounds like the know-it-all she sounded like in-the-car. Niko is also Niko2.0 again. She's at her desk where she first did her nails, except now she applies nail polish remover, then rubs them to normal. On her bed, Niko's already chosen a skirt. "Remember, Mackenzie's against you, but I asked around and the other girls like you, but, you know, even though they like you, they're not standing up to Donna."

Niko's right.

She sits beside the duffle, then bends over to her knees. Her super-long hair touches the floor. She motions her head back and forth like a broom. "Okay, I get it."

"And can I ask you something else?"

"Sure."

"I need you to cut me some slack."

She stops sweeping. "I know, it's—"

Niko interrupts. "I invited you to Coeur d'Alene and to meet Scott tonight."

She's up again, throwing hair over her face, then patting it down her neck. "Sometimes your trying feels like you're trying for yourself."

"Look, you can't imagine how pissed Donna was when I went to Sadie Hawkins with you instead of the Bitches."

Formals are, for all intents and purposes, the biggest part of her life. If she applied the time she spent daydreaming about dances, then, well, she'd be a lock for valedictorian. Knowing that, she skipped Homecoming. Niko was new to the Bitches. *I was too afraid to go without her.* It drove her to delirium, so when Sadie Hawkins came, she expressed this to Niko. She was prepared for Niko2.0. "I'm in the Bitches, but you're still so popular!" or "Ask the boy yourself! It's good for you!" Anything so Niko could seem supportive, but not really be supportive.

She was surprised when Niko not only agreed, but taught her how to ask out a boy. Actually, Niko asked. *Once Niko knew, I sorta asked.* It was very flattering, but she shoulda known Niko wasn't propelled by her plea for friendship. Niko had a secret. When Niko visited her locker, there were notes left in the slip. None of them trashed Kana. When Niko checked her phone, a new message was waiting. It never insulted Kana. When Niko went out, a certain someone found ways to whisper in her ear. It was not about Kana. Niko had an admirer. A sophomore boy named Hazu whom Niko ruthlessly blew off.

For one, dating him broke the Rules.

And two, Niko has no sensitivity for boys who love her.

In Niko fashion, against all her signals, she asked him to go.

"I know and I appreciate it, but stuff like these rumors, they're getting out of control."

Niko feels like a broken record. She snaps a bit, then blows on her nails. "I'm trying to stop that!"

"I know you are."

Niko tells a joke. It's how Niko redirects. "You know about BJS because of me! That's sisterhood!"

She laughs. Niko laughs.

BJS is an abbreviation for Blow Job Sounds, which consists of the guy's moans in conjunction with the girl's slobbering when she, A) swallows spit, or, B) loses suction, popping like Tupperware. It's a terminology exclusive to Niko and herself, sorta like the * or JBF in their note passing.

She can't stay mad at Niko after a joke.

"Alright, I believe you."

"So, are you gonna tell me?"

Of course, she is. When does she not?

Her hand, which was petting her hair, tugs at it, then fists it and twirls it like spaghetti. "Someone poured water through the ventilation diamonds of my gym locker. It soaked everything. I didn't get it, but then you told me how you got me on the team. Mackenzie musta been pissed."

Niko is focused. "You're sure it wasn't an accident?"

"I'm sure."

"How?"

"They left the bucket behind."

Niko is resolved. Her voice sounds slightly less convincing, since her throat's getting snagged by her collar. It buckles, so she gets asphyxiated when she removes it. "Well, that does it. They broke the Rules."

"What?"

"Donna agreed my friends were off-limits."

Niko got her own Rule? "What does that mean?"

"It means the gloves are off."

That sounds bad.

Also, her room smells of kitchen. She needs to wrap this up, do the two-step with her parents, and get to her homework. In the bra, she cycles through tops until she finds one where her boobs aren't too "out there." She has none. She keeps the bra on anyway. Maybe it'll give her courage to ask her mom for a haircut, a bikini, and a boyfriend, but before she does that, she needs a minute to accept she's in the Bitches, then determine her stance with Niko2.0.

Our friendship is so messed up right now.

Between all this, she ponders her responsibility. She hates it when Niko2.0 keeps secrets. *But I'm keeping a secret.* And like Niko2.0 often does, it's by omission. It's true. She did talk with Mackenzie in the shower, and at her locker, her uniform was soaked. She withheld the topic of discussion. She needs to tell Niko about it. And it feels like the last thing she should do.

For now, she forgets it.

"I gotta go. I'll call you back when Friends starts, alright?"

Niko grunts, struggling to strip the leather from her sweaty legs. "Oh, I forgot it's Thursday! Donna's coming over early for the party. I mean, I'll tell Donna to wait and—"

She interrupts. "It's okay."

"Are you sure?"

No, she isn't. But it'll have to do.

"Tomorrow, Kana comes home. Let's not be fighting for it."

Niko is timid. "Donna would never do that."

"What?"

Niko speaks up. "Donna wouldn't do that. She'd ruin it."

That should be obvious, but since it isn't, she thinks of it as a compliment. "I know she would."

"Are you hanging with my mom and me tomorrow?"

"Yeah, I'd like to."

Niko verifies. "Post-Prom and the sleepover are still cool?"

"Don't worry. It's different from the party."

Niko sounds satisfied. "I'll see you at school tomorrow."

"Are you forgetting something?"

"What?"

"I'll get my dad to tape the episode for you."

Niko is excited. "You're the best friend ever!"

"It's no problem."

"Please tell your dad thanks for me!"

"I will."

4.

Dinner is two rice balls, a salad with carrots and apple slices, gravy drenched pork and Coca-Cola. The soda fizzles in her neck while her stomach warms from what meat did not stick to her molars. Her tongue digs at it and fails, so her fingernail digs further. She does so shamelessly since no one knows of the dried vagina, which tastes a bit like salad dressing, on her fingertips. She would've washed, but upon reaching the table, she was instantly sick with hunger. This swim crap and Care Packages kept her from her after school routine of swallowing a handful of everything in the pantry.

I'm gonna be so fat when I'm grown up.

Eating together is a staple in her home and it's as predictable as always. Her father, alongside the paper, recounts the details of his day. He offers so few specifics it's almost like he has no job at all. He's thinking, "How long will they keep buying this?" Her mother buys it, then diverts into the nuances of homemaking, and outlines the meticulous steps involved in addressing all the (apparently) broken stuff in the house.

It's her turn.

"Dad, I need you to tape Friends for Niko."

Her father agrees, then says, "How was school?"

"School was fine."

"Did you learn anything?"

"Nothing really."

"Nothing?"

Occasionally, she debates confiding in her parents.

"Today, Niko got me into a way exclusive clique named the Bitches, but one of the leaders soaked my uniform. It scared me so I lied to Mom about my homework to skip a party." The dialogue remains internal. It's too hard to frame the discussion, as she only wants her parents' advice, not their intervention.

For its effectiveness against her mother, the silent treatment fails for her father. He needs her to be excited about school, life, anything, and she wants to support him, so she spills until he seems happy. "I began a chapter in math, there's a big test next week. And we watched a movie in Spanish!"

"A movie?"

Her father fakes like he's choking. It's part of a long running Daddy/daughter joke where, in an exasperated tone, he acts upset about how he pays all this money in tuition for her to, in this instance, watch movies.

"Well, the movie was in Spanish!"

His joke is cut off. Her mother wants the spotlight.

"Tell your father about the team."

Ugh, it begins! "I got on swim team."

"Congratulations."

Her father was once a competitive swimmer, and in what she understands from his infrequent visits to the gym, he is, despite his BMI, still faster than his skinnier, stronger counterparts. Her father is overweight like a football player is overweight. He looks athletic. She was proud of him as a kid and decided to emulate him. Along with Niko and Mackenzie, she swam for a local team, but quit after eighth grade since, according to her own observations, her butt wasn't big enough to be elite.

"It was a big surprise. I'm so slow."

Her father is confident. "It will come back to you."

"I don't know, Dad!"

Like a reflex, he fixes it. "Should you take lessons again?"

Didn't expect that. "Not really."

Her mother likes the idea. "Yes, lessons! You'll see, you're still a good swimmer."

But, I hate swimming! "Let's talk about this later, please!"

Talking about it later = Bad attitude. At least it means such to her batshit crazy mother. "The team is important. It's how you're going to become valedictorian."

"Please not this, not now!"

"You did this to yourself. Don't blame—"

She interrupts. "I know! Everything's my fault!"

"You quit Model UN and never chose anything else, so this got picked for you. Don't complain."

Beyond grades and church, the Academy holds students to a Student Value System. Essentially, it's an Honor Code, and it puts big emphasis on participation in the student community. Essentially, that's extra-circular activities, and prior to this semester, she was in Model UN, which, being an academic club, contributed towards valedictorian; whereas, her true interest, Glee, where slackers like Niko go to fuck around after dismissal, does not. Her mother, who views valedictorian as a gateway to scholarships, cares about it more than school.

That's why, when she quit, she kept it a secret.

She talks while chewing. "I'm not complaining. I don't want to talk about it is all."

Her father folds over the paper. "You didn't want to swim?"

She mumbles. "I wasn't that excited about it."

"Why not?"

Because I hate swimming! "It's not my thing, I guess."

Her father's also interested in reduced college costs, so even though he disagrees with her being forced to swim or being forced to overachieve to standards outside her own, he sorta pretends like it's no big deal. "It will come back to you."

Well, when all else fails... *Try, try again!*

She whines! "I don't know, Dad!"

It changes his opinion. "Is there nothing else you can do?"

She spits it out. If she weren't such a shill for Niko, it might have surprised her. "Actually, Niko had a good idea."

"What was that?"

"Prom Committee."

He eats over his words. "How do you get on that?"

"Niko had an idea about that, too."

"What was it?"

"I need to go to a party tonight and meet them."

Her mother is confused. "You said you have homework."

"I finished early. I want to show my interest and relax with my friends. Besides, you liked how Niko talked to Mackenzie about swim. Isn't this the same?"

Throwing her mother's logic back in her mother's face, to her mother, is the male-equivalent of a sucker-punch. It's a great way to put her mom on the prowl, which's exactly what it does. Her mother sits straighter, then talks higher. "By the time I drop you off, I'd have to turn around and get you."

"Actually, Niko can drive me back."

Another totally counterproductive sucker-punch!

I can't help it. I like hurting her.

Her mother shows none of her singed pride. She just moves food about her plate, acting like the answer should be obvious. "It's too late by then for Niko to be driving."

Her arm extends to her father. "You know Dad's right, right? I wasn't ready to tryout for swim. Do you even care how much pain I felt trying to do it?"

Her mother struggles. "I will decide soon."

"But, Mom, look at the time!"

"I said I will decide soon."

In mild protest, she pouts, then thanks to some thigh-high generated static cling, shocks herself when she touches her fork. Her mother wants her to eat vegetables. The reds, greens, and occasional yellow are in a plastic container that farts when it's opened. She giggles. "What's so funny?" "Nothing!" It's her chore to clear the table. She stacks plates, silverware, and cups inside cups like servers do. The sink is two halves. One side is filled with soapy water. The other rinses the bubbles down the drain. At the dishwater, she receives what her mother has scrubbed to a spotless shine.

"Have you thought about the party?"

"The dishes aren't even done."

"Can I get ready at least? So if you decide yes, I'm ready."

"You know I don't like you going out on school nights."

She needs to find a way around that. Cause Niko is right. *If my mom gets valedictorian, I should get something, too.* Like a Popsicle or a Fudgsicle. Her head is in the freezer while the flatware soaks the dish rag beneath it. She breaks the plastic seal, then holds it against her tongue until it's stuck. It's the smart thing to do. She's been handed a pot which won't fit. She dries it manually, returning to her point—if she got more stuff, she might want to be valedictorian.

"I was thinking, I need to get my hair cut this weekend."

Her mother is exhausted by the thought. "You do?"

"I can't have hair this long and be on swim team."

Her mother no longer scrubs, shocked to hear a legitimate reason. "I will call your aunt and we'll go on Saturday."

Hm, she should be humble and appreciative.

Screw it.

"Can we can go shopping too? I want to get new clothes for spring and summer."

"And what's that?"

"I want a bikini this year."

Unlike before, her mother washes uninterrupted. A sure fire sign of failure. That assumption overlooks how, having already been on swim, her mother is well versed in team customs. "This is for the get-togethers at Mackenzie's?"

"Exactly, I want to fit in with the girls on the team."

Her mother looks relieved again. "We will buy you one."

Okay, now she should be humble and appreciative.

Or go for the ultimate score: A boy.

It's another thing she debates confiding.

"Mom, after Sadie Hawkins, I sorta... Well, long story short, I overheard Niko, uh, doing stuff, and, okay, odd to say, but my date made it to second base. Mom, 'second base' means he felt my boobs. Calm down, it's never happened before, and it was fine, but a few days later, we found out we're just friends. That part sucked. My point is that I need a boyfriend. And not so I can sneak around, but so I don't. If I have a boyfriend, I can go on fun dates and stuff, but that can't happen when you force me to lie to you."

Yeah, not gonna happen—tonight or anytime soon. Besides, she has other business. Her voice is muffled by Fudgsicle. "I might be late coming home tomorrow."

Her mother anticipated this one. She speaks into the doors below the sink. She's trying to find cleaning pads. "I would think Niko wants to spend time with her mother alone."

"Mom, it's me."

Her mom stops searching and sounds stressed. "Okay, but be home for dinner."

"What if Niko invites me to sleepover?"

"Are you still sleeping over with Niko on Saturday?"

"Yes."

"You can't spend the whole weekend there. Pick a night."

Then she picks Saturday. Post-Prom is a part of Niko's plan.

"Okay, I want to do it Saturday because of the party."

Her mother seems okay with the decision. It's tomorrow that worries her. She is up from the sink and making eye contact. "I want you to call me if anything funny happens with Kana, and if she is drinking or anything, I'll drive you home."

Disrespecting Kana usually sparks a fight.

She hesitates since, especially lately, it's been impossible to defend Kana. In truth, Kana's never had exemplary behavior. *While my mom does nothing but.* For years, it's put significant friction between her mother and herself. It began when, as a kid, Kana asked her to keep "secrets." It hit a low when, as a slightly older kid, she was caught masturbating, then confessed to "rubbing" with Niko. Things were okay, but in eighth grade, her mother, with minimal explanation, told her it didn't matter what high school Niko attended, cause she wouldn't be.

The fight that started that day never ended.

And each fight thereafter, including Model UN, is part of it.

Every time, Mother Superior's intervened on her behalf. And for Model UN, it was no different. *It's nice because I don't have to keep "secrets" from Mother Superior.* And earlier this week, like when she was little, Mother Superior accompanied her to the chapel, where they prayed, then, also like when she was little, they talked about the things God would want, like all the information on Niko's Coeur d'Alene party.

She was (half) kidding.

She knows what God wants; Mother Superior, too. To maybe hug her mother, maybe cry, then say it. "Mom, I forgive you." Like in the car, it's messed up. Either because of Kana coming home or the Fudgsicle or just being too happy, she forgot what she's got on underneath her PJs, so when she bends to squeeze in a bowl, it tugs, then separates, the overlap of her pants and top, putting on full display the black fabric coming out of her ass and stretching to her waistline, which's covered by her garter—whose straps can be seen shaped along the outsides of her butt cheeks.

It's a bit of shock for her mom. "What are you wearing?"

She loses her breath and can't catch it. Or think.

She blurts out. "My PJs."

"No, what're you wearing underneath them?"

She's stood up and pulled down her top. "Ugh, underwear?"

"Niko gave that to you, didn't she?"

Oh, time to use the team excuse again!

"I got it from a girl on the team. We traded some clothes."

Her mother shakes her head. "It's Niko's. Why do you need that thing—for this party tonight?"

Is that why Niko gave it to me? No. Even Niko wouldn't be that shitty. "It's not for the party. It's a total coincidence."

"What does Niko have planned for tonight? Another party with no grownups before her mom comes home?"

She rolls her eyes, then tosses her hair. "That was a rumor! Nana was there last weekend, and she'll be there tonight!"

"Lie to me again and you won't leave that room."

I'm not lying!

Okay, she's lying, but the accusation is out of line. Her mom has zero proof! Other than previous proof of similar indiscretions. To simplify: thongs, boyfriends, whatever, cause a hysterical reaction in her mother which echoes another reaction her mother gave, when her mother caught her masturbating. *I had no idea it was bad.* Once she learned it was, she expressed regret, then swore to stop (2,000 orgasms later, she intends to still do that); however, she never understood it. Sure, she was a wee bit young, but...

Niko taught me about my vagina, so what?

"Excuse me for making new friends!"

"You don't need that to make friends. Take it off and bring it to me."

"Okay."

"And tell Niko she's not to give you that stuff."

"But, Niko didn't—"

Her mother interrupts. "But, nothing. One day, you'll run out of excuses and I fear that, instead of learning anything, you'll just say the same ones again."

That hurt. She's gonna cry about it later.

Her feet pound away. "Okay, I'm sorry!"

Her mother pounds, too. "Don't take that tone with me!"

"Mom, you're crazy! Not everything is about Niko!"

"Then why did you stop going to Model UN?"

If not obvious, her mother's arguments are often circular. It's because they're often the same. Since the masturbation thing, her mother's had this theory that Niko brainwashes her into being a compliant zombie. Which is impossible. Unless it's Donna doing it to Niko and Niko doing it to her. *They're different!* Except, they're not. Way back when, Niko had an unquantifiable hold on her. Sure, it became sexual, and while that's what concerned her mother, and it concerned Mother Superior, too, Mother Superior recognized it wasn't lesbianism driving Niko and her, but innocence.

Niko didn't originally conceive sex as being about gender.

And I couldn't say "no" to Niko. Or rather, I didn't want to.

Her mother, Mother Superior, even Kana—no one sees how the universe conspires for Niko. It's why Mother Superior saw it fit to suggest that separation from Niko was the key. Her mother agreed. She and Niko were put in different classes, lunches, and recesses. Years later, after these efforts failed, her mother tried to send her to a different high school. If only her mother knew she only needed patience. One day, Niko would join the Bitches, thus forcing the separation her mother was artificially trying to produce. Months after Niko actually did so, Niko rescinded it. *And as my mother would've wanted, I hesitated.* Specifically, she said, "Don't put a target on me." Turns out it was a cosmic joke. All the cogs, as she suspected, were working individually against Niko, but as a unit, each gave Niko exactly what Niko wanted.

She ended up at swim tryouts.

And it was my mom and Mother Superior who put me there.

Detour Two: Mother Superior.

Mother Superior's office is a square without excess. One wall bears a cross with Jesus attached to it and a circular print of the Virgin Mary, like a yearbook cutout, is stuck to a yellow-tinted computer monitor. The furniture is forgettable slabs of wood covered for the butt, the back, and for the elbows on the arms. Being elderly, Mother Superior struggles to sit, but she does sit and then stares nostalgically with her hands folded together, as if she were in a lazy prayer. Before she can speak, she hears a gulp of air, then the agony of withheld tears, and Mother Superior stands once again to retrieve tissue which she sets on the table.

"My dear, I'm not angry."

It's not that.

Everyone really respects Mother Superior, so when Mother Superior fetched her from class, an "oh, shit" ripple washed through the room, and since she too respects Mother Superior, after she set down her book bag and pulled on her sleeves, the tears came full force. *I messed up bad.* Well, not "bad" bad, but it feels that way. As a kid, Mother Superior was principal of the Academy's primary school. *So we've got a long history.* Now that she's caught, which she knew she would be all weekend, she feels an embarrassment that seems to subtract seven or eight years from her life.

Her voice even sounds like a second grader. "I swear it's not happening anywhere else."

Mother Superior sounds the same, second grade or not. "Not with your grades, but I met with your instructors."

For being such androids, her teachers perceive a lot.

She thinks the technical term is to "coast"—if a 3.98 GPA can be called coasting. And while it's true, she watches the clock more than the board, she also knows enough to know when she's known enough to shut down. She wasn't escorted here for her faraway brain. It's for Model UN. Her behavior there is inexcusable. She was not wronged, nor ignored. Actually, lots of cool people are in Model UN. They work hard and they believe in things and in themselves.

And I abandoned them.

"I know what you're thinking..."

Her voice trails off. Mother Superior is interested.

"What am I thinking?"

"I say 'no' to Niko now, I know no one believes it, but I do. It's not like when I was a kid—I get what people are saying."

"What made you think I was going to bring up Niko?"

"Because she told me you talked to her this morning."

To that there were few alternatives, as Niko strolled into the chapel for Monday mass with blond abominations at the tips of her hair. Niko was allowed to remain for the service, but found the vice-principal waiting at the Academy doors. *That wasn't all.* Word has spread of Niko's unsupervised Coeur d'Alene party. As of yet, the vice-principal has been unable to comprise a guest list or confirm which overblown stories are true or false.

He will find out, though. That's what he does.

Mother Superior handles it her own way.

"I did talk with Niko about this party she had."

"I don't know anything about it. I wasn't there."

"Do you know who was?"

"No."

"Do you know what happened?"

"No."

Mother Superior sounds suspicious. "You don't?"

She snorts snot, then grabs a tissue. And contemplates how to ditch this topic. Lying for Niko used to be easy, but with the Model UN thing, she no longer looks angelic. "We all know things have been different since her mother left."

"I have seen that in my conversations with her. I've also seen that she has latched onto Donna Harly."

"She has."

Bet you think, for Mother Superior, that's a bad thing. But, you forgot reputation. And all Donna's done for one. It's fooled Mother Superior good, as the poor dear has not a clue of the idiocy she implies when the words leave her throat. There's also something about her posture. For a woman in that habit, its starkness and its implication, to be so uninformed—it about makes her question everything she's ever believed in.

"I had hoped new friends, who have their priorities straight, would've influenced Niko positively."

"New friends" implies old friends, whom Mother Superior implied were the Stars. *But, not me, she'd love Niko to be like me.* However, she wants the opposite, and she wants to know if Niko is being truthful. "They've not been together as much. Donna's been busier. I heard she forgot major details about Prom, and that the dance is in jeopardy this year."

Mother Superior is caught off-guard. That never happens.

"Where did you hear that?"

"It's just a rumor."

"There've been challenges. This year's Prom was perhaps too much for the Committee to handle alone."

Niko was telling the truth.

"I'm glad the dance will be alright."

"It will be. Are you alright?"

No.

Even more tissues blot her face and her lungs heave for air. Her thoughts remain a secret. When she keeps secrets, she becomes a stressed-out wreck. Of course, that's preferable to what Niko's become. It proves a mother is more important than anything. Without one, Niko lost her identity, as well what parts of her life felt inherent. Sadly, that was only a small slice of what waited in store. This thing with Kana took on its own life. At school, at home, on the radio, and on TV—there was no escape, nor temporary refuge.

For Niko, or myself.

That's not exactly true.

Kana said it was okay to confide in Mother Superior, but it

doesn't mean she will. She keeps steady, or steadier, and is careful not to be too liberal with her arms. If she is, she'll draw attention to her pulled back blouse. A Personal Code violation is about the last thing she needs. "It's hard. Everyone wants to blame Niko, and if I say anything, it could get out and get even worse."

"Who do you speak with?"

"There's no one to speak with."

"Are you sure about that?"

Mother Superior refers to God. It's no joke. The Academy's got a faith expectation. It's a serious thing, like math. "Mother Superior, I don't know if prayer will help."

Mother Superior turns witty. "Will it hurt?"

Good point.

She wipes her irritated eyeballs. It irritates her nostrils. She's also cold. It's worse outside. The day is gray, and the bell towers, being so tall, allude that the chapel is on the Academy's doorstep. In reality, it's a ways past the courtyard, beyond the football field, and even then it's buried in and obscured by packs of evergreens.

It may end up a worthwhile journey.

Since it appears my prayers were answered.

As Niko predicted, swim tryouts were announced, along with the other announcements, before Monday mass ended. *I want no part of them.* Lest she wants to fulfill Niko's hidden objective. *Which is me joining the Bitches.* Even less does she care for Niko's true objective. *To send Donna a "message."* In her own way, she turned Niko down. She said, "Don't put a target on me"—believing without her cooperation in tryouts, Niko'd be unable to get her on the Bitches. Even with that, in prayer after receiving the Eucharist, she asked the Lord spare her this fate (and the gay rumors). She did so cause when Niko explained her plan, she heard in Niko what she heard on the night Niko told her about masturbation.

Ambition.

Niko always wins. This time Niko lost. *Mother Superior will force me to return to Model UN.* Which forces Niko's plan into hiatus. It's an acceptable compromise. "Mother Superior, I've been thinking. It was a mistake to quit Model UN. I'll apologize and I'll fix it, I'll go back."

"I am glad to hear your attitude has changed, but..."

She jumps in. "Like I said earlier, please don't blame Niko."

Mother Superior reaches out, then with her wrinkled, boney hand, holds tight to her own. "Missing your presentation alters the situation. It was, as I understand, the largest part of your project, so you've lost your academic credit for the semester."

Well, she didn't want to be valedictorian.

Mission accomplished.

I am so dead.

"Have you talked to my mother about this?"

"Yes. I expressed concern about it. For one, you're not in line with our Student Value System. And two, it was thought you excelled in Model UN, but what I heard, of how you handled this, is not what I've come to expect from you."

Mother Superior's right. It's not.

She wants to leave it that way.

"Is there any way to still become valedictorian?"

Mother Superior is quick. "I'm not speaking about valedictorian."

She is quicker. "My mother is. Is there anything I can do?"

"There is. You can become a swimmer again."

Wow, that was a short reprieve.

She has little concern for it. She thought when she ditched Model UN and hopefully valedictorian, she had the guts to stand up to her mother. *But, I don't.* And ladies swim, with its athletic credit, is a tiny miracle of sorts. You see, these tryouts are really a "secondary" tryout. At the Academy, ladies swim wins state championships, so the team is a core who's competed together for years. *As Niko and I did.* What she and Niko didn't do was tear an ACL skiing over winter break. Or get whiplash when a boyfriend, new to driving, nailed a mailbox. These injuries, as well as some others, have pushed almost the entire

JV squad to varsity.

"Okay, I'll do it. I'll tryout."

"If that's your decision, but you only need to do so if you wish to remain in the valedictorian race. Any activity will put you back in line with our Student Value System."

"It's fine. Can you do me a favor?"

"What is it?"

"Can you call my mom and let her know I'm doing it?"

Mother Superior pauses and then supposes she should. "Of course, I will speak with your mother again."

Whew. This is the type of circumstance where her mother will doubt she is being completely honest. If Mother Superior calls, then her mother will know she's not keeping secrets.

Odd coincidence.

She is near where the secrets started.

Near the edge of the Academy grounds, a cobblestone road veers through the many chapel gardens—each filled with sculptures of the Virgin Mary, the chapel's namesake—and it was in this garden, right here, where Kana pulled her aside. *I was young.* So young she felt like she'd known Niko her entire life when it might've only been three weeks. Still, she hears Kana word-for-word, almost sees Kana—in a hazy watercolor way. "Honey, I want to ask you for a big favor. You know, it's hard to explain, but Niko's life is complicated. It's my fault, not hers, but someone, a friend or a grown up or a parent, may ask you questions about Niko. If that happens, you can't answer, okay?" Kana made her promise. She did so. At dinner, she refused to tell her mother about school that day, but did tell of her promise not to tell.

Her mom got pissed.

Not at me, but at Kana—and eventually at Niko.

She forgets it as the garden, long passed, has been replaced by Cherry Blossoms. Being springtime, the petals, which are prone to falling, are more prone to sticking. Mother Superior pulls the slack of her robes. *And I keep my head low.* To make sure none get stuck to her shoes.

It also feels better that way.

It's weird being taller than Mother Superior.

"Anything you can do, things are going to be tough tonight."

"I thought you two had resolved your disagreements."

Mother Superior would think that.

She wants to leave it that way.

"We have and we haven't, but like I told you, I don't want it to become Niko's fault. She's got enough on her plate."

Mother Superior's no dummy. Being the third or fourth time she's been told to forget Niko, she decides to not. "There was some concern. You stopped reporting to Model UN shortly before Niko had this party."

Actually, it was right before. But, it wasn't about that.

It was about Sadie Hawkins.

Going with Niko was unexpected. And what happened during it was inexplicable. Niko2.0 caved to 1.0, the *real* Niko, and despite Donna's tense body language, Niko proceeded on a tear of charisma so huge she infected the students, the chaperones and, later in the car, Hazu himself. *It was the best time I had had all year.* And it gave her hope. That didn't last. The next day, Niko regressed. *And I was on the outs.* Left to closeout sophomore year working on a shitty Model UN project with time enough to contemplate her shitty adolescence.

Then, Niko said it. "I want you to come to Coeur d'Alene."

She was standing at her locker reviewing Model UN notes, mere minutes from her presentation. That ended. She double took a double take and recognized her opportunity. For while she did miss Niko, it was not only Niko. It was, in that aforementioned car, hearing Niko's BJS. Niko was loud, sloppy and farted like Tupperware; Hazu himself moaning in what was either pleasure or a gun shot wound. Really, it was how Niko let go. *Because Niko did, so did I.* On a picnic table, her semi exposed breasts were handled—for ten or fifteen minutes of the freest she's ever felt, even more than when she first rubbed.

It had other side effects.

Stuff that, being celibate, Mother Superior wouldn't get.

She wants to leave it that way.

"It's a total coincidence. I quit… There're good reasons, but I don't want to make excuses. I realized Model UN wasn't for me, but I didn't know what to do or who to…"

Mother Superior finishes her sentence.

"Who to talk to about it?"

Ergo her chapel visit.

Are all my problems so similar?

She ignores it. Those petals may not have stuck to her shoes, but a few have taken to her hair, and she extends her arms to reach them. "I guess. But I not only have to keep all this secret for Niko, but from my mom. She's angry at Niko."

Mother Superior's confused, and no less detoured. Five times she's mentioned Niko. You'd think she'd notice. "Why is that?"

Her mother blames Niko for a lot, and her mother does so because her mother views these things as Niko's intent instead of a side effect to Niko's circumstance. For instance, her mom thinks her bond with Niko was engineered by Niko. Her mom also believes her masturbation was engineered by Niko. For that, her mother is right. *Niko taught me how to do it. I didn't ask and I resisted at first.* Having lived these last few years, she knows it took only an instant for her mother to determine this Model UN situation was engineered by Niko.

And, once again, her mother is right.

It's those side effects.

When that boy groped her boobs, revolution was born. Deep down, she knew she'd never be valedictorian or enjoy Model UN or get a good boyfriend—not if she continued in her quest to be Mackenzie. It's difficult to admit, as the words are so associated with shame, but she needs to exceed Mackenzie. She *needs* to. Then, as soon as she does, she'll know her mother loves her, then a boy can love her, and she can quit this crap and get good grades at her leisure—since school, when she's not hating it, is easy.

It's the last thing her mother wants, as doing so means:

"My mom thinks I've chosen Niko over her."

"She does?"

And there's more.

"And she thinks I would pick Niko's mother for my own."

"Is that what you would do?"

No. "No."

"Have you ever told your mother that?"

No. "No."

Up close, the chapel resembles a medieval fortification. Its entrance is an arch with a cross, this time with no Jesus, cut into fieldstone above segment doors. Inside, an open ceilinged hall with three columns of pews assemble in endless rows toward the alter. It's part of the sanctuary—*it's where the mass is conducted*—lit by three, of what're all twelve, stained glass apostles who enclose the congregation.

At the front, she finds her knees, then waits while Mother Superior labors to her own. In the name of the Father, Son, and Holy Spirit, she forms the sign of the cross. Instead of hearing God, she hears herself. *How's that for an indictment?* However, God speaks volumes to Mother Superior. And the woman is catatonic over it. She peeks for signs that this pray-a-thon might conclude, and only sees how Mother Superior has, in this last year, grown an old face and a hunched back; yet, as always, her body's fat in that proportional way that looks thin.

Her appearance is of little matter. It's her presence.

Around Mother Superior, I know right from wrong.

She knows what she must do. She must forgive her mother.

After all, her mother's anger about secrets is kinda justified. As well, her mother can't deal with masturbation as a topic. And while it was wrong for her mother to ask her to stop and to inform Mother Superior about it... Hell, it was also wrong for Mother Superior to tell her masturbation was a sin, lovemaking was a duty and she could only have sex with one man. But, all these instances—including when her mother attempted to deny her the Academy—were mistakes. And Jesus preaches forgiveness. Or as Mother Superior says, "Let he who is without sin cast the first stone." Which she would never, ever do. Then, somewhere along the way, she did do it, and did it many times, enjoyed it, and still does it to this day.

Hurting her mother is like a drug. It's a five second fix. And it's a problem. A mother is more important than anything.

And I hate mine.

Eventually, Mother Superior sits back. She has a glow.

"Were your prayers answered?"

The question's rhetorical. Though, she does feel better. With that, she feels she needs to save what shards of her reputation are left. She speaks softly. This is a church. "I promise you I'll try at tryouts. I'll get back where I should be."

The problem?

Like she lied to Niko, she lied to Mother Superior.

In truth, she's already surrendered to apathy. And knows, in the same manner she quit on Model UN, she'll quit on swim—not through action, but a lack thereof. It's like Mother Superior intuitively knows this and isn't overly concerned. *She doesn't care if I'm valedictorian.* Grades, boys, thongs—they're trivial to Mother Superior, who believes God is supreme.

In fact, all that interests Mother Superior at this moment are the intricacies of Niko's situation. "I need to ask for your help and for your trust."

What an odd thing to say. "Okay."

"I'm trying to help Niko, but Niko's been reluctant—more than she has been in the past."

And I'm the tattletale. "Okay."

"Are Niko and her friends still using that bathroom?"

It's so infamous that's all that needs be said.

"If you mean the one by the pool and gym, I don't think so."

Mother Superior accepts the answer. Mostly cause she has a bigger question. "Under total anonymity, is Niko living alone?"

In a way. Niko's caretaker, whom Niko calls Nana, lives with Niko, but Nana's old like Mother Superior, and Nana's in a far more decrepit state. It's possible Nana's lost the will to oppose Niko. The Nana she knows would never allow an unsupervised party to happen, much less a weekend party.

She lies for Niko. It's what she does. "No, her Nana is—"

Mother Superior interrupts. "When did you last see her?"

"A month. I don't visit as often. Can I ask why you've asked?"

Mother Superior debates discretion, and chooses trust.

"These stories about Niko are not all accurate, but they are not all false. I believe she's using that bathroom and that she's hosting unsupervised parties at her house. In both instances, I know there is behavior of loose morality, and since it includes other students from this school, we need to stop it."

I guess I could stop it.

She's too afraid. "What will happen to Niko?"

"How do you mean?"

"She and the vice-principal aren't on good terms."

Mother Superior, with her boney hand, grabs on again. "I will handle Niko, as I always have."

Here come the compromises. It makes her fingers burn like Hell, even though Mother Superior's grip is icy cold. "Last I knew, Nana was there. But, I don't participate in these things, so I'm not sure, but there's good news."

"And what's that?"

"Her mother is coming home this week."

The type of obliviousness Mother Superior showed—back in her office—to Donna Harly, does not get shown for Kana. If anything, Mother Superior wears an unnatural anxiety, like she were in debate about if Kana should've come back at all.

"I'm uncertain about my feelings on that."

She stays resolute. "It's not ideal, but Niko will listen to her, at least at first."

"We'll see. Until then, I must implore you—if Niko is in any trouble, you need to tell me."

Tell the grownups. Get this handled. It'll be fixed.

Honesty, she thinks they'll make it worse.

"As far as I know, she's fine."

For what she really learned at Sadie Hawkins is something everyone had already exploited. *Me, I didn't see it.* As she said, when that boy touched her breasts, she knew she would never be valedictorian, Mackenzie would always be her better, and accepting this would get her a boyfriend. Most of all, she realized her breasts only got handled cause of Niko, and that made her what she always was, a follower. Which was fine, but then she had to decide: Follow God, follow Mother Superior, follow her mother, or follow Niko.

She chose Niko. *I did, didn't I?* But she never chose Kana over her mother. That she never did. No way. Not like it makes a difference. This insight—all of it—was a waste. When tryouts begin, she'll once again try for valedictorian, compare herself to Mackenzie, not find a boyfriend, and as a result, any peace inside her will be extinguished, as these behaviors are like currents. They're too strong to fight, especially when the pull is so familiar.

Mother Superior is disappointed in her.

She wants to leave it that way.

"Alright, I will trust you."

That makes her feel sick.

"Thank you."

"There's just one other thing."

Incoming! Incoming! More guilt!

She sounds heavy. "Okay."

"I'm concerned about her relationship with Haruhide."

In case you forgot, that's Hazu.

"Okay."

"Premarital sex is a sin, is inappropriate, and unacceptable for any student at this school. And I sense it between them."

Hang on. She doesn't have to lie. Niko broke up with Hazu, and this weekend, Scott and Niko become exclusive. Mother Superior has it wrong. In this area, Niko's totally innocent.

As am I.

She answers in a clear voice, without fear of persecution.

"Mother Superior, I swear to you that's not happening."

"How do you know?"

"Mother Superior, I know. Niko is a virgin."

5.

Her hand misplaces the off button for all the buttons and once it's found and her alarm silences, she sits at bedside, unable to stand. And she stands, unable to walk. At the toilet, she falls asleep in spurts. She does the same in the shower, and brushes her teeth so poorly her tongue flicks the leftover plaque. Her bedroom lights are flipped, and in a squinted haze, she dresses. Sort of. Her skirt is backwards. So is her undershirt. FixedX2. Her blouse is buttoned, her knee socks are straight—no, they're not, okay, now they are—and her hair is combed, then clipped, and finally combed correctly, then re-clipped.

The mirror says she looks acceptable—for her mother.

After I get to school, I'll have to fix everything.

Mental note, she needs to remember her makeup.

She hid it from herself last night, hoping if her mother searched her room, it'd be hidden from her mother too. But her mother did not search, and after the lingerie was confiscated, she got tired, then slept before she retrieved it. And she'll get it as soon as she packs her bag. Ugh, it's heavy; and it's worse with her books stuffing it up, as her still-sore forearms fight the zipper, especially around the VHS of Friends, its outline dug into the polyester.

It ends up not fitting. She decides to carry it.

Her mother shouts. "What's taking so long?"

"Nothing, I'm almost ready!"

"Hurry up, you've got to eat!"

Downstairs, her blue Academy one-piece, which smells like fabric softener, rests on the table beside breakfast. She recalls how Mackenzie said her fatness displaced the water in the pool. *I shouldn't eat.* Too late. Cereal is swallowed, OJ is drunk and a muffin wrapper lies beside muffin crumbs. *Why does mom cook so much?* Not like her mother notices. In the kitchen, she's preparing for the chores that'll make dinner insufferable, with a mug of coffee and one of those coupon books from the center of the newspaper.

"Get your practice schedule, okay?"

"I will."

"Make sure you get it. I need to plan."

"I said I will."

"And get me the schedule of all your meets."

"I know the drill, Mom. I've swam before."

Between this and being fat, she's already had enough of swim team today. That's too bad for her. Last night, Niko said she found out about her wet uniform by "making some calls." If the other Bitches "made some calls" then it could be "all over school." Well, not *all over* all over school, but with the people who matter. She supposes her best hope is everyone wants to be her friend, and that Mackenzie's retaliation was a one-time thing.

After all, Mackenzie does want to win State.

And she needs me to do it.

Her mother bothers her. "What're your plans with Niko's mother today?"

She's in the process of, like last night, stacking her plate, glass and silverware, then delivering it to the sink. "We don't have any. It's a play-it-by-ear thing."

"That makes me nervous."

Her mother thinks she's keeping "secrets." But this time, she isn't, at least not yet, but she wants to avoid any issues, so she pulls from her magic hat... "Niko's going to lose her appeal. Maybe we'll get her a haircut." It appeases her mother. It doesn't appease her. "Did you talk with Auntie about getting my hair cut?"

Her mother's voice is sly. "We'll see."

"What does that mean?"

"I don't want to reward bad behavior."

"What bad behavior?"

"You know what."

As if her mother would sacrifice valedictorian over black underwear. *That nobody saw!* Besides, if it's how she chooses to conceal her privates during her private time, it's none of her mother's business. Like her masturbation wasn't. *And what happened?* She kept rubbing. She intends the same for her undies, particularly thongs, which she will get, then enjoy—in her room, at school, on a date, or as part of swim team.

Wow, I wish I sounded like that always.

Whatever, she's finding space for her suit in her bag. "Mom, I made the team. That's bigger than this."

"No, it's not."

"You know, you can't keep it from me forever."

Her mother chuckles. "You weren't born with breasts."

"Exactly, I'm old enough now."

Her mother gives her a look, then circles, in pen, some deal on bathroom cleaner. "You're not. And don't accept any more clothes from Niko."

"Okay."

"There will be consequences if you do."

"Okay."

Her mother is too used to fighting over this stuff.

"Are you listening to me?"

Duh, yes.

She wants to fight. Then get impractical about the haircut she knows she's getting. *I need to forgive her.* She also needs sleep. She does neither, then deploys the silent treatment. In the car, it's stop-go. She'd stress over her mother's stubborn belief that the slowest lane will turn fast, but Prom's distracted her. *If only I had an upperclassmen boyfriend!* It's okay. Next year, she'll go. And she'll have a boyfriend. But the boyfriend part will preferably be this year, hopefully by summer break. *It's possible!* Being on swim, and the Bitches, about guarantees her a boyfriend. Note, "a boyfriend" doesn't automatically mean "a good boyfriend," as increased popularity includes parasites. It's an important factor that's actually not since her too high standards will interrupt any and all romance.

Blah, blah, blah—I don't even have a guy I like!

Her mother blocks the Academy's circular drive. It leaves her rushed. *I hate making people wait!* She frantically grabs everything and she leaves the car with her face hidden, so no one who's silently cussing at her knows it's her. It means she has to juggle this crap through the stopped open entrance. The main hallway is lean and the first bell is loud. Class starts in five minutes. She debates if she has time to visit her locker. Maybe it's best not to. But her teacher hates crap on the floor.

She shouldn't move and think.

She's hit a wall—no, it's a boy, who kinda knocked her back, which knocked out her books.

She drops to her knees. "I'm sorry. I'm so distracted."

He's on his knee, too. "No, it was I who wasn't watching."

She giggles in the way that makes him a dork and her not.

"That's sorta funny."

"Is this yours?"

It's the VHS of Friends.

"Yeah, uh, my friend and I, we watch it every week... Let me start over, we talk on the phone and watch it, but she couldn't, she had this party that I didn't want to go to, so, like, my dad taped it." *Jeez, who cares?* Wonderful. She's a loser. A bad swimmer. And she rambles like a crazy person. Not that he notices; he's looking at her breasts. *What?* It's true. When she collected her stuff, her blouse became slightly too snug, and his eyes became too stuck. As a result, her heart pumps, in cold shocks, what must be adrenaline, or onset Parkinson's, throughout her limbs. "Anyhow..."

"I should help you back to your locker."

"Oh, no."

"Well, can I help you up?"

"I'm fine."

His hand is out. "Come on."

"Okay."

His hand has taken her up. "You sure you're okay?"

Sure. "Yes."

"Look, I'll take your stuff back to your locker."

She bites her bottom lip. Distraught since he doesn't need to do that. He doesn't need to do anything. In fact, she'll take his stuff back to his locker. That's what she'll do and... Like a magnet, her chin is at the floor, but when she blinks, her eyes peek at his. His are big and blue. Also, he's tall, looks rich, and he's got slicked blond hair.

She's got no spit. "Oh, um... I mean, I think..."

Class has already started. Maybe we could hang out!

What was that?

She'll never know. Niko is here.

"There you are! You won't believe what happened!"

In her diminished state, she has zero resistance. "What?"

Niko nearly unloads a barrage of poorly planned sentences, then freezes mid-syllable and faces the boy. "Do you mind?"

"No."

He could of been rude. He chose not to. He's, like, a mature guy! And hold up a second! *I mind!* "Niko, he was..."

Niko shoos him. "You can move along, then."

Like that, the boy becomes barren hallway. The mass of her insides becomes barren too. She protests—marginally. It's all she's got. "Seriously, he—"

Niko interrupts. "I have amazing news."

"You do?"

"I found out that Mike Holler is hot for you!"

"Who?"

Niko looks perplexed. *Did I misspeak?* "Mike Holler."

Oh, Mike Holler! What a coincidence, she had no idea two Mike Holler's attended this school. *I'm such a ditz.* Plus, a new addition to the endangered species list. It's *the* Mike Holler. AKA: Donna's boyfriend. AKA: The Academy QB. AKA: The last thing she needs. As if the target weren't already enormous, and like she hadn't told Niko to stop, she's on the Bitches, she'll probably single handily screw up State, simultaneously spark a civil war for rule of the Academy, and for giggles, she's now threatened Donna Harly's relationship.

I'll be lucky to survive the day.
"Why would you do that?"
Niko looks confused. "Do what?"
"Get Mike Holler to like me! Why would you do that?"
"I didn't."
"Yes, you did!"
Niko smiles. "I really didn't! He just likes you!"
"Niko, please be lying."
Niko's not lying.
It's written all over Mackenzie's infuriated face, which she's never seen so colored, as well Mackenzie's body, which projects an unladylike stance. Of course, the same pack of Bitches back-up Mackenzie, but they might as well not.
I've never seen Mackenzie like this.
"Niko, we need to talk."
"*Again?*"
"Yes, again."
Like Niko did with that boy, she acts annoyed. "Fine, but we have class, so talk fast."
"You can start by explaining why the school thinks I'm only going to Prom because I gave Lonny a blowjob."
Niko plays dumb. "I don't know. I guess people call it like they see it. Do you have anything else or can we go now?"
Niko moves aside, but Mackenzie blocks her, still upset. The BJ rumor was the first surprise. The second one happened when she, Donna, and several Bitches arrived at school.
"You told on us to the Administration."
"You—against the Rules—soaked her uniform."
"It's different when you're on the team."
Niko acts disgusted. "How so? She stops being my friend?"
Mackenzie acts the same. "Don't bore me with semantics, and don't tell me how to run my team."
"I'm only telling you how to treat my friends."
"You know, you think you're so smart Niko, but you'll see. People have promised you more than they can deliver."
Her mouth hangs open. Mackenzie didn't just say that. She

thought when Mackenzie kept her in the showers, it was so the others could soak her uniform. It can't be that... *Mackenzie was telling the truth?* No, Niko's plan is to send a "message." That's all, and nothing else.

Good news, even Niko looks confused.

"What're you talking about?"

"I know you're trying to take over."

Niko plays dumb again. "Take over what?"

"The Bitches, I know you're trying to do it."

It takes Niko a split-second. "And you're gonna stop me?"

Mackenzie locks up all over—too shocked to notice.

Yesterday, Niko openly referred to Donna as Yeti. Today, Niko openly acknowledges her intended mutiny. Mackenzie knows she needs an insult. Likely, it'd be another crack about bra stuffing since, today, Niko's chest is its largest ever. Instead, Mackenzie backs off, showing her palms, and giving a half-convincing "I don't care" look. "You know what? Try your stupid plan. I can't wait to see your face when it happens."

With that, Mackenzie leaves, her gossip hound Bitches at her tail, silent since no one dares mutter about it. Because of this, the echoes of their shoes sound closer than they are. She's silent, too. Whoever stood Mackenzie down, it wasn't Niko2.0. It was the Niko from this last weekend.

I guess Mother Superior couldn't stop Niko.

"What did you do, Niko?"

Niko is stoic, but happy. She spent extra time on her boobs this morning. Even Mackenzie couldn't see they were fake! "Let's just say, I used my appeal to make an impression."

"How'd you do that?"

"I tipped them off to some hazing pranks at tryouts."

This is bad. "You shouldn't have done that."

"I had to. This shit with them has gone too far."

"So you took it further? How's that a solution?"

Niko looks like, "whose side are you on?" but only says, "They started it."

She hates this. She can't worry about it. She needs to know

the truth. "Are you really trying to take over?"

Niko's dismissive. "Of course not."

"Okay, cause I have to be on swim team with them."

Niko isn't concerned. "Mother Superior is involved—they can't touch you at swim."

"Well, I guess I'll take all my classes at the pool."

Again, Niko looks like, "whose side are you on?" She's also gone tense in her back. "I've got control of it."

What bullshit. And shit—class!

"Come on, let's go. I don't wanna be late."

What she wants isn't what will happen. The boy's been gone long enough for feeling to return to her face. And it's not what she feels, but what she doesn't. *I'm not wearing makeup.* She forgot it. And he saw her without it, a rolled skirt or a put back blouse. It solves the mystery of why he disappeared at Niko's first word.

He thought I was hideous.

She tries to ignore it, then ends up holding out the VHS. "I need to trade. Can I borrow your makeup?"

"Right now?"

She could bump into him between periods.

"Yes, I think I can do it before the tardy bell."

Niko hesitates. "Actually, can we talk about Mike?"

Why me? "Fine, come to the bathroom with me."

Niko scrunches her face. "Um, I'm going the other way."

They both take European history. The bathroom is there. "Why?"

"I'm meeting someone."

"Who?"

Niko struggles. "I'm going to see Hazu. We're ditching."

"I thought you two weren't dating anymore."

"We're not—we're just friends."

She wants to believe Niko. She does.

But, she can't.

In the car after Sadie Hawkins, she heard Niko and Hazu.

At first, Hazu was getting Niko hot. Kissing her, sure, but

also to Niko's glee, divulging his deepest sex fantasies. He said he'd change the girls' uniforms to their underwear. "That's so dirty, Hazu!" And, he said, if a girl gets in trouble, she should shave her pussy for the class. "In front of everyone?" He said yes, and added that girls should have mandatory classes on stripping. "Oh, you're so bad, Hazu!" And the Academy should have a designated room where the girls have to fuck the boys. This time, Niko said, "No, no." So Hazu offered an addendum. He said the girls had to give blowjobs.

"Okay, yes!"

Hazu appeared. His hair was messy and his shirt barely on. Niko was next, her cheeks splotched and her dress below her belly. Like a bitch in heat, Niko commanded them outside. "For just five minutes!" At that point, she was disgusted, yet fascinated by what she heard. Turned out it was comparatively tame. For what followed was *in-san-i-ty*. She only knew it was over because Niko kicked open the door, then leaned out to spit cum on the pavement like a big leaguer would chew.

As she sees it, that's not a friends dynamic.

"Niko, be real, are you seeing Hazu again?"

"No, we're just friends!"

She feels the need to state the obvious.

"Cause you can't date two boys at once."

Niko's already taken off down the hall.

"It's not like that! We're friends!"

6.

In European history, in science, in Spanish, and mathematics, she thinks and is taxed. The teenage mind is underdeveloped. Fortunately for her, her chest is overdeveloped. *I lucked out there.* And not solely because of that boy. Like, boobs are, by themselves, a fun topic. Go ahead, try to deny it. She dares you. Yep, that's what she thought. And that's what she knew. And not to bring him up again, but that boy knew it too.

See? Everybody likes boobs.

Back to him. And his hotness. It's revitalized her and when he sees her next, he might want to take her someplace, then, like, the next weekend, he might want to take her to another place. By dismissal, she's plotted out the entire relationship. It's why, after she visits her locker and releases another blouse button, she searches the social sciences wing, the library, and the length of the main hallway.

He's nowhere to be found.

Undeterred, she does a second pass, then loiters at the main entrance. *He bumped into me here. He might come back.* He doesn't, so she debates a third trip, but forgets it since Mike Holler and his boys showed up. To escape, she cut across the courtyard, heading for Niko's locker. It must be where Niko is since Niko didn't visit her at her locker.

Or she's with Kana already.

There you go. In her boy-mania, she forgot about Kana.

That makes her feel like shit.

"Here you are! I thought you might've gone outside!"

Niko is unresponsive and tense. As well, her backpack is at her feet and her locker is shut. It's strange. On Fridays, Niko can't bust outta here fast enough, but today, Niko removes from her bag, at a tortoise's speed, what she will not need for her homework, followed by what homework she knows she won't finish. And comes to a complete stop on each number on the combination lock. Like in Driver's Ed. *Or so Niko told me.* It's nothing like the Niko who went toe to toe with Mackenzie.

She was about to mention it, but a folded note fell to the floor. It's one of the letters Hazu leaves.

Niko knows to explain it. "It's not what you think."

It must not be. Niko said—this morning—it wasn't. And that was good. Hazu will lose it if he learns he's Niko's #2.

"What is it?"

Niko blinks heavy. "It's... We're friends!"

"A friend who leaves you a love letter?"

'Love letter' was hard to say. She was respecting Niko.

"It's not what you think."

"Is that letter why you're acting so weird right now?"

Niko slams her locker. It sounds more violent than it was. And it was hardly violent since Niko immediately hid her face. *Is she crying?* She tries to follow Niko, but Niko twists, then talks like she's got a cold. "Seriously, it's not what you think! Like I said, we're friends!"

"Are you okay? Did he do something?"

"No, it's not like that. I keep saying—"

She interrupts. "Then, what is it?"

Niko's hands are in her hands. Her eyes look of terror.

"What if she's not there?"

Of course, Niko's scared about her mom.

Is there nothing I won't make about boys?

Back to business, she'd love to tell Niko her mother awaits her, but she isn't certain it's true. "If something went wrong, Mother Superior would've told you, right?"

Niko still looks frazzled. "I guess you're right."

There. Nothing to worry about.

I swear, if Kana's not there, I'll stop believing in God.

"Don't worry! Let's go."

With that, Niko2.0 turns on—alive in speech and manner, bragging about her big plans for the Bitches, then discussing how Mackenzie's threats are total bluffs before beginning on

Mike Holler. *And his feelings for me.* Which she considered when she wasn't considering that boy. Like, she's not gonna date Mike Holler—his status with Donna notwithstanding. And Niko needs to know that. This seems like as good a time as any. Or not. Niko's newfound confidence evaporates twenty feet from the parking lot.

Niko breathes deep, then bolts for the pavement.

She just caught up. "Do you see her?"

"No, I'm looking."

This can't be happening. "Maybe she thought we'd meet her at your home."

That kinda thing worked on Niko when Niko was twelve.

Not so much any longer.

"I guess."

"Well, I can call my mom and—"

Niko interrupts. "I see her!"

Niko sprints down the steps, then slices between students and parked cars, zigzagging so hard she needs to hold down her skirt before she finds a break in space, then goes full on towards a white Mercedes. With no loss in speed or intensity, she pivots at the trunk, then at the passenger door, where she bursts into the car and plows over the center console—into her mother's arms.

It took a microsecond for Niko to cover the distance.

And it was proceeded by a sonic boom.

She believes in God, by the way. And thanks Him for giving Niko her mommy back. *I need to forgive my own.* She forgets it, standing guard beside the car until her emotions are sorted. Not to compare her grief to Niko's, but if this saga is over... She keeps it together, then sneaks into the backseat. Niko's lost it, holding Kana like she was saved from a burning building.

It's kind of beautiful to watch.

She coughs. "Kana, it's great to have you back!"

Kana's voice cracks. "You girls are so lovely sometimes."

Niko's not done with Mom mushiness. "Did you miss me?"

"Yes, baby, I missed you."

"I wasn't certain. I heard from you so infrequently."

Kana's voice cracks again. "Baby, I was embarrassed."

"No, Mom, don't be embarrassed!"

Kana struggles even more. It's unusual. Kana always keeps her cool, but in place of it, Kana covers her eyes with black sunglasses. "Honey, with everything that's happened, I thought you were just better off without me or—"

Niko interrupts. "No, Mom. That's not true."

Okay, her mother was right. *I hate that.* Clearly, Niko needs this release. *And I'm interfering.* Before she can suggest her exit, she finds tissues in her hands. They're from Niko, who's searched the compartments over for them, and who blots at her eyes.

Kana has accepted some. Then, Kana finally sees.

"Darling, your hair is gorgeous!"

Forget it. Nothing fixes Niko like hair compliments.

"Mom, I wanted you to see it before we go to the salon."

"The salon, why?"

Niko falls onto her mother like an injured maiden. "I gotta cut off my tips. They violate the Personal Code!"

"I'm sorry, baby."

She whines! "Mom, I wanna go to a different school."

"I don't know about that. Your father prefers the Academy."

"Then I wanna drop out."

Kana never finished high school.

"Baby, you're very close to graduating."

Minutes later, the car is in drive, then in line at the stop sign. Fighting through quaint suburbs, past poorly constructed public schools, and stopped at 7/11 for candy and slushees. Sugar'ed up, the car is in drive once again, then in line at a different stop sign. At the skyscrapers in the distance is Seneca Avenue. It's an exit that enters into downtown. Stopped for pedestrians, in a building's shade until the car is taken, and at the end of an elevator ride, is a fancy salon whose amenities seem like a standup picture book.

It's stuffed full of weeks old appointments.

It could take hours, but a single drop of Kana's glasses and Niko's hair is washed, a free stylist is found and a powwow commences around a chair that pumps Niko tall.

That's not all Kana gets for being Kana.

For instance, at the Academy, students and parents glanced at Kana, curious about the reunion behind the window tint. Then, at the 7/11, the Indian attendant acted disinterested—until his face lit up. At the valet station, the valet himself held the car door with an extravagant bend, then another valet held the building door with another extravagant bend, and a third held open the elevator.

Worst of all is the hair stylist.

He's a fit, flamboyant homosexual with too-groomed facial hair and perfect fingernails. He also wears shoes with a slight heel. He's mistaken this haircut as a platform for his "visionary" hair techniques—hoping Kana will pronounce him a raw genius, then hire him as her personal stylist, or at least allow him to claim her kid as a client.

Kana seems somewhat receptive.

Unfortunately, Niko's deaf to all his suggestions, then when Kana suggests exactly the same, she loves it! Of course, Niko's oblivious to her favoritism and blind to his subtle observations of such—choosing, instead, to suck on sugar while she mixes and matches, like carpet samples, hair style picture books. It takes time and the continued trampling of his soul, but Niko decides, and the stylist, unable to take credit for his own ideas, asks an assistant for clean scissors.

(Or a shotgun, it was a bit slurred).

Finally, as the floor becomes predominately blond, Niko turns into a total blabber-mouth. "Mom, please don't make me go back to school! Everyone is so evil! They pick on me!"

Kana is supportive. "That's so insensitive of them, honey."

"You don't get what I've had to do to fit in! If I hadn't, I'd have never survived the semester."

That statement reminds her of boobs.

Not her own, but the overabundance of Niko's lack thereof.

In the three-sixty twirls from her salon chair, ajar to Niko's, she notices how they're a comically large C-cup. She wonders if Kana notices. On her next twirl, she peeks, and sure enough, Kana's discreetly peeking. Kana's got a poker face about it. *So I got one, too!* On her next twirl, she forgets about it to checkout Kana, who sits on a bench, her well documented body in a mid-length skirt, tall heels, and a floppy top.

She decides to be Kana when she grows up. It just launched a thousand (failed) diets. One of them fails this instant, as she stuffs her cheeks with 7/11 candy, talking with her mouth full. "Kana, it's true some girls, who were jealous, are being—"

Niko interrupts! "They were jealous and hated me for it."

She decides to finish her interrupted sentence.

"They were jealous, Kana, but Niko shouldn't quit school."

Niko protests! "Like you would know what it's like."

She is a bit offended. "What does that mean?"

Kana ends it.

"Baby, we'll talk about it. We have lots to talk about."

It doesn't end it for Niko.

"You talked to Mother Superior, didn't you?"

"Let's talk about it later, baby."

Kana held firm. So, indeed, she did talk to Mother Superior. To surmise, it probably went something like this: "You have another opportunity with Niko and this time you must commit yourself. Niko's in trouble. The risks she takes are not amount to any possible gains. I don't know if you believe this, but you could lose Niko for good this time." Mother Superior speaks frankly to Kana, as Mother Superior is, in a way, the patriarch of Niko's family. (Since Niko's father, the fuckhead, moved to Japan). Mother Superior has to be, as Kana can't be, not even if Kana wanted to.

You see, in about three hundred days, Niko will reach the age Kana was when Niko was born.

That's an unnerving thought.

Niko's cell phone rings.

"Hello?" – "Like I'd know that, it—" – "Donna, you're Prom

Princess, who could touch you?" – "Well, some might argue you took tryouts too far and some other girl, who didn't make the team, told on you." – "I'd never call you Yeti. Mackenzie's losing her mind." – "Yes, I did call him today." – "Why would I tell you?" – "It's not a conspiracy! I wanted to be prepared." – "Alright, we'll talk later."

Kana is the one who asks the question.

"What was that, baby?"

"It was nothing, Mom."

"That seemed like an argument."

"It wasn't."

"Honey, how serious are your issues with kids at school?"

Niko smiles big into the mirror. "Mom, you can tell Mother Superior it's people's stupid drama, that's all."

Kana is unfazed. "She's worried about a boy you're seeing—Haruhide, was it?"

Niko erupts in laughter.

The stylist erupts in horror.

His face is beat red, and his body contorts, in what resembles a slow motion sports play or a complex kung fu move. Either way, it ends with Niko's hair still level, and in his insistence that, should Niko want ears, she'll keep her head straight.

Niko ignores his bitching.

"Mother Superior's so wrong! He's a friend—a protector."

The statement makes her ill.

Hazu's not... Let's start over.

She's not been entirely candid about Hazu since Hazu wasn't Niko's boyfriend anymore. But, when she said he left constant notes in Niko's locker, constant messages on Niko's phone, and constantly found Niko outside of school—that could've come off as more romantic than she intended. Niko's told her that, in some of the letters, he's written that if he loses Niko, he'll kill himself. And if Niko doesn't return his phone calls, he loses it and bitches her out in front of everyone. And half the times he finds Niko outside of the Academy, it's to criticize her choice of friends, clothes, or to accuse her of dating other guys.

You know, like a fuckhead.

Basically, Niko can't see how Hazu treats her like property. It's because he treats her like really nice property and Niko's flattered by crap like that. It's another reason friends is unlikely. *I'm stupid.* They're not friends. Kana seems to agree, and like her mother, verifies everything Niko says.

"Is that true?"

To lie for Niko. To not lie for Niko.

It's never really a question.

"They're just friends."

Niko holds her hand out like, "It works when you listen to it the way I want you to!" "You see, things are fine!"

Kana isn't convinced. "So you're not seeing anyone?"

"Sorta, but it's not Hazu."

"Who is he?"

Niko stretches her limbs every which way. "Ugh, he's cool."

Once again, Kana verifies everything Niko says.

"Do you know anything about him?"

This one is tough. She's not sure what lie Niko wants told.

"Sure, well, his name is..."

Niko jumps like she's been blasted by electricity. It's stolen everyone's attention while Niko flips around, collapsing over her chair's top rail. The stylist also collapses—into shellshock, preparing his defense for the police, then the tabloids, as he's sure Niko's throat has been slit wide.

Again, Niko can't be bothered by his bitching or his PTSD.

"Troy! His name is Troy!"

Kana accepts it. "Well, we'll talk about Troy later."

"Oh, you know, there's not much to say!"

Of course, there isn't. Niko just invented him.

It confuses her.

Lying about Hazu is logical. Lying to Donna is similar. And in order to do so, Niko needs to lie to all the Bitches, which pretty much involves lying to the whole Academy. These lies, to Niko, are ethical. One protects her love, which Niko believes no one should have power over. The others dethrone Donna, which Niko sees as a moral imperative. But why change Scott to Troy? As far as she understands it, Scott's only a spoil for Niko, and in no way vital to her scheme.

The recklessness of this lie highlights a larger problem.

On a scale of genius, Niko fits in somewhere between child prodigy and mad scientist, but while handling Niko2.0, Niko's also handled Donna, Mackenzie, Mother Superior, Hazu, Scott and her "source." It's so eloquently plotted. Then again, Mackenzie said it. "I know you're trying to take over," and, "People have promised you more than they can deliver."

And what Mackenzie said in the showers.

She questions what she already knows is true.

Niko's losing control. And Donna's going to win.

Detour Three: The Future.

Upon her waking, her arm's numb, her throat's hoarse, and a throbbing storms her temples like melted taffy. She also needs to pee piss and drink water so urgently she might do so concurrently, and she will do so as soon as the circulation reaches her arm. It hurts worse than her head. And other things she's too lazy to list. It's her first hangover in some time. It sucks, and the toilet seat is cold. She is cold, too, from what sweaty parts of her shirt stick to her gross skin. Her bladder is happy, though. Niko's will be soon. The hyperaware ninja, who seemed so deep in sleep, walks through the bathroom door, to plop herself on the sink, her thong rung down to her knees and her wrist dug into her eye socket.

It bothers her a bit. *She could've knocked.*
"That party was massive."
"It was."
"Mike seemed to like you."
"The party" was post-Prom. As planned, she attended it. And it was fun. Like Niko said days ago, the Bitches—outside of Donna and Mackenzie—seemed to like her. No one brought up the wet uniform, nor did they get upset when Mike spent so much time with her last night. *I was almost flattered.* He was kinda cute, dressed in his prom tux that was disassembled at the neck, the wrists, and un-tucked from his waist. Plus, he took her mind off the blue eyed boy, whom she had wasted the afternoon irrationally hoping to bump into, then became sorta bratty when she didn't.

"He was alright, I guess."
Niko knows about the blue eyed boy now.
"But, you're all on this other guy, I take it?"
It makes her embarrassed, so she embarrasses Niko.
"What happened to you last night?"

"What do you mean?"

"You got, like, really upset."

Belligerent says it better, but Niko's feelings matter again.

"What was I upset about?"

It's hard to describe.

She rarely parties with Niko2.0, so maybe this Niko drinks heavier than her former. Although, if yesterday was the norm, Niko's own Yeti-like nickname is soon to follow. Because whatever happened, it destroyed Niko in a "yelling-at-the-walls" fashion. Perhaps Niko's still destroyed, as Niko's curled her chin into her neck, keeping her face to the mirror while beating her thigh against the counter to shake loose her pee, then washing her hands and her face in the sink that washes the yellow away.

Okay, she's not looking, I can stand up.

She reaches for toilet paper, then faces the wall to cover her personals before she speaks. "I don't know, you wouldn't tell me, but you were so drunk, and even after the party was over, you kept drinking."

"I did?"

"Yeah, I was worried."

Worried about more than the alcohol. She saw a lot.

Niko giggles. "That's cute, but as you can see, I'm fine!"

So fine Niko returns to bed.

Maybe things are fine.

(She's lying).

Okay with it presently, she washes her own hands, wipes her oily face on the hand towel, then flicks off the light. Inside Niko's closet, she exchanges her thong for one of Niko's. And does the same for her socks. When she opened the drawer, two empty liquor bottles rattled each other. They're gone when the drawer is closed, and she stretches an undershirt to her belly, ripping her shorter hair through the collar.

Oh yeah, I got a haircut and new clothes, including thongs.

She was way happy because all these freedoms came mama approved, and in only the day she's had them, she's seen her mother's complaints. *It's like Niko and I have no boundaries.* She probably shoulda figured that out sooner, but she figures it's why Niko's bathroom intrusion irked her. Or why she thinks, in the future, she should, A) build a makeshift bed on the floor, or, B) stay in Niko's room past the French doors, but not, C) sleep in the same bed with Niko.

And bring her own change of clothes, she'll do that now.

And, okay, she's got to say it.

What's up with those empty bottles?

When she saw them, her heart leapt into her throat.

She was gonna ask about it, but saw Niko on her cell phone.

"Mom, I thought I might reach you, call me back, okay?"

Hm.

What destroyed Niko could've been her mother. Yesterday, Kana left... To work. Niko wore a brave face. It allowed Kana to go without regret. It also reinforced all of Niko's suspicions. That her entire life was fake and thereby worthless. *To me, Niko2.0 is the fake one, but to Niko, it's 1.0 who never existed.* After last night, it's clear that 1.0 is unsalvageable. *And with it, that part of my life.* Who knows, maybe that's why the A), B), C) is in her head. She's finally accepted the truth. And if it's the truth, then all that's left is damage control.

She leans against the doorframe.

"Why are there empty bottles in your drawer?"

Niko lies. "It's nothing. I had to hide them from Nana."

She knows it's a lie. "Is it cause your Mom left?"

"No, it's not."

It's "not" like Niko's "not" dating Hazu.

"You can tell me. I swear it's okay."

"It's not my mom, I mean it."

"Then, what was it?"

Niko turns to the wall like she did to the bathroom mirror or away from her school locker. It's uncommon for Niko to be so outwardly emotional. Niko builds impenetrable walls so no one sees her pain and no one can screw her over. Niko was taught this by the best, her mother, and it's something Niko has, throughout the years, perfected.

Until Donna Harly came along.

Niko snorts. "It's like this year will never end."

"What do you mean?"

"It's nothing."

"No, tell me, what do you mean?"

It comes in a whisper. "Mackenzie was right."

"What?"

Niko's louder. "Mackenzie was right."

"Right about what?"

"Donna knew about my plan. She was ready."

It started a day or so before the party. Signs that Donna had her own plan. It reinforced Donna's authority, and according to Niko's source, sending Donna a "message" wasn't sufficient any longer. People needed more. So Niko deduced a modified plan allowing said people to see her rise in conjunction with Donna's fall. Also, Niko accelerated the timeline, promising—the boys, the Stars, and Scott—to seize the Bitches, then cut Donna out.

Its failure ends the shortest membership in Bitches history: *mine*. It also means Niko's been excommunicated.

"Do you want to tell me what happened?"

"You were right."

I was? "I don't understand."

Niko almost curls in disgust. If she has to hear those words, "I don't understand" or if she must explain herself anymore... Like she didn't already feel like a freak all the time. She wipes her eyes again and wishes she were wearing her fake breasts. "I played so many sides against one another that, when it was time for everyone to do their part, no trusted me, and they waited for everyone else to go first, then no one went at all."

Oh yeah, I did say that. "What're you going to do?"

"It doesn't matter."

It "doesn't matter" like Kana leaving "doesn't matter."

"Niko, you can tell me. What's going on?"

Niko meant it. It doesn't matter.

At least the specifics don't. She got bitchy for sure, but who cares about that? She drank too much. Maybe she even yelled at the walls. Either way, what fragments of her meltdown are in her head are enough to be big time gossip, and by tomorrow, Mother Superior will know about it, and Mother Superior will also know with Kana gone, post-Prom was another unsupervised party. It ups the consequences. Suspension, expulsion, Administration intervention. It's too big for Niko to acknowledge. It makes her feel cold and sick. As it's also too late. To change it so her mother never got in trouble. To stop herself from becoming Niko2.0. To take back what she did in Coeur d'Alene. And to forget what happened at post-Prom.

Hopefully, it's not too late to fix what has been broken. That was Niko's final thought, last night, before she went black. "Maybe it was for the best that Donna knew."

"How so?"

Niko balls up, her knees to her chin, and her arms clutched like a vice around her shins. "I've thought a lot about how you said I was becoming like Donna, and I don't want to do that."

There's no way to praise Niko without sounding sarcastic. She tries, anyway. "I'm glad to hear that. I mean it."

Niko seems to believe her. That turns Niko shyer. Holding shut her eyes to hold shut any tears. "I didn't mean to use you. I guess I was afraid to lose anyone else, but now that it's over and things are going back to normal, I feel so guilty."

"Guilty?"

"I've done horrible things."

Horrible things? "I don't understand."

Niko sniffles. "What if I'm changed? What if I can never be good again?"

She is stuck in the doorframe. It's too hard to move, so she reassures Niko from a room away. It might as well be an ocean. She's pissed at herself over it. What makes it worse is that it's not Niko. She figures her help is useless. It's best to be distant and offer meaningless advice. "Don't be so critical. Whatever you did, you were confused."

"You don't understand. You just don't get it."

She only wishes that were true. "I think I have an idea."

"You do?"

After midnight, the party shifted gears.

What started as a high school romp transitioned to people who were not in high school and not from Prom. Along with them came the shady elements that fascinate the Yeti. As she shifted though rooms, in tag with Niko, her absentee friendship became stark. Niko would drink, then sing, then dance, and drink, then snort a white powder. That wasn't the worst. On the deck, she bore witness to the nightmare that was Niko2.0. She would've never guessed, but she should've known, or had a premonition—somehow Niko must have dropped a hint.

"I saw Scott."

Niko sounds dead. "I know you did."

She leaves the topic alone. "I saw something else."

Niko sounds cold. "I know you did."

"Was it cocaine?"

"Yes."

She knew that. Unlike her mother, she confirmed it before getting angry. The countdown is on, however. For Niko, of all people, to use cocaine. Pair it with those empty bottles and it's... *I should've told Mother Superior everything.* "If you made some small mistakes, then—"

Niko interrupts. "I need to tell you something."

"Okay."

Niko breaks into shivers. "I can't say it. I tried like twenty times this week and I can't say it."

"Just tell me."

"If I tell you, you'll think I'm ugly."

That's probably true. "Please, just tell me."

Niko hiccups air that she chokes on, then coughs a fit.

"It's that I'm not really a virgin any longer."

In retrospect, she shoulda shown more sensitivity. And she should've left the freaking doorframe, joined Niko on the bed, and tried to solve this. But in the moment, she had little in her mind, save her doubt, and less to do, beside put her hands through her hair and cover her fallen jaw.

Why would Niko do that?

Sure, Niko stuffs her bra, advocates frequent masturbation, and makes BJS, but that's not intercourse. As backwards as it sounds, Niko's love for sex enhanced her desire to stay a virgin. In fact, on several occasions, Niko's told Hazu it's not gonna happen, at least not yet, and backwards as it sounds, Hazu's respected that. He's a creepy SOB, but it's not in him to force Niko to have sex. If you saw them together, you'd get that.

If it's not Hazu, then it leaves only one other.

Like with the coke, she confirms. "Hazu or Scott?"

"Scott first, but them both."

What? "You've done it with them both?"

"After you fell asleep, Hazu and I hooked up."

"Last night?"

"Yes. He's my boyfriend again."

That's good news, but only if it means...

"So you and Scott aren't together?"

"No."

It's another moment where sensitivity was appropriate. She was too relieved. "Thank God. You've got to stay away from him, like for real, understand? That guy is trouble."

Niko hides her face again. "I know."

"It's... He's a grownup. You're too young for him."

"I know."

"I'm not trying to hurt your feelings, it's that—"

Niko interrupts. "I only dated Scott to hurt Donna, but I lost control and I..." Niko wipes her eyes, then cries tears like sneezes. "It was supposed to be Hazu. After this was all done, I was gonna be with Hazu. That's what I wanted."

Yeah. Good time to leave the doorframe.

I'm a shitty friend.

"Is that why you hooked up with him?"

"Yes."

"Did you tell him about Scott?"

"I told him I was a virgin. He can't know. It'll kill him."

Or it'll get him to kill Scott. Either way, it's a bad outcome. It's also beside the point.

While tons of stuff happened in Coeur d'Alene, the biggest—what caused the blond tips and the "message" idea—was, at some point, Niko became Niko3.0. Another bastard child from another bastard identity crisis. The first one caused by Kana. And the second by Scott. Sadly, the incidents are mirrors. In both, Niko could've wallowed in self-pity, yet despite being the victim, Niko acted like the perpetrator. In the fall, Niko took it upon herself to join the Bitches, then when that failed, Niko decided to destroy the Bitches, and by accident, with Scott, destroyed herself.

Throughout such, Niko never shed a tear. Not one.

Niko's too-flexible self has gone into a too-tight roly-poly ball. Finally separated from the doorframe, she holds Niko. It sounds dramatic and it feels awkward, but she fights it and her belief she's messing up, cause Niko needs dramatic examples. Niko needs... *A mom.* This is it. This is what Mother Superior, Nana and her own mother have felt all these years they've substituted for Kana. *Now it's my turn, I guess.* It's left her to wonder if this Niko, Niko3.0, who cries into her shoulder like she might not stop, believes in anything at all, or if Niko3.0 is simply a Niko who accepts chaos as life's only truth.

She can't let that happen.

"Listen, whatever you did, anything at all, during your time in the Bitches, or for Donna, or something that hurt me or yourself, just forget about it."

Niko gasps for air. "I can't."

She gets it. And wears her motherly voice again. Already forgiven Niko for all that's been done, and ready to tell Niko all Niko needs to hear. *Maybe I'm ready to forgive my mother for doing the same.* "It's in the past, it's over. You're not bad, you've not changed, and if you wanted Hazu to be your first, then he was your first. It can still be your choice."

Only a virgin could think that.

"I wish, but it'll never be that way."

"Then forget about that, too. And forget about Scott. As far as I'm concerned, he's a shithead."

"He is a shithead."

Niko is crying pretty hard again.

She is holding Niko tighter.

"Believe me, one day, you'll meet a boy who'll treat you like a princess, maybe even Hazu will do it."

"No. I don't want to be a princess any longer."

Every girl wants to be a princess.

"You don't?"

"No."

"Then, what do you want to be?"

"I want to be a Queen."

7.

After a dozen near misses, the stylist has finished. Niko's hair, previously at her shoulders, still remains such on either side of her forehead. The rest tapers shorter to the rear, and at front, Niko has bangs cut to her eyebrows. In true Niko fashion, this style obeys the Personal Code while doing an "in-your-face" to the Administration. For this the stylist has done well, and while he'll receive no credit for the cut, he'll at least be the recipient of a substantial tip. Or not. As Kana requests he break the hundy in her hand and minutes later his assistant is back with the bills—while he still waits for that shotgun.

(Cause all he wants are his brains blown all over the floor).

He smiles goodbye anyway, then encourages each to return. It's washed out by Niko, who's had a mini-meltdown at her phone, which keeps buzzing. This continues—on the elevator, down Fifth Ave, even at this intersection where the crosswalk is seconds from turning. The strange thing is that in between Kana's phone also buzzes.

Kana doesn't seem to notice.

"Who's calling you? The person you were arguing with?"

Niko's dismissive, so obsessed with her haircut she stares at her semi-transparent reflection in the store display windows. "It's someone I need to talk to, but this isn't the time."

"Is it this Haruhide person?"

"No, Mom! I said we're not even that close."

Niko's phone buzzes again. Then, Kana's does.

Kana ignores it. "Seriously, honey, who's calling you?"

Niko gets defensive. "I could ask you the same question!"

This logic breaks Kana, but only momentarily.

"Niko, be honest with me. Is it that boy?"

Niko ignores her. "Speaking of boys, there's a boy named Mike Holler. He's the hottest boy at school, but not in the 'he's actually hottest' sense, just he's the prototypical..."

Niko carries on for three paragraphs that last a city block—wowing Kana with Mike's various achievements. *And nearly wowing me.* Yet, her opinion of him is the same—Mike, even if nice, is an airhead for dating Donna. Besides, there's the blue eyed boy, and he'd never date anyone in the Bitches. *Except me!* How she knows, she is not sure, but it gives her confidence that some boys are redeemable. Or that some don't ever need to be redeemed.

Either way, she's unreceptive to Niko's Mike ranting.

Kana notices. "Baby, you're forgetting an important part."

Niko's almost offended. "What's that?"

"She might have an existing crush."

She's not surprised Kana knew. *We're sensitive types.* They have also got a shared facial expression thing that Niko has difficulty recognizing. "I might have a tiny one."

Now Niko's legitimately offended. "You have a crush and you didn't tell me?"

"It's small and it's not a big deal."

Kana disagrees. "It's always a big deal."

"I guess, but he won't like me, and—"

Niko interrupts. "Why not?"

"Why not?" is how Niko got Hazu. For Niko, it works. For her, it's different. The blue eyed boy... He's hot. Not that she's shallow like that, but he's too pretty for her. She knew it this morning, then purposely forgot it during her daydreaming, and after school when she searched for him. But, she knows this won't happen. She knows it because, when someone's too good for you, you just know it.

"I don't know."

Niko speaks as if her life hung in the balance. "Who is it?"

She goes for honesty. "I don't know."

Niko almost faints. "What? How do you not know the name of a boy you're crushing on?"

She shrugs her shoulders. "I really don't."

Niko speaks, once again, as if her life hung in the balance.

"Tell me something about him."

Niko probably knows him. If not, Niko'll play detective until she does. She prefers Niko didn't, but like with her uniform, this secret won't last long. "You met him this morning."

"The rude one who wouldn't leave?"

He wasn't rude! Take it back! "Yes, it's him."

Kana's intrigued. "Do you know something about him?"

"Yeah, I know a few things."

"Like?"

She shares Kana's interest. *"Like?"*

"Well, he's in astronomy with us."

In an instant, she paints her class, and while insignificant faces are drawn in obscene detail, he cannot be placed. "I've never seen him there."

"I guess he wasn't there today, but he usually sits in front."

Kana gets excited. "If he's in your class, it will be easier to learn about him."

It will. "Is that all you know, Niko?"

Niko catches herself in another window, then swivels her neck to follow herself around. "I know one other thing."

"What?"

"He and Mackenzie hate each other."

Wow. Forget this "not getting him" shit...

It's like we're soul mates!

"Over what?"

"I don't know, but it's a longstanding feud."

She wants more information. It doesn't happen.

A passerby points toward Kana. It's followed by an awkward exchange of waves. Kana gives a smile for an apology. When you're Kana, that means, "Intrude on my personal space." The passerby does exactly that. It attracts some skater boys. Then the catty glare of their teenage girlfriends. The most intrusive are a pack of Japanese exchange students who offer things like receipts to be signed. It takes a while before Kana pulls away, and even longer before she again finds anonymity, but by then Kana's withdrawn.

"That was strange, after all this time."

Niko sounds happy. "See, Mom! Everyone still loves you!"

Kana keeps to her reliable smile, then supplies her credit card for every whimsical purchase. It's not the same. Kana's posture staggers and her voice is jittery. It ends in a specialty boutique for swim wear. *Niko knows about the haircut and the bikini, I told her during her haircut.* Upon arrival, the sales attendant offers drinks. She declines. Niko does, too. Kana says yes, and once Kana has water, she drinks it in gulps, then puts a prescription bottle back in her purse, but not before she swallows several pills.

Niko is concerned. "What're those, Mom?"

"They're for my back, sweetheart."

"Still? I thought it might be better with your time off."

Kana shrugs. "I guess not."

"Well, so long as everything's okay."

Kana never answers. Her phone is buzzing again, and she's too weak to ignore it. "Honey, I need to answer this."

By request, the store supplies Kana with a private room while Niko wanders the perimeter, inspecting the mannequins who wear the spring line, then checking the racks to see if it's available in her size. Dismayed it's not, Niko talks. "I'll never forgive you for withholding your secret crush."

"I've only had it since this morning!"

"Well, I'm sure you'll get him."

"How do you know that?"

Niko sighs. "The reason I told him to scram was because he was giving you this dopey, love struck look."

I thought it was only me! "Really?"

"Yep! Maybe we'll call him tonight and hang up on him."

Hanging up on boys is a long practiced sleepover prank. It has also happened infrequently since Niko joined the Bitches. She supposes these things will become standard again. And she'd very much like that, but... "I can't sleep over tonight."

"Why not?"

"My mom said I can do tonight or Saturday, but not both."

That response makes sense, but Niko's still down about it. "Oh, I see."

"Really, Niko, it's not a big deal."

At first, Niko accepts that, then over two seconds, Niko goes through the same process as Kana did the last hour. Her posture turns sad and her voice is jittery. "I don't understand."

"What?"

"No one seems excited that my mom is home."

That's not true. "I'm excited."

"No one mentioned anything about it."

"Who didn't?"

"No one. The only ones who care are you and Hazu."

Hazu? What does he care for?

She never gets the opportunity to ask the question.

Niko's phone rings. This time, like Kana, Niko answers.

"Hello?" – "I told you, I'm with my mom, I'm not answering the phone." – "She's great! She wants to meet you." – "Oh, it's a possibility." – "I ran it by him in case." – "Don't be upset." – "I'm not with him." – "I'm not seeing him tonight."– "I haven't decided." – "Yes, I'll let you know when I do." – "Bye."

With that, Niko hangs up, and what happened with Niko's posture and voice gets worse. She tries to be sensitive about it. "Was that Donna or Hazu?"

"Hazu."

"Can I ask what he wanted?"

"This morning, I realized I don't want to do post-Prom with my mom home. I'm too..." Embarrassed. But, Niko doesn't say it. "I mean, I told everyone we might need a lower profile."

Sounds like a plan! She wasn't interested in a crazy Bitches party anyway. She notices a swimsuit, a ways away, she wants to check out. She drifts in its direction, hoping Niko will follow. "I think that's for the best."

"I know, but everyone got upset, so I asked Scott if we could have it there, but then Donna found out and got angrier."

Um. "But, he's your boyfriend."

"Yeah..." Niko thinks better of it. "Anyhow, it made its way to Hazu—now he's pissed I called Scott."

Jesus Christ, Niko.

There's really no other way to put it.

"Why would Hazu be pissed? You're not dating him, right?"

"We're friends, but he's having trouble adjusting. He says he's not over me."

Of course, he's not. The little psychopath never will be.

"Niko, can you explain something to me?"

"Sure."

"What do you see in him?"

Niko breaks into a series of expressions that fail to describe an answer. Then she gets distracted by a new bikini. It's a low-cut bottom that's checkered black and white on the ass like a racing flag, with a strapless top. Niko wants to try it on, but like the other suits here, even if it were in her size, it wouldn't fit. Nothing fits. It makes Niko wonder what's wrong with her body. It shouldn't take this long to hit puberty.

Niko could hate herself over it. She often did.

Then, she found Hazu.

"He likes me this way."

"How do you mean?"

"He likes it when I go goth. He wants me to do it more."

I didn't expect to hear that.

Nor did she expect this bikini to look so good up close. It's a bit off the checked flag one. It's basically strings with a cup of fabric over her bust, then her beaver. She's usually too shy for this type of suit, but either because of the color scheme or because she thinks she can wear it in a way other girls cannot, it kinda speaks to her, and dares her to be different.

She wonders if that's a good idea.

She also wonders if she could be more self obsessed.

Am I joining the Bitches? Or am I becoming my own 2.0?

She ignores that thought. "I guess that was where you were headed before you joined the Bitches."

"There's something else."

"What?"

Niko's quiet. "He likes it when I don't stuff my bra."

Oh my God. *Did Niko just admit that?* "He does?"

"He thinks I should stop. And he said if he hears anyone making fun of my breasts, he'll kick the shit out of them."

She freezes.

"Kicking the shit" out of people is a Hazu solution. It means he's a terrible boyfriend, but she gets it. Even if deep down Niko knows it's wrong, it's hard to forget a boy who'll stand up for you like that. More importantly, it means Hazu dislikes Niko2.0. And supports Niko through Kana's troubles. So despite being a terrible boyfriend, he cares. No, he can't. He's a boy, and a jerky one, worse than Mike Holler and his "boys."

"So what're you gonna do?"

Niko's gonna change the subject.

"That's what he wants to know, but I don't know, so it's just how it is." Niko is close to surrendering to emotion. It never happens. Niko flicks whatever switch is inside of her, then acts like she didn't just say her breasts, the ones hanging from her this moment, are fake. "Anyway, I've got something for you."

"You do?"

"Yes, I've held onto it since I don't want my mom to see it."

"What is it?"

"If I give you it, you can't ever speak of it to anyone."

A chill runs down her back. "Okay."

Niko looks all about, like she worries spies have binoculars pointed at her. Assured, Niko reaches into her Academy skirt, toward the pocket that lines the right side. When Niko removes her hand, it's a fist, which Niko displays before turning it over, unfolding her fingers like flower petals in sunlight. In Niko's palm lies a golden key. There's nothing extraordinary about its surface or its size. It looks like any old key.

Niko's face says otherwise.

"This is the biggest secret in the Academy."

"What does it do?"

"It opens the locked bathroom by the pool, near the gym."

I knew it! Donna and Mackenzie were in there!

"Where did you get it?"

"Donna."

"And no one knows?"

At that, Niko closes her fist. "Not all of the Bitches have this key, most don't know about it, but you're my best friend, so I want you to have it."

She feels a bit numb. "Okay."

Niko holds out the key. When it's accepted, Niko doesn't let go. "I never meant to put a target on you. I mean it."

She nods. The key is in her own pocket.

Meanwhile, her mind has gone back.

To yesterday at home on the phone, then in the car after tryouts, or in the hallway with the Bitches, to discovering her wet uniform, then stops in the showers. She was being blasted by a full on spray that was half steam when it touched her skin. Because the showers themselves are akin to lampposts with four nozzles pointed in four directions, Mackenzie pushed the tab beside her, which shot more steamy water that Mackenzie stood underneath. They've often been icy to one another, so she ignored Mackenzie, but Mackenzie did not ignore her.

I've got to say something.

"Niko, I've got to tell you something."

But she does not.

Kana has returned and looks terrible.

"Oh, are you going to try that on?"

Kana refers to the string bikini. And, yes, she is.

"I just need to find a dressing room."

The sales lady shows her to it. She feels a bit dumb since it was behind her, but she forgets it. Bathing suit wearing will do that. Inside, she's careful with her blouse, then with her skirt, so her mother will not scold her for wrinkles, and when her bra hits her elbows, she realizes she can hear Kana.

"Niko, honey, I need to tell you something."

"Sure, Mom, what's up?"

"There's a party in New York tomorrow, it's important I see these people, but then I'm coming right back to be with you."

Niko quivers. "But, you said you aren't leaving anymore."
"I have to, honey. It's a sponsor dinner."
It's tragic.

When Niko gets hurt, she refuses to feel any of it. It's Niko's survival instinct, and it's exactly what Niko does when she panics. So Niko copies what she did when looking for her mother in the parking lot. "Well, bring back a lot of free stuff!"

Inside the dressing room, what should be Niko's tears fall.

No way is Kana leaving Niko so soon.

She can't believe it. She just can't.

The bikini sits on the bench. There it stays. Until she's back in her bra, her blouse, and her skirt, taking time to buckle her shoes. She leaves the dressing room, uncertain how to pretend she doesn't know. It's ends up being easy. Kana is so tortured by this that she turns away from Niko. In actuality, puts her back to Niko—then beams!

"Did it look good?"
She shrugs. "Not really."
"Really? You seemed so sure you'd like it!"
"It was alright, I guess."
Kana fears the silence. "I'll buy it for you."
"It's okay. My mother wouldn't—"
Kana interrupts. "I insist—for taking care of Niko."
She blinks over to Niko, who faces a rack of swimsuits.
"Thank you."
Kana has her hand in her purse.
"And don't worry about your Mom. It'll be our secret."

8.

Things have reached a critical level.

On her bed lay her yearbook, it's opened on the page where the blue eyed boy, whose eyes are chrome, is crammed into a tiny rectangle. Never worry, he's still pretty. And he puts heat in her. It's fine. She's well-ventilated. For while she did swap her wrinkly, floor-discarded uniform for a camisole, she forgot pants. It leaves her free to pull aside her panties, which allows maximum application to the pillow that's jammed into her.

She hasn't masturbated. (Not to climax, anyway). She just likes the pressure. It feels like the hug that should be his arms.

Or it did.

Maybe a minute ago, when her lungs got cloudy and her chest struggled to operate, sex fantasies encroached on her love. Like, it was reckless of her to run with those books. He agrees. She's been a "bad girl" and he needs to confiscate her blouse. (It makes sense since he liked her boobs). Some other stuff happens too, but it's too naughty to share, and disgusting like the stuff Hazu tells Niko. *I can't stop thinking it. My brain won't...* She was excited when her boobs got grabbed, but this is different. She doesn't know what to do—with her hands, her mind, her feelings...

They all want to explode. As does her door.

It's her mother. And her mother knows something's up.

"What're you doing?"

She has ripped aside the pillow, herself white as a ghost.

"Nothing."

Her mother is too much of an ass to accept that.

"Where are your pants?"

Or her mother can't understand.

She did rat me out for masturbating. "I was changing, but I had an idea for a project and I was afraid I'd forget it, so I tried to find it in the book."

Halfway through her fumbled lie, she set aside the yearbook, facedown. It's too thin and too big for a text book, but it might pass the sight test. Her mother's uninterested in it and talks while she, behind her cabinet door, slips into pajama pants.

"Did you have fun?"

No. "Yes."

"Is Kana doing better?"

No. "Yes."

"I imagine Niko was excited."

Yes. "Not really."

"What did you three do?"

Stop asking so many questions! "I'm afraid to answer."

"Afraid of what?"

This is why she never confides in her mother.

Like Niko destroyed her lingerie escape, her mother destroys this boy escape. Kana would not ask about this afternoon. *No, she'd ditch me for a party.* What she means is Kana, unlike her mother, can read things like body language. And hers says, "Leave me be!" At least until she processes. She's serious, that boy was all that was helping. If there's one thing worse than her wet uniform, it's hearing Kana's ditching Niko.

Her anger at Kana has somehow become anger at her mom.

I wonder how often that happens.

"You."

"I asked what you did, that's all."

"Don't worry, I didn't smuggle anything into the house."

By instinct, her mother scans the area—for shopping, duffle, or any other type of bag. While there's nothing visible, her mother knows it's there, yet she practices restraint, choosing to hang the crumpled uniform. "I want to trust you, but every time I think I know what's going on, it changes. Whether it's what you wore yesterday or the makeup you put on at school."

Ah! "None of that is about you!"

"You're playing games with me and—"

She interrupts. "And what game is that?"

"Is this haircut, that underwear, even about swim?"

She rolls her eyes. "God, you're paranoid!"

"You're trying to get a boy to like you."

"I..."

Her mother gloats. "I was a young girl once, too."

It stings.

A boyfriend has been the priority. It's hard for one not to be since she thinks boys aren't as bad as their reputations. But maybe her mother is right. Boys are bad and school is good. *Fuck that.* She wants to wear a thong, not be a stripper. She wants a haircut, not a Mohawk. She tires of these extremes. *And my mom's a hypocrite!* Look at her! Done over in her Connie Chung hair and her fancy clothes.

Her mother never leaves the house!

"So what? What's so wrong about that?"

"Your grades are lower and you quit Model UN."

She defaults into the silent treatment. Her mother leaves. She'd sulk longer, but in ten minutes the fight will resume. In the interim, she has some safe pillow time, so she wedges it in her clitoris. Instead of pleasure, she feels frustration, over how this picture and its crappy resolution blurs his distinguishable features. Looks like everything at the Academy is first-rate but the Goddamn yearbook cameras.

Hey, he may be in the student directory.

(206) 333 – 1952.

What a stupid idea. She's already picked up the phone five times. One time, she entered half his digits. Five more minutes on the pillow and she's determined to call. To say hello. Or to thank him for his help. It's only when a male, clearly young, answers that she realizes he never introduced himself, so this implies she was spying on him and that's creepy...

It's also stalkerish. Something Hazu would do.

She hangs up. The phone rings back.

*He *69'd me!*

What to do? Pick up and hang up? What if he calls again? Answer? *No!* If she lets it ring, will he give up? What if he doesn't? Then, her answering machine identifies the last name of the residence, so if he searches his own yearbook...

It's too late.

The phone's been answered. And her father is shouting!

"You know it's for you! Why didn't you pick up?"

She can't speak, so she listens.

"Hello? Hello? Isn't anyone there?"

Her brain releases enough dopamine to sedate a dinosaur. It turns her to the grins one gets after escaping certain doom. "Oh, my God, Niko, thank God, it's you."

Niko is confused. "Why? What happened?"

"I called him!"

Niko gasps. "What did you say?"

"Nothing, I hung up!"

Niko laughs. "You dork!"

Hey! "Shut up!"

Niko laughs again. "Okay, I need to tell you something."

Niko implies Kana's abrupt departure. As anything bad is best ignored, Niko and Kana never mentioned it, so she did the same. The illusion didn't last. Whatever those pills were, they knocked Kana out. *That's when I heard my mother.* "I want you to call me if anything funny happens, and if she is drinking or anything, I'll drive you home." Well, it was Niko who drove. Once Kana was in bed, Niko drove her home.

My Mom has yet to freak out about it.

"Niko, I overheard that Kana's leaving. It hurt me, too."

Niko laughs some more. "Oh, that? I'm fine with it."

You are? "Really?"

Niko continues to laugh. "Yeah, she'll be back Sunday."

It's still no laughing matter.

She hears whispers. "Is someone else there?"

"I'm sorry, Hazu's being a jerk."

That and he's—along with Niko—drunk. She knows because, upon examination, Niko has a slur. It worsens now that Niko's admitted he's there, and Niko whispers a response before she gives three quick, openmouth kisses. (Like BJS, openmouthed kisses have a fart). What can't be heard is Niko's wrapped in a blanket and in Hazu—crammed into the back of his 7, and but for her panties, she's naked. What's great about that, for Niko, is how—before they engaged in an extended oral examination of each other's genitals—those C-cup breasts were tossed in the dumpster behind the Thai place where they ate.

Hazu did it, even though Niko begged him not to.

"Why're you with him?"

"I'm taking him to meet my mom."

"I thought you told her you weren't dating him."

Niko gets a tone. "Technically, I'm not."

That's so gross. "I'm hanging up now."

Niko talks fast. "I'm serious. I need to tell you something."

"Fine."

"With my mom leaving, this might be my last big party, so the plan's changed. Tomorrow, I'm taking Donna down."

She slides off her pillow. "Down?"

"Yeah, I'm going to take the Bitches from her. It's... It has to be this way. And my source says I have to do it now."

Oh yeah, the "source." Forget being angry over this Hazu bullshit. *I've got my own.* She meant to tell Niko all day... She didn't know how to say it so things wouldn't get worse. She's gotta say it now. That key on her desk wasn't free.

I'm in the Bitches. I better start acting like it.

"I have to tell you something."

"What?"

"When Mackenzie was distracting me in the showers, she, like, said she knew you were gonna take over. I didn't get it cause you didn't tell me at first that it was part of your plan."

Niko feels legitimate concern. It's why Niko disregards it.

"It doesn't matter."

She begs to differ. "Donna knows, so does Mackenzie. It wasn't a bluff—what Mackenzie said this morning."

"How can they know? This part just got invented."

She knows that, too.

"Your source isn't your source. She's working for Donna."

Niko sounds too innocent. "That can't be."

She doesn't know how to put it. "Niko, you tell these people so many different things. Are you sure they'll listen?"

Niko sounds too innocent again. "They don't trust me?"

She dislikes how that sounds.

"You just need to be extra careful."

The call is over.

She wants to get angry at Niko for lying about Hazu. She cannot, and not because of her own lies. You see, after Sadie Hawkins, Niko gave BJS, but when Niko was done, Niko shouted, "Ten more minutes!" What followed was the four collisions necessary for a girl to remove her undies, and what followed that was Niko moaning in either pleasure or child birth. It was an eternity before Niko subsided, and longer before Niko emerged, wrapped in a blanket, to pee in the bushes. She knew what happened. Hazu went buffet style on Niko's twat. Very fair, and unexpected, of Hazu. He never seemed the type to take pride in a woman's pleasure. Regardless, she didn't understand why Niko did it—any of it. Now, she supposes, she doesn't understand why Niko does anything for Kana.

But, I still let my boobs get felt up.

And here she is, sitting on pillows, obsessed with this boy since Kana's lies hurt that much. And yesterday, to escape the shame of her uniform, she wore that lingerie. So explains what drives Niko to Hazu. It isn't love or lust or poor morals—it's pain. It's the hurt and it's what one does to alleviate it, even if only temporarily. At least Niko's actions are redeemable, as the lengths Niko will go for Hazu are equal only to those which Niko will go for Kana. *Would I go as far for my mother as I would the blue eyed boy?* She might. If her mother didn't hate things like thongs or masturbation or...

That's not right.

Her mother saw her on the pillow, and at some point, her mother left a bag on her desk. Inside it is the lingerie, washed and folded, Niko loaned her. And it... You know what? Girls are complicated and too complex. It's not worth figuring them out. *I'm lying.* Girls are simple. As simple as it's obvious. Kana betrayed her. *And I betrayed my mother.*

When she hid Model UN.

When she hid Niko's situation.

When she hid the lingerie.

That she's currently hiding the bikini Kana bought her.

It's the "secrets."

They've lead her to the downstairs couch, otherwise known as a minefield. It takes a sec, but she says it. She gets misty. "I got the lingerie from Niko."

Her mother is emotionless. "Thank you for telling me."

That wasn't all she came here to say. "Do you ever see stuff from my perspective? You're stricter than the Academy. All the girls wear makeup. I'm not doing anything weird."

"I think some of it is okay, I don't like the speed."

"The speed?"

Her mother takes a moment to lower the TV volume, but it can still be heard in the background. It's not about anything, but the noise will fill the gaps. And there will be gaps. Her mother's in one, as she considers what to say. "With Niko, you get whatever you want, when you want it. You want a haircut," her mother snaps her fingers, "and I'm supposed to take you. You want lingerie? You borrow it until you get permission, which is like not asking permission."

"But, Mom..."

Her mother interrupts. "It's disrespectful."

Okay, she gets that. "That wasn't my intention."

"You have to think before you make choices."

"I know." She catches herself. This is her pattern. She agrees with her mother to bypass any dialogue. Her mother knows it, too. She tries to be mindful of her tone. She's tired from a long day and she fears it'll translate to her words. There. That was the thought she needed. *I need more rest.* She rids the thought from her, then focuses herself—physically feeling the pressure to move forward. *It's been two years. Like rest is gonna make a difference.* "You can ban me from seeing Niko, so I don't ask cause then it becomes Niko's idea."

"It isn't?"

She wants to implode. "Mom, that's disrespectful."

Her mother surprises her. "I shouldn't blame Niko. Some of those things are your idea."

A concession. One step from an apology. How unfortunate, as she only desired cooler tempers, not for her mother to admit fault for anything. Primarily because she's not ready to. Too late now, the ball is, so they say, in her court. The words don't come. In fact, she enjoys the high ground, then thinks—and she's disgusted with herself over it—if she wanted, she could hurt her mother hard. Or she could forgive her mother, if she even knows how.

She's tried all week and it ends at the same place: "secrets."

One day after her talk with Kana in the chapel gardens, Mother Superior fetched her from class. In her office waited Kana, dressed up in skintight jeans that were buttoned way too high and a shirt that fit her bust like it was made of elastic, but her face was flawless and her hair, on one side, was braided so her ear and its giant earring were visible. Next to Kana was her mother, conservatively dressed with a fair amount of make-up and hair like she were about to begin as a substitute. She was in her elementary jumper. Everyone took turns talking, and when it was Kana's turn, Kana said, "Honey, it's okay to talk about Niko with your mom or Mother Superior. I didn't mean them." She knew enough to agree, but like any astute kid, she recognized that Kana's concession was like when a grownup forces her to apologize for something she isn't sorry for.

I knew Kana didn't mean it.

Also, she knew this meeting happened because her mother tattled to Mother Superior. Tattlers can't be trusted, whether it be about Niko or not, so she decided to trust Kana. She'd keep all the secrets. She'd lock her mother out. *I... I did lock her out.* Wait, that can't be true. She never picked Niko or Kana over her Mom. *Except I did.* And her mother, never one to give in, fought to get her back—from different classes, to the masturbation incident, to separate high schools, to... All her mother's sins were mistakes, so were Mother Superior's, maybe Kana's, too.

Her sins are unique, as it's the original sin.

I started it.

Now that Kana's abandoned Niko—*along with all my faith in her*—she sees. She also hates the secrets. "Kana bought me a bikini. You won't like it, but I had to accept it."

Her mother does a short nod. "Please bring it to me."

Wow, that was easy. It's just as well. *I'd have to seriously shave for it.* "And my reason for wanting a haircut or a bikini isn't swim. I knew you couldn't say no, so that's why I said it, but I want them and thongs, so what makes that okay?"

Her mother is rock solid. Like she fears movement will release whatever fit fired upstairs. "There must be rules."

"Like?"

"What Niko gave you was too adult. You're not old enough for it and Niko also isn't, but I'm not her mother. You give that thing back to Niko, and if we buy you underwear," her mom's not gonna say thongs, "then we do it together. On the condition that's all you wear, I see you in anything else—"

She interrupts. "I can follow that rule, I promise."

"And don't pressure me to make decisions."

No secrets. No games.

That's gonna be hard. "I'll try to stop."

"We both need to be comfortable."

"Can I ask when we'll go?"

"Tomorrow after your haircut."

So she is getting the haircut. She knew that.

"Can I ask one more thing?"

Her mother wants to launch into a speech about how it's never enough, but once again... "What?"

"Can Niko please drive me to school?"

Her mother rubs her temple. "I have to think about it."

"But, Mom—"

Her mother interrupts. "I said don't pressure me to make

decisions."

With that, she shuts up, then stands up and backs away, a little surprised this dialogue didn't degrade into an argument. (Her father, who's been hiding in the kitchen, must be short of breath). Either way, she still hasn't forgiven her mother. It stops her at the stairs. At one time, as a little girl, she thought people who held onto grudges for years and years were stupid babies. *Looks like I'm a stupid baby.* If she told her mother she forgave her, it'd be over.

It's what she should do. It's the right thing to do.

She about-faces. "Mom?"

"Yes?"

She knows she's not gonna say it.

At this point, she's more comfortable hating her mom.

"Nothing, I'll see you tomorrow."

Part I (Cont.): Junior Year.

IX.

The sun fries white the blue sky as birds chirp like summertime, tucked away in nests on the branches of these infinite evergreens stuffed as tightly as the cigarettes in her soft packs. A soft pack right beside her, calling to her—nothing more than a jackhammer hangover. Already dehydrated, sweat trickles down her sleek curves as her body, which smells like coconut suntan lotion and Niko's peach scented shampoo, deepens in tone. In that suit made of some suspicious stuff that hugs her breasts like one of those beds on TV that promise a bowling ball can be dropped from a ladder without Tom's knowledge.

She flips onto her stomach, holding her girls in place while she clears herself of her bikini strings. She does not want to have tan lines for Prom, *if* someone bothers to ask her. This love business interceded; nevertheless, Prom remains a priority and should he ask, fret she will not. Her dress and her shoes already reside in a mall boutique, hanging lonely off a plastic mannequin with no eyes or mouth. They sing to her. *Don't wait for the boy to ask! Just buy me!* It's an enticing melody, and on her every mall venture, she checks out its price tag.

It's pricey. And her body is sleepy.

Between prolonged blinks, she watches the water volleyball game. It's Niko, Mackenzie, and Tom versus Timmy and Clyde, who think they're the North Seattle Community College water volleyball champions. Timmy shouts things like "Set!" and Clyde spikes the ball and crashes into the water. She ogles his shirtless body without his notice since her sunglasses are the disguising type. She thinks he's thin but not works out thin. He looks better with his guitar. Finished with him, she spies on Tom. He looks good without a shirt, except his arm. It's scarred all over and her spying has given her ample chance to review it. Also, he and Mackenzie are acting like team sports require conjoining.

SS1 has noticed. "Sykosa, you let him do that?"

SS2 agrees. "Yeah, you let him do that?"

The Sluts are lined up 1-2-3. SS1's in a skimpy number with no makeup. SS2's the same. SS3's in a one-piece, partially in the shade, as she fears cancer or something impractical.

"I don't let him do anything."

SS1 yawns. "My boyfriend has called me twice today. He says he's going nuts without me."

SS2 yawns, too. "Yeah, our boyfriends have called us twice!"

As stupid as they are, the little hoes make an excellent point. "We're not like that with each other."

SS1 yawns again. "Whatever."

SS2 yawns too. "Yeah, whatever!" Then, after some seconds, she pokes Sykosa and whispers. "It's alright, you'll get him!"

Niko lays her palms flat on the poolside and lifts herself in a blur. Water fallen like that girl in *Fast Times*, only Japanese and in a silver bikini. Her thumbs roll underneath her bottoms to release her vacuum packed ass cheeks before she puts her hands on her sides and pouts like her mother does for all those cameras. "Are-you-gonna-come-in?"

"I'm not interested."

"Why?"

Tom—*no, he wouldn't do that*—shouts! "What? It's so easy!"

"I know how to swim, Tom."

"What's it about, then?"

It's about how she's never entering the water with Mackenzie again! "Leave it be, okay?"

Niko sits Indian style. "I can't believe he said that."

"It's alright." Or it's not. Like, why is she the only one who sees? The ocean tastes like piss, pools feel like chemical spills, and lakes are sewage dumps. All an ocean, pool, or lake has done is force her to wash her hair. She likes water that's hot. Steam-covered mirrors, cloudy shower doors, bath robes, and fancy smelling soaps. She'd like to kiss him in a bath, or fuck him in that lagoon, which is the pool. *Whose side are you on?*

"The only thing I like about water is—"

SS2 interrupts. "Psst, Niko!"

Niko turns around. "Beautiful, what's up?"

"You're so beautiful in your bikini!"

"Aw, gorgeous." Niko slinkies herself over and kisses SS2 on the forehead. "Let's make love later, honey."

"Okay, Niko!"

That's a joke.

She mentally separates from the Girl-to-Girl Male Attention Supplement Session—too confused to be anywhere physically near human affection, artificial or otherwise, and in need of Niko. For one, Niko's experienced, but also her best friend and something like Tom professing his…emotions—she can't even think the "L" word—after a page of details she fails to notice about herself feels like best friend territory. She won't mention anything within earshot of the Sluts. As a result, from the start, his confession backfired. She stayed with Niko all night in the wake of Scott and avoided Tom, including when he suggested she share the guest room he had claimed as his own.

That said, before she ran off to the main suite to be with the Queens, she kissed him, and then, this morning, he gave her a long hug in the second dining room before grabbing her butt. *It's a good sign, I think.* "What's there to do but swim here?"

"We can hike a trail. I mentioned it to Clyde and he might go, but we'd be limited because rock stars don't exercise. All they do is drink, party, and fuck, or so he says."

Cute. "Um, can we sneak off and do it?"

Niko winks. "Yeah."

Timmy shouts. "Aw no, you guys ain't sneaking off, uh-uh, everyone outta the pool!"

Who knows how he heard that. Niko shrugs. "Sorry."

"It's alright." She fastens her top and fluffs her hair. "I have to get a pair of shorts."

Niko glares back at the Sluts. "You guys gonna come?"

SS1 shakes her head. "Exercise, yuck!"

SS2 shakes too. "Yeah, exercise is yucky!"

Inside, she pulls cutoffs over her ass and decides against a tee-shirt cause this bikini top is too good to her ta-tas. Plus, wearing this top and these shorts while walking through the woods is cliché horror movie. Maybe she'll hear a growl in the bushes, and Tom will take her in his arms and protect her and then they'll run from the serial murderer, and in her movie, they both get away and make out in the cabin forever! Okay, not forever, but until they find a phone, and she calls Niko and tells her everything about it.

This fantasy has made her playful and full of smirks as she grabs moisturizer because, while horror movie fun is exactly that, nothing's fun about dry skin and premature aging. She spreads the liquid over the hump of her neck and down along the fencepost of her shoulder—hums, *All them bitches. All them hoes.*—and dabs a blue oil-absorbing sheet against her forehead, which always breaks out first and clears up last.

Niko waits in flip-flops and her bikini with a visor clung to her head and an old military canteen hung off her shoulder. Mackenzie waits by Tom, her tee-shirt and shorts stuck to the wet outline of her own bikini. *Of course, he's gonna waste this perfectly good horror movie opportunity on Mackenzie.* Well, if that's so, she'll spend her time with Clyde. She roughhouses him with a pansy noogie that gives him the excuse he needs to lay his hands on her, which—*about time*—is too much for Tom, who's stolen her hand, and then moments later her person.

He seems angry. "Attention starved much?"

"You were the one sounding starved last night." She thinks of her prom dress and curses. *I'll never get asked if he hates me.* She's being counterproductive. She needs to regroup. After all, he's a stupid boy, but a good boy. She brainstorms ways to drop big hints that sound like tiny suggestions. "It's nuts with the dance and everything. They said this year it's happening at some great hall we've had it at before."

Clyde butts in. "What?"

Niko butts in, too. "Our Prom's a big deal because a bunch of magazines come to photograph it. We have one of the best proms in the country. We win awards for it, and it's run by this thing called Prom Committee and it's a big deal to be on it."

Clyde doesn't care. "Mine was in the school gymnasium."

Niko figured as much, then assures Clyde that not all proms are like his prom and not to worry his sweet, burnt-out brain over it. She also mentions, "By the way, it's *Prom* not prom."

"What the difference?"

"Ours is capitalized."

"Why?"

"Because we're special!"

Clyde whispers. "Spoiled rich babies is what you are."

Niko stops in place. "What was that?"

"Nothing."

And skips off! "That's what I thought!"

Niko leads the way through the black fence surrounding her pool, across the grass and past some pushed aside branches, avoiding poison ivy and spider webs in an aggressive swagger, emerging onto a passage—more like a tunnel than a trail—as the treetops intertwine and create an umbrella over the sky. Niko reviews some forest rules like an old man who has swam the ocean his entire life, and as an afterthought, warns the kids to swim ashore if they see a shark fin. "No cigarette butts! Put them out, then put them in your pocket! Once, this woman threw her smoke out and it landed in some brush and the forest caught fire. My parents and I were evacuated."

Clyde's distressed. He's used to looking cool indoors. "Niko, there aren't any bears or anything out here, right?"

Niko laughs so hard she almost trips. "Really, Clyde, bears only show up when they want food. I don't think they're gonna bother us over Marlboro Lights."

"You sure?"

"Yes."

Timmy's worried since he knows Clyde is worried. "Baby, you know your way back, right? We've walked a long ways."

"Please, I drive further to school. You two are sissies."

Sykosa's lit a cigarette, which Clyde effortlessly slides from her fingertips into his own, hits off it and returns it. A rather smooth, albeit inappropriate, move given his age. That may be her fault; she provoked him and Tom, by coincidence, grasps her waist and tucks her into his shoulder. She figures that may be her fault, too. To fix it, she pecks his cheek to reaffirm her devotion before she jogs to Niko, leaving the boys confused as to her intentions, which is fine. It's her job to be fickle, so she knows she's special and Tom knows to take her to Prom.

She shares the cigarette with Niko. "So, does your mother even know you're here?"

To reinforce, Niko3.0 doesn't talk about her parents. It's why Niko flips around and stares at Mackenzie as she walks backwards. Niko can't place it, but Mackenzie's acting odd. If only Niko knew, Mackenzie saw Sykosa and Tom's public smooches last night. It wasn't a surprise, yet Mackenzie wasn't prepared for it, and without her Bitches, Mackenzie's decided to keep quiet about it, even if Niko tries to goad her, which Niko does.

"Mackenzie, are you going to Prom?"

"Why do you ask?"

"You've been so silent about Prom this year. Last year, I heard so much about it, I thought I was your date."

Mackenzie sounds tired. "Do we really have to do this?"

Niko backs off. She won the Academy. Everyone knows it. "Not if you don't want to, we don't."

"I don't. And let's keep it that way through the dance."

Niko whistles. "If you're too ashamed to talk about your date, it's not my problem."

"You're one to talk."

"What do you mean?"

"Where's Hazu?"

That hit Niko in the gut. Worse, there's little Niko can do about it. That stupid bitch Ass Girl took him, and it appears as if Ass Girl's taking the Bitches, too. At least, it feels like Mackenzie, who was never a natural leader, intends to defer command to Ass Girl.

"He wanted to come out here."

Mackenzie talks like it's a joke. "Sure, he did."

Sykosa wants nothing of this talk. She pays attention to the forest instead, to notice, when her elbow smacks a branch, it leaves fishtailing white scratches that she rubs off with spit. Everyone is covered in these white lines, save Niko who, from face to toes to tushie to forearms, bears not a mark. "Niko, when you told me those stories about you walking around the mountains up here, I didn't know how true they were."

"It's because I'm such a klutz in the city. I get overwhelmed by all the lights and the busy-*e*-ness." No one responds. Oddly, Niko thinks of that vampire hair boy who knew what her headband said. She sighs and forgets him. "Sometimes I think about camping for a month or something in these woods—backpack the whole thing. I'd use the time to get back into my Aikido. I miss it, but I don't have time for it anymore."

"I didn't know you liked this stuff so much."

Niko's bored with the conversation.

"Come on guys, you have to see this. It's amazing."

Niko scales the almost vertical hill in a jiff. She laughs as the others dig their feet into the soft ground and fall, trying to transfer weight. Niko suggests many smaller steps instead of giant ones. This helps, yet the struggles continue. *Particularly for me.* She steps up once, twice, and then the dirt gives and she gives with it, nearing a fit. She cannot swim (very well, anyway) and she cannot climb hills. *I'm useless.* Her palms bat the dirt off her ass, and on her seventeenth try, she follows the group through branches that open on a field of tall grass.

Everyone kind of does their own thing.

Tom wants to go to the other side of the field.

"Come on, let's go."

"I don't know. We should stay with Niko."

"Niko, you don't mind, do you?"

"Not really!"

He tugs on her like she is a ragdoll—for the third time.

She snatches back her hand, almost in fear of her freedom. She's never seen Tom jealous, but she's seen him violent, and it's maddening. She follows him anyhow—in need of another hug like last night—until their friends are specks. Somewhere along the way, she held his hand and that is what they do until she gets a hug. It ends in another ass grab. Casual conversation persists, but nothing that clarifies why he confessed his love for her, yet avoids her Prom hints. Not that she's forthcoming, as her instincts want to protect her heart, not share it.

Then, he taps her shoulder. "You're it!"

She runs after him. The grass tickles her knees. "Stop!"

"Why?"

She is out of breath. "You have to let me win! I'm the girl."

"Excuse me? I have to let you win, why?"

She doubles over. "You don't have to let me win anything." She wipes her mouth and thinks she needs to quit smoking. She's kidding. "I had to get you to stop! You're it!" She tags his waist and scurries off. A second wind finds her and his fingers still descend upon those same ticklish corners. She plants her foot and pivots across his body, seemingly eluding his grasp, but then her tit gets clamped. *Damn boyfriend gets to tag stuff no one else does!* "Missed me!"

"Naw, I got you!"

She pants. "Uh-uh, you didn't say I was 'it.'"

He has a look in his eyes. "You know I'm gonna get you."

"No, you're not." He jumps forward and she skits back. This is fun. "I'll never jerk you off again."

"Oh, that's a lie!"

The grass falls under her commotion and her stomach tightens under his fingers and her body is in the air.

She pounds his back. "Put me down! This is cheating!"

He does so and she stumbles, threading her finger through the knot of his swim trunk string. On her tiptoes, she makes out with him. He holds her. She squeezes his butt (to be even) and he squeezes her butt back (it's never even). Their noses are molecules apart. He says, "What if we were playing freeze tag and I left you out here?" She pouts, laying her forehead on his chin, distraught over his cruelty. He's regretful. "I don't know why I said that. I was thinking about last night and what I said. It was, maybe, not the best time."

"What do you mean?"

"I'd have rather told you here. I'd have rather it not been at such an average party."

Good point! Now, make it better!

She's joking. She doesn't want to talk about last night at all. Or last year.

"That's okay."

"I do feel what I said, you know?"

No, she doesn't. "Yeah, I know."

"I mean, none of my friends know about us, not even M. None of your friends, except Niko, know about us. What do we say when we tell them we have been seeing each other?"

"Seeing each other" isn't how she would phrase it. They've been kissing. And that's acceptable since nothing's slutty about kissing. (The handjobs and the humping, well... *Must you be so hypercritical?*) If he wants to get serious, then that's cool and she wants that too, but he better be serious, cause—okay, yeah—she's getting along fine, or fine when the blackness isn't about, and has tolerated being his ass candy, but no decent girl lets, "I love you," hang over a relationship unaddressed for long, so he's on the clock by his own devices.

"You think it will be that big a deal?"

"Well, everyone loves you."

"What?"

"It's..." His mind's stuck on images of her with that idiot and his guitar. He knew, sooner or later, Sykosa would figure out how hot she is. He never knew it would drive him this crazy. "People should know about us and we should start doing stuff like a couple does."

"*What?*"

"We should go to Prom together, shouldn't we?"

"Yes!"

This isn't her story. This isn't her life.

He asked! He asked! The stupid little perv asked!

She hugs him and refuses to let go, even when he tries to pry away. He whispers. "I tried last night, but last year..."

No!

She kisses his mouth to shut him up. He does shut up and it's perfect. She understands why he might think it necessary to bring up the awful past, but she wants him to know, like last night, it's not so, that she gets her duty and, furthermore, how lucky she is to have a cute boyfriend who asks her to Prom. He also finds her sexy enough to apply his fingers back to her ass.

She giggles, cause it's kinda funny.

"Why do you keep touching my butt?"

"It's your bathing suit. You look hot in it."

Ah, he likes the short-shorts! "That's funny. I bought it for this trip." She brings herself in close for another hug that goes on until she hears Niko shout, "You guys know we have rooms back at the cottage, right? You don't need to take getting back to nature so literally!" Both Tom and her laugh, and he adds a middle finger. Niko gives him the ASL sign for "fuck you" and finishes with, "We're headed back, lovebirds!" She separates from him, her hair behind her ear and his hand already on hers, then another surprise kiss that leads to a smaller surprise kiss that ends with her hand on his oblique.

She's got a lost look in her eyes.

"Tom?"

"Yeah?"

"I wanna move my stuff to your room."

X.

The bathroom walls are tuffs of rust, sanded soft as sand. In corners, sturdy green climbs up golden chains attached to the ceiling, before it falls, hanging low like the stretched curls in a woman's hair. Not far away the exhaust fan collects a mixture of smoke and shower steam, the latter stretching above her like dry ice. The shower itself is unreal. She eyed it a few moments ago, and she eyes it now—stares at Niko's silhouette, who has propped her leg upon the triangle while her arm swipes the razor that swipes her nick-free. Then, Niko kills the water to drip the floor slippery. She eyed that too a few moments ago, and she eyes it now—stares at Niko's hairy cunt and how, like an invasive species, its unchecked growth is near as high as her belly, as wide as her thighs and devours her undercarriage.

Niko hums something, like a contagious yawn:
All them bitches. All them hoes.
BUZZ. buzz. BUZZ. *BUZZ.*
The big bash will commence soon. She needs to get ready.

Especially since she did as she said. She dropped off her stuff in his room, then on the bed, he cupped her cheek and put her hair behind her ear—repeatedly. And between strategizing how to disclose their relationship, they discussed school, her Model UN project, parties, how doggie style is the position he most wants to try, video games and finally Prom and what going will be like. It made her fuzzy, so she was receptive to his kisses and to how he slowly pulled both knots from her bikini top. She thought: *I should stop.* Instead, she lay there topless, and he held her, for what felt like hours, and every now and again, his hands turned her bottoms over their elastic waist.

She trusted him to stop himself before exposing her vagina, and it was a close call, but he did stop, choosing to respect her dignity over his erection.

And she thought, *It's real. He loves me.*

Then Niko called her for girl time, and she ran, like she did last night, to be amongst the two-sprout Jacuzzi, the tall faucet sinks, the three-milled import soapbox and, in the corner, a retro-red icebox with an equally retro service station. *I want this bathroom.* She wants less confusion and occasionally materialism accomplishes that. After all, Tom's her Prom date, her boyfriend, her soon-to-be lover, and while he did the 99% perfectly, he messed up the one. *He brought up last year.* It put a pinch of the blackness in her, and once it's there, it's...

The strain of inevitability.

(Or as she knows it: the "pull.")

That means she's going to * him. Her mind has already made the decision and this is the part where she freaks out.

The big bash will commence soon. She needs to get ready.

Take a shower, do her hair, wear makeup, put on clothes, only to take them off. *I've lost to him.* And what results in her is a void that, sex or not, is here to stay. *Why must I think these crazy things?* And she wonders what he'll say when he does it and if it'll hurt and how much it'll hurt and if it'll still hurt tomorrow. *Like it has this last year.* Wow, that's harsh. *I learned from the best.* She means her mother. And she's on the self-assault train, no longer worried about the pain because the pain is constant. It runs her over and runs her down. It's so big it's almost a joke. To think that a penis might hurt her.

He'd be so lucky.

This isn't her story. This isn't her life.

You wouldn't understand.

It's not her fault. It's the blackness. It's paralyzed her. And it's terrorizing her. It's destroying her and...

&&&&&&&   && #!

She cannot bring herself to prepare for him.

The desire is...absent.

Niko wipes down the full-body mirror. She stares at her A cups and narrow hips, then gets in on those nine imperfections, as if her telekinetic intensity could reshape them. "There's a razor in the shower, but my Mom has some wax stuff too."

"The razor will be fine."

Niko stalls, something was off with that "fine." It disturbs Niko, as it reminds Niko of herself. She looks at Sykosa's breasts to forget it. "Tom sure wanted you to himself fast."

"What're you implying?"

"Hell-o, attitude much?"

She didn't intend to be so bitchy. She noticed Niko noticing her boobs, which's what Niko does, sure, but this is why the Academy thinks they're gay. *I looked, too, didn't I?* As she does again, glaring at Niko's enormous bush. *Maybe I'm why everyone thinks we're gay.* Or maybe she's in regression and now, despite a year of independence, she wants Niko3.0 to go 2.0 and steal her back. Too bad, it's too late, as Niko's covered her snatch with boy-cuts that say *Speed Racer* on the ass.

"Tom asked me to go to Prom."

Like a best friend, Niko's suspicious. "Did you bring it up?"

"No."

"He just asked?"

"Yes."

"Wow, I wonder why he did that."

"I don't know, he did. He said that, like, he wants everyone to know we're seeing each other, even Mackenzie."

"That's what you wanted, right?"

"Yes."

"Well, he's your knight in shining armor..." Niko lets the words trail off to see what response might surface. "So?"

"I moved my stuff to his room."

"You did?"

She stands there, vulnerable, and receives only a look that feels sorta mixed. Like, "I'm happy, but I'm sad," and, "I'll miss you and I love you," but, "I want you to be happy and I'll support you no matter what." To ice the discomfort, she hides behind the shower door, a silhouette like Niko. When she pulls the nozzle, four showerheads, situated at different heights and angles, kinda help it slip away and her hands peacefully work conditioner into her hair like two sticks starting a fire.

It helps.

"I love these shower heads."

"I've taken showers in there that've lasted an hour."

"Oh, I believe it!"

"Try turning the top one to rain."

"How do I do that?"

"The controllers are on the wall."

She finds the electric keypad. "If I die, leave me in here!"

"If you're gonna die, you need the 411 on Clyde first." This is another best friend thing. Niko provides boy bulletins. "While you were off with Tom, he was talking about you. He said you were hot, so he might make a move tonight."

"He mentioned he might play some songs for me."

"If you listen, tell him it's good or you'll be sorry!"

She shouts. "I know! He blew up at me for no reason!"

"Be warned, it gets worse!"

She laughs. "Whatever."

For Niko, that "whatever" didn't sounds like "whatever." It was like, "Clyde doesn't matter, my mind is 100% made up." That turns Niko protective, like she wants to steal Sykosa back. It might seem confusing, but Niko never thought Sykosa would actually have sex. Even ten seconds ago, she had her doubts. *Sykosa can't open a can of Spaghetti-Os, but she's gonna have sex?* The notion of it was too absurd to take seriously and suddenly too scary to contemplate.

"Are you sure about Tom?"

Yes. "Why? What do you mean?"

Niko is annoyed. "You don't owe him anything."

"Yes, I do."

Simple truth, she owes him.

Last year, he saved her. And got all his scars. Tonight, she imagines she'll get her own. *Don't be so crazy! You're every guy's worst nightmare!* Cause here she is under this miracle of warmth, unable to accomplish the simplest of tasks. It's weird her vanity chose now to disappear. Like it matters. He probably won't notice if she's not extra special. *But, I will.* It's enough to get her started. Her heel rests on that same triangle to lather her sloping thigh, then slide that same razor, careful around her knee, and bent over like a sack to her ankles. Her armpits are next and lastly she touches up the "big one."

She feels slightly better.

If the blackness ruins my first time, I'll hate myself.

Since her eyes are on her pussy, she might as well note that, while her bush was never as industrious as Niko's, it was still its own masterpiece. A black turf like an island all her own. It was big, strong, and sometimes it made her hungry. She thinks that'd be something Tom'd be interested in, yet she just knew he wasn't, and that she had to shave it. It went beyond intuition. It was observation. You see, Tom likes Mackenzie, and last year, on swim team, she saw tons of Mackenzie's vag.

And it's bald.

Ah, nothing is getting done!

The water dies in drips and she smacks her hands against her hips (nothing jiggled!) to reach out from behind the door. Her voice echoes like a walkie-talkie. "Can I have a towel?"

"You're so private! It's not like I'm a dyke or anything."

"I wish I could be so sure!"

"What?"

"Nothing, I was kidding."

"Don't say that, that's disgusting what you said."

"I'm sorry. I'm not comfortable like you are, ya know?"

"Yeah, it's cause my mom took me backstage to those shows when I was young. It's not cause I'm a carpet muncher."

Time to move on. (Before you see some unflattering stuff about Niko). Still, Niko's reaction is defendable, as Niko's equally bothered by the gay rumors. What bothers Niko more is how a few shitty rumors have altered their entire friendship. It's not worth hashing out at her cottage, so Niko provides a towel, then skips (boobs in skip with her) to the red icebox. Seconds later, there's the clank of a bottle and two shot glasses, which Niko bobbles as her foot kicks shut the fridge.

"What's that?"

"Grey Goose, I wanted us to drink together."

"Vodka straight?" Not her style, but it's booze and maybe, like her wine, it'll wake her from this lethargy. She hesitates, though. It was a tough night of partying, and it'll be tougher still. Her mind changes when, at her overnight bag, she sees her turquoise undies. *Oh yeah, I'm losing my virginity.* "Pour me a shot!" At the very least, it'll dull the blackness. Once she's in her undies, and covered up by a cami, she slams the drink. It tastes like nothing until her throat gags as it back spills over her tongue and burns out her nostrils. "I shoulda chased that."

"A-haha! I love you, Sykosa."

It was Niko, but she heard Tom, and her privates contracted at it. That's embarrassing. It's also progress. Perhaps this, further alcohol consumption and her panties will build the momentum and then, like, her vanity will be here. By the way, her shot glass is full—bottoms up! to inebriation, to watch Niko chug the bottle like a street wino. She wants to tell Niko to slow down. She tells herself to "shut up, please" and her self-centered moping retreats.

And she remembers!

Niko needs her own boy bulletin.

"You don't think Scott's gonna show up tonight, do you?"

"Not if he knows what's good for him."

"I was shocked to see him. It's been so long."

"You were shocked? I nearly fought him."

"I'm glad we'll have fun without him, but I wanted to ask, does Timmy know him?"

"No."

Interesting, cause she swore the person holding Niko back was Timmy and that he seemed apologetic, and not to Niko, but to Scott. "Why were they talking?"

"I don't know."

"Don't you think that—"

Niko interrupts. "It was a party, people talk. Beside, he

already agreed never to talk to Scott again."

"Cool, I just don't want anything to happen, you know?"

"I know, I know!"

Scott is a stressful topic. He also brings on the blackness.

I should've remembered that.

It's easier to cope now that another shot prances numb feet about her cheeks while she stares at Niko's still topless body, particularly at the sparkles lining Niko's neck. *You know, we're not gay. People just like to see people naked.* (So begins a long evening of drunk talk). Who knows when Niko attached it, but its chain is a white gold with randomly set diamonds until the dip in her collar where more diamonds—of different shapes, spaces, and angles—bunch like a bouquet. The price tag is beyond sanity and, outside of her 7, it's Niko's prize possession.

"Your necklace is even more beautiful than usual."

"I totally forgot!" Niko nearly drops the bottle, but saves it, drinks from it, then leaves it on the counter as she scurries to a closet where she removes a jewelry box from a safe. "I took this from the vault when I found out you were coming."

It's a gold necklace with a giant rock at her breastplate.

"I can't wear this."

"Oh, good, you like it!"

"Of course I like it, but—"

Niko interrupts. "Just when you go to sleep, put it in your pocket or in the safe. It'll lock when you close it."

It's cold on her chest. And it feels heavier than her breasts. *I look...beautiful.* She feels guilty as this entire time Niko was being her best friend and... *I was being a jerk.* "I'm sorry I did not want to ask my father to come this weekend."

"It's alright."

"It's been fun, and this place is great, and I'm happy we've spent time together. And I know Tom feels the same way, too."

"Tom's a nice guy. I mean, he's an idiot, but as far as boys go, I suppose he's almost good enough for you. I remember how messed up he was after that fight last year, at least—at least he cared, and he's always dashing into the fray like some hero!"

Two things. 1) She finds it both strange and expected that Niko would say this. There is always a .01% factor of zero logic in Niko think. 2) "Dashing into the fray" is the right way to say it, so much so that even Niko—a woman full of sycophantic tendency—cannot deny him such prestige. Okay, three things. 3) Subconsciously, she fetched her #10 foundation and has already turned half her face flawless. And 4) Thank heavens this topic has been brought up.

She needs to talk about sex.

"I gotta confess something."

"What?"

Her wrists are inverted on the counter, and her shoulders are perked like indecision. She gets a peek at Niko that, like Kana occasionally does, stops time. Niko has collapsed in a wicker chair, her left leg laid provocatively over the seat arm, her calf swinging like some bored goddess—her servants fanning her browned body and eyeing the areolas of her bare breasts. For some reason, she mentally disrobes Niko's bottoms, to see that same bush, except this time it stretches to the floor and intermixes with the vines hanging from the ceiling.

"It's that lately—"

Niko interrupts. "Can I ask you a leading question?"

Yeah, that's Intro to Law talking. "Sure."

"Why're you sure Tom wants to have sex with you? I mean, I know you guys were fooling around, but it's—"

She interrupts. "That's what I wanted to confess."

"*What?*"

"I have, uh...'worked'..." Her hands make quotations. It's cute. "...him...to..." And one more time! "...'completion.'"

Niko is slack jawed. "You've actually, like, touched it?"

"Yeah."

"I can see why you're worried."

"You can?"

"Oh yeah, they get a taste of that and it's over."

Maybe she shoulda talked to Niko a long time ago. And the fact she didn't... *It's over, isn't it?* This is now a world where she jerks Tom's dick. If she—for instance—quit swim team, she quit swim team. She can't quit Tom's dick. It's something she's done. It's permanent. Wow, what a lot to take in. And it takes her to the chapel, to the times he's asked her for her hand. *I don't mean marriage.* He's so persistent. He plows through all the potential consequences. His tunnel vision is awful.

And such a turn-on. At least for her.

"Is it a boy thing for them to get weird when they're turned on, but when it's over, they're normal again?"

Niko takes a big slug off the bottle. "I think I've determined it's caused by these damn pornos they watch."

Tom watches... "Porn?"

"Yeah."

Yeah, she knew that, or she figured it.

Mike Holler's old gang convinced her all boys watch porn.

"Yeah, but maybe it's—"

Niko interrupts. "It's not like the one I own."

Surprise! Niko owns a porno where women have sex with men they just met. It's hidden in her closet with her dildo.

"It's not?"

Niko moves to the edge and hunkers her shoulders. "Timmy showed me a tape where a girl sucked off a bunch of guys, and they, I don't know, shot on her."

"Oh."

"Now that's all he wants—on my face too."

She also knows about that.

It's outside of her sexual repertoire, but when Donna found out Niko's plan to start the Queens, she instantly dubbed them the "Bukkake Queens," a name which has stuck and has been used to describe both Niko and herself.

That said, it's gross.

"You don't let him do that, do you?"

Niko's quick. "Of course not."

A little too quick. "Niko, you didn't really let him..."

"I said I didn't, didn't I?"

Then, Niko breaks into giggles.

She's played this game long enough to know where it goes.
"He has done it?"

Niko collects herself, turning a bit smug. "Hazu used to do it all the time."

Not a surprise. There's nothing Niko won't do for Hazu.

"That's so gross, Niko!"

"You wouldn't understand." Is all Niko says and all Niko offers. "My turn! How many handjobs?"

"Two."

"That's all he's asked for?"

"No, that's all I've given him."

"Has he fingered you?"

She tightens up. "I'm not answering that."

Tons of people would read that as, "Yes." Niko knows it's, "No." "You're gonna sleep with a guy you won't let finger you?"

"I don't see them as one and the same."

"You don't want to feel good?"

"I don't see sex as being about feeling good."

"What's it about?"

Love. "I don't know! Stop it with the questions already!"

Niko hands over the bottle.

"Then, don't worry over Timmy. He's a sweetheart."

"No, he isn't."

"You said it yourself, he goes back to normal."

So she did. "Makes you wonder if it's worth it."

The statement is immense and of no more importance than the fresh cigarette between her fingertips. She is too drunk to stand, and she sits on the floor, half of her horrified and the rest absent. Unable to resist the fear that last year will replicate itself. Maybe for the guilt. Maybe for the pain. Maybe as an excuse to visit the stall in the secret bathroom again. Although, one has to argue, eventually, negativity becomes the appropriate lens. But, it's too late. She remembers Niko with Scott, Hazu, and Timmy, then remembers her own boy, her test score, and how, last year, he bled on the Academy floor, beaten nearly to death, and it's...

The strain of inevitability.

(Or as she knows it: the "pull.")

That means she's going to * him. Her mind has already made the decision and this is the part where she freaks out.

The big bash will commence soon. She needs to get ready.

The anger surfaces slightly. She plays it off as discontent, or boredom, or "being a girl." Typically, this provokes the Pep Squad. Perhaps her breath might be heavy. Her eyesight could mix. Then, behind the chapel, she can rebel with him. She thinks again of Niko3.0's big, hairy overcompensation. *Can you keep a secret?* Niko2.0 had no bush. She was bare, as was Mackenzie, and all the Bitches. *I did it, too.* It was a Rule. Cause Donna was primarily a drug addict, but she was also a pervert. *And she made Niko do some...uncool stuff.* So you can see why she thought the density of Niko's bush meant something, that her own meant something.

She sees things clearer now.

Shave your crotch. Don't shave your crotch.

Wear makeup. Don't wear makeup.

Dress up or dress down.

It's all the
    @@rf

same. And her desire...her need to make it make sense, to make it focus, is false.

Tom fucked me a year ago.

She was too selfish to let him do it. And the void inside her is a void because her virginity, outside of her intact hymen, no longer exists. It belongs to him.

And he deserves it like he always wanted it.

From a girl who loves him.

From a girl who lusts for him.

From a girl who would die for him.

She knows it now.

Tonight, I'm gonna be pretty.

Just-you-watch.

XI.

Yeah, vanity won.

Got her to get that rosiness on her cheeks, that obedience in her hair, lips lined in that shiny shade of fruity pink, nails painted like cherry blossoms and dressed in a skirt which stops far short of her knees, strappy sandals and a white formfitting long-sleeve that's too long in the sleeve. It bunches at her wrists in a way that makes her appear clumsy and child-like while the neckline dips in a near fatal *v* like a runway to her chest. In fact, it seems, be it clothing or carriage, she's become obsessed with the presentation, or the various color schemes, of flesh itself.

That is for later, however.

For now, she sits in a French Provincial loveseat, trimmed and legged in mahogany and upholstered in a textured fabric of white flower bouquets. Lost in the glare of a fifty-some inch TV with peculiar dimensions. Niko says it's a "widescreen." It's supposed to be a big deal, but as far as she can tell, it turns thin people fat.

Click!

Past CNN, MSNBC, Mtv and E!

Unable to find a program nearly as interesting as the show playing within her gaze. Tom and Mackenzie standing by a keg, driven in from town, which rests in a steel tub amongst pounds of ice. "M, can you believe it? I told her I loved her!" "She believed you?" "Yeah, she totally bought it!" "Tom, I can't wait until we're finished destroying Sykosa's life, then we can be together." "I can't wait, either." That was the conversation in her brain, and it is with the blackness. It's circulating inside of her. An anxiety she is too practiced to let show on her face. *When did I become so practiced?* It goes unanswered, as the whole thing is overplayed. It's unlikely Tom's saying anything of the sort. In fact, his mood appears somber, and whatever's happening, Mackenzie's not happy about it.

Good.

She'd continue watching, but she cannot. Clyde's sat beside her, his dirty hand brushing her knee. She pulls back, taken aback and frankly tired of his frankness. His response is to smile that smile that's bound to work on some girl tonight. For his sake, she hopes said girl is over eighteen.

He persists. "Are you drunk?"

"No."

"I thought Niko and you might have started early."

"No."

"Is that what you guys usually do for parties?"

"No."

He sits back nervously. "Well, I just finished putting stuff away for the party."

That is true.

The cleared out bookshelves are two shades of exposed and dusty brown, the priceless art is stored, and large furniture blockades certain sectors of the cottage. It's left her feeling slimy. She doesn't know why. No wait. *I do*. Niko's parties are better described as mini-riots, and while she's accustomed to Niko closing off her mansion in Seattle, she's unaccustomed to the sight of it here.

"This party sounds big, even for Niko's standards."

"Sure, of course."

"Sometimes Niko gets caught up in this stuff, and she doesn't think straight, ya know?"

"Don't worry, it's taken care of, everything's gonna be fine." He looks at her eyes and finds himself hypnotized by her concern. "I think I've figured it out!"

"What?"

"You're, like, Niko's conscience!"

Lord knows, Niko needs one—pronto. Not to say she doesn't trust Niko—of course, she trusts Niko, she just doesn't trust Niko. She doesn't trust Clyde either; however, he isn't privileged enough to know what, or what not, to lie about. He has also adjusted in his chair as if her tits were in his face. For good reason, she adjusted in her chair, cause her tits were in his face. She leans back, then she blinks below, to see what she never considered. The chain of her necklace also forms a v and the rock is centered above her nipples. She looks to his eyes to see him in a panning stare of her crotch, then her legs, then her breasts.

It's awkward.

She waits anyhow, until he has finished undressing her.

Any second now.

Annnnnnnnnnnnnnnnnnnny second now...

There.

"Clyde, I need to ask you something."

His responses are delayed. "Yes?"

"Do you know this guy Timmy was talking to last night? The one Niko got pissed at?"

"Oh yeah, that guy. What was his name?"

"Scott."

"Yeah, I had just met him, so did Timmy."

"You guys don't know him?"

"No, but he and Timmy were really hitting it off."

"How do you know that?"

"I teased the faggot about it."

"How so?"

"Well, here we are at this great party with all these beautiful girls and he's trading digits with another dude."

"What did Niko say about him doing that?"

"She was pissed! I tell you what, you know Timmy, he's so full of shit—he's so crazy for Niko, she's all he can think about. He had no idea Niko knew that guy."

Alright. Niko's story checks out.

Speak of the devil, Niko plops herself into a low back chair, trimmed and legged in the same mahogany and the same textured fabric. Niko's bored, so she'll fidget until the party starts. "I'm drained and this party hasn't even started. All the swimming and the walking, I have no energy left. *No energy. No energy. No energy.* That could be a song, don't you think?" No one responds. "Forget you guys."

"Ya know, the party, it..." Clyde chokes up on the sofa and produces a few tablets, pharmaceutical in appearance, from his pocket. "...hasn't started yet."

She has done this once.

Niko's done it more. "No shit, I knew you guys could score some! Please, can I have one?"

"Shh, I took these from Timmy's stash. He's been guarding the shit like gold. I only have the three, the third one I was gonna give to him, but I'm gonna let you have it, Sykosa. You tell him and he's gonna get seriously pissed at me."

Niko has already swallowed.

It pressures her. "When we're high, he's gonna notice, no?"

"Yeah, but I won't care then."

He said it directly to her breasts. Never even started at her eyes, or anywhere in the facial region, so while she wants the pill, and what she expects will also be its effective usage as a blackness inhibitor, she ponders its true cost. That word "cost" spikes the blackness momentarily. It curls up her throat like vomit. *Maybe I shouldn't.* Besides, in wake of her concern for the house and Scott, drugs seem irresponsible. It feels like a solid decision, but then her nerves, already fired up over Tom and what might happen tonight, what should happen tonight, what will happen tonight, *what happened last year*, urge her forward. If she swallows it, things'll be less intense—both now and later, when they're alone.

She makes a deal.

"I only want half, not the whole thing."

Clyde seems happy. "Cool, more for me."

The pill is split. By chance, it went 70/30.

She took the 30.

Neither here or there

It's sped up or it's slowed down.

She's at a loss for when these people arrived.

They're in the pool, the lagoon, the hot tubs—some are even on dry land. Leeching on each other's shoulders and pocketbooks. Bumping into her, stabilizing her, handing her drinks, then telling her to take shots. Never mind, she knows these people. They're the Sluts. *We're such better friends when we're wasted.* And none of it comes close to the translucence behind her closed eyes, when her inner-ears skew her balance or whatshit—anatomy, you suck!—and she flies, spins, rides, and the world is the tortoise and her heart races like the...the... rabbit—hare, see here, hare, she meant hare! Damnit, she lost, the tortoise beat her, and the floor beats hip-hop that blares! *All them bitches. All them hoes.* As she hums like a homie and sings like a deaf! She finds this song's message disconcerning, but she's no more concerned than to favor her disconcern over her originally conceived concern of humming, you know, like a hummingbird, breathing the smoky air, and at night, without streetlamps, neon store signs or car headlights, the sky is the darkest shade of black.

Clyde finds her. His eyes are red. "Everything sucks?"

Her foot stomps on the diagonal deck boards. "Everything does! I've never found anything I enjoy! I get up every morning and dread my day. And my dad's an asshole. A major asshole, but my mom's worse."

She bulldozes through topics and he yawns internally. It kills him how girls like Sykosa's tight ass have to be talkative and bitchy like Niko's juicy cunt, and not just Niko, this Asian jailbait—they all come with baggage and it drives him insane! He has pledged such an allegiance, one that says if he were not so damn horny, he'd swear off women, but he is horny and, be it as such, (her legs in that skirt, her breasts in that shirt, *they* do not bore him) these moments have become his favorites. A development in his loins telling him he will sleep with a girl, or at least she'll suck his dick—it's a matter of listening long enough, caring enough, and watching her succumb.

God, he can't wait till he's pile driving her.

The bitch is really asking for it.

He grips her hand and pulls her inside, and she slips through the crowd until she's ordered to sit on a beanbag. She pulls her skirt forward and delicately lays her legs. He has his guitar. *What a cool magic trick!* The case is a worn thing with threads sticking out of it and some bumper stickers that are stuck to it. They read, "Eat Shit" and "Socialism Now!" He sits Indian-style with his instrument (*ah, double entendre!*) in the hammock of his thighs as he toils with his hair between strummed notes and delicate adjustments to the silver tabs.

His hand is blurry across the strings.

Gray skies in my silver tongue
Feeling young in my run with my rum
Over green hills, I see the sun
Believed I was right
Believed you might...

Don't ever think you've got me now
Don't ever think you know me now
Don't ever think you'll win this war
Cause I'm in love and it's just too much

Overcome by rage, I surrender amongst the sage
Feeling of birth, while coasting onto the earth
Rejuvenation comes from an unknown
And I see through the trees
That you still know me
There is nothing we won't do
Nothing we won't say
Darling, ain't it funny
How things end up this way?

Don't ever think you've got me now
Don't every think you know me now
Don't ever think you'll win this war
Cause I'm in love and it's just too much

Because my life you see
Is meant to be, atop a bounty
Of a world brand new
Beyond all constraints...
And in celebration of the one...
Who comes to learn
And to be

Cause I'm in love and it's just too much
I'm in love and it's just too much
In love and it's just too much
It's just too much
Too much

Her mouth's without adjective. Truly one of the most overly stupid tunes. He's possibly the worst songwriter whoever lived and... Who cares about that, it's being sung to. It's having a boy sing to her such gentle words. Like being in the middle of class and receiving a dozen of the reddest roses from Tom...

Tom?

Come to think of it, she hasn't seen him in a while.

Clyde strums his next tune over the synthesized music from a spy video game. The British assassin (under Tom's control and beer-glazed pupils) kills enemy agents with his snappy handgun. Tom cannot concentrate with that moron's guitar playing and his eyes loom from the TV to the beanbags, at a Sykosa ready to fall out of her skirt. He wants the assassin to jump out of the TV screen and shoot Clyde...or at least punch him. He tries not to be jealous like this afternoon when he grabbed her and she got pissed.

It's hard cause he feels...

The assassin bleeds on the television screen.

He throws the controller. "I'm taking a break."

Mackenzie follows him. "Lost your concentration there?"

"Yeah, I guess."

"Well, let's go to the kitchen, get some pizza, and I'll drink beer! Then you'll have three of your favorite things."

"M, you're the greatest."

She spins round, then flings her hair like girls in shampoo commercials do, ready to hang out, but his attention is absent. He watches Sykosa. How she smiles and giggles, how her shirt, at the right angle, partially exposes her breast, but especially at how her mysterious eyes lie beyond her mess of lashes.

Mackenzie is worried. "Are you coming?"

"Uh, yeah, I am." He stops. "Actually, I don't know."

"Tom, about what you said earlier—"

He interrupts. "Can we talk about that tomorrow?"

Tomorrow? "Sure."

He turns towards Sykosa. "Okay."

"Tom!"

He turns towards Mackenzie. "What?"

Mackenzie stares at him, thinking, *She acts different around you.* She's too chicken to say it. "Nothing."

He says a quick goodbye, forgetting how it was he who asked Mackenzie to come when she got pouty about not going, and now he's ditching her as he crosses the room, coming up on Sykosa's rear, aware by her demeanor that she is on more than alcohol. He heard her mumble about ecstasy once.

He stutters, one hand in his pocket. "Sykosa?"

"Oh, Tom, where've you been?"

"Around. Listen, I thought we could hang out."

"Yeah, sure!" She hurries to her feet, then balances against his arm. "Clyde, don't go pass out while I'm gone!"

"I won't."

They end up by a gray post of deck railing, beyond the reach of the wall lanterns, where her free hand desperately clings to his belt loop while she chats him up like a girl. "My God, Tom, there was this girl and she's somewhere at this party, but I swear she looks like garbage. She's got a low-cut shirt, but her boobs are all floppy and under her armpits!" She covers her mouth as if she were surprised at her supreme diss! Returning her hand to the place of origin, his belt loop. "Anyways she's one of those girls who thinks she's so hot and she's totally not. Don't you hate girls like that? But, like, right, she was doing something, what was it?" She stops. And then gives up. "Hm, I don't remember, isn't that funny?"

"What're you on?"

She talks like a doll. "Nooooth-ing."

He whispers. "What did you take?"

"A happy pill."

His fingers play with the edge of her skirt. "Does your happy pill make you happy?"

She recognizes this part. It's when they play. "Yes."

"How happy do you want to get?" He intended that to be a euphemism for sex, so he should seem cool and experienced. He pinches her stomach, so she understands. "Huh?"

She frowns. "Don't do that."

"Why not?"

"Because I'm not supposed to have any fat there."

"It's called skin."

"No, it's fat, but thanks anyway." She shakes her hair and her eyesight gets dizzy. "Wanna kiss?"

He leans in to kiss and kiss and kiss!

(She cannot feel the blackness anymore).

His hands reach to her hips and instruct her off her heels. Stronger. Tighter. To give in and disappear, and she wants to meet her soul mate and love him always. Also play games like these. What're they called? Foreplay. *I'm having foreplay. Little old me, having foreplay.* It sounds strange, but it feels right. And she starts to think devilish thoughts. Like how far could she take him? How many times could she look into him? How often could she smile before his eyes get hungry and his mouth quivers and he breaks down (and he takes her)?

When he will confess such wonderful feelings!

She thinks she better scrunch his shirt and she better play.

Boys are fun. "Say something!"

"I want you."

"What would you give to have me?"
He stutters. "Anything, take it."
"Anything?"
Girls are fun. "Anything."
Oh, that makes her wilt. "What else?"
"I told Mackenzie you're my girlfriend."
She skips a second. Her hair feels fried. "You did?"
"Yeah."
Then, that means he's made a decision.
She sounds very girly and raspy. "When?"
"Before the party, when we were outside together."
That's what he was doing? "You really did that?"
"I don't want to lose you." To Clyde.
"I don't want to lose you either." To Mackenzie.
It's finally fair.
He needs the security she needed all along.

It's left her short of what to do. She no longer feels playful, but she doesn't feel bad. She needs a minute to collect herself. Yep. A minute—during such he holds her. At first, she doesn't comply, standing stiff, but soon his tenderness gets to her. Like, it's been hard. Ignoring some of the careless things he says, or some of his thoughtless behaviors—occasionally, she thought she had hardened to him, that she would never truly feel for him. And like she said, it does take a while, but her arms hold him back, and her shoulders change so that he can position her into his chest. Somehow his heartbeat sounds in rhythm with the music she barely hears. When he separates, her breaths are staggered and her cheeks are bright red.

"I love you."

It's hard to repeat that. It also reminds her of the blackness.

The pill has done its job. She feels it, but doesn't. *Maybe I should use them more often.* Wow, that's a dangerous thought. "You're too nice."

It doesn't detour him. He's looking into her eyes.

"You're gonna be beautiful at Prom."

She hopes so. "We'll see."

"You're so...beautiful. Even now, you're beautiful."

"Oh."

He puts her hair behind her ear, then runs his thumbnail back along her cheek. "I mean it, you're beauti..." He struggles. "I can't think of another word."

She smiles like a goofball.

Translation: You're really beautiful, too.

And he is! Something about how the shadows lie along him has turned an already attractive boy to near perfection. *I can't believe I got a hot boyfriend.* None of the Sluts—or Niko—have ever dated anyone as cute as Tom. It's something she fails to notice about him often enough.

"It's okay."

He's cupped both her cheeks. He seems really nervous.

"Will you follow me some place?"

"Yeah, where?"

"It's a place for you and me."

"Okay."

He's less nervous now, and holding her hand as they go.

On the way, she looks back to see that the cottage, save window slits of manufactured yellow, has disappeared into the night. Her heels are stuck in the soft ground and her ankle rolls onto its side. She tells him they should go back. She'll sprain her ankle. "We should go back. I feel like I'm going to sprain my ankle." "We can't." She wonders why not. "Why not? Let's go to the room." "The hallway's blocked." That's true. He insists they're close. "We're close, it's there." He stops at some equally spaced trees, which means they haven't left Niko's property. He already has a blanket hidden and, before he unfolds the sea green fleece, he tosses aside what rocks and woodchips are on the ground. After he assists her to her ass, and she is busy verifying all her parts are covered, he gets a small cooler.

There's beer inside.

He's opened one for her and it tastes good going down.

"Can we try something?"

"What?"

"I wanna try the thing where we lock arms and drink from the bottle."

He's disappointed. He'd hoped she meant to try something with his penis, but he notices that locking arms will give him a bird's eye view of her breasts. He does love her breasts. So much so he can't both focus on them and drink. They mess it up and she laughs. Subsequent tries are also a disaster, but they figure it out when he grabs ahold of her butt to hold himself steady. She's enthused by his hand and how it grabs her butt. No shame. Smack! Grab her butt. Eventually, the attempts to drink topple her to the blanket. On her back, her head is leaned to the side, as he's on his side, they stare each other in the eyes while he again tells her how beautiful she is.

During this, his hand exposes her stomach, then his palm gently moves about it. It stretches all the way around to her back, splits her breasts and caresses her neck, then follows a path along her side to her knee, to return to her stomach and brush up against the underwire of her bra. It's kind of a tease. And it's a bit frustrating after a few minutes, as her breasts have become enraged by his denials, but it's helped by his long kisses. Even those only work less, as his conquest is now her skirt, which when returning from her knee, he either A) drags it up one millimeter, or B) reaches deeper into her thighs.

It's starting to get to her. She thinks dirty thoughts.

Like, what if she made his face her pillow? Would he like it? *Should I say that?* Instead, his hand gets so close to her vagina that she contracts. She knows what to say. "You're not supposed to touch that."

He smiles. "Oh, yes I am."

He kisses her.

She waits until he's done before responding. "Uh-uh, not unless I say."

It's almost too late. His pointer and middle fingers trace the outsides of the turquoise. He gets so deep he feels the fabric's edge. She looks up—his elbow is at a hard angle and the last she sees of him is his wrist. *Oh, my God, a boy's gonna touch my vagina.* The anticipation mixed with the fear, or the blackness, mixed with the desire almost causes her to kick her hips to help him out. But, she forces the energy into her stomach—where she restrains it, including her breath, while his hand fully distributes itself upon the entirety of her twat.

It feels like he's about to boost her onto a chair.
Then, it feels like a million miles per hour.
She moans. "Uggggggggggggggggggg-h!"
She covers her mouth in embarrassment.
She had no choice. He "tugged" at her and...
It was the right part to tug.
He looks her in the eyes. Then, he tugs again.
"Mmmmmfffffphhhh!"
And he tugs again and again.
Her neck snaps. "Ohhh—HHHHhaaaaahhh!"
He gets it. And continues.

It weakens her hips and her legs wobble, opening. He moves on the invitation, and she welcomes it, if she could speak. Or concentrate. His tugs are uneven. They put pleasure deep in her vagina, then around her inner right thigh, her tummy, her left arm or...well, sometimes they don't do anything at all. He tugs and she feels nothing. Either way, it's too scattered, and it's... She grabs his wrist, then with force, moves him north an inch and left a centimeter and... Oh, much better. That's much, much better. More like a dome, encasing her hips, radiating like warm, tingly pulses. Soon, it's not localized enough, so she drags him two millimeters down, a tad right, a tad left, right again, and again, right, there, there, right there right

There there there there!
"Oh, Tom. Oh, oh, ah, oh."
He had no idea she was a moaner.
"I told you you'd like it."
"Ugh. Ugh. Ugh. Oh, Tom. Tom, ugh."
"Just keep going? Like this?"

It's so good she forgets about her directions and throws back her arms. In all the times she's... "Oh, ah! Ahhhh! Ugh! Ugh!"

...masturbated, she's never felt... "Ko. Ka. Ah! Ah! Ah! a-H!" ...like this, it's never been... He decides he's a professional and digs behind her panties where his finger rubs her like a floor waxer. It hurts and he lost the spot. It's gone. Along with the pleasure in her body. It just turned off. Or reset. She doesn't know. But, he's not done. Too happy, he's touching her pussy all over, every part of it, including when he nestles his fingers against her entrance, like he might finger her. *I take it back, that feels good.* But, she takes hold of him, then looks at him in a way that says it's over. "You can stop." He retrieves his hand and she closes shop, wrapping his fingers in her own.

He has a request.

"Do you mind if I see it?"

"See what?"

"I wanna look at it."

Oh... Maybe later. She wants to cuddle!

She shakes her head. "No, come here."

For her, that's it. She may have moved into his bedroom and sent out a thousand signals and hallelujah! for her lack of specifics. She won't have sex. This was too special.

He has a different opinion. "That's it?"

That's it? "I let you touch it. You've been dying to do that." His prick presses against her. *Oh, yeah.* What a poor boy, he thought she would forget him. *He's so cute!* She sits up and acts goofy. She feels goofy. It's strange, but... She wants to jerk him off! She wants to see him squirm, moan, then come all over the place. She can't wait. So she gives him a determined look as she rolls her sleeves up her forearms, then collects her hair in a tail that is held in place by a tie from her wrist. She smacks like the bubblegum of a truck stop waitress. "One handjob coming up! Come on, off with yer pants!"

His head hits the ground with a thud. His expression looks like he knew this would happen and he's fed up with her. He wonders why he is so unlucky with girls.

He releases her hand.

"Are you pretending we weren't gonna do it?"

Never mind, maybe she doesn't want to jerk him off.

Just like before, she's reset.

The goofy energy has become pouty. And the blackness has become large. *I'm letting him down.* After last year, after all he did... *I need to be better. I need to.* Her fingers met in her lap. They pick at her nails. "It's not you or anything."

He asks a dumb question.

"Do you have fun with me?"

It hurts her feelings. *Why're you implying?* "Yeah, I do."

He talks like he didn't hear her. "I mean, when I was at your house, and we were at your bedroom door, or in the field... I want you so much. More than I've ever wanted anyone."

That's so sweet. "I've seen that sometimes—"

He interrupts her. "Are you mad at me?"

What? "Mad?"

"For what happened... You were having such a good time and then I—"

She interrupts him this time. "No, Tom. That was great."

"It was?"

"Yes, I had no idea that could even happen."

He looks confused. "So, we should do it, right?"

She tries to see his eyes. He's hiding them. She adjusts her position so she is closer to him, then she tries to reach him, but it feels like she's failing. The physical symptoms are here. She struggles for air. "Tom, it's not... I just gave you a handjob last week and now we're at sex? Is that normal?"

Then, he becomes mean.

"Sykosa, who gives a fuck about normal?" Her head bows. One of her oversized sleeves un-bunches to her wrist. He stays quiet and counts the stars—pissed off at himself. He shouldn't have said the f-word. It came out wrong. *God, whenever I'm around her, I feel like I need to apologize up front.* He doesn't apologize, only couples his ankles, one foot straight up and the other skewed left, to straighten out his back. His voice relaxes, and he speaks fluidly, trying to show it was something beyond his control. "See that in the corner?"

"See what?"

"That *W* looking thing. Do you see it?"

She fears, if she looks up, the blackness will commandeer her gyroscope and she may fall over. She doesn't, but she does feel a tad of vertigo looking at the sky. "Cassiopeia?"

"You know that constellation?"

She laughs. "Duh, I took astronomy with you last year!"

He thinks about it. "Yeah, we didn't know each other yet."

The laugh ends up being mutual. After it's done, she feels the need to cuddle again. This time, he's receptive, so she nestles into his shoulder and lays one leg over his own. And remembers her trick, *Relax*. They lay silently. He finishes up one of the beers. She has her eyes closed. He's gotten her to thinking—visualizing, actually. Of being at her bedroom door, or in the field, or in the cottage, but also of their first kiss, and the first time he told her she was pretty, the first moment she felt herself falling in love and the moment right before she did.

She goes back through all her memories.

All the way until she reaches last year.

Then, she shuts down.

Relax.

"Tom, why did you come behind the chapel a few months ago? I mean, we'd never been close and then you were there."

He knows why he came. To kiss her. That's what he did. He told himself to be a man, go behind that chapel and do it. "I don't know. Before I went, every time I would see you, I had to have you. You were so stunning and... I mean, I had to... I felt like you weren't safe if I wasn't watching you."

Well, he's got a point about that.

She forgets it. "How did you remember my room so well?"

"That was easy."

It was? "What was your favorite part about it?"

"Being on your bed."

"Why?"

"Because I want to have sex in it."

It makes her laugh. He's so weird sometimes.

She gets quiet, satisfied with his answers.

He's not satisfied, however. He wants her to continue talking about fucking. If he can't get any, then hearing her cute voice speak of cocks, cunts, and cum is a fine substitute. He'd also consider it a personal triumph if he can get her to talk about blowjobs. And if she'd consider eating the cum off her hand after she gives him a handjob. That would, like, make every bad thing that's ever happened to him okay.

Also, it'd be nice if she'd give him that handjob.

He'll gladly accept it now.

"What do you think it will be like? When you have it?"

"I don't know."

He interrupts. "You don't think about it?"

All the time. "Sometimes."

He's put his hand in his hair. "You're so innocent. How can you not think of it?"

That kind of annoys her. Her voice is a crack catty. Also, she has a bit of a headache. "I'm not all that innocent. I've seen a porno. I know how it works, okay?"

Never mind. This is better than blowjobs.

She watches porn!

"Which one?"

A weak ass one, according to Niko. "What do you mean?"

"What was it called?"

She's confused. "Pornos have titles? Like movies do?"

"Yeah."

She laughs again, then lifts a hand to God. "Why would you title a porno? It's porn."

"Well, they come in volumes, like one, two, three. So, like..."

Her same hand storms his eyes, fingers lined one against the other in the symbol for STOP—not entirely ready to learn the grim reality of pornography and men. "I was getting by fine without knowing the titles." He has indeed stopped. And she realizes she's freezing. She rolls the blanket over her, then rolls onto him, so her stomach is atop his, and her chin rests on his breastplate. She looks into his eyes. "What was I saying?"

He teases her. "You were saying how porn titles upset you."
Her face scrunches thin in agitation. "Before that."
"Oh, about how you think about sex 'sometimes.'"
Oh, yes. That.

She can tell her discretion is bothering him. She supposes she gets it. And in its own way, this conversation is necessary. It's clear he needs to talk about sex in this relationship. It's suffocating him that he can't, and even when he does, he can't get a straight answer from her. *We can't do anything together if I won't be honest.* She thinks if she needs to hear the titles, she will. Or answer his ridiculous questions, she'll do that, too. Plus, it'll keep her mind occupied by him. That's a good thing. If he gets the opportunity, she imagines he'll manage to steal her, like he always does behind the chapel.

She gives no emotion with her face. "I think about it. I do."
"What do you think about?"
She's not answering that.
"What do you think I think about?"
Here is it!
"Do you think about giving blowjobs?"
Yes. "Yes."

The following conversation is better stated in a paragraph.

He asks if she thinks about blowjobs often, if she'd give one on her knees, if she would give one in a car, in a movie theater, in her bedroom, at a party, in a pool, before classes, after classes, between classes, would she swallow or would she spit. He wants to know if she masturbates, how she does it, where she does it, and if she'll do it for him. Then, he says: "*Barely Legal*," "*Gangbang Girl*," and, "the one with Pamela Anderson and Tommy Lee." He explains: "The girls do everything." "The camera gets it." "It's called the Money-shot." "Yes." "Yes." "*No.*" The porn talk goes on until, kinda out of nowhere, he asks if she's ever gone panty-less to school, would she let a boy give her a breast examination, could he finger her at a dinner table, and would she ever strip for a guy.

If for some reason you need to know, her responses were:

Yes. No. Yes. No. Yes. Yes. Yes. No. No. No. Doesn't know. Yes. "I don't want to say what, but I do use something to help me." "In my bedroom." "Someday." "I don't get what Barely Legal means." "Okay, so in a gangbang, there's only one girl and a lot of guys?" "The Pamela Anderson one? I heard about that." "Do all the girls have sex?" "And the camera always gets the guy going inside her?" (And since Niko put the thought in her head). "Do the guys, like, cum on the girls?" "On their faces?" (And since the Academy is convinced Niko and her are lesbians). "Do you watch girls have sex together?" "Do you watch guys having sex together?" Then: Yes. Yes. No. Yes.

She tried to hide her fascination at the porn talk.

It's really taboo—so it's interesting to hear about.

It also makes her forget the blackness.

A time later, she unfastens her bra so he can perform a breast examination. In determining her good health, he pushes them, pulls them, circles them, grabs the nipples, jiggles them, enters into a prolonged dialogue with them, and in general, makes a total ass of himself. In order for him to do so, she put her arms on either side of him and lifted herself like she were doing a girl's push-up. It allows her to lower her breasts onto his face, then per his request, shake them. When he's done, he looks like he's gotten the best Christmas gift ever. She feels happy. Santa knows, she wishes she had something that made her that happy.

Here comes the part she wasn't expecting.

She's convinced—100% positive—all this has satisfied him and he could have no further energy for sex, so it's quite a surprise when he says, "We should have sex."

Somewhere in her brain, she's learning. This moment will be the rest of her life, with Tom or anyone. Constantly fighting off advances. Just when she suspects she's in the clear...pow! Like a train wreck, it's about his penis.

She's putting a bra strap over her shoulder. "What?"

He sits up, then stares. His hands are out. "No games. No nothing. Let's just do it and get it done. It's too much pressure with all the build up. Let's just...and be done."

She puts in place her other strap. "Tom, I don't think—"

He interrupts. "Don't worry, we'll do it slowly."

You should do it. Stop being selfish.

She doesn't listen. "Tom—"

He interrupts. "I'm serious—relax and don't think about it."

She looks out into the trees in the distance. She thinks about it. And she needs an answer. "Why do you want to do this?"

"I love you."

Such a dirty trick, she's annoyed. "Tom—"

He interrupts again. "I didn't want to say it. I wasn't going to, but I do. I love you. I loved you ever since—"

She interrupts. "I know."

"Then, what's the problem?"

It's that her headache has been accompanied by a panic she contains. *Why're you waiting? Just do it.* "It's just..."

She stops herself.

She sees his hand. It's odd. She saw it on her breasts, but she didn't see what she sees now. *The scars.* She knows he's telling the truth. He does love her. It isn't a matter of that. Nor is it that the blackness is here. The pills... They made her forget it, but they also made her more susceptible. She's further along in the process than she realizes. *Stop being so useless.* These thoughts are only somewhat darker than the pool of blood he left behind that day. And it brings some perspective. What did he say? The games? He's right. Her behavior only makes sense to her since only she knows of the blackness. To him, she's screwing with him. As she knows, and he knows she knows, it's not sex he needs to talk about, it's last year. He needs to talk about the scars and Donna and Mackenzie and Mike and all the details stuck permanently in his head.

Like a selfish brat, she hasn't let him. It's too painful.

He's talking again and holding her hand. "We're supposed to be together, Sykosa."

This isn't her story. This isn't her life.

Actually, it is. I totally agree with him.

Her face is distressed. "I know we are, Tom, I know it. It's not about that."

"That day, last year, I knew I had to save you."

She whines. "I know."

"I was scared, but I knew it. I knew it."

She whines more. Her vision gets splotched. "I know."

"When I think of it, when I see—"

She interrupts. "Okay."

He's confused. "What?"

She looks at him plainly. "Okay."

"You'll do it?"

"Yes."

"Really?"

She won't lose to the blackness with him here, nor will she give him a moment's thought that when he saved her, he didn't actually save her. That part of her was gone. She won't put it in his head, not when it's so important to him that it not be in hers. And, by the way, who's to say. Maybe he wants sex for a reason(s). Maybe they're the same reasons she wore this shirt, shaved her pussy, asked her parents if she could come here—all for him, so he can get better. Maybe her vagina can fix what her cowardly love cannot, and he deserves to be fixed, even at her expense.

If you were there when it happened, you'd understand.

I gotta do this.

She looks at him plainly again. "Do you want me to take off my clothes? Or do you want to do it?"

"No, I can do it."

He moves toward her. She holds out her hand. "Take off my shoes, alright?"

"I won't forget your shoes."

His lips brush her lips. She doesn't kiss back. If she starts to feel, she'll get overwhelmed, and he'll be upset again. She tells herself: *Don't feel.* And: *Just do it.* She's motionless while he undoes the straps of her shoes, then allows him to grab her shirt, her arms above her and the cotton catching her hair.

She screeches! He crawls into his shell.

"Actually, can I leave it on? It's cold."

He nods, yet says, "Will you take off your bra?"

That annoys her. *It'll be over soon.*

Arms inside her shirt, she pulls out her bra before reaching inside the top. By accident, her breasts fall out the bottom. It stirs him and he bunches the loose fabric at her sides. She's frozen. So is he. Until, in concert, her arms mindlessly lift and the fabric lies inside out on the ground. *Okay, that was weird.* She pats down her hair, watches as he removes his own shirt, then touches his chest before she lies on her back, elbows dug into the ground, to elevate her butt and allow those hands to bunch her skirt with her panties, then—as one unit—strip both down her thighs, past her adjoined knees, towards her ankles and, afterwards, he stares between the small gap in her legs.

She prefers he not make a total ass out of himself.

"Are we going to do it?"

He nods, then removes his pants, then reaches in his pants. He's holding a condom.

"Just give me a second."

She hears the aluminum seal rip and feels better. At least he's still protecting her, still worrying. *Don't think. Don't feel.*

"It's good that you brought it."

He seems good at getting it on. It only takes him a second. He's near her again, trying to separate her legs only to find a lifetime of negative reinforcement has flooded her. (As a little girl, every time she sat or lay, her mother hit her thigh and told her to keep her legs crossed). She cannot open them. She cannot even breathe. The fuzzy vision is full on. She only kinda makes him out.

I can't do this.

He whispers. "It's alright, there's nothing to worry about."

He succeeds since her muscles have turned to jelly. She stares at what hangs between his legs, black in the night. It looks bigger than it felt. The thought scares her. *Shut up, it'll be over soon.* His hand has taken it, then lowered it; and that does it. Now a penis has touched her vagina. It scares her, and she looks away. *Don't think. Don't think.* He pushes her lips apart and she pays attention to every part of her body but it. He digs further, inward and she scrunches her cheeks. *You're not a slut. He's earned it.* That thought accomplished the opposite of its intent. It lets loose the blackness to parade around. It's not... It's not like usual. The drugs, or the alcohol, like before, it's put, like, a padded wall between it and... *Shut up.* Shutting up returns her to her vagina, where his digging is now pushing, and his pushing is quick and jaded. *It's just a penis. That's all. It's nothing else.* He's making progress, yet still struggles. A tear is down her cheek. He's too preoccupied to notice, and she wipes it away.

I don't want this.

"Stop!"

He does as he is told. "What?"

She breathes heavily. She feels stupid. *It's not about you. It's about him.* She finds resolve. "Nothing, keep going." He's against her entrance again. He's having difficulty again. *It'll be over soon.* She closes her eyes. Tries to count to ten. Ignore the blackness. *Stay disconnected.* Her throat burns. *Why can't he hurry up?* With every false entrance, she becomes less confident in the procedure. Let something *in* her? What crazy idiot thought that was any way to reproduce? She pulls back her soaked hair. Maybe her sweat, maybe his. No, it's tears. She's crying.

I don't want to. I don't!

"Stop!"

"What is it?"

Again she gasps for breaths between words. "Can't I just jerk you off or something?"

"What?"

"I'll give you a blowjob. You've never had that before."

A bit to her surprise, he agrees.

She sits up and wipes her eyes. She does it in that quick way which makes it look like something got in her eyes and not that she was crying. He's on his knees and he asks what he should do with the condom. She looks at him confused. It's gone. Once it is, she stabilizes herself against his stomach, and leaning over from her own knees, puts his penis in her mouth. He moans instantly. She tries to go as fast as she can, but her teeth brush against him every fourth movement. That's wrong. To fix it, she tucks in her chin and opens her jaw until it pops, then flexes her lips a tight seal. He gets even louder with his moans. Her tongue gets salty. She thinks it means he's ready to go, so she goes faster, but nothing happens until he uses her hand to jerk him off. That makes sense, and she does it herself. He must be close. He sounds like this behind the chapel, but his hips get a bit too active and he falls out of her mouth.

Just as well, she's starved for air.

She forgot to breathe.

He waits as she catches her breath. Before she starts again, she looks up at him. He's looking at her. It's intense. And a bit scary. But, it's not, because his mouth is on hers, and when she's not kissing him, she's breathing into his mouth. *You shouldn't kiss him—not with your mouth, not now.* He's got his hands somewhere on her body. She can't be sure. They're everywhere. In her ear, he says, "I love you, Sykosa. I love you." Her tummy gets tight at it. Her mind gets dark from it. She wants to say it. She wants to. *He needs to hear it.* She should fuck him. Fuck him now. Fuck him before he bleeds to death. But, she doesn't, she just puts him back in her mouth, then goes at his penis with all the speed, intensity, and meager skill she can. It's no different from busywork. It keeps her here, but inside, the attack has started, and if not for the fact that she was constantly moving, she would be unable to be still. *Keep going.* Which she does, and doesn't relent, not one iota, until the cum, which usually flows down her hand, fills her mouth in globs.

She doesn't leave him until he's stopped.

They look at each other momentarily.

For some reason, she swallows. She didn't think about it,

and it wasn't too bad, but he came a lot, so she had to lap the inside of her mouth with her tongue, then swallow again. That time she looked like she had taken bad cough medicine.

He reaches out to hug her. She feels no better in his arms.

The hug is too warm, too tender—too loving.

She breaks into tears.

Don't lose control. Don't show him. Don't let him see...

He's confused and trying to calm her, holding her again. "What's the matter?"

She whines. "I'm sorry, I just couldn't, I don't know why."

"Couldn't what?"

"I told you you could, and I... I'm always screwing up."

He holds her intently. "No, this was fine. It's nothing."

Except, it's not. It's almost like a metaphor. He needs. She promises. And then never delivers...ever. Meanwhile, he's the one suffering and the one apologizing. She cries, losing herself to convulsions, unable to oppose their explosions. She talks like nothing's wrong. "We'll do it later. I said I will and I will."

"No, it's alright."

She sniffles, and considers it, then rejects it. *I ruined it. Our first time and I...* "No, you're gonna be mad, you will be."

"I'm not gonna be mad at you. I'm not."

When he said that, he put his hand on her cheek.

She felt the scars.

And the glass. Of the third pane of glass window.

Tearing her to shreds like it tore him to shreds.

@@rf

"Just don't be mad at me, okay? Please don't."

"I'm not."

"Tom, I..."

Blackness.

XII.

By morning, she has and has not become herself again.

The thought, as she stares in the mirror like she's contemplating womanhood or something equally pretentious, reminds her of bad made-for-TV movies. She still stares like she stared when she stood in front of her mirror and picked her turquoise undies. She believed (somewhat) that, after this weekend, he would meet her behind the chapel and life would go on—handjobs and all.

Not true.

This sex thing won't be a one-time or even a two-time deal.

It's going to change everything. Maybe it already has.

She awoke to find she was sore as hell down there. It was a surprise—and not. Truth is, she doesn't know how far he got before she stopped him, but she remembered that, one time, it was at the very last second. *Which was, I guess, a second too late.* Even so, that's not her primary worry. Last night, she... Well, he learned her dirty little secret, the reason she waits for him behind the chapel and goes to such distances for him.

He met the blackness.

And that's going to change everything.

Maybe it also already has.

To just put it bluntly, she's horny. (And extremely volatile). Which is fine. (Maybe). She gets horny a lot. (This never ends well). She even masturbates slightly more often than she thinks is normal. (She just rubbed herself. It was uncomfortable, but she wanted to make sure everything still worked). It's not that, though, it's the timeline, or the lack thereof. Events aren't chronological. The panic will do that. So perhaps it's good to feel horny. And perhaps she's lucky that's all she feels. If she's reckless, the weight will come, then the breathing problems, followed by her skewed eyesight and her sickly tummy...

The Pep Squad is on standby.
Relax.
It cannot stop her thinking.

Obviously, she remembers the early evening, and the time on the blanket—the joy of his hand and the BJS of her mouth. Where it gets somewhat hazy is later. When she came to, she was wrapped in the blanket and in him. She offered little explanation, as her senses were not yet working together. When she got back to the party, she found a relentless (and empty) energy was driving her. She knows she went shot-for-shot with Niko (bad idea). Niko had her Aikido headband on and, after each victorious round, blew up her cheeks fat as a teapot and pounded her feet like a Sumo wrestler. Tom didn't think the game should continue. She remembers listening to him. And she remembers him protecting her from whatever dangers surrounded her that she could no longer comprehend. They got all touchy-feely at one point, but neither felt it was a good idea to risk repeating what had happened outside. He wanted her to talk about it. She refused. It happened in this bedroom, which—around 4:30 AM—he and somebody, maybe Timmy, moved the dresser to access. Lastly, she recalls her collapse, wrapped in his arms and legs, her head being pet while her mouth tasted like throw up.

Last night was eventful.

A boy touched my vagina and put himself in my vagina. I put him in my mouth and slept in a bed with him and...

(Went black before him).

She knew the E was a bad idea. She knew it.

And I did it, anyway. I'm so stupid.

She came here to get some water and to escape the bedroom, which smells rancid. She also needed some space. She needs him now. She unlocks the door to the darkness. Her eyes adjust and see him sleeping on his stomach. She climbs into bed, then lowers her giant tee-shirt so it recovers her vagina. She needs underwear. It's too hard to find them. She curls as close to him as she can without disturbing him. She cannot sleep. *I fucked up big time. He knows something's wrong with me.* He knows he didn't save her, that she is broken, and that possibly negates the value of his sacrifice.

And she did so so close to its one-year anniversary.

That makes her feel sick.

I should've just done it. It was a mistake not to.

That statement invites the blackness. It's edgier today than it usually is. It feels powerful. She's gonna need his help.

Like that, he gives it.

His tired, heavy body grinds itself to life like construction machinery and, like construction machinery, it has, with massive torque and little speed, applied her body against him. She was careful to split their legs and crossed her arms over her chest to help. He's fallen back to sleep and she refuses to disturb him. The minutes pass. It all leaves her. Her despair. Her fear. The weight she never felt but was there anyway. Her horniness. It all leaves. And the heat in the secreted liquid of her canal has become dry, in drought, burned itself up in a scorching that causes her to sweat all over.

He does, too.

It's soaked her tee-shirt. It's also too much for him. And he separates, rolling onto his back. She rolls with him and lies atop his chest.

He sounds like he's in the middle of a nightmare. "Sykosa?"

"Yes."

"I'm too hot."

She understands. "I'm going to take a shower."

"Okay."

"Do you want to sleep longer?"

"Yes, sleep. I want to sleep."

"Okay."

Her body is slick, slightly slipperier than the soap, and it, her stink of vodka, sperm and tobacco, will not wash away. It does eventually and the water stops and she drips onto the toilet seat. Her piss stinks, too. Beside the towel rack hangs a bathrobe of stitched yellow stars and silver moon pockets. It hangs from her person as she tiptoes along the bedroom floor. He still slumbers with his face seemingly happy. That's good. After all, she did suck his dick. That has to somewhat even out the freak show she turned into. *Maybe if I sleep with him today, he'll forget the whole thing.* [Blackness]. She thinks she should climb back into bed and be held by him. Instead, she searches for her clothes. It's hard since, like their bodies, their wardrobes have combined. Her bra is in his pant leg and his shirt has knotted with her grass-stained v-neck, long sleeve.

Damnit, I liked this shirt.

She forgets it.

The undercarriage of her turquoise panties is stained, north-to-south, like blood streaked snot. It's disgusting. And difficult to ignore. *That's proof, isn't it? I lost my virginity.* She goes ahead and quarantines them in a mini-compartment of her bag, then from another compartment, trades it for one of her shoplifted thongs. Then she snaps internally. *I should fuck him this moment, that way I can fuck up this pair too.* That's it. He'll fuck her and she'll lay around bleeding like a dying animal. Then, her eyes can go crazy and her lungs go... *Why even have relationships if you're gonna fuck things up like you did last night?* And, hey, it gets better, remember? This sex thing isn't a one-time thing, or a two-time thing, it's the rest of her life—so she fucked up permanently, and now might as well just resign herself, then go downstairs and fuck Clyde, fuck Timmy, and back in Seattle, suck off the Stars and every dick in sight.

Cause she's "gorgeous."

Cause she's "sexy."

Cause she's "beautiful"

She's "perfect," "an angel," for heaven's sake.

Daddy's little cum bucket.

(Did she mention the volatility?)

She tells herself to shut up. She lost her virginity. Nothing'll fix that. Besides who gives a shit if she bled a tiny bit? He bled more, and he suffered more, and he never complains about it, and he never asks for a thank you, and he never dangles it over her head, even last night he coulda used that to have sex with her. It woulda worked, and he knows it woulda, and she knows it woulda, but that's not what he did—he stopped.

And he said, "I love you."

He did say that, didn't he?

She is back at bedside. "Tom?"

He is annoyed. "I need twenty minutes."

"I love you."

Come on, say it... Please, say it!

"I love you, too."

Thank you.

"I'll bring you some coffee, okay?"

"In twenty minutes."

"In twenty minutes."

Downstairs, the television plays, on loop, the title sequence of a video game where a woman, in a red dress and black jacket, is instructed that, in order to save the world, she must arouse as many teenage boys as possible, and if she's not busy, destroy the run-a-muck Artificial Intelligence computer that's exterminated the inhabitants. Maybe Timmy was one of them. His body is up against the wall, his head draped over his shirt, where a tiny pool of drool collects. Clyde's passed out, however he fell, on the couch. Curiously, SS1 is passed out on top of him, however she fell. Turns out his smile did work last night. Turns out the girl wasn't over eighteen. Then, there's the table top, which is dusty in cocaine.

She stares at it until Clyde coughs some nasty ass phlegm.

How flattering.

Niko taps her fingers on the kitchen countertop and awaits the dulling of the coffee machine's orange light with her coffee cup impatiently clinched in her fingers. It's a clear plastic cylinder that displays a drawing that Niko drew as a first grader. A little girl in a triangle skirt whose arm elastically bends up to a man dressed in a black suit with oversized glasses. Around them, she's written, *I love my Daddy*. Appearance wise, Niko's puffy and her cheeks have that acne her makeup covers so well. She wears a pair of short-shorts and a slinky camisole, no bra.

The orange light dims. The coffee pours.

Niko tries to say good morning. It comes out as, "Ugh."

"Good morning, too." From the refrigerator, she removes an unopened gallon of milk, then some cereal from the pantry. Niko's family must pay someone to keep this place stocked even though they're never here. Rich people are strange. She sits at the island counter and decides that, even though doing so blew up in her face last night, she's gonna ignore her shaky eyesight. *Relax.* "But, I'm a bit 'ugh' myself."

Niko drinks her first sip with aspirin, supplies Sykosa her own cup, then replaces the mug for the yellow and red cereal box, stuffing handfuls down her throat. "It's not mine."

"What's not yours?"

"The coke on the table, it's not mine."

"I wasn't thinking it was."

"I didn't do any, either."

"I didn't say you did."

"I don't know where Timmy got it. I told him not to bring that stuff around me."

And yet, there it is. "You know where he got it."

Scott.

Niko's serious. "Hey, you don't know that." Then Niko chews another handful before scratching her thigh. "What happened with Clyde? You seemed totally into him, then you ditched him. He was calling you a bitch and was totally pissed off."

She has no concern in her voice. "Looks like he got over it."

Niko covers her smile. "My God, she was all over him."

She, being SS1, also has a boyfriend.

"Gross."

"I don't know, sometimes it just happens, I suppose."

"I suppose." She does suppose. As that's what happened to her. Funny, she worried if she took Tom here he'd turn into another guy, like the guys the Sluts' date. But he didn't. He tried to make this weekend special. *He asked me to Prom, told* me he loved me, told Mackenzie we're dating... And she went psycho on him when he tried to sleep with her. Then, like a total bimbo, scrambled to make up for it by sucking his dick. *Like SS1 probably did to Clyde.* Wow, that did wonders for her self-esteem. *I'm not a slut!* She replaces the monologue with chews and swallows. "I grabbed this before I came down."

It's Niko's necklace.

"Admit it, you liked wearing it, right?"

Honestly, given everything, she forgot she had it on.

"It was cool."

Clyde farts something large and smelly.

Niko laughs. "He's been doing that all morning."

"Disgusting." Timmy makes a noise that's unidentifiable as a bodily function. "Shit, what was that?"

"I don't know, but it's what woke me up."

When she took out the necklace, she took out her smokes. One is lit between her lips. She is sick over the first hit. Once it's gone, she feels a sympathy for Niko. To be with that drool hound and his loser job as night manager at the 7/11. She'd never wish that fate on any girl, well, except Mackenzie. "I'm not trying to sound guyish, but Clyde has all this baggage, and I don't have the energy for it." She ashes into an empty beer can, then brushes her wet hair behind her ear before she tightens the bathrobe over her chest. And thinks: *If Niko knew, I bet she'd feel sympathy for me.* (She's on a run of really bad thoughts). "Tom is... He only wants to be himself, and even though he isn't perfect, at least I know him."

Niko smiles. "Well, of course, you know him."

She's confused. "I don't understand."

Niko does. "You guys did it, didn't you?"

She's fast. "No."

"Yes, you did."

The cigarette makes her sound like she's wearing a retainer. "No, I didn't."

"Yeah, you did."

Fuck, am I marked or something? "I didn't."

"Swear to me you didn't."

"I swear."

Niko smiles bigger. "You're a fucking liar."

That read worse than it sounded. There's something about Tom that makes her lie, even to Niko, who should always know the truth. "Okay, yes."

Niko grabs her arm like she was dying. "Did you enjoy it?"

"It was alright."

"Enjoy it, alright? Don't be one of those girls who can't."

She stutters. What a strange thing to say. "O-okay."

Then, Niko remembers that Sykosa's kinda a baby. "It hurt, didn't it? You shouldn't worry because—"

She interrupts. "Well, it was kind of an accident."

"What do you mean?"

"We started and I wanted to stop, but we didn't in time."

"You wanted to stop?"

She doesn't want to explain it. She tries to sound like its no-biggie while she looks at the cereal box as if it said something important. "It was weird, okay? We did other stuff, but I think we went too far beforehand. I think it happened."

Niko's unsure how to behave. "Are you okay with that?"

No.

And not necessarily for the reasons she might've expected. All the terror in her considered, there's no legitimate regret to having lost her virginity to Tom. If anything, she thinks back to earlier this week, when she was deciding on the turquoise, and how excited she was. *Part of me wanted to do it.* However, that part wanted none of the blackness involved. *Maybe I should have sex.* Upstairs. Now. She said she was "horny" earlier and she is, but it's not a fidgety horny. It's a... "Pull." She feels the pull. It wants her to sleep with him. She ignores it by eating cereal, then asking for some of the aspirin that Niko took.

"Can I have some of that aspirin?"

Niko gets a naughty look. "I have something a bit better."

Who knows where Niko got it, since Niko is barely dressed, but her hand holds a 3/4th consumed bottle of whiskey. Its cap already spins on the counter after being spun off the bottle. Niko spices up her own coffee, then sucks down on the only cure for a hangover she knows—getting more hammered. Once Niko's finished with her a gulp, she liquors up Sykosa's drink.

She's obliged. "Thanks."

The coffee, which was a bit strong, now tastes sweet, maybe syrupy, like it were mixed with honey. Not surprisingly, as well against anything any adult ever told her, the second it washes her tongue, she thinks clearer and the fog of the morning lifts. She wants to gossip. "Did you do it last night?" While this question is gossip, it's also rhetorical. Like Timmy, or Niko for that matter, would skip on the statutory rape. She'll skip on hearing about it. "What I meant was..."

Niko's already answered. "Nope."

"You didn't?"

Niko shrugs. "He was too drunk to get hard."

She smirks, then buries it. "Really?"

"His loss."

"Or your gain."

Niko looks playfully hurt. "You're such a bitch."

She smiles. *I sorta am.* "I'm sorry."

Niko also apologizes. "I'm sorry, but I gotta know—are you gonna do it again with Tom?"

Her thoughts are quick and decisive.

Yes.

In real life, she shrugs. "If he wants to."

"Well, he's gonna want to, so—"

She interrupts. "I want to."

The answer confused her. It's not so bad since this time with Niko has pushed the blackness to the backburner. She still feels it. It doesn't normally work like this. The blackness wins, then leaves. Its victory last night has somehow carried over to this morning, as has her decision of sex. And it is a decision. If she goes back to Seattle without the deed done, it puts many things in a precarious position.

That's not what I meant.

She means that...

"Niko, did you ever tell Hazu about Scott?"

Niko gets a serious look. They don't talk about this.

"No, why would I?"

She gets apologetic. "I'm sorry, I shouldn't've—"

Niko interrupts. "Yeah, you shoudln't've."

She drinks. "I'm sorry."

Niko focuses. She's sucking at helping out. Typically, these issues are her own. Niko feels responsible. It was her idea to come out here and to invite Tom. *I practically engineered the entire thing!* Now Sykosa's been... She didn't want Sykosa to lose her virginity this way. Aside from her own responsibility, Niko feels resigned. As Niko sees it, when it involves Sykosa and Tom, even when it's foolproof, it's always a disaster. It started last year and it continues to this day.

Now Niko has to go along and fake it.

Niko coaches herself: *Stay cool, help her sweat it out.*

This is Sykosa.

Niko knows, somewhere, the chick is losing it. "Eh, I was out of line. And I've never told Hazu. Why do you ask?"

"I was thinking... Tom doesn't know. He thinks we didn't do it. If I went upstairs and I—"

Niko interrupts. "You don't have to do that."

"I know, but—"

Niko interrupts again. "Do you feel the same about him?"

"What do you mean?"

"I know you have quasi-semi-warm-feelings for him."

That's right. Niko doesn't know she's in love with him, and he's in love with her, and... She needs to recommit to this friendship. If she listened to Niko and trusted Niko, instead of always thinking about Scott and last year, then... *That was an important question.* The answer is yes. She does still love him. And she's still grateful for what he did for her last year. And she still wants to go to Prom with him.

I did let him see the blackness.

Maybe that was also her way of saying, "I love you."

"Niko, I have to tell you something."

"What?"

"I love him." She hears no response, so she looks to Niko to see that Niko looks no different. "You knew?"

Niko shrugs. "It was obvious."

This isn't her story. This isn't her life.

I should've done it last night. I messed up.

The conversation gets quiet. Her cereal has turned itself fat and bloated in the milk, so she abandons it, then shares another smoke with Niko while they finish their coffee. The smoke curls up her hand and into the sunlight where it looks like something more mystical than smoke. It feels like what sharing a beer must be like for boys. The microwave reads that twenty minutes was ten minutes ago.

Niko tries to stop her. "You don't have to go."

Her answer is stupid. "No, I said I would bring him coffee."

"He'll be fine."

"No, I said I would."

Upstairs, she stands before the door and tries to compose herself. Maybe plan out her actions, exactly how it'll happen. Any plan she devised turns to crap when she finds him not in the bed, but the shower. She hears it and sees the sliver of light from underneath the bathroom door. She stands at the door and listens to his body obstruct the shower water, changing the intensity of the sound as it hits the ground. She plots again. If she walks in without the robe, it'll send a strong message, but maybe he doesn't want that. She settles for interrupting—the rest is up to him.

She is at the shower door.

It takes a while for him to see her through the glass.

When he opens the door, he's facing her. He's wet from head to toe, his blond hair pushed behind his ears and its bottom flirting with his shoulders. There's soap on those shoulders, and it follows several paths, sometimes becoming patches that've not washed away along his chest and stomach. It's particularly sudsy at his cock, which is where he's been washing, so it's already pretty meaty, and it twitches once or twice after he tugs free the robe belt and sees her naked body.

He grows fully hard when he's holding her against him.

And she forgets everything.

"I thought you were gonna bring me coffee."

"I did. I just thought you wanted to sleep."

He agrees. "I did."

He also wants to wash her, which he thoroughly does. It gets him all the opportunities he could want to feel her boobs. Then he spends time with her butt, which he gets her to bend over for. He goes longer on her pussy, rubbing it somewhat like he did yesterday. It doesn't work like it worked yesterday, and in some respects, the shower might've been annoying, had he not also discovered if he massages above her collar, into her neck, she loses her balance, and that she's sensitive on the insides of her wrists, or that she gets flush when he scratches her knees.

They also talk.

"So a blowbang is when the girls only sucks their dicks, but the gangbang is when she fucks them."

He laughs. "I think you're figuring it out."

She went back to the porn talk since she liked it last night.

And he likes it, too.

She's also sitting on a corner of the shower while he washes her ankles. "How many guys are there?"

"At minimum, four. There's usually more."

"How many guys have you seen be with a girl?"

He laughs again. "Maybe thirty."

She's shocked. Also mildly at her language. She can't talk like this normally, but the academic nature of the conversation has given her free reign to say things. She likes it. "Thirty? I don't get it. They stand around waiting?"

"Well, she can do several guys at one time."

She's confused. "How does she do that?"

"Well, she has two hands, and a mouth."

"She'll jerk off some, blow one, and have sex with another?"

He corrects her. "Two will fuck her."

"How does that work?"

"They use her butt."

Her mouth drops. She whispers. "They do anal?"

He smirks so large he blushes and hides himself. "Yes."

She bets he thinks she didn't know about ass fucking.

What did you think Ass Girl's nickname means?

"I didn't see that in the porno I saw."

He extends a loose invitation. "Well, come over sometime, I'll show you it."

It may've been a loose invitation, but it was a serious one. She keeps herself silent about it, not wanting to over commit, though she can envision circumstances where she'd watch porn with him. She forgets it. She's not done with the porno stuff. She does stop while he redirects the water on her ankles, then stands up as he says he wants to give her a splash down. "So when do the guys come on her face?"

"At the end."

"What do you call it?"

He turns off the water and shakes out his hair. "You know what it's called. Let's not go there."

She does know. "Yeah, cause a certain friend of yours calls me it all the time."

He tries to be diplomatic.

"And, as I understand it, you call her a Cokehead Bitch."

She pouts. "So?"

Again, he tries to be diplomatic.

"Please don't get me in this shit between you two."

She doesn't want him to. She only wanted to tease him. She will handle Mackenzie and the Bukkake Queens nickname herself. The shower is turned off and she's dripping on the mat. He's toweling her off and having fun feeling her all over again. She's a tad surprised she isn't interested in covering up. He's also erect, like really erect, and has been for some time. He's not done anything about it, and she's uncertain if she should, but she's decided to wait.

It's better when he's ready.

In the bed, he gives her a big hug, and she hugs him back. His erection digs into her stomach, and when he moves, it leaves behind a sticky spot.

They're still talking.

"I've always wondered, like, what you knew about what goes on between all of us girls."

He is diplomatic again.

"I know enough to know I don't want to know any more."

His penis now leaves a sticky spot on her thigh.

He's losing interest in conversation. He's feeling her breasts and she is nestling into his neck and stroking his hair with her hand. Pretty soon, he starts to touch her butt too, this time in the sexual way, and she feels his jaw tremble a bit when his fingers find her vagina to be already several degrees hotter than her body. It gets him too hot and he puts her hand on his penis, she grips it and starts to tug slowly.

He's fighting it. He doesn't want to give in.

But he's a boy, and he does.

He's breathing hard. "I want to have sex."

"I know."

It's like he didn't hear her. "I know some stuff happened, but I still want to, and I think, maybe, I was so close—"

She interrupts. "You didn't."

"I didn't?"

"No, we stopped in time."

For her, this means they should move forward. For him, it provides pause. He thought if he could convince her he got in last night, she would want to do it this morning. But, all in all, he feels weird about it. Last night... Well, he doesn't know how to describe it. She lost control, then she was lost. She passed out and he didn't know what to do. He means, sure, he made sure she was breathing and everything, but for about twenty minutes, she was gone, just sleeping, but it wasn't sleeping.

He thought she might mention it today.

She hasn't.

She's so weird sometimes.

He barely speaks. "I still want to, but if you…"

He can't say the word "can't." He doesn't even want to put it out there. Not that either notices, but she's still jerking him off. And thinking: *Okay, just do it. Do it.* She doesn't know what to say, so she says, "I feel fine."

It's all he needs to hear. He leaps from the bed, then at his bag, goes through all the zippers until what is in his hands is another aluminum seal that he's broken. She watches him unroll it over himself. Her stomach gets tight. *Okay, it's a thank you for last year.* Her breathing has got a bit heavy, but she doesn't think it's blackness breathing, just normal stuff. *I already lost my virginity. I can't lose it again.* But, somehow, like last night, it's started to replicate. She's no longer on her side, but on her back, and her legs are fully spread.

He sits up between them. He's looking at her pussy.

It's just a penis. And it'll be over soon. Relax.

He lowers himself to her, and then lies himself on top of her. She feels his chest on her own and puts her arms at his sides and tries to keep them steady. *Relax.* He is trying to keep his hips up, but he's never done this before, so it takes him a moment to find stability in his knees. Then he has to fight her legs, which've waned shut. He tells her she needs to open further. *Do it! Open you legs!* It takes a lot, and they open, yet it feels like she opened her heart—it's her chest that's open. *It's the one year anniversary. This matters.* She scrunches her face, then resists her own hip contractions when she feels his penis against her vagina, moving around, looking for the grove that signals her entrance.

He digs.

I can't do this! I can't do it!

"Stop!"

He does.

His voice isn't that sensitive. "Sykosa…"

She opens her eyes and tears, which she didn't know she was holding onto, fall down her temples. He's still against her, his hand also still at his base, ready to guide him in. She forces her arms outside of his own, then locks them around his neck, pinning him against her, and he does his best to hold her back.

She puts her cheek in his own.

"I'm afraid, Tom. I'm afraid."

He tries to be supportive. "I swear, I'll go slow. It'll be fine."

"No, Tom, it's... I'm afraid."

"Sykosa, you're—"

She interrupts. "I'm afraid they'll find me."

Tom shakes his head. "No, they're gone. They're all gone."

Donna. Mike. Lonny.

It's true. They're all gone.

Last year happened and they disappeared soon after.

She cries more. "You don't know that. You don't know if I'm safe. Nobody does."

"You're safe with me. I'll protect you."

She gasps for air. There are no thoughts in her head.

"What if they come back? What if..."

Tom whispers. "Then, I'll kill them."

It's a terrible thing to make him say. It's also the only thing that makes her feel even slightly better. Just the promise he'll do it—it means ... She can feel her body again, she can feel how warm he is, how cold she is, and she can feel every one of his scars running along her. She opens her eyes to find he's looking at her. She touches his cheek. "You love me, right, only me?"

"I love you."

He tries to kiss her. She turns her face away.

"Okay."

He doesn't know what that meant.

"You're ready?"

She wipes one eye. "Yes."

"Okay, I'm going to start."

He shifts around in the bed and he reaches back down.

He's almost there again.

Wait...

"Stop."

He stops. "Sykosa, maybe this isn't—"

She interrupts. "That's not what I meant, I... I meant I love you, too."

She hugs him again, then kisses his cheek and holds him close to her. Her thoughts have changed. *He loves me.* And she knows he does. And she knows she loves him. And as much as she wishes for this to be romantic and problem free, she'd have never found Tom otherwise. *Relax.* This time it works. Her legs stay open. They're still nervous, but they're open. She stays steady when she feels him against her. *Stay calm.* It takes some time. No different from yesterday, he's struggling—digging and turning and retrying and...

He finds his stride. His force is grand.

She jumps. "Ouch!"

He freezes. "You're alright, right?"

That's funny. She didn't think it would hurt.

Maybe I was a virgin?

Too late, she's definitely not one anymore.

"It was a surprise, that's all."

He withdraws enough so she feels her canal close without his presence, then she scrunches her cheeks, and she struggles as he goes back inside her. The second time, a little deeper. Then, a little deeper on the third. Like her fingernails into his back, a little deeper. All the way until his hips hit her hips and his force forces back her knees. God, it hurts. It really does. Especially when he starts the full motion, it's like paper slicing down the middle and her hips scoot up the bed to spare herself the agony. He follows her up, then he grabs onto her, and she grabs onto him.

"Are you okay?"

She is.

He hasn't moved for five seconds. Already it hurts less.

"I think I'm fine. We just needed to stop for a second."

That was true.

She slides back down the bed with him, then hugs him in such a way that, when he hugs her, he is really holding her in place. *I need him to help. I can't do it myself.* And she closes her eyes as he begins to go at her again. The soreness is there, and it's far worse than this morning, but otherwise, she's lubricated him, and everything's working better. He's getting in and out, and she's dissociated the pain. All she feels are his movements, and all she concentrates on is the changes inside her, the wideness of her canal, and trying to pin-point exactly how deep he's gone, so she might be able to point there later. Finally, it gets to a point where she can think, and she thinks nothing useful—just, *I'm having sex.*

Actually, she *was* having sex.

He's moaned directly into her ear and spasmed like a gunshot! (She doesn't like how that read). He's also collapsed on her and his heart beats down on her breasts harder than his hips did her own.

She feels smothered. "Did you enjoy it?"

"Yeah, it was nice."

"Good. Can you get out?" He carelessly pulls himself free. She gasps and holds him in place! As it is, once he's gone, she feels her vagina return to its original shape, like memory foam or something. It still hurts. Her poor and injured organ needs time to mend. Her breath is short, and she feels normal again. He's sat at the edge of the bed. She can see he is covered in red splotches. She touches his thigh. "It didn't hurt as much as I thought it would."

He looks back at her. He wants to say something. Instead, he holds out his arms and pulls her in close. She's crushed into his collar. "That was great. You were perfect."

I was?

She feels girly, and she smiles, then surrenders to cuteness.

"Aw! You were perfect, too!"

XIII.

Interstate I-90 West to Seattle is a vast nothingness of desert rock with scattered patches of farming amongst the pertaining dust. Air that cracks the skin and bloodies a nose. She wants to saddle up her horse and go hunting for Injuns. And this fantasy is as good as any, especially since fantasies are all that remain. Scratch that. Complications are all that remain. Complications and feelings. Frustration. Over how her fingertips are without the cigarette that lies between Clyde's own. (She left her pack with Niko). Clyde notices, and probably thinks she's itching to hookup with him, no longer afraid of the rock 'n roll and jealous like a woman over his hookup with SS1.

He is wrong, as he is so often.
And what was that word?
Frustration.

As not only does she not get to smoke, she doesn't get to have Tom. He's not far. From the back row, she sees his reflection in the window, one row up with Mackenzie. He had a choice of where to sit. And that's where he sat. *Or where Mackenzie led him.* They came downstairs, him carrying their bags and herself giggly and happy and... Mackenzie dominated him, then cornered him in the car. It's almost exactly what Clyde did to her on the way out here. It drove Tom crazy; yet, if she mentions this, she's gonna hear how it's different cause, "Mackenzie's my friend. Clyde isn't your friend."

Don't get mad at him.
This isn't real. It's a stupid game.
Clyde did it to get Tom upset and start a fight.
Mackenzie did it to get her upset and start a fight.

Knowing not to get angry and not getting angry end up being two different things, especially when not getting angry involves, A) riding bitch between the Sluts, SS1 passive-aggressively slugging her, shouting, "No, Dawson's a horse-face!" while SS2, on the lap of SS3 with her legs laid across all them, says, "No, he isn't!" "He is!" "He isn't!" "He's a horse-face!" and, B) being separated from him for this massively long car ride, with only a sore vagina to remind her of how close she had felt to him, has gotten her to do exactly what she shouldn't. She's listed every single thing that must change in their relationship. It's funny... She thought things were fine, but now that they've had sex, or she should say: if they're ever to have sex again, she can see things are gonna have to change.

She ignores it for a more pressing concern.

The van is toast. No one wants to admit it.

Niko admits it. "Something is wrong, now pull over!"

Timmy's busy slapping the steering wheel like a jockey slaps his steed, bent over like a jockey, too, to investigate the gauges he cannot read. "It's not a big deal. I'll figure it out."

"What's wrong? Your engine looks like it's on fire!"

"Funny joke, now seriously, what is it?"

"Do you ever look at the road when you drive?"

Timmy looks up. "Ah, my car is on fire!"

"That's fucking awesome!" And that was fucking Clyde! The douche muscles his way between the front seats, then against the front console, to see white steam burst from the grooved hood. "Do you think it'll blow up?" It's a bit like crying fire. At first, the panic is contained. Then, somewhere along the way, all senses are lost and nine skulls kick forward. It's the brakes. They've locked. And they've done so without regard for Clyde, whose face smashes and streaks the windshield in boogers and teeth. Once the van skids to a stop, it explodes with kids instead of flames. Clyde is between the front seats, rolled over on his side. "You asshole! You fucking prick!"

Timmy pulls up his sagging skater shorts. "What? You said the van was gonna blow up."

"Fuck you, asshole!"

On the shoulder, Niko watches smoke shoot from this twice-rolled-over beast, and she wishes for her RX7. On this straightaway, she could push 130mph, maybe 140mph and more importantly, be in her bed in her bedtime clothes, salting some low butter popcorn and sucking on frozen bananas, swearing to stave off the alcohol with another drink. Niko forgets it, then prepares herself for this latest crisis. It's difficult for her. After Sykosa's confession this morning, Niko felt uncharacteristically guilty and has been moody and cruel all afternoon.

Niko tries to rein it in. She fails.

"What the fuck is the matter with you?"

Timmy puts his hands to his chest. "Me? What did I do?"

"Who knows how much damage you did while you kept driving like a moron. I told you to pull over."

Timmy shouts back. "I was trying to fix it."

"Like you would know how!"

"I know how to fix my car, alright? Don't tell me about it!"

Mackenzie hears this and gives Tom a look.

He responds. "Why're you looking at me like that?"

"Nothing."

"Come on, M, I hate it when you do this."

Unmoved by the Mackenz-ian drama, Niko yanks the lever that dislodges the hood, and underneath said hood, feels for the release latch. "Let's see what damage your stupid ass did."

Clyde laughs. "Dude, you're such a woman, you know that?"

"Fuck you." Timmy ushers Niko aside. "I got this, baby."

Niko's quick. "No, don't do it."

Timmy lifts the fiberglass corners and bonfires of steam, which volley for the free air, envelop his face. The hood smacks shut and he smacks the pavement, grabbing at his skin and cursing manically, then loses it when he hears Clyde laughing. "Shut the fuck up! I don't need your fucking voice."

Niko approaches him. "Let me see, what's wrong?"

"My face, it's burned."

What a wuss. "You'll be fine."

He points to a rosy blemish beneath his nostril. "Niko, tell me the truth. I can take it. How bad is it?"

"That's not a burn."

"What is it?"

"It's your acne."

Clyde's out of breath before the first laugh leaves his mouth. "Oh shit, I can't believe you said that!"

Timmy and Clyde continue their fight while Niko resumes her analysis, save her efforts are again impeded. "Niko, how long will this take?" It's Tom. Somehow, Mackenzie convinced him to handle this situation. "Niko, Mackenzie's worried about school. Attendance is important to her." In response, Niko stares into the engine bay to coax her brain into a viable solution. It upsets him. "Niko, answer me."

Answer, Niko does. "I'm not talking to you."

"But, what about..."

"*But, what about...*" Niko disappears under the hood. The cigarette muffles her voice. "Unless you have some expertise I'm unaware of, could you give me some breathing room?"

"Can you at least guess how long it will take?"

"*No, I can't!*"

Tom returns to Mackenzie. "I tried! She wouldn't tell me!"

"Unreal! Who takes a trip if their vehicle is unreliable?"

"I know, but the best we can hope for is..."

It doesn't matter how that sentence ends, or any thereafter; none will deter Mackenzie from her spoiled princess routine. At least Mackenzie has a routine. Something to rely on. Like how Timmy and Clyde—who've already made up—share slugs off a flask. Or how the Sluts—who're worried the others will resort to cannibalism—have crowded together. *Safety in numbers!* Everybody gets something. And she gets loneliness.

That's unfair. She needs something.

Him! That's what she needs!

By chance, his bum rests on the sandy shoulder. She joins him, sitting Indian style. Given the condition of her cooch, it's not a great position, and her body tells her that. She abandons it and sits on one leg. "I'm sorry about Niko."

"What was that about?"

"We talked this morning about some stuff."

His hands hold up his face. "About us?"

She sounds soft. "She needs time. Too much has happened this weekend."

"You're telling me. The van."

Even here, she smells broken car. It should worry her, and she's sure it will soon, but for now she's happy to be separated from the Sluts—it doesn't matter why. "Yeah, weird, huh?"

"It sucks is what it is."

"Hey..."

"What?"

"Do you love me?"

The words seem to bring him physical discomfort.

He says them, anyhow. "I love you."

"Good, then feel better!"

The results are inconclusive.

She decides it probably isn't the opportune time to list her grievances with their relationship. Or to behave as if she has any. She kind of wobbles closer to him, and he gives and sets himself next to her, putting his arm around her. He's in shorts and a hoodie and, for some reason, not very warm.

He whispers. "How are you?"

"I'm fine."

"Everything's okay, like, physically?"

It is.

Other than feeling sore, and sore might be understating it, she feels fine. Her feet work. Her hands work. Her eyes see. If she didn't know she had sex, she might not think she had sex. In truth, she subconsciously operated under the assumption that losing her virginity would be like a war wound—it'd be traumatic and involve a lot of blood, and like, she'd need a field medical kit. But, aside from her blood-spotted panties and the toilet paper she wiped herself with after, there hasn't been another drop, nor was there any on the sheets.

In retrospect, that seems normal.

How else would girls survive this for millions of years?

Her body knew this was coming, and how to handle it.

She shrugs. "I'm fine, no problems."
"Can I ask you something?"
"Sure?"
"Did you, like, enjoy it at all or—"
She interrupts. "In a way, I did."
They're interrupted by Mackenzie.

The perpetual third-wheel, who can't sit since she's chosen a Bitch's-style skirt and top outfit with exposed legs, holds out her cell-phone. For being so bratty, Mackenzie looks perfect. It's the sign of a fantastic makeup job, and Mackenzie must've put in an hour. Also, her retro flip hairstyle is in tremendous shape, considering the weather and the wind and the general discomfort of the car ride. "Tom, I can't get into roaming!"

Tom extends a hand. "Let me see." He examines the phone, and while he does, he explains, "Neither Mackenzie or I have good reception out here. We can't call for help."

Mackenzie reiterates that. "Trapped, that's us."

She begs to differ. "I know no one believes it, but Niko's good at this."

Mackenzie doesn't and lets it be known. "Sure, she is."

Tom doesn't say anything. He's looking at the phone.

She insists. "No, I mean it. Niko'll fix it, you'll see."

Mackenzie ignores her. "What do you think, Tom?"

"I don't know. Maybe if we tried it away from the road."

"Then can we try that?"

He agrees and stands. When his back is to her, Mackenzie gives her a snide look before snatching his arm. *What a bitch.* She reminds herself not to get angry over this, but it puts one or two new things on the grievance list.

It also leaves her alone.

Her wrists hit the dirt, launching her off her ass to wander back to Niko, who's climbed onto the doorframe to look down on her subjects like a politician. Perhaps for effect or by coincidence, Niko has turned on the headlights. The low-beams backwash onto her. It looks really cool. "Look everyone, here's how it is. A coolant hose has blown. The leak is slow and we've given some time for the engine to cool, so if we can get it to start, we can drive slowly to the next gas station. We may need to stop if it overheats again, I don't know how many times, but when we get there, and if we can be inventive with what the place has got, we can jury rig the leak and buy enough coolant to refill us all the way home."

The group agrees, except Timmy.

"Uh-uh, that's not happening!"

"Oh yeah, and what's your problem with that?"

"The problem is that it's my van."

"Baby, we know that."

"No, you don't understand. I won't let it happen."

"Because it's your van?"

"That and you aren't frying the engine because your friend got burned last night." He means Sykosa and her coquettish behavior with Clyde and Tom. Apparently, it has led the group to several different conclusions about what happened. The majority opinion, which was subtly suggested by Clyde during a smoke break while reassembling Niko's cottage, was an emotionally distraught Sykosa hooked up with Tom only after Clyde rejected her for SS1. Everyone was quick to believe Clyde since, sometime that evening, it became clear by noise alone that he was making it with SS1 in the lagoon. It's made this moment incredibly awkward. And put a spotlight on Timmy's stupidity. He tries to rally the group anyway. "I mean it, we all know it happened, and it's what's driving this—"

Tom interrupts. "Fuck you, man!"

Tom scoots chest-to-chest with Timmy.

Timmy's staring him down and pointing his finger, which he's hanging high and letting move with his words either like a diva or like it were an inverted handgun. "No, fuck you cause we're not fucking up my van!"

"I don't care. You don't talk to her that way."

"Don't fuck up my van and I won't have to!"

Niko's between them. "Let's get home, alright?"

It suffices.

Tom loads into the van, followed by the rest. As predicted, the engine overheats again and is turned off again, then run again, overheats again, and finally, manually pushed down an exit ramp—the only sign of civilization, save the 747s rumbling above—to stop at a dilapidated foodmart. The pushing part strained her abdominals. It forced her to shut her butt. It's poop, but also gas from all the drinking. It's hit in urgency, and before she expels it, she watches SS1—who stands in sunglasses, sports bra, and a thong riding visibly above her waist—and SS2—dressed the same, but in a different color scheme—put on a public spectacle.

Truthfully, it's a miracle the Sluts lasted this long.

"Niko, am I trapped out here?"

"Yeah, are we trapped?"

Niko ignores them.

"Niko, don't ignore me!"

"Yeah, don't ignore us!"

Mackenzie's in on it. "I think it's a good question."

Niko's dumbfounded and infuriated. She's yelling at them, but she's really yelling at Timmy, who keeps getting in her way. "For a pack of retards all dying to get home, you've all got fucking asinine opinions that cannot go unvoiced."

Regardless, *that* did not help.

SS1 loses it! "I knew this would happen! I knew we'd need the boys to fix something! We never should have come out here by ourselves!" She's on a roll, bunching her face and crying like a baby. "This is your fault, Niko! You're the reason we're stuck out here! You're the reason that..." She screams. "I want my daddy! Do you hear me? I want my daddy!"

SS2 collapses. "Daaaaaaaaaa-ddy!"

Niko nearly slaps the 'ho. "Shut your fucking mouth!"

SS2 straightens up—frightened. "Sorry, Niko."

Niko wears regret. "Come here, honey." SS2 prances beside her and Niko uses her arm to hold her close. "Let's see if we can't find what we need inside, alright?"

"Okay, Niko!"

Once Niko's gone, hostilities fizzle.

That'll happen when the smartest person you've ever met, who also declared your existence to be a waste to all evolved life, disappears. But, it's understandable. Everyone, including Niko, is too hung over and too underslept to be friends. And she still needs to shit, and this is as good a time as any, so she follows Niko. Inside, the store clerk, a redneck behind bulletproof glass, is halfway into a practiced speech about kids, like them, who stop en route to Seattle, peruse the post cards, try on sunglasses, spin round the personalized novelty plates and leave with pockets lined in cheese ball and candy.

He's really passionate about it.

Niko's unimpressed, mumbling through her teeth. "I need duct tape, cleaner, paper towel, coolant, a flashlight, gloves, and something I can create a splint with."

The clerk, clearly intimidated, directs her, then looks back. He's white as a ghost.

She understands. "I was wondering if I could have a key to the bathroom."

The key is along a bay beneath the glass.

"It's behind the utility shack."

"Thanks."

She exits the store, and once the door jingle finishes, she hears Tom's voice. He's at a picnic table with Mackenzie. "Yeah, it's stressful, but please don't upset Niko, Sykosa says she can fix this." Wow, he listened. That's attractive. Though, while she agrees Niko's their best shot, she thinks she should be beside him, and Mackenzie should be kicken' it elsewhere. She hears him again. "It's stressful, but please don't be upset, I'm trying, I am." It's a whisper that's invented in her head.

Her eyes curl over her shoulder to see him. Mackenzie's staring at her. She darts her head around.

Damnit, why does she always win?

Quickly, she applies her hair in a ponytail, that way when she looked, it was to her fix her hair. Still, the embarrassment is real, and she can't shake the premonition that Mackenzie—

being the gold standard—is going to steal Tom from her. Losing Tom makes her reconsider the list of grievances and... Damnit, Mackenzie won. The bitch has undermined this great, significant day. To hide her anger, she quickly—too quickly, actually—cuts between gas pumps to the toilet, where she's gonna be emotional about this. Halfway there, she realizes she shoulda asked the Pep Squad to tag along since some nausea sets in, and she feels strained for breath at the edge of her lungs, and her eyesight—which, now behind the utility shack, stares at the scuffed door handle—loses its edge definition.

It's stupid that the blackness would be provoked by this.

I need to sleep for, like, a year.

The blackness may be here, but so is he. He followed her when he noticed her fleeing from the gas pump. She's receptive to him instantly and clutches him and forces the grooves of her jeans into his own. Finally after this time away from him, she gets what she needs—a long, meaningless, directionless, sexless hug. She doesn't care how scientifically improbable it is, it soothes the soreness in her groin and almost distributes the pain so it's less of a burden, then flushes it away with the relief her body feels to not be supporting its weight alone.

He's overwhelmed by all the estrogen of this afternoon, but he guesses he understands. In the bedroom after they finished, she was almost afraid to go without touching him for longer than ten seconds. "Is this because of the van? I'm sure it'll be fixed soon."

"I guess, maybe, a little bit. No."

"What's it about?"

She whines in a whisper. "Can't you see what she's doing?"

"Who? Mackenzie?"

"Yes."

"Please don't involve me in this stuff between you two."

His tone was diplomatic like this morning, but it also had an edge to it. *He's been telling Mackenzie the same thing.* The little bitch is trying to break them up! "She wants to break us up, I know she does. She wants you to leave me."

"Sykosa, she's just worried—"
She interrupts. "Please don't."
"No, you need to hear this."
This isn't her story. This isn't her life.
I swear if he defends her...
"Please, talk about something else." He has nothing to say. She says something. "It's cold." He disrobes his hoodie. It's gray, and, in red, the Academy logo is over his heart. She pulls her hair from beneath the collar, her arms slipped through the sleeves. It smells like him, like boy. Or rubbed off girl. Or more accurately, rubbed off Mackenzie. She's back in his arms. "You aren't cold, are you?"
"No, I'm fine."
She sounds concerned. "You sure? You can have it back."
"No, I want you to have it."
"Thank you."
"For what?"
She feels no need to answer and doesn't, but when she puts her opposite cheek by his chest, she sees his arm in his undershirt. He rarely wears short sleeves. The scars are too numerous and some too deep for public display. Though, a lot of the superficial cuts—leaving scars barely impacting the surface—seem to have resolved themselves back to skin. She's surprised she hasn't noticed before. "These have healed well."
"You think?"
"Well, better than I thought they would."
He is timid. He's tried and failed so many times at this.
"I got them in a fight last year."
"I know."
"You were there, I saw you."
"Yeah, I was."
"You know, tomorrow is—"
She interrupts. "How much school did you miss?"
"I mis—"
She interrupts again. "Three weeks, I knew that."
He almost sounds surprised. "You did?"

"I know it all, Tom."

In a few minutes, she poops, or farts a lot, and in the few minutes after, he buys two microwavable burritos. They spin in the microwave and they wait by the foodmart window. At the van, Timmy distracts Niko with his belief that his years at the 7/11 out-qualifies her expertise. Inside it, Clyde strums his guitar—*cause I'm in love and it's just too much*—for SS1, who stares like a groupie. SS2 also stares like a groupie. SS3's along for the ride. Mackenzie's in the front, her head in a schoolbook. *He's with me.* They're wedged between a coat stand of lunchroom-size potato chip bags and a cabinet of print media.

"That's Niko's mom, right?"

She looks at this magazine rack full of racks, specifically at the rack on *Redbook*. "Yes, that's Kana."

"I think people might be forgetting what happened."

Hopefully. Probably not.

It's hard to forget the biggest story of the year.

Last year, early in her sophomore year, a tabloid published pictures of Kana at a party. No big deal? Well, it so happens Kana was in her underwear. That's just the start. The signature photograph had Kana bent over a cocaine filled table-top with her boob popped out. It was obviously gravity being a bitch, but the news stations had to mosaic it, which made it risqué, and that made it—follow her here—the signature photograph. It also didn't help that Niko's father wasn't at this naked, drug bash. What proceeded was Kana's stay at an in-patient rehab clinic, the duration of which became extended since the only time Kana left was when she checked out, got wasted, then checked back in when more pictures were published.

"Don't mention it. You'll make Niko uncomfortable."

"I won't."

She decides to obsess about Kana. It's easy to do since, if she had one or two features of Kana's, it'd be Mackenzie thinking she was the gold standard instead of the other way around. "She's natural. She hasn't had any surgery or anything. I mean, that's her. She looks like that all the time."

"You look better."

She looks like a blob, and in his sweatshirt, as if she were trying to hide that she's fat. She still likes wearing it. "Thanks."

"I'm serious."

"I know I don't look like her."

"That's unfortunate for her."

"What?" The comment confuses her. It's not blatant, which is typically his style. "Are you saying that—" She interrupts herself with a grin. *Good boy.* "Aw."

She manhandles him close to her again. At first, he thought it was cute. Now, it worries him. He would think the longer and the harder she holds him, the less she would need to do so, but it seems like whatever owns her right now owns her damn good. So he holds her back, holds her tight, then wills away the resulting erection by thinking of video games and fat girls. That's only 50% accurate. Inside, he really wants to fix it, to fix her, and to do it now. He wants to tell her about last year. He wants her to tell him what it was like for her. Then, after that, she can suck his dick like she did on the blanket, or he can fuck her until he comes, or...

Look, he's gotta say it already...

All day long, every time he sees her, he gets vivid images of her fucking thirty guys. And her doing "anal." (He even thought it in her own voice). Or, sometimes, he can't stop wondering if, even by the tiniest probability, any of those lesbian rumors last year were true. He could walk into a room, maybe, and, possibly, see Niko and her, buck naked, sixty-nineing or putting dildos in each other or... He wonders what it might feel like if Sykosa exchanged sex for whatever parts are broken in the van with that redneck asshole and...

No! What he meant was...

The words never come. And when they do, they're wrong.

Fixing Mackenzie is easy. Fixing Sykosa rips him to shreds.

She makes him feel too much. And that makes everything so much more complicated. Even now, he knows it's a bad idea to bring this up, but he's gonna do it anyway. Because she made it sound like she needed it, and because his stupid ass can't ignore it. "I know you're upset about Mackenzie, but you two have had problems forever and—"

She interrupts. "You're not sitting by me in the van."

That was impulsive. She regrets saying it.

He doesn't, as he knows what she's talking about.

After they slept together, she had a "way" about her and once Mackenzie caught its scent, Mackenzie had a "way" of separating them. Mackenzie got by him in the van and he thought he should sit by Sykosa, but it took ten seconds to decide. By then, he didn't want to move cause he didn't want anyone, especially Clyde, to know he knew he made the wrong decision and... This whole agonizing trip—he's wished he was with her.

"I'll sit next to you."

That surprises her. "You will?"

"Yes, I didn't... I hadn't spent much time with Mackenzie this weekend and I guess... I don't know."

It's gonna be hard to ignore the Mackenzie problem since he's conceded it's a serious one. She talks carefully, unsure how many of the grievances she should list. "You're gonna have to try harder, much harder."

"I know."

"I don't feel like your girlfriend sometimes."

One of his hands has released her to rub his eye into his eye socket. He's also trying like hell to hold back a yawn. He's so tired. "And that's because of Mackenzie?"

"I think...if you do something with, I mean, like, anything you do with any other girl, I should get to do it, too."

"Like what?"

The first grievance that comes to her is also the dumbest. "You talk to Mackenzie on the phone."

He throws his hands in exhaustion. No, wait, in joy. He's smiling. "I do, but not like you think."

On rare occasion, she's okay with being wrong. This would be ones of those times. "How do you talk to her then?"

He holds her close, and when he talks, it's softly like she

does. "On the Internet. She has AOL. We IM."

She's miffed. "I have AOL."

"You never mentioned it."

"Duh, I need it for school."

"Not everyone..." Strike that. "What's your screen name?"

"It's Sykosacess."

He smirks. "As in princess?"

She feels dumber. "Maybe. What's yours?"

"ThomasBuilt."

Never mind, his is dumber. "That's your screen name?"

"Yeah, and when we get back, I'll add you."

She likes that.

She never uses the Internet, but she'll start. "Okay."

"Is there anything else?"

She thinks there is. It shoulda occurred to her long before.

"I don't like how you waited so long to ask me to Prom."

He pulls away from her a bit, then holds his place. "I wasn't certain you would go."

That's stupid. "I'm not stupid, Tom."

This time he does pull away. One hand goes back into his eye, the other goes through his hair. "It's... You won't talk about last year, so I didn't know if you wanted to go or if you never wanted it mentioned."

"I kept bringing it up."

"Yeah—about how dumb the other girls were acting over it."

He's got a point. She lets it die.

Though, she knows this talk isn't over—not by a long shot. It's enough for her for now. Besides, the microwave bings and Tom shuffles hot burritos between his hands as he transfers them to a flimsy paper plate. She eats in small bites, and despite the indigestion, the warmth is disarming. Outside, they talk about school while she smokes a cigarette. It's been a long time since she last smoked, and the buzz is like a freight train. It also helps with the indigestion.

She looks out at the group.

The Sluts sleep in the van, all leaned against each other for

support. Mackenzie has a textbook pointed at a cabin light, ignoring Clyde who's—*overcome by rage, I surrender amongst the sage*—made her his next conquest. She has to imagine Tom wants to save M from that loser, and he does want to save M from that loser. He also wonders how many girls Clyde gets by sheer shamelessness. He reminds himself it doesn't matter.
    He has a girlfriend.
    But, why can't I let Mackenzie go?
    As for Timmy and Niko, they crouch together by the engine.
    "Baby, please just let me finish."
    He insists. "No, I can do it. Let me."
    "Fine."
    He does it. "Alright, what's next?"
    "This right there."
    Timmy waits. "Niko?"
    She's so defeated—she could die! "Please, just do it!"
    "No, wait, I wanted to say... Well, thank you."
    "What?"
    "Thanks for fixing my van. I love you, girl."
    This time Niko is dumbstruck. "Thanks?"
    Timmy forgets he said it. "You said this right here?"
    "Yeah."
    He does that, too. "Okay, what's next?"
    "Nothing."
    "Nothing?"
    "Turn it on."
    He's in the drivers seat. The engine is loud on start. "Yeah baby, I knew it! I knew it!" Louder is his stereo. He's pumped it up in triumph. *All them bitches. All them hoes.* It stirs everyone awake. "What did I tell you all? What did I say?" No one knows. He knows. "I said it wasn't a problem, and it wasn't a problem. I handled my business!" He pounds his chest, howls to the moon, then screams into the backseat. "Who's da man? Huh, suckers? Who's da man?"
    SS2 shouts! "Niko!"

XIV.

The students kneel in pews, fingers folded over fingers in worship as the Monsignor, dressed in robes, goes in peace to love and serve the Lord. Cotton mesh kneelers are kicked forward with little order and bang like distant buck shots. Followed by the shimmy shaker salsa of hundreds of cotton uniforms in a procession of rows, from back to front, towards the exit. The whispers start. The whispers multiply. In the lobby, it happens. The teachers, in professional attire, attach themselves to the stragglers. This is no surprise, people. We have Monday mass every week. It's time for class and not congregation.

She congregates, anyway.

Herself and Niko and Mackenzie and Ass Girl and the Sluts by a painting of the Virgin Mary. Jessica, or "Cow," needs to flee the chapel since Prom Committee has a daily meeting. It's just as well, the Queens should always outnumber the Bitches.

It's the truth.

Ass Girl shivers. "I can't believe it's so cold! It was so hot this weekend! You guys need a better heating system."

Mackenzie's got this. "They want to, but it's impossible without destroying part of the building, and you can't do that! Our chapel is too important."

Mackenzie's mother is head of the PTAA (Parent-Teacher Academy Association). It's called the PTAA, instead of the PTA, for the same reason prom is Prom. As Niko said: "Because we're special!" But, that's not what Niko says. "Who cares how much it costs? Look at my hands!" Everyone does look at Niko's hands. It seems, at first glance, that Niko only wants to gloat about her shiny, new (definitely Personal Code violating) French manicure; however, closer examination shows, sure enough, tiny red rivers have surfaced upon the prevailing beige.

Ass Girl is distraught on her face. Her hands look the same.

"I never noticed! Do you guys think that, like, this is medically okay? Or do we need to see the nurse?"

No one has a response for that.

Mackenzie tries. "We'll be fine."

"This stuff doesn't happen in Texas. I'm so unprepared."

Niko is confused. "Unprepared for what?"

Ass Girl forgot. Oh, never mind, she remembers! "Like, you'd think they'd make makeup for this. Yo, Sykosa, you're smart, what do you think about it?"

I don't.

She hides her annoyance. "It's impossible. It would rub off."

"Uh-uh!" Ass Girl raises her finger. "They could make it non-rub off makeup. Why couldn't they do that?"

That statement nearly keels her over her grumpy self. As it is, her eyes lose traction and fall out, to roll beneath Ass Girl's skirt. Say what stupid things Ass Girl will, she has a nice ass. A nice ass which bottlenecks at her waist, then opens up at her All American double Ds, up towards her elegant neck and finishes with an all-Holy combination of platinum blond on blue iris.

Basically, Ass Girl's got Barbie puking in the toilet.

And a bit more than that. School has only been in session for fifty-five minutes, yet the gossip has already circulated far and wide—this weekend the senior boys listed the twenty hottest girls at the Academy. The entire list hasn't leaked yet, but word is that Ass Girl debuted #1, SS1 was #3, and in what baffles her, she was #11. Niko wasn't on the list. *Boys are so predictable.* What's also predictable is no one will bring it up, and everyone knows it's gonna start some shit.

She ignores the elephant, too.

"But, it'd have to be, like, industrial strength to work at all." Ass Girl is beat. "I don't know, but I want them to make it!"

SS1 rubs her hands to counter her pastiness. "Why do you have something against them making that?"

SS2's teeth chatter. "Sykosa, what's up? It's a cool idea!"

Morons!

She ignores them, as she has all morning, to glance around

for Tom. Last night, he spent the duration of the ride beside her in the back row. She leaned against him, and he put his arm around her, and eventually she fell asleep to the rhythm of her thumbed bra strap. At Niko's, they hugged before Niko drove her home. At home, her mother offered no hugs, but wanted about thirty gazillion questions answered. She apologized for being late, then lied that Kana flew out at Spokane and Niko and her had to drive home alone. Upstairs, she realized she stole his hoodie, the one smelling like him, or more accurately Mackenzie. She slept in it. And that made her feel warm.

She wishes she had it now since she cannot have him.

In the interim, she decides to stop being a bitch, even though she's right, it would totally rub off. "I've been wanting to try these new color-changing contacts. I heard you don't even need to have bad eyesight, you just can wear them."

Ass Girl is excited! "I love those!"

"Oh, you have them?"

"Can't you tell? My eyes are green today instead of blue!"

Truth be told, when she did that description of Ass Girl, she never noticed Ass Girl's eyes. That part was from memory. The part about Ass Girl's ass? That was thoroughly verified. *I'm such a perv.* "Oh yeah, they look great!"

Ass Girl is cheerful. "I'm testing colors so my eyes won't contrast my prom dress."

SS1 loves that! "I never thought of that."

SS2 loves that, too! "We never thought of that."

Morons! She writes a mental note to think of it. "What does it look like?"

"It's... Well, you should come over sometime to see it."

Um. "Okay."

"It's too bad you're not going to Prom!"

"Actually, I'm going."

"Really? With whom?"

"Tom."

"Tom who?"

There're other Toms? "Uh..."

"Mackenzie's Tom?"

No, not Mackenzie's Tom. "I wouldn't put it like that."

Mackenzie giggles nervously. Obviously, Mackenzie thought he was Mackenzie's Tom, too. What she never thought was how much Sykosa would slut it up this weekend. That's fine. Boys fall for whores, but they don't love them. Mackenzie knows Tom will get bored when his new toy loses its luster. Mackenzie knows, deep in her soul, that she'll win. "I thought you told me he hadn't asked."

"He asked after I told you."

"He did?"

Her eyes roll. *Yeah, when he told you we were dating!* God, the delusions Mackenzie tells herself. "Yeah, he did."

Ass Girl is excited! "You should come with Mackenzie and me and our dates, you know, in our limo!"

She stumbles. "Su...sure, I don't think Tom would—"

Mackenzie interrupts. "I'll tell him the details."

"I bet you guys are cute together!"

Since Ass Girl mentioned it, they are. "Thanks."

Ass Girl contains her curiosity. Like, why did Sykosa say yes to Tom? *Does Sykosa have a secret crush?* Oh, the possibilities set Ass Girl afire. She needs to know what Sykosa thinks about Tom, then "coincidentally" get in a conversation with Tom to compare findings. "Hey, I didn't even know you knew Tom that well."

She puts the piece of her hands between her pointer finger and thumbs along her book bag straps and yanks. "We've been, like, er, talking for some time, him and me."

SS1 giggles. "Talking, ha!"

SS2 crouches close to Niko to share heat. "Yeah, talking!"

Niko looks pissed. "Shh!" Then, she cups her hand over SS2's ear and whispers a message that SS2 then whispers to SS1. "Not in front of the white girls."

Ass Girl pouts, uncomfortable to be outside of the inside joke. "That's cute! Do you think that he *likes you* likes you?"

"*Likes you* likes you" means non-deniable affection of the

semi-committal sort. "Well, he's my boyfriend."
    Mackenzie looks like she joined Barbie at the toilet. That is sorta odd. *He told her about us, didn't he?* Or maybe he pulled the famous boy cop-out. The, "he told her, but didn't tell her," trick. She feels like a bitch. She has no reason to doubt him.
    Don't let Mackenzie destroy your relationship!
    Ass Girl notices. "How long have you been dating?"
    "A few months."
    "I can't believe you didn't tell me this!"
    I was supposed to? "Oh, well, we kept it a secret."
    "Yeah, a big secret! You've been seeing Tom longer than I've been seeing Hazu!" That brings up a good topic! "We celebrated our three-month anniversary!" By the way, if Ass Girl knows Hazu and Niko were dating before she moved here, Ass Girl does a brilliant job of hiding it. "Look what he got me!" It's a diamond tennis bracelet that's back up her blouse. It also violates the Personal Code. "Isn't it sweet?" Quiet. *I'm bragging too much!* "Well, I want to take you dress shopping, Sykosa!"
    "Thank you, but I already have my dress picked out."
    "You're like me, better to be prepared!"
    "Yeah, I suppose."
    Niko is tired of this stupid bitch.
    Time for revenge.
    "By the way, how was your party this weekend?" Gossip says Ass Girl's party was a let down. Without the Sluts, half of the Stars no-showed, which means voices said, over cell phones, "This party is lame. What's going on where you are?" It reminds Niko that the Academy belongs to her. This pleases Niko. Ass Girl might have a great ass, but in all seriousness, her parties are shitty. In Niko's world, this makes sense, and it appears, by Ass Girl's resultant shyness, that Ass Girl has indeed been introduced to Niko's world, and it slammed the door in her damn face. "Mine was the greatest party ever! We had lots of college boys! It has never been this massive before."
    "Oh, maybe next time we'll be able to coordinate, that way we won't have opposing parties."

"Fuck that, mine always come first! I mean, Goddamnit..."

"Young lady, what did I hear?"

That was the vice-principal. (Herein known as: Veeps).

He's snuck up on Niko, and he did quite well. As a physical structure, he's a short man who projects stern discipline in his mantle. His most relatable feature being his bald head, and its glare often invites speculation a waxer is involved. As a thinker, Veeps is from the school that people want the opposite of what they express. So to say, he made this grand entrance for Niko, and not himself, because he knows Niko wants it this way. And when Niko goes straight as steel, as she just did, it confirms for him all he has ever thought was true about nature.

And Veeps knows a thing or two about nature.

He goes hunting every winter break.

"Nothing, sir."

"That was not nothing I heard."

In the Academy, the g-word is worse than the f-one. "I'm sorry, sir. I shouldn't have used the Lord's name in vain."

"Especially not in this chapel."

"Yes, sir."

"Niko, and this goes for all you girls, if I hear one additional iota of profanity, there'll be disciplinary action, understood?"

Niko swallows. "Yes, sir."

"I'm serious."

"Um, I was too, sir."

Veeps misunderstands Niko. He thinks she talked back.

"Niko, how many demerits do you have for this semester?"

Stuff like this sometimes provokes Niko to stray from the respectful student path. It's well known that sometimes—okay, most times—Niko blasts off, thus this macho crap often feels like a countdown.

Niko, do what he says!

For Niko's on the Academy's radar. Not only for being a free thinker, or a misbehaved free thinker, and a woman whose sexual appetite could swallow $5/6^{th}$ of the boys at this school, but for being infectiously so—or an "enabler." You see, it isn't solely about cusses or truancy. One time it was how Niko stopped wearing bras to school. Really, it's last year, when—after Tom was safely in the ambulance—this entire troop, minus Ass Girl, sat before Veeps, all saying the same.

"Sir, there was nothing between Mike and Tom."

"Donna's eye was black?"

"It just happened, sir, we don't know why."

Conspiracy was afoot, and yet, conspiracy it was not. Whatever ties her to her classmates—perhaps the uniforms, the hierarchy or the subtleties of social interaction—decided to hide the truth.

Veeps decided to blame Niko.

"Four, sir."

"We spoke about what happens if it becomes five. What you need to do—what all you girls need to do—is to hurry to class and show us you're serious about your responsibilities."

He leaves them be. And no one speaks. No one moves.

Except for Niko. "Fucking prick."

She touches Niko. "Let it go. He's trying to upset you."

"Trying? The rat fuck was putting the screws to me." Niko's lips layer and her brow straightens. Then, she shakes. Seconds pass. It's like an eternity. "He wants profanity? I hope Jesus butt fucks him until he bleeds to death."

Pause.

Okay, that quote might sound contrived, and it is. Niko's tailored it to break Veep's monotonous face. It is vital to Niko that she be able to break people. The reasons are complicated, but not illogical. It spurs from (big surprise) last year. It's also one of Niko's few tells. While most will fall for this phony statement, and you will see how far that fall is momentarily, that Niko spoke such only proves this isn't Niko. This whole façade is Niko3.0 and it's vital to remember this because, if you forget, you lose yourself in Niko's spell and, once lost, you'll do whatever Niko says.

Play.

"Are you crazy? What's the matter with you?"

"What do you care if I say it? I hope Jesus—"

She interrupts. "Shut up."

Mackenzie has lost color. "Niko, that's disgusting."

Even the Sluts agree.

"Ugh, that's so gross."

"Ugh, Niko, we're so grossed out!"

Ass Girl's jaw hangs like an asphyxiated fish. "Niko, we can't be friends if you're going to say things like that."

Pop. The weasel goes free. Stepping forward like Veeps upon Ass Girl's frightened face. "Be your friend? How stupid can you white girls get?"

Ass Girl stands her ground. "It has nothing to do with that, and some of us at this school are actually Christians, okay?"

"What're you gonna do about it? Tell the vice-principal?"

"I might."

Sykosa splits Niko and Ass Girl. "Please, don't tell on her."

"Why not?"

"It's not what you think it is."

Mackenzie gets in a second too late, like usual. "We should go to the vice-principal, maybe even the Administration."

Now, she's pissed. "Mackenzie, just please..." It's not worth it. She turns to Ass Girl. "You don't know what this is about. You don't understand."

"What don't I understand?"

"It happened last year on this Monday."

Ass Girl is confused. "What happened last year?"

No one wants to answer. She didn't tell you earlier? That was the elephant, not the who's hottest list, which will be dealt with in the next few days, she's certain, but for now, last year is why Veeps is trigger-happy, why Niko's aggravated, and most of all, why she wishes she had seen Tom. Perhaps in memorial, or fear, no one wants to discuss it, and the girls separate.

She heads to the secret bathroom. Niko goes with her.

She lights a cigarette, then gives Niko the pack.

Niko lights. "Sorry about that."

"You know, I'm Christian too, and you know I pray at mass.

And besides, the Bitches don't need that sorta ammunition against us!"

"You're right. And I love Jesus."

Lies! Filthy, filthy lies!

She hits off the smoke. "No, you don't."

"Yes, I do, and I'll say I'm sorry in my own way."

"That's not good enough for them."

Niko is defiant. "Well, it'll have to be."

"That's not what I meant."

She meant the omnipresent overseer, the Administration. It's the bureaucracy that operates the Academy.

Mother Superior, along with her other duties at the abbey, directly oversees the operation of the preparatory Academy and its primary schools, and for such she is part of the Administration, formally known as a regent. The Monsignor is also a regent, albeit one whose duties do not include the Academy. You see, the Academy's a fraction of the parish itself; which, in conjunction with the Archdiocese, manages an endowment funding a university, two hospitals, countless charities, and the maintenance of Seattle's finest churches, including the St. James Cathedral and the Academy chapel.

She would joke of La Cosa Nostra, and it'd be funny since it's partially true. Once you're in this community, you never really get to leave, and many don't even try. That's why you never piss off the Administration. They're too powerful.

And they were pissed about last year.

And we got lucky.

Niko remains defiant. "What they think doesn't matter."

"It should."

"Why?"

"Because you can't change the world, you'll only get kicked out of school. I mean, you're just like Mike Holler or Donna and the rest of them. You can't do whatever you want."

Niko hates it when Mike Holler is brought up. Because, like, Mike's not the answer and, whenever he enters the equation, the problem skews. And no one seems to get that, most of all

Veeps. Like a gullible twerp, he fashions himself a crusader for justice, but what he seeks is not what he imagines, and should he find that out, his dissatisfaction over his failed conquest will leave him thirstier for the next.

Maybe they all, Niko included, lied to prevent a bigger war. That is why Niko concedes now. "You're right."

Niko means that. She knows it.

"You're gonna have say something nice to Ass Girl."

"I will."

"And Mackenzie's gonna have to be there to hear it."

"I will." It seems like enough, so Niko forgets it, then ashes her smoke before one-handing her bra through her sleeve. She tugs on her sweater vest to see if her tits make any impression. *I'm never gonna make the list.* Speaking of lists, Niko reaches into her knee sock. "I got it, by the way."

Niko always gets this stuff!

"I don't care."

"Your butt got a 10."

Wow, a 10? "I'm not interested."

"Your tits got a 10."

Another 10! "Boys are sick."

"And your face got a 10."

Wow, three 10s! "Wait, how did I end up eleventh?"

Niko giggles. "You got a 2 on the slutiness scale."

Sweet! "Well, at least boys get some things right."

"You've never made a list before."

"Yeah, I wonder why."

Niko has her thoughts. "People know, but they don't, about you and Tom. It's kinda up'd your profile with the other boys now that they think they have a chance."

That's gross, more than what Niko said.

On the other hand, Tom snagged himself a 10.

Good for him!

"It's a stupid list anyways."

"Still, it's a problem. It reeks of the Bitches."

It does? "How so?"

"They wanted Ass Girl #1."

"Why would Ass Girl want that? It doesn't seem like her."

"She probably didn't, but Jessica did."

Niko is smart. She should do Model UN.

When Donna disappeared, only Jessica and Mackenzie were left to lead the Bitches, and they don't possess the punch Donna did. Ass Girl changes things. Sure, positively nothing is Machiavellian about Ass Girl, but Ass Girl needs only to be a figurehead to—oh, the irony—threaten Niko's Queens in the same way Niko threatened Donna's Bitches. The way it looks, Ass Girl's popularity will keep rising, and it's obvious Niko will be powerless to slow it, and it seems like, unless Ass Girl checks herself or Niko backs off, the Academy could be in for another turf war.

In fact, it's already begun.

In some ways, I'm more vital to the Queens than Niko. Her undying loyalty to Niko is the glue that keeps the others stuck. Jessica knows this, and it explains why Ass Girl is so interested in shopping for dresses or sharing limousines.

"I've noticed they want to separate us."

"That's old hat. We can deal with that. But, this list..."

Here comes a sad, totally un-feminist truth about life.

If you don't have boys, you don't have anything.

"I think I get it."

"The Bitches are stockpiling penises, and who knows who we lost while we were partying in Coeur d'Alene this weekend. I mean, I'll always have the Stars, but have we paid enough attention to the spillover from Mike Holler's old gang?"

This is gonna break Niko's heart.

"Are you sure you have the Stars?"

"What do you mean?"

"Hazu is dating Ass Girl."

Niko is serious. "He would never double-cross me like that."

How love makes one blind, and it's blinded Niko too long.

The Stars get into some uncool shit. It could be described as "juvenile delinquency," but that overlooks how, a lot of times, they're outright criminals. One weekend it's graffiti, another it's small-time dope dealing, the next illegal racing, and the one after that, petty burglary. They're a gang after all, and while no single member is pathologically evil, it feels like—when assembled—the Stars are solely destructive.

And Hazu only gives a fuck about himself.

"If you're sure you have him."

"I'm sure."

The first bell rings.

"You go to class, I'll be along."

Niko hits off her smoke again. "Don't worry about it."

She insists, reminding Niko of her demerit situation. Not like she's a Niko-level super-genius, but last year, Niko won after bankrupting, for their swim team antics, Donna and Mackenzie's creditability before the Administration. If Niko loses all her leeway, the Bitches will have all the leverage.

Niko agrees, but isn't worried. "It's one class. Besides, I'm not going anyway."

She's not? "Where're you going?"

"Hazu and I are going to hang out."

"Niko..."

Niko smiles. Her smoke is squished and her book bag slung over her shoulder. "We're only friends this time! I mean it!"

Niko's gone. Soon her own cigarette is, too.

Being late to bed last night, or what was technically early this morning, meant she woke up later than usual, so her person is a bit dirty and her hair knotty (for Asian hair, anyway). It's better this way. If she had woken up with time to preoccupy herself, she'd have thought more about it. *The one-year anniversary of last year.* As it is, ignoring it hasn't been hard. The second bell hasn't rung and she's certain the names, "Mike," "Donna," and "Lonny," won't even be spoken (by anyone other than her). Her mother mentioned nothing. Niko did the same. As you heard, the other girls were mum. Of course, the Academy followed suit. And Tom's not even here to not receive the plaque no one's giving him.

Turns out that's the price for being a hero.
Everyone pretends you died anyway.
She won't.

Unlike this weekend, the blackness doesn't own her anymore. She got home and got in her bed and she ate a good breakfast and... Tom may be her hero, but nothing beats home and nothing beats Mom and Dad. She feels safe and totally stable. Thus, she's free to show Tom how important he is to her—without actually saying it. All he has to do is show up for school. Since he hasn't, he won't be in American history, so she doesn't want to be either. She exits the secret bathroom, then cuts along the courtyard. The pathway to the chapel is empty, so she walks it, and at the chapel, hides behind it. She smokes a cigarette she only half-finishes since subsequent cigarettes never give her as powerful a buzz. The isolation works for her, though. It drops her into a deep meditative state.

When he arrives, it takes a while for her to break it.

"I saw you weren't in class." ¶ "I thought you might be here." ¶ "I left before class started." ¶ "Look, I know things were strange yesterday." ¶ "Some of that stuff I said at the foodmart, I'd like to say it again, but differently this time." ¶ "I thought about it a lot, I've got a lot to say."

She listens. "Like what?"

He holds out his hands.

"You're right about everything. I'm wrong about everything. Whatever happens because of how I've handled Mackenzie and our relationship, it's my fault. I'm sorry you think I don't love you. I asked you to Prom and I told you I love you and I told Mackenzie we're dating because I want you that badly."

She smiles. Boyfriends are wonderful sometimes. Anyhow, his apology is still appreciated. As well, his timing—for once—is impeccable. This way, when she takes off her clothes for him next, she won't question it.

"Okay."

"'Okay' like okay or 'okay' like not okay?"

"Okay."

"Okay?"

She chuckles. "Okay!"

"Alright, then."

He steps forwards, so does she and she ends in his arms. It's a good hug—nothing to write home about, but it suffices. She pulls away and he kisses her. She uses her tiptoes to reach and she stumbles. She'd have never fallen. But, he still grabs her, then yanks her in close. When the kiss ends, she's crushed against him, and his arms are using tremendous force to ensure she stays that way. He only need do it for a minute—soon, her cold body matches his warmth, and her muscles go limp, then mold. She can hear his heartbeat and she recognizes that her own heartbeat is in progress to matching it.

She smiles.

(Boys are such narcotics!)

"You didn't go to mass this morning?"

"I had a doctor's appointment."

"What for?"

He holds up his scarred hand. "One-year checkup."

"Is it okay?"

"Yeah, it's fine."

It doesn't feel fine.

She wants to ask a question. "Can it happen again?

"Can what happen again?"

"What happened last year. Can it happen again?"

He is definite. "No, it can't."

"Well, not here, but somewhere else—in a different school."

His tone is the same. "It won't happen anywhere else."

If she could have anything of his, it'd be his courage. She tries to have it. "If you need to talk about it, I understand."

He knows she didn't mean it.

"I'm starving. Let's go before the cafeteria stops serving."

"Okay."

She breaks away from his grasp, then tosses her cigarette butt into the brush. All the while, he fills her in on what specifically he thought about last night, and how he thinks this weekend was fun, but maybe it'll be a while before they do anything like it again, and she agrees with everything he says. It gets to the part where she knew it would get to, and she's glad he brought it up now.

"After school, do you want to meet back here?"
"Where else would we meet?"
"Well, my mom doesn't get home until six or seven."
He means: "We can have sex in my room."
Good thinking on his part. They need a place.
"Okay."
He kisses her. She kisses him back.
They both put their hair behind their ear.
This is her story. This is her life.
It's sex. And it's what we do now.

An Open Letter From Niko:

I just finished *Sykosa*. Let me tell you, I am awesome! I knew I was cool, but wow, I'm mammoth! And not to be too critical of the author—who's clearly trying too hard—but Ass Girl is way ugly, and that bimbo poses no threat whatsoever.
    My Queens are untouchable!
    Did you like Sykosa? She's neat, but she buries her feelings, and maybe for good reason. One-on-one, few would shame her for being herself, but one-on-anything-over-three, and the opposite is true, which is why, ta-da!, she buries her feelings.
    (See! I'm a good writer, too!)
    For reals, this is why you probably heard of Sykosa when a friend whispered about her in your ear like she were a dirty secret. It's cool, she appreciates your discretion, especially about the parts where she's *'ing, but you gotta understand, if you don't support her, then no one will, and she'll disappear, cause she's not the type to rebel by singing bad, yet addictive, pop music in her underwear.
    She can't even be in her underwear around me!
    I speaketh the truth, so if you love Sykosa, be a leader and...

<u>TELL-SOMEONE-ABOUT-HER!!!!!!</u>

It's not hard, and it's kinda awesome to be that outgoing.
I'll see you for Part II!
(That's what these next few pages are! ^_^)
Arigato,
Niko
P.S. Donna Harly bites.
P.P.S. I'm really freaking cool!

An Excerpt from Part II.

Prologue: When It Started.

He's dead.
    That's her first thought.
    She just saw a person die—right now.
    And Mike Holler and his cohort, Lonny, are not beating down upon a boy who needs to learn a lesson. They're beating down on a dead body. It's... People don't bleed this much. Yet, it's seemingly everywhere. From the moment that boy's fist smashed the third pane of glass, the glass—which never cut so bad on TV—ripped him in two. The uniforms at the Academy, for the boys, include a sorta dirty white button down, not quite gray, but dirty white—but his shirt is dirty red. That same red that gets into the floor tiles, like the grout, things that conventional cleaners won't be able to wash.
    It's starting to smell.
    (What feels like minutes has been probably seconds).
    She looks around.
    Donna Harly's on the floor. She got tackled hard, like one does in a football game. It knocked the wind from Donna and she huffs for air like she cannot breathe. Half of her face is black. All around Donna are people who are watching. They occasionally say things like, "Oh my God" or utter some half-scream. Mostly, everyone's has the same face they give the TV. Save for one. (The biggest phony of them all). He's in his suit and tie and it's cut tight and he rushes the hallway, compelled to action.
    Veeps.
    There's a hiccup, though—as there's a choice.
    There's the boy. There's Donna. And there's something else.
    It's not a perfect world.
    She repeats:
    It's not a perfect world.

Made in the USA
Charleston, SC
09 February 2013